HAPPY ARE THOSE WHO THIRST FOR JUSTICE

A FATHER BLACKIE RYAN MYSTERY

HAPPY ARE THOSE WHO THIRST FOR JUSTICE

Andrew M. Greeley

THE MYSTERIOUS PRESS

New York • London

The Mysterious Press, 129 West 56th Street, New York, N.Y. 10019

Printed in the United States of America

First Printing: September 1987

10   9   8   7   6   5   4   3   2   1

Library of Congress Cataloging-in-Publication Data

Greeley, Andrew M., 1928–
    Happy are those who thirst for justice.

    I. Title.
PS3557.R358H35   1987   813'.54   87-11139
ISBN 0-89296-180-5

Book design: H. Roberts Design
Map by Heidi Hornaday

For Dan and Joan

Monsignor John Blackwood Ryan, Ph.D., is far too wise and far too gentle to be like any existing rector of Holy Name Cathedral. Sean Cronin is too courageous, honest, and outspoken to be like any known archbishop of Chicago. All the other characters in the book, Ryan clan or not, are imaginary, fictitious, made up, and otherwise products of my fantasy. Anyone thinking otherwise is wrong, that's all.

THE BEATITUDES

This series of stories, featuring Monsignor John Blackwood Ryan, is based on the Beatitudes from Jesus's Sermon on the Mount. A variant form is found in Luke's so-called Sermon on the Plain, which is accompanied by parallel Woes. I choose Matthew's version, which is probably later and derivative, because it is so much better known.

The Sermon on the Mount is not, according to the scripture scholars, an actual sermon Jesus preached but rather a compendium of His sayings and teachings edited by the author of St. Matthew's Gospel, almost certainly from a preexisting source compendium.

The Beatitudes represent, if not in exact words, an important component of the teachings of Jesus, but they should not be interpreted as a new list of rules. Jesus came to teach that rules are of little use in our relationship with God. We do not constrain God's love by keeping rules, since that love is a freely given starting point of our relationship (a passionate love affair) with God. We may keep rules because all communities need rules to stay together and because, as ethical beings, we should behave ethically, but that, according to Jesus, is a minor part of our relationship with God.

Nonetheless, some Christians, early on, went back to the rule game,which attempted to bind us so that our proper behavior would bind God. Often religion was pictured as a sort of contract: We keep rules and God keeps His promise to us sort of like giving back to a Professor in our tests, the material we have transferred from his notebook to our notebook.

In such a framework, the Beatitudes were converted into

new rules, much tougher than those revealed on Sinai. All right, some Christians said, ours is a much tougher religion. Jesus and the Father, one might imagine, are not amused.

In fact, the Beatitudes are descriptive, not normative. They are a portrait of the Christian life as it becomes possible for those who believe in the love of God as disclosed by Jesus. If we trust in God, we are then able to take the risks the Beatitudes imply, never living them perfectly, of course, but growing and developing in their radiant goodness and experiencing the happiness of life that comes from such goodness.

"Hunger and thirst for justice" is often interpreted as a passion for political and social justice either, as in the 1930s and 1940s, for the church against authoritarian governments or, as in the seventies and eighties, for the "poor," in whose name the church has exercised a "preferential option," against the middle class. (Be it noted that the church exercises said option without incurring any obligation to pay its own employees any more than poverty wages.)

Such an emphasis is not so much inaccurate as incomplete. The justice of which Jesus preaches in the Sermon on the Mount includes political and social justice but is not limited to it. Rather, those who hunger for justice are those who hunger for what God wishes in all aspects of personal and social life. In the individual's personal life it is passion to do that which one does best and in which one finds the greatest challenge and excitement, because they are clearly what God wants and expects.

Monsignor Ryan's reference to God as "Lady Wisdom" is based on the analysis of the figure of Wisdom in the Jewish scriptures by Father Roland Murphy, O. Carm., in his presidential address to the Society of Biblical Literature (*Journal of Biblical Studies 104*:1985, 3–11). Wisdom, always presented in the Bible as feminine, both in grammatical gender and in characteristics, is the self-disclosure of God through the order and the inviting attractiveness of creation. Imaging God as both Man and Woman is a theme throughout the Catholic tradition. In the Middle Ages, mystics and theologians described God variously as Father, Mother, Spouse, Friend, Knight, Brother, Sister. They told their people to drink milk from the breasts of God our loving Mother. Pope John Paul I reiterated this theme in one of his audience talks during his brief September pontificate. Survey research indicates that some 32 percent of Americans (38 percent of Catholics) picture God as equally mother and father, or even more mother than father.

—AMG

DRAMATIS PERSONAE

Violet Elizabeth Harrington Enright, matriarch

Most Reverend Henry "Harry" Harrington Enright, D.D., son to Violet

Dan Harrington Enright, Ph.D., son to Violet

Lena Enright, wife to Dan

Edward Harrington Enright, M.D., son to Violet

Minerva "Minnie" Enright, wife to Edward

Rita Enright Downs, daughter to Violet

William Downs, Ph.D., husband to Rita

Fionna Downs, daughter to Rita and William, granddaughter to Violet

Vincent Nelligan, banker to Violet

Richard Nelligan, grandson to Vincent, suitor to Fionna

Carlos and Tomas, servants to Violet

Luisa Flores, servant to Violet, foster sister to Fionna, by decree of the latter

Mary O'Brien Feehan, nurse to the Harrington Enrights

Mary Kathleen Ryan Murphy, M.D., psychiatrist to Fionna

Joseph Murphy, M.D., husband to Mary Kathleen

Sean Cronin, Cardinal priest of the Church of St. Agnes Outside the Walls and, by the grace of God and the tolerant inattention of the Apostolic See, Archbishop of Chicago

Monsignor John Blackwood "Blackie" Ryan, S.T.L., Ph.D., rector of the Cathedral of the Holy Name, brother to Mary Kathleen, gray eminence to Sean, scholar to William James, M.D.

Edward P. "Ned" Ryan, Old Fella to Blackie and Mary Kathleen

Sundry members of the Ryan and Murphy clans and citizens and officers-at-arms of the city of Chicago

HAPPY ARE THOSE WHO THIRST FOR JUSTICE

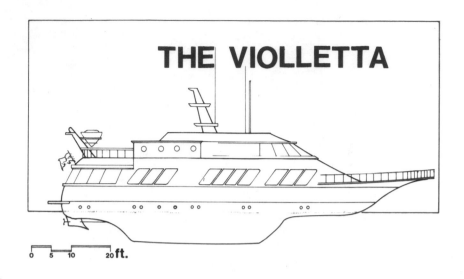

THE VIOLLETTA

0 5 10 20 ft.

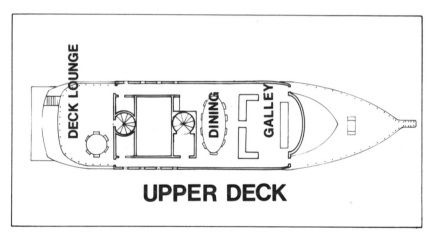

DECK LOUNGE

DINING

GALLEY

UPPER DECK

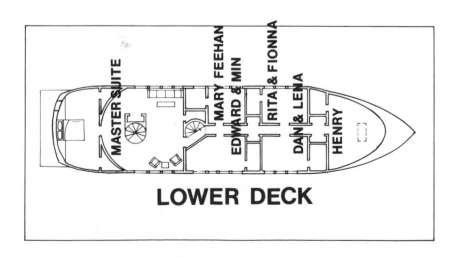

MASTER SUITE

MARY FEEHAN

EDWARD & MIN

RITA & FIONNA

DAN & LENA

HENRY

LOWER DECK

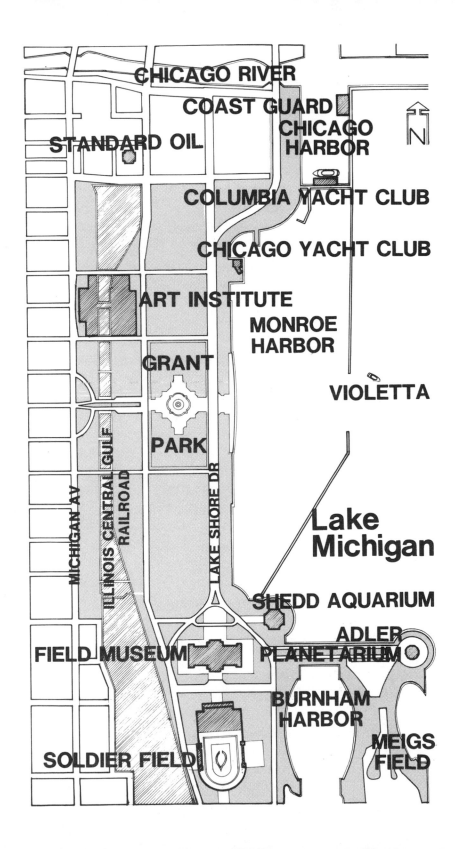

OVERTURE

Fionna Downs

"I'd like to kill her," Fionna Downs muttered through clenched teeth.

"Oh, Señorita Feehona," Luisa Flores pleaded plaintively, "do not say that." She whispered in Fionna's ear, a deadly hiss of a water moccasin: "Let us kill her for you!"

Fionna's grandmother, Violet Harrington Enright—an overweight Queen Victoria as Empress of India in flowing cream caftan—waddled down the pier toward her yacht. Determined on an implacable progression to the royal barge, she was oblivious to Fionna's rage.

Murderous anger toward a devouring matriarch, Doctor Murphy, Fionna's shrink, would have said.

The *Violetta* was berthed temporarily against the pier of Montrose harbor. The skyline of Chicago was soft rose and gentle gold against the pale blue sky of an early August, apartments and condominia to the west and Lincoln Park and downtown to the east, the latter guarded by the John Hancock Center burning crimson in the light of the setting sun.

Not a night for murder, Fionna reassured herself.

"Don't ever say that again." Fionna pulled away from the immigrant girl, fifteen and totally gorgeous in her comic-opera naval uniform, like really voluptuous, you know? "You have to learn, Luisa," she said, adopting her school-marm tone, "that in this country we do not settle family feuds by murder."

As much as we'd like to, she added to herself.

Luisa drew away from her, big brown eyes filled with tears. Damn, why must the child be so sensitive?

The lushly built Mexican girl played many roles in Fionna's life, of which maid was the least important. She was, depending on the moment, friend, confidante, foil in rock-music discussions ("Luisa, 'Born in the U.S.A.' is degenerate Springsteen! How many times do I have to tell you that you should listen to 'Born to Run' instead?"), little sister, pupil, and according to Rick—Fionna's boyfriend—(with a twinkle in his totally cute eyes) salve for Fionna's social conscience.

"It would not be a great sin to kill her, señorita, she is mean to everyone."

"Shush." Fionna tried to sound gentle. "She's my grand-mother and I love her. . . . Look at her, she's hammered already. Can't face her family without being hammered."

Mary Feehan, an elegant grand duchess whose gray linen dress matched her neatly bound gray hair, walked next to Grandmother, hand gently at her elbow. A strange pair, Fionna thought. The closest to a friend poor Grandmother has—a woman who has never had a lot of money but who has the class that Grandmother's money cannot buy.

"Tons of money," Fionna said, smiling at Luisa, "and not an ounce of class."

Luisa, now restored to favor, beamed happily.

"You and your mother have enough class for many fami-lies, Señorita Feehona. Doña Rita is truly beautiful tonight."

Fionna's mother was wearing a black strapless dress made of cotton gauze with a flaring rose and gray scarf at the waist.

"Pretty shoulders and boobs," Fionna observed, the ex-act comment she had made when welcoming her mother on board *Violetta*. Rita Downs had blushed at the compliment, heaven knows she had heard few of them from anyone since her husband had left home eight years before. "We should look like that when we're as old as she is."

Rage surged through Fionna's body again as she thought of the loss of her father.

"We must do the Nautilus every day." Luisa laughed happily. "Sometimes twice a day."

Well, she didn't cry this time, Fionna mused. I'm not old enough to play the mother of a sensitive teen.

Mother superior, Doctor Murphy would have added, matriarch in training.

Since she was a little girl, Fionna had known her family was strange. Violet Harrington Enright's determination to dominate the lives of her children and grandchildren seemed weird even before Fionna knew of other families with which to make comparison. But only at Stanford—Leland Stanford Memorial University, Rick called it with a chuckle—did she realize just how strange they were. Sometimes she feared that she would end up as crazy as the rest of them, Mom included. Rick, however, had assured her—holding her chin firmly in his big, strong hand—that she was disgustingly sane.

He absorbed her in his wonderful smile, which filled her with a warm glow and made her body behave like that of a woman about to make love. Not that there was much chance of Rick doing anything in that line till they were married.

Fionna longed for Rick like she yearned for a glass of water halfway through the minimarathon she had run in Palo Alto the previous year. He gave every sign of the same thirst for her. The devouring, consuming look in his eyes whenever he kissed her made Fionna's speeding heart jump like her Mercedes on a gravel road.

If Grandmother really drives him off like she did Daddy, I'll totally murder her.

"Easy does it, Violet." Mary Feehan spoke with a serene West of Ireland accent, gentle and melodious like the woman herself. "It wouldn't do now to fall climbing on your namesake, would it?"

The *Violetta* was eight years older than Fionna, purchased in 1955, a couple of years after Grandfather Enright had died. According to Fionna's mother, the ninety-five-foot powerboat was used several times that summer. Since then, it rode every summer, burnished and polished, at the family mooring in Montrose harbor. Grandmother made substantial annual payoffs to park-district employees for the mooring, although she used the boat only twice each summer for her family overnight rituals.

It was gross, Fionna had told her grandmother, to own a boat like that and not use it.

"You can use it as much as you want after I'm gone," she would reply, making Fionna feel guilty as always when Grandmother spoke of her death. "If I decide," she would usually add, "to leave it to you."

As long as Fionna could remember and as long as her mother could remember, Grandmother had "guilted" the family with threats of her death and hints that she might change her will. Fionna was now, according to Grandmother's broad hints, the principal beneficiary of her endlessly changing will. But she could fall out of favor as easily as anyone else in the family.

"It's a roulette game, kid," her father had said. "Whoever is lucky enough to be in her good graces the day before she dies will win the whole pot."

"I'm perfectly all right, Mary." Grandmother brushed the nurse's hand aside. "I'm not old enough yet to need someone's help climbing on *my* boat."

Fortunately Mary's hand remained a few inches away from Violet Enright's arm. Grandmother stumbled and almost fell between the boat and the dock. Mary and Fionna pushed and pulled her safely on the boat.

"Look at them," Grandmother snorted, "every one of them up there watching me and hoping I fall into the lake. Everyone but you, eh, Fionna darling? You wouldn't push me in the lake, would you?"

"Only if you pushed me first." Fionna kissed her on the forehead.

"See what I mean, Mary?" The old woman cackled. "Isn't she the only one in the family who has my kind of guts?"

"Would I want to be after fighting either of you?" Mary winked at Fionna, hinting that in another hour or two of steady drinking Grandmother would have to crash, leaving the rest of the family to their own fights.

She's right, Fionna thought as she and Mary guided Grandmother to the waiting ranks of the family, lined up like a naval crew for guest inspection.

Fights with Rick after coming home in June with her college degree and her literary ambitions had driven Fionna to Doctor Murphy's office.

It was impossible to fight with Rick because he would never fight back. "You're not angry at me," he would say. "You are angry at her."

"I *am* not," Fionna would insist furiously. "Grandmother and I are buddies. I'm the only one who understands her."

She knew very well, however, that Rick was right. Her attempts to make him fight her were foolish. And dangerous, because she might lose him just as she had lost her father.

So, fearful that she was becoming as crazy as the rest of the family and terrified at the prospect of losing Rick, she hied herself to a shrink. Jeannie Ryan, a classmate at Stanford, was dating Tim Murphy; she said that Tim's mother was totally neat. So, stretched out and twisting on Doctor Murphy's couch, Fionna fought with her too.

"She manipulates you all with a mixture of fear and guilt," Doctor Murphy's cool crisp voice had pounded accusingly against Fionna's brain. "With enough love thrown in— like you'd feed a silly puppy a doggie cookie—to keep you from ending the relationship."

"How do you know so much?" Fionna had shouted.

"I know the Irish matriarch's temptation from the inside, young woman. Just as you do too when you're playing mother to that poor Mexican child."

"I love her!" Fionna squirmed uncomfortably on the hard leather couch.

"She drove off your father, ruined your mother's life, interfered in everything you've ever done, and is now trying to take Rick away from you. You love that?"

"You don't understand how hard her life has been."

"Granted that she tells you fun stories about the old days, granted that she's been very generous with you, granted too that she's a sad and lonely old woman. Nonetheless, you are furious at her and even more furious that you can't admit your fury even to yourself."

"I do really love her." Fionna felt totally miserable. "I DO."

"Presumably they taught you about ambivalence in your psych classes at Stanford."

"Leland Stanford Junior Memorial University."

"Pardon?"

"That's what Rick calls it."

"Ah, Rick . . . you love him, of course?"

"Really!"

"What if your devouring grandmother does get him fired from his job and forces him to leave Chicago?"

Fionna clenched her fists angrily. "She wouldn't dare."

"It sounds to me like she has already begun." Doctor Murphy was implacable. "What happens if you lose Rick because of her?"

"I'll murder her!" Fionna had bolted upright on the couch. "I'll totally murder her."

Then she had collapsed into tearful hysteria, sobbing uncontrollably in Dr. Murphy's arms.

"Are all us Irish women like that?" she had asked when there were no tears left, only a few sniffles.

"Our hungers to protect our own by dominating are terribly fierce," the doctor had said mildly. "We must learn to control them."

"Will I end up that way?"

"That's what we're working on here. Now, young woman, back on the couch."

I wish she were my mother, Fionna had thought. Then, from her class on Freud, she remembered that they called that "transference." I'm supposed to wish that, am I not? Does she wish that I was one of her daughters? I guess she's supposed to feel that way too.

Still wheezing from her exertions in boarding the

Violetta, Grandmother, Mary Feehan at one arm and Fionna at the other, worked her way down the line of her family, waiting patiently on the foredeck in the last rays of the setting sun. Unerringly she went to the jugular vein of each of them, reducing each to the condition of a child who has been punished by ridicule.

"Well, Henry," she said to Uncle Henry, who was a bishop sent home in disgrace from the Vatican, "I see you're wearing your pectoral cross and French cuffs, even on the yacht. Do you sleep in them? Hasn't that terrible Ryan priest thrown you out of his rectory yet? You do get thrown out of a lot of places, don't you?"

Bishop Henry blushed painfully. "Monsignor Ryan is the perfect host, Mother."

Monsignor Blackie Ryan was the rector of Holy Name Cathedral and also Doctor Murphy's brother.

"And tells everyone behind your back that you're a pompous failure."

Fionna did not know Monsignor Ryan, but from the way Jeannie Ryan described him—she was a "very distant" cousin—she was sure that he would say no such thing. But Uncle Henry, a tall, handsome man with a touch of gray hair above his high forehead, was surely afraid that everyone was ridiculing. Grandmother had him.

"Monsignor Ryan," he said, his face still the color of the bit of purple under his Roman collar, "is a perfect gentleman."

"He doesn't look like much of anything." Grandmother turned away from Uncle Henry. "Of course, it isn't enough to look like a cardinal to become one, is it, Henry?"

Fionna's mother, pale and frightened, was next.

"Where did you get that terrible dress, Rita? It doesn't fit you at all, and you'll catch your death of cold if you don't put on a sweater. Anyway, there aren't any men in our party who will ogle you this evening. Except maybe Carlos and Tomas." She gestured at her chauffeur and houseboy, who were dressed in hot and heavy naval-guard uniforms like the one Luisa was wearing. "Would you like one of them in your bed tonight, dear? I'm sure they'd be happy to oblige even if I tell them you're not very good in bed."

Mom turned pale and shut her eyes.

"I'm sure I'll be warm enough without a sweater."

"Sure? Well, maybe. But a Latin lover might warm you up too."

Poor Mom looked like she wished the boat would sink under her. Why did she care? She had only to look in the mirror to know that the dress was perfect for her. But not once in her forty years had Grandmother said a nice thing about her clothes—except when she bought Mom something gross that hid her durable natural beauty.

"Don't you hate her for what she has done to your mother?" Doctor Murphy had demanded. "Or are you happy that you have replaced your mother as the favored daughter?"

"I have not!" Fionna had screamed, knowing that she had done just that. And that her mother did not seem jealous.

I could kill you for what you've done to her too.

A couple of drinks and Mom—a very short hitter—would escape to her bedroom, lonely, hurt, unhappy.

Evil old bitch. I should have let you fall between the boat and the pier. I'd love to hear you scream in pain.

Before supper was served, Mom would find a sweater and cover her bare shoulders and her lovely boobs, hiding her attractiveness. Did Grandmother resent her only daughter's beauty?

Why didn't I think of that before? Damn you, Doctor Murphy. You've made me think of so many things I don't want to face.

At her graduation, Mom and Dad seemed to be as much in love as ever—their eyes filled with longing for each other, not unlike the longing for her in Rick's eyes. Fionna was pretty sure that they had spent the night together in Mom's room in the Palo Alto motel.

"You still love her, don't you, Dad?"

"It doesn't make any difference as long as the old gal is

alive. And, Fee, to tell the truth, I think she is going to live forever if only to keep us apart."

"Daddy!" She had exploded in Grandmother's defense. But that was before Doctor Murphy had made her look honestly at her own emotions.

Would I kill her so Dad and Mom can get together again?

Is Luisa right? It wouldn't be a terrible sin, would it?

"You're fatter than ever, Dan." Grandmother was working on Uncle Dan, a professor of English at De Paul, who, when he'd been a Jesuit, was lean and ascetic and who now, as a married man, had become an untidy slob. "The suit doesn't fit you either. If you're not going to diet, you should at least buy clothes that fit you. And for the love of God, Lena, make him take this suit to a cleaner and get it pressed before he tries to raise funds for his magazine. No one with money will give it to a sloppy ex-priest."

Grandmother had hit home again. Uncle Dan's white trousers and dark blue, double-breasted jacket were both unpressed and too tight. And he was having trouble raising money for his proposed Chicago literary magazine, a project for which Grandmother wouldn't give him a single one of her many dollars.

"We have an endorsement from Saul Bellow." Uncle Dan fidgeted nervously in his tight clothes. "That's pure gold."

"Fool's gold, if you ask me. Can't you keep him slim, Lena, like you are? And that's a clever dress you're wearing. I think it's so wonderful the way you make things yourself. That *is* burlap, isn't it? Natural cloth, like natural food, wheat germ and such, I presume?"

Double blast at Aunt Lena. The poor woman, with snapping, hateful eyes, looked like a skinny little boy planning ways to get even with a bully. And her short beige dress, which did hang on her like a burlap bag, had probably cost a couple of hundred dollars.

Grandmother didn't give Aunt Lena a chance to reply. Her sons' wives were dismissed with one quick attack so that the deck might be cleared for return engagements with her sons.

"You look worn out, Ed." She focused her attention on Uncle Edward, a surgeon at Northwestern Hospital, a beaten-down man with a large, handsome head and a small wimpy body. "Another hard day at the hospital? Too much sex? Or another batch of losses on the exchange? A little harder to operate there, isn't it?"

Half hammered or not, Grandmother was knocking them down like pins in a bowling alley. It was no secret, according to Rick, that Uncle Ed had been losing heavily in the options market and in gold trading at the Board of Trade. Nor was it a secret that his mother was refusing to make good on his margin calls.

Moreover there were rumors that Uncle Ed was having love affairs with male orderlies at the hospital and that Aunt Min, frustrated in her marriage bed, was sleeping with every man she could seduce.

"Actually," Uncle Ed stammered, "I did rather well in gold today."

"You never did well in anything," his mother sneered. "And that's quite a dress you're wearing, isn't it, Min? Doesn't leave much to the imagination. If I were you, dear, I'd be a little more careful about ... what's the term, Fionna? ... letting it all hang out, especially since you don't have all that much to hang out. But then tastes do change, don't they?"

Aunt Min's white minidress was held in place by thin white straps, which were about all there was to the dress above the waistline. Unlike Mom, who managed to look chaste in the most revealing clothes, Aunt Min, whose figure was less than spectacular, usually looked like a tart. Which arguably she was.

"Better not enough, dear," Aunt Min fired back, "than too much."

"Matter of opinion, dear." Grandmother laughed genially. "Dear God, Vinney." Vincent and Rick Nelligan were at the end of the receiving line. "You look terrible, ten years older than you actually are. You should see a doctor, Vinney, you really should."

Vincent Nelligan, who did indeed look like a respectable retired banker with one foot in a fiscally solvent grave (on which he might have earlier foreclosed a mortgage) had been Grandmother's financial adviser and ally for fifty years. He coughed nervously.

"Always joking, Violet. In fact, I am as sound as a T bill, if not sounder."

"Not with that hack. You should have an X ray of your lungs on Monday. Lung cancer can be cured if you get it early. . . . And you, young man"—this to Rick, resplendent in a dark blue sport coat and light blue trousers—"I hear your career has run into some obstacles. Don't let poor Vinney down like your father did."

Rick, six feet three of point guard, was wearing his nerd glasses, but at least Fionna had been able to talk him out of a vest under his sport coat. He winced at the crack about his father. "Business is fine, Mrs. Enright," he said in his firm, resourceful yuppie voice.

"We'll see about that," she said, laughing happily.

O'Rourke Feed Grain had pursued Rick and not vice versa. The only reason they were debating whether to get rid of him was that Grandmother was threatening to withdraw her massive trading account.

I'll murder the bitch, Fionna thought, as she stood on her tiptoes to kiss him.

Rick bent his head to brush her lips. But Fionna didn't let him get away that easily. She crushed herself against his lean, tough body and imprisoned his lips with hers. He stiffened in surprise and then responded passionately to her passionate onslaught. She forced her tongue through his lips and assaulted his tongue with demanding fury.

Maybe he will sleep with me tonight. Oh, shit, there isn't room for them on the boat.

"Tell the captain," Violet Harrington Enright bellowed,

"to get this damn boat out on the lake before my grand-daughter and heiress turns the deck into a bedroom for her paramour."

Fionna turned away from a flustered Rick. "Grand-mother, if you keep saying things like that, I'll be sorry I didn't let the boat crush you against the pier."

She was surprised at the ferocity of her anger. There was a moment of dead silence on the deck. Then Grandmother laughed and tottered away. "See, Mary, she's a bitch just like me."

Later Fionna went belowdecks to change for a swim off Monroe Street before supper. Mary Feehan stopped her. "I've got her resting in the salon," she whispered. "You mustn't mind the poor woman, Fee, she's lonely and un-happy and too much of the drink has been taken. She doesn't mean those terrible things."

"She took away my father." For once Fionna was able to resist the quiet serenity of her nurse. "She's not going to take away my Rick, even if she is my grandmother."

Fionna heard her voice choke, a kind of sob of guilt. Mary was watching her very closely.

"I don't think she'll do that, child. Now run along and dress for your swim."

In the cabin she was to share with her mother, Fionna changed into the bikini Rick had given her as a birthday present last month.

"Wow, Fee"—Mom came into the cabin—"totally cool. It will give your grandmother fits."

"Brazilian," Fionna said. "You could wear it too."

Because your grandmother is the absolute ruler of the family, Doctor Murphy had said, your mother is more like an older sister, isn't she? A weak but pretty older sister of whom you have to take care?

She's neat, Fionna had insisted. The only one in the family with class.

There are worse things, Doctor Murphy had chuckled, that a girl your age might say about her mother.

There's no point in hating her, Fionna had replied.

"I don't think I'll try it just now." Mom had considered the bikini with a critical smile. "Try to stay out of Grandmother's way."

"If you wear that sweater"—Fionna slipped a terry cover-up over her head—"I'll totally disown you. Put it back. It isn't cold at all."

Rita Downs considered the sweater and then her daughter. "The conversations with Doctor Murphy seem to be having quite an impact on you, Fee," she said thoughtfully.

"Good or bad? . . . And put it away."

"Yes, ma'am." Mom folded the sweater back into her nylon case.

"Good or bad?" Fionna insisted.

"I like you this way." Her mother grinned. "And that was some exhibition with poor Rick. You'll drive the boy out of his mind."

"That" Fionna kissed her mother's cheek—"is the general idea."

While she and Rick were swimming in the warm waters off Monroe Street harbor, under a dome of stars and skyscraper lights, Fionna thought about the stories Grandmother told about the days when she was young and in love with Grandfather Enright, on summer vacations in northern Wisconsin. And the stories about how much she missed him when he went off to war, leaving her with three little boys—and then a baby girl conceived on his last leave. She seemed to remember those days fondly. Were they too distant for her to remember what it was like to be young and in love? Or did the pain of the years since then extinguish all memory of youth?

Dear God, protect me from that.

And help Doctor Murphy to teach me how to protect myself.

"That was some kiss, Fionna." Rick helped her climb the ladder back into the *Violetta*. "I think you're trying to seduce me."

"Really!"

"What I really think is that you were defying your grandmother." He touched her face gently.

Fionna fell apart as she always did when he touched her that way. "Do you mind? I mean, I don't want to use you. . . ."

His hand slipped down her throat and brushed the top of a breast. "Not in the least."

His hand remained there. And time stood still for Fionna, heaven and earth blending. A thirst partially quenched, a glass half full and half empty.

Fionna waited till he removed his hand and then picked up her cover-up. Who needs a robe to stay warm, she thought, when your lover touches you that way? She was about to say something witty when Grandmother stumbled out of the door of her specially made two-floor salon.

"God in heaven, girl," she yelped, "you look like a tart in that thing, a Clark Street whore!"

The sound of Grandmother's voice caught the attention of Fionna's three uncles who had been lounging on deck chairs on the other side of the yacht.

Calmly, though she felt killer rage in every cell of her body, Fionna handed her cover-up to Rick.

"You're envious, Grandmother, because even when you were my age, you couldn't have worn a swimsuit like this. Or any kind of swimsuit without looking ridiculous. I'm not a whore. I'm a virgin who intends to become a wife to the man I love as soon as I can, no matter what you say or do. Don't get in my way or I'll kill you."

She turned on her heel and stomped down the companionway, Rick trailing dubiously behind.

"Pretty strong, Fionna," he murmured.

"You know what I am, Rick. Like Doctor Murphy says, I am at least as terrible a matriarch as Grandmother. If you don't like it, now is the time to ship out."

"I like it." He turned around and drank her in again with his powerful, hungry eyes.

"Then more affection, please, before I burst into tears."

Once more his fingers traced the outline of her face and throat and chest and came to rest, this time on both her breasts. She responded by standing on her tiptoes and kissing him as she had on the foredeck.

"Your mother . . ." He freed his lips.

"She won't mind." She recaptured them.

The door of her cabin opened and Mom emerged. Rick's fingers deserted her flesh.

"Sorry, Mrs. Downs."

"Don't apologize to me, young man," Mom laughed. "You know by now exactly what you're getting into."

"It won't be dull, ma'am."

"Tell me about it."

"Geeks!" Fionna protested as she dove into her cabin and a cold, cold shower.

Later at dinner on the foredeck, with Carlos and Luisa and Tomas serving the food and pouring the wine, Fionna wished that her family could show a little class. Gleaming crystal and white linen tablecloths, sparkling silver, waves lapping against the boat, star-drenched darkness beyond the multicolored foredeck lights, the silent walls of the skyline, boats drifting by with their green and red lights flickering, handsome men and beautiful women (and she included Mary and Aunt Min in the latter category)—all the raw material for a perfect romantic evening, especially with Grandmother safely tucked away in bed.

On her right, Bishop Uncle—always ill at ease with women—spoke of his years as subsecretary to the Papal Nunciature in Ghana and made the job sound totally BORING. On the other side, Uncle Ed talked to poor Rick about the prospects for a rebound in gold, which Rick knew was no way going to happen.

Dullsville. And I'll never get Rick away from Uncle Ed either.

Neither the cold shower nor the California Cabernet (which she had ordered from Dad's favorite winery) had done much to cool Fionna's deliberately roused passions.

"Your body is designed for coupling, childbearing, and nursing, young woman," Doctor Murphy had observed.

"And your hormones drive you toward such activity, especially at your age. They don't determine your destiny, of
course—Old Sig was wrong about that—but they create a
very powerful propensity. You shouldn't be surprised about
the physical components of your affection for Rick."

"Do the hormones weaken as you grow older?" Fionna
asked, hoping that they didn't.

"Not that I've noticed." Doctor Murphy seemed amused.
Lucky Mr. Doctor Murphy. "Not unless you drown them
with drink or fat or drugs or despair."

Despair—that was Grandmother's problem. And maybe
the rest of the family too.

Across the table, Uncle Dan was talking about a writer
whose books were much more successful than his own.

"Classic symptoms of paranoid schizophrenia, Fee, a
highly organized set of distorted beliefs by which he attempts
to explain everything that happens to him. He suffers from
delusions of both persecution and grandeur, rejection of all
authority, and inability to maintain close relationships with
others—Oedipal conflicts and a loveless childhood, you see."

"Really." Uncle Dan had taken a few courses in psychol-
ogy in graduate school and delighted in psychoanalyzing everyone, especially authors, both living and dead. Fionna
liked him much better as the cautious scholarly priest who
had been so kind to her when Dad left.

"He's quite skillful at employing defense mechanisms
and delusions to control reality. He is not without intelligence, and he is thus able to mask his psychosis and give the
appearance of somewhat eccentric normalcy. He also is very
clever in using generosity to buy friendships. However, he is
a profoundly unhappy man and, of course, as you perceive,
Fee, has powerful if latent and unacknowledged suicidal
tendencies."

"Really!"

Fionna had asked Doctor Murphy about her uncle's
analyzing people, since he had many different explanations
for Mom's inability to sustain a "permanent relationship of
intimacy with a man." (For example: "The reason, Fee—and

I'm sure you'll not be shocked—is her unacknowledged desire for lesbian intimacy.")

"Horse manure," Doctor Murphy exploded. "Sorry, Fionna, that's the only dirty language I normally use. What I mean—"

"I know what you mean," Fionna giggled. Doctor Murphy joined her.

Uncle Dan was nice beneath all the horse manure, but the layers were getting thicker every year.

"His books sell well, don't they, Uncle Dan?" She put on her innocent face.

Her uncle's big brown eyes widened. Then he rolled them in mock despair. "Any literate person, Fee, knows that the reaction of semiliterate American readers is irrelevant in determining the quality of a writer. Almost by definition a writer who is popular with readers is irrelevant to students of serious literature."

"The reader be damned?"

"Precisely," he smiled triumphantly, missing her irony.

Fionna, who wanted as many people as possible to read the books she intended to write, withdrew mentally from the BORING conversation to fantasize about a story, a technique she used often at family gatherings when she and Rick were separated from each other.

Had Agatha Christie ever written a story about a murder on a ninety-five-foot power yacht?

Probably. She'd set her mysteries in just about every place a murder could occur.

Fionna intended to write mysteries. Also SF, Western, fantasy, horror, and spy stories. Also serious novels. Whatever they were. Tonight she would think about a mystery set on a boat like the *Violetta*.

Suppose that someone wanted to kill Grandmother. How would they do it?

The easiest technique would be to push her over the side of the boat when no one was looking. But Grandmother would make a loud splash and an even louder screech unless she was totally wasted from her vodka martinis.

There was, of course, the gun in Grandmother's cabin, given to her by, of all people, Bishop Uncle.

She glanced at the handsome man next to her, with the sad, sad eyes. Something terrible had happened in his life. Would that give him motive for murder? Could he blame his mother?

Offhand, Fionna couldn't think of a reason, but since it was a story instead of real life, she would make Grandmother the one who had wrecked his career in the church. There was no reason that she could see why one would want a career in such a horrible institution, but Bishop Uncle did and that was sufficient grounds for murder.

Luisa had cried out in horror when she had found the automatic in the bag of Grandmother's things that she and Fionna were unpacking earlier in the day.

"Nine-millimeter Beretta." Fionna had pretended to be sophisticated, but the weapon scared her too. "With a silencer that is longer than the gun." She picked up the pistol and held it almost lovingly. Compact, cleverly designed death. You could solve a lot of problems with it. She stared at the weapon, fascinated, hypnotized.

"Put it down, señorita," Luisa had pleaded. "It is evil."

"Yes, it is." Fionna had shuddered and quickly stored the pistol in a drawer next to Grandmother's bed. "But it helps her to sleep at night. That's all it's for."

However, it was readily available for Fionna's mystery.

A locked-room mystery in Lake Michigan? Using the silencer, someone might shoot Grandmother—she shivered with inappropriate delight—throw the weapon out of the window of her cabin, sneak out the door, lock it from the outside and maybe even go over the side of the boat in a wet suit like someone in a James Bond movie.

Only, the temperature of Lake Michigan according to the weather radio was seventy-two degrees, so you wouldn't need the wet suit.

Except maybe as a disguise.

Now who might the killer be? Well, there were lots of people with motives.

Bishop Uncle to restore his career. Uncle Dan because he needed the money he would inherit for his magazine. Uncle Ed because he needed the money to meet his margin calls. Aunt Min because maybe Grandmother was going to tell Uncle Ed about her love affairs. Aunt Lena because Grandmother still wanted Uncle Dan to return to the priesthood. Rick because . . .

No. Rick would not be a suspect and that was that. Totally.

Mom because she wanted to return to Dad and would never be able to do it while Grandmother was still alive. Carlos and Tomas, or even Luisa? No, it was cheating to make servants the murderers. Mr. Nelligan and Mary Feehan? No reason for them. But what if . . . Fionna pondered . . . what if they had been lovers long ago and Grandmother had prevented them from marrying?

No, too much like a Harlequin romance.

WELL . . . who has the strongest motive?

You do, geek. You inherit most of the money now. But if you stand by Rick, you could lose it all. You'd keep Rick, get Daddy back, liberate Mom, and satisfy your murderous anger.

I'm not that angry. . . .

Doctor Murphy seemed a little afraid of how angry you were.

Don't be silly. It's only a story. In some mysteries the attractive young heroine is the killer. Why not in this story?

Then Grandmother—the real one, not the one in the story—stumbled back to the table. Half wasted, but coherent enough. "The drink doesn't interfere with her thinking, at all, at all," Mary Feehan often said. It did, of course, but not very much.

Grandmother slumped in her vast chair at the end of the table and began to drink the coffee that Luisa, in fear and trembling, and Mary, in cool serenity, brought her. She mumbled and grumbled but did not seem to want to talk to anyone. The boring conversations began again, hesitantly for fear an unfortunate word would send Grandmother off on a tirade.

She looks so old and sick and unhappy and fat. Dear God, please don't let that happen to me.

Once Grandmother had been young and filled with expectations of happiness in life. Where and why had her dreams gone sour? Did the dreams of all women turn sour?

Luisa and the two men began to clear the table. The anchor slipped noisily into the water. The first day of the party was coming to its usual end—Grandmother wasted and everyone else frightened.

Fionna considered the women around the table, stirring their coffee or nibbling at the remains of the melted parfaits. How many of them had seen their dreams turned into nightmares?

Mom? Slightly tipsy as she always was after two drinks, she was daydreaming at the end of the table. Mom spent her days reading, watching public television, and going by herself to serious films at the Biograph and the Fine Arts. Fionna's fantasies were intermittent escapes from boring reality. Mom's daydreams were her reality.

Aunt Lena? Watching with hurt, hateful eyes for a hint of a slight because she had married a priest, the poor woman didn't realize that no one gave a damn anymore.

Aunt Min? Brittle, nervous, a little cheap. Did not her high-pitched laughter probably hide pain over her husband's failures as an investor and a lover? And how did she cope with her three kids when Uncle Ed was stewing about margin calls and maybe his favorite orderlies?

Luisa, trembling as she removed the dishes, lest she break something and be humiliated again by Grandmother? Poor child, might she not one day find herself on the road back to Mexico if Grandmother, wasted out of her mind, called the INS?

What chance do any of them have? Fionna wondered. What chance did they ever have?

The only one who was happy was Mary Feehan, with a fine husband, a healthy bunch of kids, and real cute grandchildren. Yet she too seemed to have some mysterious, unhappy secret.

I don't want to be like any of them, but what chance do I have?

"My dear, it's time we be leaving." Vincent Nelligan had shambled up to Grandmother. "It is a long ride back to Lake Forest. Richard and I will return first thing in the morning. . . ." His weary voice trailed off into a raspy hack.

Grandmother glared up at the frail, bent old man who hovered over.

"You can come back, but keep that dumb punk off my boat. I didn't want him here tonight and I don't want him around here tomorrow. If my granddaughter does not give him up, I will destroy both of them. Count on it, Vinney. I'll get rid of both of them."

Fionna was something of a short hitter too. A couple of glasses of wine, however, did not make her sleepy as much as pugnacious.

"Shut up, you drunken old hag," she shouted. "You hurt my lover and I'll kill you." She stumbled up to Grandmother and shook a fist in her face. "If he doesn't come back tomorrow morning, you'll never live for the return trip to Montrose. You're dead. History. Archives."

Grandmother leered at her, pleased that she had goaded someone into an angry reply. "You'll die first, my dear, I've killed smarter men and women than you."

Fionna shook the old woman's shoulders, rock solid mounds of bone and muscle. "I'll break your neck, you sick old bitch."

Even in her temper tantrum, a voice in the corner of Fionna's head observed that (a) she'd made Grandmother happy by losing her temper because that's what the party was all about, and (b) she really wasn't as mad as she sounded.

Grandmother cackled joyously and threw a glass of red wine on Fionna's peach-colored dress. Fionna went for her eyes.

Mom, of all people, pulled her off. She turned to fight with Mom.

"She's ruined your life, I'm not going to let her ruin mine."

Then Rick took over from Mom and dragged her back, kicking, scratching, screaming, to the aft deck.

" 'I'm gonna liberate you, confiscate you,' " he imitated Bruce Springsteen in "Rosalita."

Rick was such a nerd when Fionna met him that he didn't know beans about rock music. She had patiently educated him—and astonished him with her photographic memory for lyrics—and now he had very discriminating tastes. He liked the Talking Heads for example and not the Beach Boys or the Monkees.

So Fionna stopped fighting and cried in his arms.

So much crying these past few days.

Then Luisa and Mary Feehan joined them and made Fionna take off her wine-splattered dress and put on her terry cover-up. "Use salt and then soda water," Mary told the distraught Mexican teen. "And don't worry about Doña Fionna, she'll be all right."

"Sure she will," Rick insisted.

Fionna wasn't so sure.

"Your grandmother is back in bed now. Sure, she didn't mean it. Too much of the drink was taken, that's all."

"She did too mean it." Fionna cowered under her robe. "She did too."

"I'll come back tomorrow with Grandpa." Rick kissed her gently. "Don't worry, Fee. It'll all work out."

"Only when she's dead."

"Now don't say that." Mary made her sit down on a deck chair. "The poor woman has had such a hard life—"

"And she wants everyone else to have a hard life too."

"You just sit down here and watch the stars and calm down." Mary ignored her complaint. "And like this dear boy says, everything will work out all right."

"And I do love her too." Fionna tried to lay back in the chair. "I hate her and I love her. Oh, Mary, I don't know what to do."

So Rick left, after another kiss, and Fionna and Mary sat watching the stars.

"Sorry, Mary," she said finally. "I grossed out. I'm as short a hitter as Mom."

"You're both sweet wonderful women. Now, don't you think you ought to get some sleep? Your grandmother didn't mean any harm. It's just that she loves you so much."

Fionna wanted to argue that it was a hell of a kind of love. But she was too tired.

First she went to the bridge and made a phone call on the *Violetta*'s ship-to-shore phone. She waited twenty minutes for a response to the message she had left. The conversation helped a little.

Then she shuffled down to the cabin she shared with her mother, tiptoed into the tiny room so as not to wake Mom, undressed in the dark, pulled on her sleep T-shirt, and fell into her bed.

Mom was asleep in the next bed, breathing softly. Fionna twisted and turned, but sleep would not come.

So she decided to continue her fantasy that she was living in a mystery novel.

What were the other suspects saying and thinking?

Uncle Bishop would be kneeling on the prie-dieu in his room, head in his hands. What did I do wrong? he'd be asking God. What was my mistake? Why did my mother interfere and make everything worse? I became a priest to make her happy, but she's never satisfied with me. Will she ever leave me alone? Will I ever find any peace?

Fionna considered thoughtfully: Uncle Bishop was not a very good suspect.

Fionna rolled over, searching for a more comfortable position on the hard bunk.

Uncle Ed and Aunt Min, in their stateroom down the hall, were much better suspects.

AUNT MIN: She wants you to turn over all your money to her? What kind of a man would do that?

UNCLE ED: It's either that or face a grand jury.

AUNT MIN: I'll have to ask her permission to buy a dress?

UNCLE ED: I don't think it will come to that.

AUNT MIN: And she'll pick schools and spouses for our kids?

UNCLE ED (trying not to sob): She thinks I'll never be more than a little boy.

AUNT MIN: If you let her run your life, you have the courage of a little boy—a little coward at that.

UNCLE ED: Do you want me to go to jail?

AUNT MIN: She won't do that . . . will she?

UNCLE ED: You know what she's like.

AUNT MIN: I wish she'd die.

UNCLE ED: Don't say that, she's my mother.

AUNT MIN (sarcastically): I know, you love her. I still think we ought to find a way to kill her—and not get caught.

UNCLE ED: Don't even think that!

Then they would have a big fight.

And no reconciliation and lovemaking after it.

No way.

Great suspects.

Same for Uncle Dan and Aunt Lena. She'd egg him on like she always did.

AUNT LENA: She's not going to give you that money. You're entitled to it. Look at all the crap that's published. You have a right to an audience. Take the money from her.

UNCLE DAN: As my friend Saul Bellow would put it, the path of a genius is a rocky way.

AUNT LENA: Fuck Saul Bellow. He doesn't have any money. It all goes for alimony, like he says in his books. Your mother is filthy rich. Take it from her.

UNCLE DAN: She's the last of the great characters. Means well. Of course, Studs wants to interview her one of these days for his book on Chicago. And Jim Squires promised me a feature article in the *Trib*.

AUNT LENA: You're dreaming. And even if they do those things, she still won't give you enough money for the magazine. I hate her. I wish she were dead.

UNCLE DAN (only half listening to her because he is so busy listening to himself): Don't say that. Maybe she'd go on the board of the Friends of the Public Library. . . .

AUNT LENA: She hates me. We ought to kill her. Then the money would be ours.

UNCLE DAN: Most of it goes to Fionna.

AUNT LENA: She's a little bitch, but she's generous.

Fionna pondered the last line. Yes, she supposed she'd give Uncle Dan the money for his magazine. Why not? It wasn't much, and it would make them happy.

Let's see who else? Mary Feehan?

Such a nice, gentle lady? She couldn't kill someone, could she?

Well, in a lot of mystery novels, it was the lovely lady who seemed so good who was the real killer. Trouble was . . . Fionna rolled over again . . . how could you find a motive for Mary?

WELL . . . it was kind of funny that she kept coming back to visit. Like maybe Grandma was blackmailing her?

Not very likely. But maybe . . .

Then she imagined Rick and Mr. Nelligan driving back to Lake Forest in the chauffeur-driven Lincoln.

RICK: Grandfather, I am not like Bill Downs. I will not give up. No one will take Fionna away from me. Even if I have to kill her.

MR. NELLIGAN (hardly listening): She drove all my children away. You're the only one I have left.

RICK (cool and reasonable): I don't think I'll have to kill her, but Bill Downs didn't have the courage even to think about killing her.

MR. NELLIGAN: Downs was smart, he escaped while he could. I should have done that, Rick. You should too. Fionna is not worth it.

RICK: She is totally worth it.

Nope, Fionna decided, Rick would never use the words "totally worth it." And he wouldn't think about killing anyone, would he?

Poor dear boy.

She smiled contentedly. Well, it was nice to think that he might become violent to protect her.

Would he really?

No way.

Okay. It's only fantasy.

In the servants' quarters Luisa might be talking to Carlos and Tomas.

LUISA: She is a *muy* bad woman. Maybe we should kill her for the Señorita, even if she does not want us to.
Would be difficult?

TOMAS (rubbing his finger along the sharp edge of a knife): For *hombres* like us it would be like slicing a piece of ripe fruit.

Fionna shivered. Carlos and Tomas were scary. And, anyway, it was bad technique to make the servants the criminals.

Who else?

Poor Mom. She's probably dreaming about Dad. Like every night I bet. She has tons of reasons for wanting to kill Grandma. What was it Rick said about her? "The fires are deep, Fee, but they're like an acetylene torch. If someone ever touches the right switch . . ."

"Not Mom," Fionna had replied. "No way."

But she wasn't so sure about that. If Mom did it, Fionna would never tell.

Well, that's the whole list of them. Like the house guests at an English country home on a weekend. Except it's a boat off Monroe Street in Chicago. And two of the suspects aren't even here.

Wait a minute, Fionna Marie Elizabeth Downs. You forgot someone. The best suspect of all.

Who?

You know whom.

I hate her! Fionna sat bolt upright in bed. I hate her!
She's done terrible things to everyone. Totally.
And she'll do the same to me too!
I want her dead more than all the others!
Fionna pounded the bunk furiously.
If I kill her, everyone else will have a little extra chance
at the happiness Grandma took from them.
She collapsed back on her pillow, wanting to cry and not
finding the tears.
God damn her.
Should I call Doctor Murphy again?
You'd only be a pest. She's entitled to a weekend away
from her patients.
But she said to call. . . .
Fuck it.
Don't use language like that.
I still wish she was dead. I might kill her after all.
How?
I'm the mystery writer. If I do kill her, it will be in a way
that I'll never get caught.
A perfect crime.
That's what they all say.
Except I'll REALLY commit the perfect crime.
Like maybe a locked-room puzzle that no one can solve,
huh?
And Doctor Murphy will laugh at you when you tell her
about this fantasy. And you'll have to tell her because you
promised.
Finally Fionna drifted off into a restless sleep, like she'd
had too much to drink. She dreamed all night that she had
shot her grandmother and pushed the dead body into the
waters. Then Grandmother rose from the lake and pulled
Fionna in after her.

JOE MURPHY'S STORY

1

"How often are matriarchs assassinated?" my wife demanded, brushing her gold and silver hair with impassioned fury.

"Rarely, if I remember the data correctly." I put the book I was reading next to me on our bed. "Only when they deserve to be liquidated. Are you expecting someone to attempt to dispose of you?"

Outside, under a cover of late-August stars, in which it was alleged you might find Halley's comet if you tried hard, the waters of Lake Michigan licked softly against our beach. It was the kind of warm summer night toward the end of August, to which you wanted to cling as you would to the last taste of a Sachertorte—so my wife had said earlier when we were climbing out of our pool, not yet disturbed by the late night call from her answering service.

The Ryan family's metaphors usually referred to food.

Tomorrow, free temporarily of all responsibility for our children, we would sail our thirty-two-foot boat, *M.K.*, across Lake Michigan to Monroe Street, mostly because it was there.

"I am not a matriarch!" Mary Kate slammed the brush on her vanity table. "I will not permit you to label me!"

In her family all women are matriarchs, including Brigid, our teenage daughter, currently on a visit to California. If our as-yet-unborn grandchild should emerge as a baby girl, she would be a matriarch the day she arrived.

"Would you believe a good as well as beautiful matriarch?" I asked tentatively as I eased my way to the side of
the bed.

If you have any sensitivity at all, you learn after almost
twenty-five years of marriage to read the signs. If the hair-
brushing ritual at the end of the day is performed with the
woman partially or totally naked, a nude or bare-breasted
Juno or Diana, the message is that if you don't make love to
her you may have to face a divorce lawyer the next day. If the
woman is wearing underwear when she attacks her hair, she
is indicating her availability should you be interested. If she
is bundled up in a robe, she is implying that while, of course,
if you insist, she loves you too much to flat-out refuse, she'd
much rather fall asleep immediately without any preliminary activities.

A frail summer nightgown on a humid, sensuous, sleepy
August night, with just a touch of dank autumn smell in the
air, is a more ambiguous communication, one demanding
cautious hermeneutics. When it is combined with a banging
hairbrush, the message is probably that while you are not
her training analyst, she is worried about a case and wants
to talk shop—and very likely be loved afterward for purposes
of reassurance.

Why else marry a man who is a psychiatrist like yourself, especially if you're a classic Freudian and he is a
"Jungian eclectic"?

I knew all the signals and what I was supposed to do in
response. Nevertheless, our marriage was in a phase when I
was tired of the signals, tired of the response, tired of the role
into which I had been cast, and tired of the woman who had
cast me in that role—as desirable as she was and as much as
I loved her.

I tell my clients that a good sexual relationship does not
guarantee an easy marriage. It only makes the end of the
marriage intolerable.

I was especially tired of the agonistic, dialectical style
with which the Ryan clan—and especially its principal
matriarch—approached life. Could not she once, just once,

come at reality in some other modality besides the argumentative?

"I am not," she huddled under the protection of folded arms, "a devouring mother."

I sat next to her on the vanity bench and touched an ice-cold shoulder blade. "A matriarch is not necessarily a devouring mother and certainly not one against whom a person would feel murderous rage."

If I could have imagined the trouble her case would cause for us, I would have been less flippant in my tone.

"How can you tell?" She tried to shrug my arm away from her stony shoulders.

"Mary Kate!" I used the tone of voice one must sometimes use with a mate to indicate that a certain kind of behavior is intolerable. A husband cannot respond to a plea for consolation when his preliminary efforts at response are fought off.

Was I tempted not to respond?

Only in remote theory. Argumentative or not, my wife is irresistible. Which made my resentment against my role as the saint who put up with her peculiarities all the more intolerable.

Not that there were not rewards in being a saint to her woman-who-would-try-the-patience-of.

But that wasn't my Mary Kate either.

"Sorry." She leaned contritely against my encompassing arm. "I'm worried."

Heaven knows she had reason to worry, though not that she was a devouring mother.

"About a case?" I began the task of massaging the tension out of her neck and back and shoulder muscles, with fingers searching for the depths of her fear in a mix of implacable demand and delicate reassurance, a combination which I am sometimes able to approach. "Someone with murderous rage against a devouring mother?"

"Grandmother. . . . I don't know why you put up with me." Her body slowly relaxed against mine. "What do you Jungians know about devouring mothers?"

"In the myths they are not ritually murdered. Quite the contrary." I brushed away a white strap, the better to massage her shoulder and eventually to gain access to one of her sumptuous breasts—what else does a man want on a hot summer night, especially if the breasts have to be as mysterious and wonderful as those of my wife? "In Mexico and the Middle East and in the Kali cult in India, for example, you cope with them by sacrificing children to them. They are too strong to kill."

"Bitches," she shivered.

"The structure of the myth"—I removed the other strap—"correlates with an experience with which humankind is all too familiar: mother love and mother protection running out of control and destroying those it purports to love and protect."

Mary Kate's body no longer enjoys the youthful perfection it possessed on our comedic wedding night. But it has been fiercely disciplined against the erosion of time, and those marks which time has managed to impose on it only make it more appealing. Fully clad, she turns my knees to water. With her gown hanging from her waist as it now was, her back arched against my chest, and her slick, perfumed body defenseless to my desires, she drives me out of my mind. I began to stroke her breasts, lightly at first, then with insistence and implacable demand.

It is conventional to say that the first thing you notice about my wife is her scorching blue eyes. But if you're a man, the first thing you notice is her breasts, whether you're a young resident in Little Company of Mary Hospital twenty-five years ago or a teenage boy watching Biddy Murphy's mother put on a life jacket on our water-ski boat. I cupped my hands around the suntan lines of both breasts. She smiled affectionately at me, a hint of a modality much deeper than the dialectical. It was the same smile I had seen the first day at Little Company and on our wedding night when I began to explore for the first time her full wonders.

Each time I see that smile, whose meaning I've never understood and never asked about, I feel like an adored pet, an amusing little boy, a plaything which she enjoys enormously.

It is not a feeling that I want to protest. Or even could protest if I wanted to.

"Am I like that?" She continued the discussion as though we were around a conference table instead of in the midst of intense foreplay. "I mean, I do interfere a lot. With our kids. I was a bitch about Caitlin's marriage, wasn't I? And with my brothers and sisters and their kids. And even Dad and Helen and the little family...."

She meant Ned Ryan's children by his second wife.

I lowered my lips to one of her breasts, tasted the suntan line, and then took possession of a hard, jutting nipple.

Mary Kate had played many different womanly roles for me during our life together: mother, spouse, virgin, wise woman (to use my Jungian paradigms), and also colleague, friend, lover, orgy partner, adviser, buddy, adversary, critic, back stiffener, inspiration. But among the many dimensions of wifehood, the most important often seemed to be the mother role. She was the tender, caressing, nurturing mother who brought the gentleness to my life that I had never experienced as a child.

She was never more completely what I needed as a man than when I was a child at her breast.

God, I think, designed the womanly breast more for husbands than for children.

And this was a part of me that I yearned to share with her, had to share with her at this age of my life. She had sated my hunger and thirst for laughter and vitality and fun, but somehow refused to cast herself in the role of wife/mother for me.

Presumably there were hidden dimensions of her selfhood that I had resisted sharing too.

I removed my tongue from her nipple so I could answer her question. "The line between protectiveness and possessiveness is sometimes thin. You normally walk it with great skill. It's hard to let your daughter and confidante go."

My fingers slipped down to her well-muscled belly. "You released Caitlin with grace."

More grace, I could have added, than any of us might
have believed possible. More grace than the perceptive
Caitlin had expected. More grace even than the bride's
Jungian father displayed through the whole ecstatic agony
of losing your first daughter.

"Strong women are bitches." She pulled away from me
and turned to explore my face with tear-filled blue eyes. "I
hate them all."

"The other option is weak women who are leeches. We
Irish prefer the former." I recaptured her, turned her
around, drew her back against my chest, and reasserted my
rights to her breasts. "Tell me about the case."

"A woman in her late sixties; widow for thirty years;
made tons of money in real estate, much of it dishonestly, I
suspect; amoral—bribes, lies, cheats, steals; totally domi-
nates her children and grandchildren; makes decisions
about schools, careers, spouses, homes, even clothes, and tol-
erates no dissent." She sighed in response to the now vigorous and determined demands of my fingers against breasts
and belly. "She threatens to destroy the professional career
of an unapproved suitor and drive him out of town. All her
life my patient has been caught in this woman's prison. Now
she wants out—the patient is a kid a little younger than
Caitlin—and does not know how to escape. Hence murder
fantasies."

"You're worried that she means them literally?" I
paused in my pilgrimage across the gently curving plains of
her belly to the sacred forest swamp of her loins because it
was this fear that had begun the discussion and I did not
want to hurry its conclusion.

My wife hesitated. "I don't think so . . . but she is very
angry. There is a remote chance she might kill the old
woman."

"And you're worried about your professional responsibility?" I kissed her neck very gently. "What would the family do if you shared their fears with them?"

Mary Kate stiffened in my arms, angry and frightened. "The old lady would go after my license. She might even try to have me killed."

Foolishly I did not take that remark literally.

"So you certainly have no obligation to warn her."

"I guess not." She relaxed fully into my possession. "I love you so much, Joe Murphy."

"And I you, Mary Kate Ryan Murphy." I again assaulted her face and her throat and her mouth and her chest with my kisses. "And you are a good matriarch—you don't deprive anyone of their freedom."

"Only," she sniffled through her tears, "because I have a strong husband to draw the line and love me anyway. Why can't the goddamn Irish produce enough strong men to go around? Why are Irish men so easily intimidated? Do I intimidate you?"

Brusquely she pushed away her nightgown and let it fall on the floor next to the vanity. She sighed deeply, exulting, as she often does, in her nakedness.

"All the time," I admitted honestly enough, as my fingers and lips preempted her most intimate womanly secrets and made them my own once again. I played with them, fondled them, teased them, caressed them. "You're a challenge every moment we're together."

"I don't mind being a challenge." Her body twitched as little, tormenting charges of electricity coursed through the nerves in her thighs and back, preludes to a much more powerful charge of energy that was yet to come. "But I don't want to be a castrating bitch."

"As ought to be obvious at this moment, woman, you're not."

My own eyes were misting, as they often do when I am confronted with my wife's piquant mixture of passionate strength and anxious vulnerability, a glorious woman and a frightened child, an earth mother with hunger for the absolute, for which I am momentarily a more or less satisfactory substitute.

After all these years together I am still awed by the

magic I seem to be able to work on this brilliant, tough, magnificent woman, a giant in our profession, important in our city, indefatigable in controversy, and uncannily skilled in making the sick less sick and even, on occasion, well.

All her poise and self-possession, all her aloof dignity, all her often furious strength collapse when I undo a button or a zipper or a hook, or brush against a breast or mischievously pat a rump or squeeze a thigh. With the most abject and suppliant admiration in her eyes, her lips surrender to mine; her mouth opens and her jaw drops at my touch; her breasts absorb my playful hands and demand their sustained attention; her nipples rise to my lips; her body twists and squirms to my tickling fingers; her loins flood at my probe; her body arches against mine; her legs part readily to receive me; her eager groans respond to my thrusts, and on the mountaintop of our pleasure she cries out in painful delight at my love.

And then, sometimes with ribald laughter, sometimes with pathetic tears, sometimes with a mixture of both, she thanks me for my patience and forbearance in loving her.

And I am her equal in nothing of which I am aware— although the mythology in her family holds exactly the opposite.

Before we could continue this always new scenario, the problem of the matriarch archetype had to be resolved, temporarily at least.

"It's such a thin line"—her hands on mine, not to impede but to encourage—"you can't be sure when you're protecting and when you're possessing, when you're helping them and when you're hanging on to them too long."

We clung to each other silently, listening to the lake and waiting for the next phase of our passion. Her lips tasted of vodka (one) and salami (one sandwich without the bread) and faintly of chlorine from our pool.

"A matriarch who can give herself, as you're doing now, will never be a devouring mother."

"She can't do that unless she lucked out in her man." Mary Kate stood up and took my hand. "My patient's grandmother didn't. He was a wimp. I married"—she grinned impishly—"a rapacious pirate who would not tolerate a devouring mother."

We embraced vehemently, summing up in an instant all the ebb and flow of passion in our marriage.

"Stop tickling me, beast," she insisted.

"I will not . . . cut it out . . ."

She jabbed her finger at my ribs. "See you don't like it when I—oh, Joe, I love you so much. . . ."

Struggling, wrestling, giggling, we fell to our bed—that same couch of luxury, as the old spiritual books would have called it, in which three of our four children had been conceived. Caitlin in all probability was the result of a honeymoon romp on a Caribbean beach. Or rather a night of romps, the precise number of which we had not been able to count.

Fortunately for me, our wrestling did not include the karate Mary Kate and Brigid had taken up last year after Caitlin saved Brendan Ryan's life in a fight in the Karwick Plaza parking lot. All one needs is an aggressive wife who is not only big and physically strong but in training for her black belt.

That night in late August, however, she was in a submissive mood. As I was arranging her limbs in an appropriate pattern for the final act of our drama and tormenting her loins with my kisses, she murmured, "You'll never let me become a devouring mother, will you, Joe Murphy?"

"Not a chance! Now forget about your case and think about me."

"Not much choice, is there?" she groaned complacently.

Mary Kate fell asleep immediately after our interlude of passion. She slept, as she always did after lovemaking, soundly and serenely. "It beats martinis and you don't wake up at two o'clock sober and there's no hangovers," she explained often.

It was my turn to worry.

My woman is a pro, quite possibly the best analyst in Chicago, smarter, more sensitive, and more brilliantly unorthodox than I could be in twenty lifetimes. She worries about her cases, more than I do, mostly because she is a woman and women worry. But her fear tonight was different. It didn't quite make sense. A young woman felt murderous rage against a domineering grandmother. Fair enough, but such situations are no more unusual than the rising of the sun in the morning. Among the Irish it was a commonplace, maybe one family in five had a devouring mother messing around with and messing up the lives of her children and grandchildren.

What was so special about this one?

I stirred uneasily, as a shade flapped against a screen in a light breeze.

The matriarch's appetite must be especially voracious and the young woman's hunger for freedom at least as voracious.

The Ryans were a hungry clan too. One ought not to be deceived by their casual, comic upper-middle-class professional pose. They were voracious—not, to use Ernest Bloch's phrase, hungry for more of what they already had, but for what they did not have. Money didn't drive them. They lived as comfortable professionals well below the possibilities of their incomes.

What did they want then? For what did they hunger? Excitement, adventure, novelty, romance. Most of their generation of Chicago Irish had been hounded by the fear of enjoying too much the things one likes to do, because, if one is to believe Mary Kate, they were either overstimulated or understimulated as babies.

No one would say that the Ryan clan was afraid of challenge or stimulation. They were all hungry. Mary Kate to be an analyst, Eileen to be a federal judge, Packy for political power, Nancy for a writer's reputation, Blackie the priest . . . well, God knew what he wanted other than a second dish of chocolate ice cream, but he certainly wanted it.

Despite the idyllic weekend on which we were embarking and despite the exhausting satisfaction of our romp, our marriage was not in particularly good shape. The silver anniversary was drawing near, as was my mate's fiftieth birthday. A grandchild was on the way; Caitlin, in a typical ploy, had conceived earlier in the marriage than she had been conceived, breaking all the mores of contemporary childbearing (which said you did not, repeat *not*, become pregnant immediately after your wedding). M.K. was already older than her mother, Kate Collins Ryan, had been when she died. Our professional careers were more demanding and less satisfying. The nest was emptying rapidly; in another year, when Biddy went off to college, it would be quite vacant.

I don't think we disagreed any more than we had in our earlier years. But the disagreements seemed never to be resolved. She had favored strictness with the older children, I leniency. Now she belabored me that I was being far too harsh on our contentious, outspoken Brigid, who thought, I argued, that rules were made only to be broken.

And she worried about the relationships between our two sons and their young women friends, fretting about whether Tim and Jean Ryan were rushing toward marriage too hastily and Pete and his Cindasoo far too slowly.

She would become indignant when I suggested that she would advise any client who was the mother of two such young men that they would move at their pace (and their women's pace) and not ours.

It did not help that we both knew that we could survive this crisis of multiple turning points. Of course we could, but it would require hard work and painful honesty. We seemed to have no time for either.

We had so little time—in both our days and our lives.

When you're both psychiatrists, the only difference it makes at such a time in your relationship is that you know more explicitly the problem which you're facing separately instead of together.

Death.

Even the Ryans are mortal and must contend with the anguish of mortality approaching.

What happens to the hungry when they grow older?

They become more hungry.

Challenge, excitement, novelty. All right, but that is much better than devouring your children.

A strong woman, in the absence of a strong man and a hunger for new stimulation, would of course turn upon her own and consume them.

What was so unusual about this case, however?

What did Mary Kate say when I raised the question of conferring with the family?

"The woman would go after my license"?

What kind of an idiot would do that in response to a well-intentioned warning?

A name flashed across my mind.

Enright!

Was Mary Kate mixed up with a rebellious Enright?

I felt sweat at the back of my neck. Mrs. Harrington Enright would indeed stop at nothing if she felt her brood of chicks and chicklets was in jeopardy.

Nothing.

The Ryan clan was tough and loyal. But a fight with the Harrington Enrights, a family for whom ethics hardly existed?

I considered my sleeping wife's pretty, innocent face. A chill slipped through the screens and across our bed.

Quite irrationally, I was afraid, for the first time in our marriage, that I might lose her.

■——————————————————————————————■

2

On Sunday morning we woke to find Mrs. Harrington Enright towering over the bulkhead of the *M.K.*, an angry lioness going about seeking whom she may devour.

"Your services are no longer required, Doctor Ryan," she howled, now more like a hyena or a coyote than a lioness.

"This is your recompense." Her murky blue eyes were dark, obsidian pools of rage and hate, two hard blank stones of cheap costume jewelry.

Mrs. Harrington Enright managed to tower even though she is a short, solid, compact building-block version of the devouring matriarch. She was not much over five feet high and gave the impression, without ever suggesting the unspeakable word "fat," of being almost as broad—solid muscle, solid strength, solid woman. Perhaps her regal impact that morning was aided by the flowing lemon-colored caftan she was wearing and the matching lemon scarf around her almost nonexistent neck.

One could also not avoid being impressed by the motor launch that had brought her to the *M.K.*, a fourteen-foot boat piloted by a young Hispanic dressed like he was perhaps Admiral Dewey. Mrs. Harrington Enright sat solidly in the launch like a cube-faced, cube-eyed Cleopatra on her imperial barge.

My bare-breasted wife struggled out of my arms, looked about for a garment, threw a robe around herself, and shoved open the cabin door.

"I beg your pardon?" A sleek, sinewy woman tiger whose whisper was more terrible than Mrs. Harrington Enright's howl.

I'll bet on her.

"A thousand-dollar bill, Dr. Ryan. If you continue your efforts to destroy my granddaughter's sanity, I'll have you disbarred."

"My surname is Murphy. You disbar lawyers not doctors. My husband and I are on our boat in Sunday-morning privacy. And I will not discuss my patient with you."

Oh boy, duck.

"A thousand dollars, Dr. Ryan," she screeched, throwing the bill on our carefully polished teakwood deck. "And leave my family alone, or no one in your family will be safe."

Hugging her robe close about her, my sleepy-eyed, tousle-haired mate scooped up the money, tore it in two, and threw it into the calm water of Monroe Street harbor.

"Fuck off, you castrating bitch!"

Language I have heard no more than once a year in our marriage.

"You and your family will regret that obscenity for the rest of your lives!" the sawed-off lioness bellowed. She swatted her pilot on the shoulder, and the Harrington Enright launch departed in a burst of angry sound.

"Get stuffed!" Mary Kate yelled after her, sounding very much like her teenage daughter, the ineffable Brigid. "And leave my kids alone or I'll blow your brains out."

Mary Kate stormed back into our cabin.

"Hooray for our team," I shouted tentatively.

"Wipe that amused, proud grin off your face, Doctor Murphy"—she whirled on me, her robe falling open—"or I'll tear you apart just like I did Grover Cleveland."

I yawned contentedly. "Unless you tie the belt on your robe, I think there'll be other activity first."

"Don't you ever get tired of being a rapacious pirate, tormenting your poor, modest, captive matron?" She swept off her robe like a sweaty goddess of the hunt returning from chasing lions and flipped her panties aside with a single swift movement.

"No," I said mildly as she threw herself on top of me. "Though I think there's some weakness in your metaphor."

"I want my men naked." She tore off my shorts. "And thoroughly aroused."

I have never been able to understand the psychodynamics that constrain my wife to desire abandoned sex with me when she is savagely angry at someone else. Not that it is necessary that I understand. Or even relevant.

But then I don't understand her very well despite our quarter century together.

Thus, she had argued with frantic piety for that entire period of time that she was five pounds overweight. When the new standards came out during the summer of 1985, she was then, by official definition, no longer overweight. From the Olympian heights of my psychiatric wisdom, I predicted (to myself—to mention it to her would have cost me my life) that she would promptly add five more pounds—a modification which on her tall, classic figure and large frame would not have made an appreciable difference, not as far as I would notice.

She did not, in fact, gain an ounce. Indeed she lost two pounds.

I suspected (again I would have jeopardized my continued existence by vocalizing this suspicion) that she knew what I was thinking and was determined to prove me wrong.

So that fateful Sunday morning in Monroe Street harbor she besieged me, assailed my defenses, battered down my resistance, and captured me with especially dissolute tactics—all the while assuring me, as the sweat gushed off both our bodies, that she loved me beyond description, that she did not know how or why I put up with her, and that she could not survive without me.

None of which I can comprehend. I know what the words mean, but I cannot grasp the reasons behind them.

She saved me from being a desiccated, stuffy academic. And still does. Every day.

Not since the day she agreed to marry me have I been able to understand why this Irish Diana—Maeve or Morrigan or one of those, I suppose—should choose me to be her lover.

In the autumn of 1960 a new group of medical school clerks appeared in the corridors of the psych unit at Little Company of Mary Hospital. Although I was only a second-year resident I was deputed to supervise their six weeks in the unit—which meant that I must awe them with my greater experience and wisdom and knowledge. Since most students were frightened their first time on the psych floors, that did not promise to be too difficult a task.

I saw her at the other end of the corridor and heard her laugh and revised my strategy. If I were not careful, this loud, shapely blonde with her devastating humor and distracting breasts would take my program away from me.

As I said before, I noted her flawlessly carved breasts before I saw the mischief dancing in her eyes. I was a male member of the human race, how else would I react?

And maybe, looking back on it now, a touch of interest in me. But I was not then the kind of young man who thought that such a woman could possibly be sexually fascinated by me.

Twenty-three years old, her mother dead a year, Mary Kathleen Ryan knew already that she was a woman of enormous personal power. She did not yet understand the nature of her influence on others and was awkward and unfocused in the exercise of her talents. Intelligence, wit, ambition, intense sexual energy, all packaged in a lush and supple body: Miss Ryan needed to learn restraint and self-discipline.

Or so I told myself.

She also scared the hell out of me.

"Miss Ryan?"

"Yes, Doctor Murphy?" Blue eyes dancing impishly.

"Do you think you might modulate your voice in the corridors of this unit?"

"I'll try, Doctor Murphy." A quick hint of pain in the same blue eyes, enough to break your heart.

"You'll have to do better than try, Miss Ryan."

"Yes, Doctor Murphy." The imp bounced back. "Why do you talk so funny, Doctor Murphy? Are you from somewhere strange?"

"I was raised in Boston."

"Well, you're honest about it."

Much laughter from the other students.

"I don't want this program"—my face flaming—"to become a wrestling match between us, Miss Ryan."

"That might be fun."

More laughter. First point to Miss Ryan.

I grew up on the poorest block in South Boston. My father worked on the streetcars. I was the youngest of eight, the only one to go to college and that by playing basketball at BC. I got into Harvard Medical on their last scholarship in my year, against the admission committee's better judgment because they didn't want too many Boston Irish scholarship students. I had little experience with women and none with middle western Irish aristocratic blondes.

I was not sensitive enough to the nuances to realize that the Ryans were not aristocrats, only upper-middle-class professionals.

Our power struggle in the LCM psych unit could be judged by someone favorably disposed to my side as at best a draw. She didn't take the unit away from me, but she did instruct and supervise the other students at least as much as I did. She was smarter, had read more psychiatry books, possessed sounder instincts, and exercised the indomitable willpower of a team of veteran Missouri mules. By sheer force of character and against my diagnosis she brought a frail girl only a couple of years younger than herself back from the edge of permanent catatonia.

After the first four weeks of the program she had also figured out how to manipulate me. I'm unclear even today about the precise strategy, but I think it involved (and still involves) sad eyes and a vulnerable smile.

I told myself that I would be happy to see the last of her, even if her departure meant that my deliciously obscene dreams about her went away.

And I did delightfully obscene things to her and with her every night in my dreams.

"Doctor Murphy . . ."

"Yes, Miss Ryan."

"I didn't want to leave without thanking you."

"You're quite welcome."

"I've decided that I will do my residency in psychiatry."

If I had followed my angry impulses I would have given her the usual lecture about why women should stay out of the field—pure chauvinism, though we didn't have the term in those days. My life would have been very different.

"I'm happy to hear that, Miss Ryan." I rose from my desk and extended my hand. "You will be a notable addition to the specialty."

"And, Doctor Murphy"—she shook hands firmly—"you still talk funny."

"The difficulty with your presence on a psychiatric floor,

Miss Ryan, is that you create sexual tension that can only be resolved by a lifetime in the marriage bed."

A crude and stupid comment, right?

She considered me as if I were a Maxwell Street merchant offering her an allegedly mink coat at a bargain price.

"All right."

"I beg pardon?"

"That *was* a proposal, wasn't it?"

My cosmos collapsed beneath my feet. "Remotely I suppose. That *was* an acceptance?"

"Most proximately!"

Instead of embracing her, I collapsed back into my chair. "I can't believe my good fortune."

"I'm the lucky one, Joseph Murphy." Her eyes filled with tears, not the last time I would see that phenomenon. "Don't you ever forget it."

I was a dull, dry academic, a pipe smoker without the pipe, on my way to the cynical boredom of a permanent Irish bachelor's life. Without much ceremony and without the slightest hint from me (of which I was aware, anyway) that I might like the ride, I was dragged on a roller coaster of passion and laughter and excitement.

And, somehow, the Ryans define me as the gentle saint who puts up with their kookiness and keeps M.K. in line, more or less. Their definition obviously is not true. But we all need myths.

It was repeated again that morning in August of 1985, in the cabin of the boat that bears her name and which she gave me as a fiftieth-birthday present.

"I didn't hurt you, did I, Joe?" She was still panting from our exertions.

"Call intensive care. We both need it."

I struggled to realign my pulse and respiration. On other occasions my tiger lady was as gentle as a mother touching a newborn's smallest finger.

I'd given up trying to predict.

"I really mean it." She laughed happily. "I don't want to hurt you."

"Have you ever?"

"I can't believe that I become that crazy."

"I can."

She snuggled closer to me. "If it were not for you, I'd be as bad as that poor woman."

"Nonsense." I kissed her lips lightly. We had to get beyond this saint/demon role definition.

"It's *not* nonsense. Look at the way I interfered in Caitlin's romance."

"Your exact words were 'Caitlin, if you let that red-haired giant get away, I'll never speak to you again.' "

"You know what I mean. I'm only a thin line away from Violet Harrington Enright."

"A light year."

"A millimeter. . . . Anyway, let me see what I can produce for breakfast. You looked starved."

"That's not necessary. We can go ashore to the Chicago Yacht Club. I'm not hungry."

"I *am*." She bounded out of bed and wrapped a navy blue towel around her waist. "We can eat brunch later on. I adore their pastries."

"Mary Kate."

"Yes, master. I recognize the commanding tone."

She sat on the edge of our bunk, ready to be commanded.

I rested a hand on either breast, in affection rather than desire. "You are not in the least like Mrs. Enright Harrington . . ."

"Harrington Enright."

She can't resist corrections. None of them can.

"Precisely. As you well know from your own practice, not all women, not even all strong-willed dominant women, become devouring mothers."

"I interfere a lot. . . . Hey, what are you doing to my tits?"

"Playing with them, as ought to be obvious. To return to my point, you usually resist the temptation to dominate." I pressed her breasts against her ribs, affection and desire now. "And when you succumb, you quickly recover. Your life history and your behavior patterns are not at all like hers. Interference, as you call it—concerned involvement, as I might call it most of the time—does not mean domination. I'd like to see you try to dominate, really and seriously, any of the clan. Eileen? Blackie? Ned? Come on. Manipulate a little, maybe." I grinned. "Not dominate."

"I'm not talking about psychiatry." She bowed her head and, stubbornly, would not look at me.

"What are you talking about?"

"Grace."

"Grace?"

"There but for the grace of God . . . you know."

Silence. The lines on the mast above us creaked softly. A drop of perspiration formed on her neck and slipped down her right breast.

"All right," she continued. "If I should ever freak out, it won't be quite like poor Vi. But if she had the right man in her life, she might not have freaked out either."

"We don't know that."

"And if I haven't freaked out yet"—she kissed me almost sadly—"it's because I've had the right man in my life. Now, unhand me, sir." She slipped away and tightened the towel at her belly. "I'll fry us some bacon and toast some English muffins with raspberry jam from Grand Beach and brew us some Earl Grey."

You see?

Have I ever won an argument?

Like the clerkship program, I sometimes manage a draw.

Still, she had touched on a truth that would be decisive in the maelstrom into which we would plunge before that glorious Sunday was over. As Blackie would express it, the men in the lives of hungry women are the difference between life and death.

For the women, he would add, his pale blue eyes blinking furiously, and for themselves.

We had sailed over the day before in eighteen-knot

breezes and four-foot waves, a stimulating and exhausting eight-hour technicolor challenge that permitted neither me nor my one-person crew a moment's inattention, lest the snarling, charging whitecaps surge over our gunwale.

The wind pulled her hair into an unruly, slightly tarnished halo and turned her face a youthful crimson. In white jeans and blue windbreaker—color coded to match the eyes, of course—she scampered around the deck in response to the captain's (my) orders, as if she were a demented adolescent, very like our own demented Biddy. There was no time for romance, save for an occasional quick brush of arms or touch of bodies or meeting of fingers when she passed me a cup of hot chocolate.

I did have time to note that in occasional interludes of tranquillity as she tightened the jib sheet, her face still reminded me of a Botticelli goddess. It was not a face much accustomed to tranquillity.

I resolved, nonetheless, that we must not wait till the symbol of the silver anniversary dinner to face the task of restructuring for the next quarter century.

I didn't want to lose her, you see.

The fairy-story skyscrapers of Chicago loomed up in front of us against the red and gold sky—not Beirut on the Lake, as the Lady Jane Byrne says, but Camelot on the Lake.

"This is how we'll go to heaven," she shouted, "not paddling down the Styx but sailing across a big lake in a spanking breeze toward a city of ivory and silver."

When we finally anchored at the family's hereditary mooring in Monroe Street harbor, we were too tired for the supper we had planned at the Yacht Club, too tired even for lovemaking. We ate salami sandwiches, drank Diet Cokes, stripped off most of our clothes, and collapsed into sleep, to be awakened the next morning by Mrs. Harrington Enright.

The Ryans had always been boat freaks, hence the membership in the Chicago Yacht Club. Ned Ryan had raced to Mackinaw before and after the War. (World War II is always "the War" to those who were in it.) The kids messed around with beach boats almost as soon as they learned how to walk. But there was too much of Great Depression Boston still buried in the corners of my soul. I could only look at the white sails pasted against the azure waters of the lake with feelings of inferiority and envy.

Besides, the family was not interested in serious racing. "Too much work," Ned had said, sighing contentedly. I agreed. But it seemed to me that if you were to have a sailboat of your own, you ought to be serious about it and that meant serious racing, right?

So I watched and envied and felt sorry for myself.

And didn't tell anyone.

The *M.K.* appeared at the doorstep—quite literally on a flatbed truck—of our home on Longwood Drive in Chicago on my fiftieth birthday.

"You don't have to race it," my wife told me. "You can just sail around in it and fondle your wife and enjoy yourself."

"I can fondle my wife even without the boat."

"But not on the lake."

Thus are Depression Irish nerds civilized.

And humanized.

We went out into the street, where our kids were already climbing over the *M.K.*

"Unlike its namesake," Caitlin sniggered, "it's second-hand."

"And unlike its namesake," Brigid snickered, "it's REAL old."

"And like its namesake," their mother added, "it will need constant care. Come on, you guys"—to our two sons who were already scheming on ways to race it on summer weekends out of New Buffalo—"figure out how we're going to transport it from here to Grand Beach."

"Call the Coast Guard," said red-haired Pete, who had begun to have a thing going with a petty officer, third class, at Michigan City named Cindasoo McLeod. From Stinking Creek, West Virginia.

Thus my wife and I, now dedicated day sailors, came to be in Monroe Street harbor on that August morning. Clad in swimsuits because it was going to be a hot, still day, we ate breakfast on the foredeck of the *M.K.*, enthusiastically devouring our bacon and English muffins and drinking our Earl Grey tea. M.K., the wife to be fondled not the boat to be sailed, babbled about the feats of the pastry chef at the Chicago Yacht Club. I watched through binoculars the activity on *Violetta*, the ninety-five-foot power cruiser of the Harrington Enrights, anchored beyond the inner breakwater like an overgrown child excluded from the company of normal-sized kids in the harbor.

"A woman can't be all bad if she owns a boat like that," I murmured as I examined the teak and mahogany superstructure of the luxurious craft. "If I live to be sixty, will you give me one?"

"Quiet." She jabbed a finger into my ribs. "It's really gross, Joe. I mean, she keeps it up in Montrose harbor. A couple of days each summer she's driven there from her Edgewater Beach apartment—worth two-point-five million, as she will tell you—in her Silver Cloud Rolls. Her dark-skinned crew putt-putts down here, she sits on the afterdeck under an umbrella, and the family comes on board to pay court to her and spend a happy overnight pajama party. Then they disembark and the crew putt-putts back to Montrose."

"Truly gross," I agreed. "When you give me a boat like that, we will putt-putt around the world."

"What are you doing?" she demanded.

"I thought this boat was for fondling my wife."

"In Monroe Street harbor?"

But she didn't try to stop me.

I brought the remains of breakfast back to the cabin, washed the dishes carefully—such a pragmatic feminist am I—and returned to the deck, my wife, and my minor sexual amusements.

With the other hand, however, I watched through my binoculars the crowd on the *Violetta* as they downed drinks and hors d'oeuvres at an astonishing rate. On Sunday morning.

Maybe it was the way to survive one of Vi's boating parties. She sat under a lemon yellow umbrella that seemed to match her caftan, a dark-skinned attendant in elaborate naval uniform on either side. Queen Victoria could not have had more ceremony, though the late Empress of India was much better looking than Mrs. Harrington Enright.

"The fat, long-haired one—probably in pink and white striped seersucker shorts?" Mary Kate sighed contentedly as my fondling continued. "That's Doctor Dan Harrington Enright, Ph.D.-type doctor, professor of English at De Paul and self-proclaimed 'Chicago writer.' Sometime lean, ascetic, dedicated Jesuit till he decided to let it all hang out. Which, as you can see, he did. The dumpy woman in the too tight jeans who watches him with furious jealousy is his wife, Lena, a professor of biology at the same distinguished university."

"Uh-huh."

"The tall man with wavy black hair, turning silver though you probably can't see it, dressed in black trousers and a clerical white shirt without a collar?"

"Bishop Harry Harrington Enright?"

"Got it. Joe . . . we can't do two things at once."

Virtuously she replaced the strap of her cream-colored swimsuit.

"Why not?"

"Playing with me in Monroe Street harbor on Sunday morning?"

"I don't think anyone can see us."

"The voyeurs with telescopes in the John Hancock?"

I removed the strap again. "Tell me about the bishop."

"You know the story. Brilliant, handsome young Vatican diplomat. Perhaps destined to be the Cardinal O'Connor of the Middle West. Got a little too involved in the dealings of the Vatican Bank and what Blackie calls the shadow world. Allegedly diverted money to Solidarity in Poland. Which was all right. Got caught. Which was not all right. Sent home in disgrace. Named auxiliary bishop here because Cardinal Cronin was willing to take him back. Does confirmations and things but has no power. Maybe you can smell his Aramis scent from here."

"Sad-looking man, even at this distance. Two priests in the family?"

"Right. Their mother consecrated them to Mary at their birth. Whether the mother of Jesus wanted them or not, she got them. Vi did a lot of double thinking when Dan departed from the Jesuits, but since he's her son, it became officially approved to leave the priesthood. I don't think she chose Lena for him either, which must gall her. But she and Lena share a taste for large jewels, so I guess it's all right. She did choose Minnie, though. Do you see her? Fancy, artificial affair, probably in black pajamas or something of the sort."

I moved the glasses to the left. "Yeah, sexy if you go for the type."

"You'd better not." My hand was temporarily brushed away. "Unless you like nymphos. You see, Vi defines something as real and it becomes real—this is all from common knowledge, not from my patient, by the way—so she defined Minnie as the woman for poor Edward Harrington Enright and she remains the woman for him. Eddie may be AC/DC and Minnie may be a punchboard, but neither reality exists because Vi says they don't."

I found Ed Enright, a colleague at Northwestern Hospital, though he never speaks to me. Or anyone else who is not a surgeon like himself. Or even a surgeon who is not a Republican far to the right of Jack Kemp. He is a good surgeon if unfortunately a stereotype—no, a caricature—of the surgeon myth: a waspish, arrogant little man with big head and small body and a face that makes you think of Rock Hudson, God be good to the poor man, until the illusion is shattered when you see his ridiculously puny body.

He appears on TV frequently, like a sawed-off Moses striding down from Sinai to denounce the legal profession and lead the fight against malpractice suits. To give him full credit, no one has won a suit against him.

"Poor Ed, a pathetic little man for all his bluster."

"If I were manipulating—your word, Doctor—that family, he should have been the priest and Harry should have been the politician and Dan should have been a bartender." Mary Kate rearranged her position on the towel but not so as to disturb my hand. "Do you see a pretty woman, very Irish looking, kind of beaten up?"

"Late thirties?" The woman, wearing a print summer dress, was sitting on a deck chair apart from the others, chin on her hand, reading a book. She didn't seem to be downing the Scotch and the martinis with the rest of them.

"Older than that. My patient's mother, Rita Downs. Husband deserted the ship, so to speak, eight years ago. Gave Rita a choice—Mom or me. The little fool took Mom. Lives with her, a fate worse than death."

"Any hope?"

"The husband has not remarried. Lives in L.A. Would take her back tomorrow, according to my patient. Do you see Fionna? Cute little button, round face, black Irish?"

I found an attractive child in a string bikini sitting next to an austere young man in whites and a dark blazer. He wore thick, horn-rimmed glasses.

"With a boy?"

"Rick Nelligan, O'Rourke Feed Grain, you know the Board of Trade money machine. Computers and math models. Wants to marry her. Grandma's opposed, of course. Threatens to destroy him. He encourages my client's determination to be a writer. He wouldn't be on the boat except he's Vinney Nelligan's son. Do you see Vinney? Courtly old banker type? He's been Vi's spear carrier for years."

"Yeah, he doesn't look very happy."

"No one has ever seen him look happy. What do you think of my client?"

"Nice figure, neat tits, luscious ass."

"Men!"

"Probably too young and too soft to fight Grandma off?"

"*Wrong!* I thought so at first too. Tough as they come. Vest-pocket matriarch. All of Vi's genes. That's why I worry about her murderous rage."

"Oh. Is young Nelligan up to that?"

"Best that's likely to come along. The kid has a chance. But maybe not if Grandma lives."

"Other grandchildren?"

"Dan and Lena don't have any kids; Ed and Min have two daughters and a son. All nerds, all securely in the slots Vi has picked out for them. My client is an only child. She's probably permitted on the yacht because she's the favorite. Grandma made the others nerds and despises them for it."

"There's another woman on the deck. Gray hair, dignified. Nice figure too."

"Lemme see." Mary Kate squirmed around, grabbed the binoculars away from me with one hand and kept my caressing paw in place with the other. "Oh, she's here again, is she? Now that's interesting. Mary Feehan, Mary O'Brien Feehan. A nurse who took care of Daniel Enright when he was dying back in 1950. Married a Chicago fireman after Daniel's death. Had some money, which someone wisely invested. When Tom Feehan retired as battalion chief, they bought themselves a gorgeous home on Lake Corrib in County Mayo. Her influence is hard to figure out."

A hippie ex-priest with a jewel-crazy wife, a discredited bishop, a bisexual surgeon whose wife was a nympho, a lonely and beaten woman, a feisty granddaughter with a threatened lover, a somewhat sinister banker, and a mysterious visitor from the County Galway—a nice crowd I thought for a Sunday-morning drinking bash.

And—the words flashed quickly through my head before I dismissed them—for a murder.

3

"The trouble, darling"—Mary Kate touched my hand softly—"is that we're both afraid of death."

Then the shot rang out, loud and clear, across the purple, late-afternoon waters.

On the *Violetta* a girl had begun to scream. And then a second girl.

Time stopped, frozen in a frame.

Earlier we had debated between a swim and brunch at the Chicago Yacht Club. The delights of the pastry table won out easily, although my wife justified the decision on the grounds that if we ate first, the wind might pick up and we could sail along the lakefront instead of swimming, which we could do anytime at Grand Beach.

Single-handedly she demolished the pastry table.

"I permit myself only two drinks a week," she chortled as she speared a second French doughnut, "and karate. So I can eat all the pastry I want."

"Good news for the bakeries," I murmured.

We paddled our inflatable dinghy back to the *M.K.*, hauled up the anchor, and under auxiliary power picked our way out of the harbor and around Navy Pier—an elongated Sears Tower phallic symbol thrust arrogantly by the Burnham plan into Lake Michigan—to the breakwater-protected cove next to the filtration plant on Olive Park.

We passed close to the *Violetta* which was defiantly anchored near the entrance of Monroe Street harbor, as if it were daring anyone to complain that it might be obstructing traffic. Mrs. Harrington Enright continued to reign and rule under her lemon umbrella. Glasses were still clinking busily. A couple of her guests had put on swimsuits. My wife's patient was swimming by the bow. As we eased our way around them, Bishop H. Harrington Enright boarded the launch to be ferried back to shore. Perhaps to await the phone call of forgiveness from the Vatican.

Mary Kate was wrong about the wind and the United States Weather Service was right: There was not a hint of breeze. We anchored opposite Mies's legendary 900 North Lake Shore Drive apartments ("Less is a bore!" Caitlin had dismissed the famous architect's functionalism) and dove into the placid waters. We swam around the boat till we were exhausted, climbed back in, finished off the salami, and drank the last of the Diet Cokes. Behind us the skyline, presided over by the slender mass of the John Hancock Center, shimmered in humid pastel mists, a light-drenched Impressionist painting.

I turned on the portable TV to watch the Bears' last exhibition game at Soldier Field, three miles away down the Drive.

"I need a nap," Mary Kate announced. "Since there's a football game on TV, I presume I won't be disturbed for other uses."

"I never use you," I replied, not—to my shame, be it admitted—looking up from the screen.

Jim McMahon had told Johnny Morris on Channel 2 earlier in the week that exhibition games were boring and that he never took them seriously. Sure enough, he threw two interceptions in the first half. At the end of the half, the Bears were losing 6–3. I turned the game off in disgust.

Even though it was still contended that I talk funny, I have so acculturated to Chicago that only the Celtics retain my loyalty. So, with a convert's zeal, I was more frustrated with the Bears than lifelong fans like my father-in-law, Ned Ryan.

"This will be the year, Joseph," he had insisted the previous weekend. "The kid is hungry."

"He's a flake," I insisted.

"He's the best quarterback since Sid Luckman." The Old Fella's eyes glinted. "And, like I say, he's hungry. Make your reservations for the Super Bowl in New Orleans now. Helen and I will be staying at the Roosevelt on Canal Street. Fine old place."

"You'll notice," said his normally quiet wife, "that he knows already where the game will be."

I took a nap too. And awoke to discover Mary Kate back on the deck, a matching black and white skirt over her swimsuit, hard at work on her fingernails.

"Maybe we should tool back to the harbor and drive home."

"I won't fight it. Two days without a shower are a long enough experiment in primitive living."

One of the family cars, the Mustang convertible, I

thought, had been deposited at the Yacht Club so we could drive back to our home on Longwood Drive in St. Praxides parish.

We dragged up the anchor, I turned on the fan to air out the hold and then started the auxiliary engine. Mary Kate took the helm for the return trip around the pier. She was as good a helmsperson as I. Maybe better.

"First weekend on the silver anniversary honeymoon?" I sat next to her in the cockpit and broke through the somber silence that marks the end of the weekend for most husbands and wives.

"So much to deal with," she shuddered. "I'm afraid to start."

"We love each other too much to lose each other now." I extended my arm around her. "We'll both mature."

"I hate maturing." She rested her head on my shoulder, eyes still carefully on the weekend water traffic at the head of Navy Pier. "It hurts."

"I wonder if reorganizing a marriage is easier or harder for people with a good sexual adjustment."

"We don't have a good sexual adjustment, Joseph." She dodged around a lumbering cruiser. "He's drunk, I bet. . . . We have a permanent adolescent sexual crush. Which is not necessarily bad."

"It forces us to face our problems."

"It sure does that. I can't make love like we did this morning—stone sober at that—and just drift along." She grinned rakishly. "Can you?"

"You were the aggressor," I said, without much conviction. My hand found its way to her thigh.

"Hi, Doctor Murphy!" a young woman shouted near us on a power launch.

We both looked up, since the cry could have been directed at either of us. Beyond the outer breakwater, a line of smaller boats, sails fluttering in nervous protest, were struggling to form up for the beginning of a race. Late-afternoon contest for young sailors.

"Fionna Downs," Mary Kate said, frowning, as she returned her patient's enthusiastic wave. "On the imperial barge going back to Grandma's battleship, perhaps for the long voyage to Montrose harbor. She doesn't look like someone in the grip of murderous rage, does she?"

"She looks like a young woman in love."

"She certainly does. Put your hand back on my thigh, Joseph Murphy. You know how melancholy I become at the end of the summer."

"The young woman who looks like a fleet admiral that's piloting the launch?"

"Luisa, I suspect, Vi's maid. It amuses her to dress the servants up in heavy uniforms on hot days. Since they're probably illegal immigrants, they don't have much choice but to do what she tells them. Looks like the chicklets have departed—most of them, I daresay, feeling no pain."

"And if they're driving home, they're endangering the safety of sober and respectable Chicago Bear fans."

"Ha!" She laughed. "And you were saying?"

We were only ten yards behind the Harrington Enright yacht, the name *Violetta* elaborately embossed on its stern.

"I was saying that maybe we ought to begin our summit meeting about the second quarter century."

Then she said we were both afraid of death, and the shot rang out, echoing and reechoing over the waters of the lake, as it would in a mountain canyon. Two women were screaming.

"Fionna!"

The frozen film frame dissolved. Fionna was screaming hysterically amidships. Luisa, screaming too, ran up to her from the stern.

"You killed her, *muchacha*," she shouted. "You killed La Señora!"

All around us boats were coming alive. We were only thirty yards at the most from the *Violetta*. The sails on the boats in the race beyond the breakwater flapped weakly.

"We'd better help, Joe." Mary Kate knifed our boat sharply to the left, ran it toward the Enright yacht, slammed the engine into reverse, and turned at the last moment so that we drifted gently alongside the larger craft. I shoved our fenders over the side to cushion the light bump and leaped up into the *Violetta* as if I were once again the agile guard of BC's basketball team.

Mary Kate threw a line around a cleat on the rail of the yacht and made us fast to it as I scrambled on board. We had made our joint decision to intervene without reflection, a decision which I was to regret in the next couple of days.

The two young women—hardly more than children, it seemed to me—one in blouse and jeans, the other in her naval officer's gold-braided dress, were clinging to each other in noisy hysterical embrace. Fionna Downs was holding a small automatic—a 9mm Beretta if I remembered my James Bond films correctly.

"What happened?" I shouted.

Luisa turned her tear-streaked face to me. "The *muchacha* killed La Señora. Poor *infanta*. La Señora deserved to die, but you should have let us do it."

"Where is she? I'm a doctor."

Magic words, huh, guys? Medicine man, go work your miracle and bring the dead back to life.

"In the salon, señor, at the back, uh, the stern!" She waved her hand wildly.

I raced back along the deck—between midships cabin and the rail—and down the companionway to a gangway through the central bowels of the boat. Even then I decided that what Luisa had said to me was privileged communication.

I hesitated in the gangway. It extended up to the bow. To the left were two doors on either side, to the right a massive oak door across the width of the gangway. The salon, presumably.

Locked. Not just shut and perhaps stuck. But solidly locked.

"No, señor," Luisa shouted down the companionway, "the open door is up here. Hurry. Maybe La Señora is still alive."

I clambered back up the companionway. The open door

I had missed was on the port side of the stern. As I dashed through it, I noted a key in the lock.

The salon occupied two levels of the whole stern area of the yacht. Tiny portholes circled the top level, where I entered, letting in light from the deck. Three huge picture windows, all tightly shut, provided a striking surrealistic view of the Chicago skyline in the pink and gray gauze of a dying summer. The walls of the luxurious room were paneled in solid mahogany, the carpet was a rich peach, and the sheets and comforter on the king-sized bed beneath the stern window were a dusky rose with stripes that I believe would be called French vanilla.

Nice taste in colors. Anything goes so long as it says expensive luxury.

The room smelled of sulfur and heavy perfume, the former on top of the latter. The two aromas were stifling— sweet and sour pork. No circulation of air. Everything closed up tight.

These impressions and reflections came later. My attention was riveted by the cubelike body, in a frilly and elaborate rose and vanilla gown, lying in the middle of the bed, a broken doll out of place on its oversized couch. As I plunged down the companionway to the deck of the salon, I had little doubt that she was dead.

I refused to consider what that might mean to Fionna and Mary Kate. It was critical that my behavior be completely professional. Nothing that the police or the State's Attorney could fault later on.

So long have I been in a family that, as Ned Ryan says, "is cursed by too many lawyers altogether."

And one Father Brown.

I tiptoed toward the bed, careful not to step on any evidence. The bullet had entered her head just above and a little behind her left eye. It made a small, neat hole, slightly larger, I imagined, than nine millimeters. There was very little bleeding. I touched the hand of the corpse. Still warm, of course.

A hard blow to the head and then, as your brain exploded, nothing. Except, if we are to believe the testimony, a figure in white light at the end of a long corridor. What would that person have to say to Mrs. Harrington Enright?

Probably would have to listen for a while first.

Searching for a pulse was a gesture done for the police and the State's Attorney. I didn't expect to find it and I did not find it. Nothing more could be done for Violet Harrington in this life, besides committing her sad little body into the earth from which it had come.

I looked around the salon, noting carefully the details. No one there as far as I could see. Picture windows and portholes closed, probably from the inside unless some Spider Man–like creature had clung to the outside hull. Had they been open earlier in the day? I couldn't remember. Mary Kate would.

The solid oak door on the lower deck was firmly shut. It did not move when I kicked my foot lightly against it. The smaller door at the top of the companionway down which I had rushed flipped back and forth as the boat tilted lightly with the movement of the lake. No other way out.

The door to the bathroom was open—pink tile and enamel with a tub almost as big as the bed. No one in either the bathroom or the tub.

Closets on the bulkhead under the companionway. Sliding doors. Open. I looked in without touching anything. Possibly the biggest collection of pastel caftans in all the world. No one hiding among all the swirly frills.

"What if someone had been hiding?" Mary Kate would demand later that night.

"I would have called on you for some karate," I said, shivering, like a true hero, at my first thought of danger.

My eyes searched the room again. I had answers for all the questions that the police might ask.

No, one more question. I glanced at my Casio musical-alarm wristwatch—a Father's Day present from Brigid. "It plays Beethoven's 'Ode to Joy' on your wedding anniversary, DADDY!"

4:05:45. The shot must have been fired no more than five

or six minutes before. Dear God, poor Fionna. I hoped she would find herself a good lawyer.

I went back up on deck, where Mary Kate, a matching black and white blouse over the top of her swimsuit, looked like she was prepared to attend a very formal luncheon. Somehow she had found time to run a comb through her thick silver-gold hair.

She was also in charge. Naturally.

"Dead?"

"Very."

"I called Cindasoo on the radio. She's in charge this afternoon over in Michigan City. She's notifying the police boat."

If the Ryans can do something directly or indirectly, they always and instinctively choose the latter.

"The girls."

"In the galley up front. Keep them away from the vultures." She nodded at the ring of power- and sailboats surrounding *Violetta*. "Stand off, please," she commanded them in her Ms. Commodore voice. "The police boat will be here shortly."

Some of the boats backed a couple of feet away. Outside the breakwater wind was filling the sails of the craft in the race—a light breeze, nothing to clean away the pink and gray Disney World mist that seemed to be creeping down the sides of the Sears Tower directly opposite us, like a dress skirt falling to a woman's knees.

"Is she dead?" someone demanded.

"Reporters even in the harbor." Mary Kate turned her back on the vultures in firm disgust. "She says she didn't do it, Joe."

"Do you believe that?"

"I think she's too hysterical to make it up. You understand that there's enormous ambivalence. Grandma has been generous, so you love her, especially because you have been told all your life that you love her. Grandma has been domineering, so you hate her. Grandma is an obstacle and a challenge, so you fight her, think even of destroying her, feel guilty about your murderous thoughts. And then . . ."

"The gun was in her hand."

"I made her put it on the deck. For the fuzz." She pointed to the Beretta, propped up against the cabin wall. "Looks like a toy, doesn't it?"

"What did she say happened?"

"She opened the door, after Luisa unlocked it, looked down the steps. Her grandmother was asleep."

"Companionway."

She smiled briefly at my correction. "You're getting to be as bad as I am. . . . When she got to the foot of the companionway, she heard a shot. She looked at her grandmother. A hole had appeared in her forehead, and there was a gun on the floor next to her bed. Even though she reads mysteries and wants to write them, she 'freaked out'—her words, of course—felt a compulsion to grab the gun, picked it up, and ran screaming up the . . . companionway for Luisa."

"Mary Kate, there was no one else there. I looked."

She shrugged her broad shoulders. "I'm inclined to believe her."

"The police never will."

She nodded her head gravely—already, I knew, profoundly worried that she had failed in her own professional responsibility.

And perhaps remembering her promise to blow out the brains of Violet Harrington Enright.

Not a reassuring memory as the blue and white police boat, its sapphire lights flashing ominously, threaded its way through the circle of boats that imprisoned the *Violetta*.

No one, I reflected, could possibly escape from the yacht without being seen by most of the boaters in Monroe Street harbor.

4

"I'm afraid that I'm going to have to call Homicide, Dr. Murphy." The intelligent and soft-spoken young black sergeant who was the "captain" of the police boat shook his head sadly. "This one is beyond me."

"I understand, Sergeant Barry." Naturally it was the other Doctor Murphy to whom he was talking. "Please do so at once."

Our goal was to take the sobbing Fionna to Mercy Hospital for a night of psychiatric observation and care before permitting the cops to drag her off to 11th and State, police headquarters, a few minutes away from the harbor. Given her hysterical condition, it was not an unreasonable request. The captain of the police boat, however, could hardly authorize such a move.

I had learned from Luisa, a light brown and pretty child, who was very frightened of the police—surely she was illegal—but had recovered some of her composure, that there were only two keys to the salon, one in the possession of "Señora Enright" (an increase in tears) and the other in Luisa's purse. Luisa, Carlos, and Tomas had taken Dr. and Mrs. E. Harrington Enright, the last of the party, to the dock, Carlos and Tomas had been dispatched by taxi to procure a bottle of J&B Scotch and Monday's *Tribune* and the pilot for the yacht, while Luisa purchased a bottle of Advil and returned to the dock to wait for the launch. Then the *muchacha*, the Señorita Fionna, had appeared on the dock, very agitated. She must *"Please, por favor, Luisa"* see her grandmother at once.

So Luisa, who could drive the launch at least as well as Carlos and Tomas, drove the Señorita to the boat. While the Señorita went to the back of the boat to see her grandmother, Luisa went to the galley in the front to take a Coca-Cola out of the fridge. The Señorita rushed into the galley to say the door was locked and her grandmother would not open it. Would Luisa please open it with the other key?

Luisa broke a rule and opened the door. Then she quickly ran to the companionway leading to the launch. She must return for Carlos and Tomas. She did not want to hear another fight because they made her cry.

Then she heard the shot and Fionna's screams. She returned to the door of the salon and looked down the steps. She saw the hole in La Señora's head and knew she was dead. No, Señor Doctor Murphy, she did not go down the steps of the companionway. She was more afraid of La Señora dead than alive. Had she not opened the door so the *muchacha* could kill her?

When Sergeant Barry came aboard from the police boat, I whispered to him about the two Hispanics who would be waiting on the dock for the launch—unless they had already seen the crowds around the *Violetta* and fled.

He nodded somberly. If they were undocumenteds, they had probably left Chicago already. It would be next to impossible to find them. Luisa would have to face the *policía* by herself. I made a mental note to see what Ned Ryan could do for her after the problem was settled. The Chicago police would not be eager to turn a key witness over to the tender care of the Immigration and Naturalization Service.

It was after seven-thirty when the harbor tender brought out the homicide detectives. The lake had already turned dark purple, and the haze around the city was changing into a dirty black, a curtain for the day and for summer. So soon does summer end, downhill after the twenty-first of June.

The lieutenant in charge, one Amos Worth, was white, young, intense, and officious. Night student, I wagered, at John Marshall Law School who did everything strictly by the book. As sure as spring would return next year, he and Mary Kate would not like one another.

"She is still hysterical, Lieutenant, in no condition to be questioned at this time."

"She's an alleged perpetrator, Ms. Murphy."

"Talk English, Lieutenant. And it's Doctor Murphy."

Are you ready for it? Around the neighborhood and at Grand Beach, I'm Doctor Murphy and she's Mrs. Murphy or, sometimes with Biddy's friends—and at the latter's insistence—*Ms.* Doctor Murphy. Far from being offended, the first American-born woman, to say nothing of the first Irish Catholic, to be certified by the Chicago Institute for Psychoanalysis, is amused. But standing outside the galley on the foredeck of the *Violetta,* she gives a smartass cop with a brush haircut, square chin, and painfully frowning forehead the full *Doctor* Murphy treatment.

"Is the alleged perpetrator under your care, Doctor?"

"Who alleges she perpetrated anything?"

She hadn't added *asshole* yet. She would, my wife who deplores scatological and obscene language.

Me ride to her rescue? You gotta be kidding.

"This young woman"—nod at Luisa—"said that—"

"Did she see the crime?"

"I presume not." Deeper frown. "Again, I must ask you whether Ms. Downs is under your care."

"Of course she's under my care, asshole; I am a doctor. I come upon a hysterical young woman and assist her. She is under my care. Did they teach you to add two and two in the academy?"

"Mary Kate . . ."

"I'll take care of him, Joe."

No doubt about that. Sleek tiger, right? Fearsome matriarch, right?

"If she's not under your care on a regular basis, Doctor Murphy, then I must insist on interrogating her now."

Wrong word, buster.

"She is under my care on a regular basis."

Worth tried to digest that. Note that she did not mention the Ryan family connection; Ryan clout was as awesome as ever in Chicago. You do not waste clout on an insect of a homicide detective.

"That's a funny coincidence, isn't it?" Lieutenant Worth finally figured out what to say and said it with a sneer. "You just happened to be here when she kills her grandmother."

"What do you mean by funny, Lieutenant?"

"Well, just kind of odd, you know, funny."

"Are you suggesting that I might be an accessory alleged perpetrator?"

A husband wants to ride to the rescue of his woman when she's under assault by such a birdbrain, right?

Forget it.

"Try suspect," I suggested helpfully. Both of them paid no attention.

"You make whatever you want out of that coincidence, asshole. I am telling you that the young woman cannot be interrogated—to use your Nazi word—at this time, and you will have to overcome my objections to an interrogation by physical force."

"Mr. Murphy?" He turned to me. Worth's experience with badgering alleged perpetrators was probably limited to poor people not capable of fighting back or junkies on drug highs.

"I'm Doctor Murphy too, Lieutenant. I have never changed my wife's mind, and in this matter I don't intend to try. I concur in her judgment that Ms. Downs is too distraught to be questioned. Both of us would be compelled to testify to that in court should the matter arise."

Mary Kate's eyes danced with glee as they had the first afternoon in the corridors of LCM. I fell in love with her all over again.

She grabbed my arm when Worth withdrew to meet Dr. E. Harrington Enright and his wife, the first of the family to arrive.

"Great, lover. I forgot the courtroom bit. We must get that child into the unit at Mercy at least for the night."

"He'll fight it all the way."

"So much the better. I'll be too busy to wonder about my fall from professional responsibility."

Guilt would come later.

Ed Enright immediately began to berate the police in a voice which sounded like an Islamic call to prayer. He seemed to believe that, if they had not killed his mother, they were at least responsible for not protecting her.

"Her blood is on your hands, Officer," he shouted at the hapless Lieutenant Worth. "I hold you personally responsible for her death. I'll see that you lose your job for this failure. I am an important man in this city and I will not be flummoxed by corrupt police."

E. Harrington Enright, M.D., ignored us like we were infected with the Black Death. But then he always ignored psychiatrists, especially when he suspected that they might be Democrats.

Mary Kate's judgment about Fionna was unassailable. Like many strong women and unlike most strong men, Fionna could resonate emotionally to tragedy. If you discover the body of a mother figure you both love and hate with a bullet hole in her head, you quite properly become hysterical.

And if you have put the hole in her head?

Well, suspect or alleged perpetrator, in our society, you are still innocent until proven guilty, despite newspaper headlines and TV clips convicting you before you are even indicted. And you don't have to help the police prove you guilty.

Fionna was an irresistibly pretty young woman, an Irish porcelain doll with pale skin, dark blue eyes, jet black hair, and delicate facial bones. A lovely, well-crafted exemplar of the species. The kind you would want to bring home to mother. (Not, God knows, the kind I brought home to my mother, who promptly hated my outsized doll because "she puts on airs.") Tears did not dim or smear her beauty, because she wore no makeup. Nor did hysteria hide the hints of intelligence in her high, mobile forehead.

Indeed, a matriarch in the making.

She insisted over and over, "I did not kill her, Doctor; I did not kill her. I only wanted to tell her that she was not a real grandmother. I mean, I often felt like killing her, but I never would really have done it. I didn't kill her, did I?"

No, you don't let the police question someone that confused.

Bishop H. Harrington Enright, clad in a clerical suit,

pectoral cross, episcopal ring and (indeed) wearing French cuffs with the papal coat of arms, was more courteous than his brother. After he had performed the church's last rights for his mother, he joined us on the foredeck, a tall, handsome, sad-faced example of all that *Romanita* used to mean.

"Doctor Murphy"—a nod at Mary Kate—"Doctor Murphy"—a nod at me—"I am very grateful for your assistance to my mother. I regret that it was too late, but you acted with commendable professional zeal. I am also grateful to you for ministering to my poor niece. I am sure that the unfortunate child is quite distracted. . . ."

He spoke as if he were translating at a papal audience, a task which he did indeed perform during happier days in his career.

"With your brother's permission, Doctor Murphy, I will be saying Mass the day after tomorrow at the cathedral for Mother. I hope you will pray for the repose of her soul."

We shook hands and returned aft. I imagined the choir singing "Ecce Sacerdos Magnus" as it did when Richard Cushing, sometimes sober, sometimes not, entered the chapel at the preparatory seminary in Brighton where I survived for three long years.

"A millennium older than the Punk," Mary Kate whispered. "Is it the same church?"

"He's hurting real bad, M.K. Real bad."

"I know it."

The D. Harrington Enrights arrived. The police had not yet located Rita Harrington Enright Downs, Fionna's mother. It did not seem to matter. Nor was the mysterious Mary O'Brien Feehan present.

Vincent Nelligan, his face gray in the dim lights of the yacht, was the last one to climb slowly up the companionway. Although he walked as if he were entering the dining room of his Chicago club for a formal dinner party, his face was a solemn mask, like that worn by African or Asian tribal chieftains.

It was almost dark now. Lights were blinking on in the skyline, the temperature was falling quickly as it often does at the end of August. The ring of boats around us began to dissolve. Running lights on and sails down, the long-distance racers, practicing for the Tri State next weekend, glided into the harbor, sleek ghosts appearing in the dark. On the shore blue lights of squad cars and patrol wagons glowed fitfully. TV camera crews were testing their floodlights.

It reminded me of Venetian night, not a murder setting.

The only sounds, other than the hum of traffic on the Drive (which will stop only the day after the Final Judgment) were the uneasy lappings of the lake against the hull, the bumping of *M.K.* against the fenders separating her from the yacht, and the harangues of Dr. E. Harrington Enright aft.

"Prosecution," "fullest extent of the law," "electric chair," "death sentence," "callous murder" were his most frequent words.

"Surgical profession having its say," I whispered, because the night and the situation seemed to call for whispers.

"I wouldn't want my daughter to marry one."

"Señora Doctor, what will happen to me?" Luisa asked timidly, fearful that the gringo police would blame her for her employer's death.

"Nothing, dear." M.K. put her arm around the child. "We'll take care of you."

Carlos and Tomas had not returned.

Half asleep on a cot we had pulled out of the servants' quarters and into the galley, Fionna turned fitfully. "I didn't kill her. It was someone else."

There was a stir aft, and a number of men moved in our direction.

"Worth," my wife said distastefully. "Wish me luck."

"Okay, but you don't need it."

"I'm afraid, Doctor Murphy," he began resolutely enough, "that I'm going to have to read her her rights."

"A hysterical young woman, deep in shock? Lieutenant, you must be out of your mind."

"Then I am going to have to bring her over to 11th and

State and book her on a charge of murder one." He continued doggedly. "In the absence of her mother, Mrs. Rita Enright Downs, you may accompany her if you wish. She may call an attorney. You may call an attorney for her in her name. Now stand aside, please. I intend to read her her rights."

He was clutching the little plastic card that the Miranda decision imposes on the police.

"And I will gladly testify that she is incapable of understanding her rights at this time."

"Be that as it may," he hesitated, trying to link what he had learned at the police academy and in law school with Dr. E. Harrington Enright's demands, "I still intend to make an arrest at this point in time."

"You're blowing the State's Attorney's case right out the window, Lieutenant." Mary Kate was working the restraint bit, content perhaps that she was to accompany her patient to 11th and State.

"That will be for him to determine."

She delivered her last jab with a complacent smile. "I am warning you in the presence of a witness, Lieutenant Worth, that Ms. Downs is not capable of understanding your warning. If you proceed, you'll never make captain."

Mess with the Ryans, will you?

"I'll take that risk, ma'am."

So he stumbled through the Miranda warning in an incoherent monotone. Fionna Downs, rumpled and bedraggled, peered up from her cot, confused and frightened.

"What is he talking about, Doctor Murphy?" she wailed.

In front of witnesses at that.

"Don't worry, dear, I'm coming with you. And you too, Luisa. Handcuffs, Lieutenant Worth?"

He did not dare.

"Ah, that will not be necessary. I do not believe that the alleged perpetrator is dangerous."

"Tell me about it." And to me: "Would you take care of the home-front situation till I get her into the hospital? I'll be home when I'm home."

I kissed her. "Carry on, Doctor."

She sighed wearily. "This one will take a long time to sort out."

As the police and Mary Kate and the two young women approached the companionway to the waiting police boat, they passed the silently watching mourners of Violet Harrington Enright.

"I didn't kill her," Fionna sobbed. "I didn't. I only wanted to tell her that she was not a real grandmother."

An odd plea.

And, as it turned out, a fateful one.

"Doctor Mary Kathleen Murphy is responsible for my mother's death," Ed Enright thundered at the camera. "She's as guilty as my miserable niece. She should be indicted too. I will sue her for ten million dollars. I will have her banished from the medical profession. I will destroy her. My poor mother," he sobbed, "was a saint murdered by demons."

Cut to a slightly confused Sunday-night anchorman. "We asked Doctor Murphy about this charge when she left Mercy Hospital where, under police guard, Fionna Downs is undergoing treatment for shock."

Cut to Mary Kate, lovely, self-possessed, aloof in her black and white ensemble, a grand duchess leaving a ball. She listened to the question thoughtfully.

"Rather surprising to hear such a statement from a man who is a leader in the fight against malpractice suits, isn't it?" She smiled beautifully. "Poor dear man is surely beside himself with grief."

Applause from all around the parlor of the Murphy home on Longwood Drive. The whole clan was there: elegantly pregnant Caitlin with her red-bearded husband Kevin Maher; Biddy and her Aunt Trish (who is the same age); Pete with his sexy little Coast Guard person, Cindasoo McLeod; Tim with his distant (distant enough, Blackie says) cousin, Jean Ryan; Ned and Helen.

And the so-called head of the house, who turned off the tape.

"You were definitely slandered, Mom." Kevin, who teaches law school at Valpo, might well have been searching for a pike. "No doubt about it."

"No-'count, mess-ahead molly-jogger," Cindasoo agreed. "You sure were scrumptious, Doctor Murphy, a real lolliper."

Cindasoo's Appalachian English is authentic. Her use of it, when she can speak perfectly good standard English if she is of a mind, is a put-on in which our whole family revels.

"With your permission of course"—Ned smiled blandly, an ancient but healthy benign leprechaun—"I'll file suit tomorrow morning for slander. There were excusing circumstances, but hardly for a murder charge. Say ten million?"

"The poor bastard." Mary Kate, exhausted and battered, no way the grand duchess on the screen a few minutes ago, was slumped into my easy chair. (Mortal sin under most circumstances.) "Do we have to?"

"You have a professional reputation to protect, kid," I said. "This sort of thing can stick if there is no response. A woman analyst . . ."

"Fifteen million." She perked up instantly, ready to do battle for her profession and her sex.

"We'll force a public apology." Ned leaned back on the couch, pleased as Punch, whom he also resembled. "The malpractice charge would never stick anyway and with our countersuit he'll have to drop it."

Ah, how the Ryans love a fight.

"I may be guilty." The wind went out of her sails. "My patient did talk murder. I didn't think she meant it."

"Dear, how could you know?" Helen, her stepmother (only two years older), pleaded. "A doctor can't be a spy."

"It's a judgment call," I agreed.

Blackie stirred in the far corner.

Blackie. Of course. I forgot to mention him. He is, by his own admission, an easy person to forget, even when he is wearing a Chicago Bears windbreaker over his collarless clerical shirt, and a Jameson Irish Whiskey cap that wishes all a Happy St. Patrick's Day. He claims that people board the elevator on which he is riding and think that it's empty.

Monsignor John Blackwood Ryan, S.T.L., Ph.D., rector of the Cathedral of the Holy Name, expert on Alfred North Whitehead and William James, *éminence grise* to Cardinal Sean Cronin. A.k.a., among his siblings, the Punk.

My kids claim that he deliberately cultivates the bumbling bumpkin Father Brown image because it suits his purposes. Mary Kate, who knows him better, says it a little differently: "The Punk was born with the persona, he developed the personality to fit it."

Alone of the clan, he is short and rather dumpy. Unhandsome, with thin grizzled hair, a high forehead, and nearsighted blue eyes blinking behind thick, rimless glasses, meek-voiced, and mild-mannered, Blackie is, by universal agreement of womankind, definitely "cute." "Like totally," according to teenagers, with whom he has a special rapport because, as Biddy contends, "Uncle Punk will always be, I mean really, a total teenage priest."

Need I say that the comment is intended as the highest praise?

And if Sean Cronin is to be believed, he has also one of the finest minds in the Catholic church. "Listen to Blackwood," he said to me once with a typically sweeping wave of his hand. "He's almost always right. Seldom in error and never in doubt."

On my first date with M.K., the evening of that fateful day I seemed to have proposed marriage and been accepted—"quickly," as she said in my arms in the country club parking lot that night, "so you wouldn't change your mind"—I met the Punk, then a first-year seminarian. He opened the door at my knock, a copy of *The Spy* by James Fenimore Cooper in his hand, finger marking his place. He looked like an ineffectual cherub.

"I'm Joe Murphy."

"You talk funny." He stepped back to let me in the house.

"I'm from Boston."

"You are honest about it." He repeated Mary Kate's cheap crack with an elfin smile.

He led me to a chair and resumed his reading.

"Are you going to marry her?" He peered over the top of his book.

"Unless she changes her mind."

"No chance of that." He smiled like a benign little Buddha. "Great! You're just what she needs."

It has become gospel truth in the clan.

Physically he is still an elf, a Buddha, a sweet-faced, ineffectual cherub. "The Punk never changes," Mary Kate complains. "He'll never grow up."

He adopts with me the pose that he and I are the only sane ones in the family. It is perhaps a reasonable position. The opposite stand is taken by Eileen Ryan Kane, the federal judge: "The Punk is crazier than most people think he is."

In any event, while we were debating the suit against Ed Enright, he slipped out of the parlor. I heard him on the phone in the hall but could not distinguish his words.

"Whom did you get to defend her?" the Old Fella asked.

"Patty Slattery, the young associate from Minor, Gray. She's good and young enough to relate with Fionna, which will be important."

"Oh boy," Kevin Maher exclaimed, "she's the kind who give us redheads our reputation."

"Poor Al Worth wished I was still in charge when she started to chew ass. The State's Attorney is going to have one hell of a fight on his hands."

"Did she insist on the paraffin test?" A slim, white eyebrow lifted a centimeter above Ned's frosty right eye.

Blackie had slipped back into the room, unnoticed by all but the so-called man of the house.

"Yes," Mary Kate nodded. "I wasn't sure . . ."

"Smart girl." Ned nodded his approval.

"What's a paraffin test, Daddy?" Trish demanded.

"It's a pretty good way of telling whether someone fired a gun in the last twenty-four hours. It picks up the traces of carbon imbedded in your skin. Not perfect, but it will do."

"But won't that give them more evidence?" Caitlin looked to her husband, rather than to her grandfather.

"It's a clever, calculated risk, dear," Kevin replied, sounding like a law teacher, but not a pompous one, "as Ned hinted. They have plenty of evidence and are likely to find more. So they didn't want the test lest it cut the ground from under them. On the other hand, Patty Slattery knows that the odds are she'll have to plea-bargain for a lighter sentence, diminished responsibility, something like that, to get the poor young woman out of prison, maybe in a couple of years. But if the test is negative, she might get her off with probation or win an acquittal from a jury."

"I hate to think of that poor child in jail for even a week." Mary Kate began to weep softly. "The dykes will destroy her. And it's my fault. If I had been smart, I would have—"

"No, it's not," I interrupted her, knowing she would cry herself to sleep after the others left. No professional practice committee could ever be as harsh in judgment as my wife is on herself.

"Quite right." Blackie sighed his huge West of Ireland sigh, which sounds like the advent of a serious asthma attack. "Mary Kate's diagnosis was patently correct. The fabulous Fionna did not shoot her grandmother. Dad, will you communicate to Ms. Slattery and such others who may be pertinent that under no circumstances is she to be left unguarded for a moment. Her life may be in grave danger."

NED RYAN'S STORY

5

I knew her as a young woman, all right, Johnny. But it was a long time ago. A long time ago. Some of my contemporaries, those that are still around, tell me that it seems to them only yesterday that Gabby Hartnett won the pennant in 1938 for the Cubs with his famous home run in the gloaming.

I tell them that it seems like a century ago instead of forty-seven years.

So, yes, I knew Vi Harrington and Daniel Enright when they were kids. Daniel and I were about the same age and we lived in the same neighborhood. They were Republicans, as was your mother before she became a Communist. I try to hide that from the kids, Caitlin and that lot, you know. I mean, that she was a Republican when she was young.

His father, old Dan Enright, grandfather of that flaky ex-priest, made his money in the Metropolitan Sanitary District—Chicago Sanitary District we called it then. He was a trustee, which is a joke if there ever was one, because you couldn't trust him with the eraser on a pencil. Sounds kind of strange, doesn't it? Like saying a man made his money in stocks and bonds, except from a government job. He was not the only one, of course. Sewer Pipe Ed Kelly, who was mayor back in the thirties and forties, made a fortune in the same job. The rules were different in those days. If you didn't become rich in such a job, people thought there was something wrong with you.

85

So Dan lived the good life, big home in Old Austin, summer "camp" up near Eagle River, a fleet of Packards, winter vacation in Florida, all through the Great Depression.

Today he'd be indicted by Thursday evening. In those days it was considered to be part of the political game. He was admired and respected as a successful man, president of Holy Name Society at St. Catherine's, papal knight eventually. Not everyone approved. My family sure didn't, but we were not about to suggest that he be sent to jail. Or to keep me away from the "camp."

How can I tell you what the "camp" was like? An enormous house, kind you couldn't put up for a couple of million today, rustic looking but solidly built. Driveway with a locked gate. Big park all around. Huge chunk of lakefront property. Their own electric generator, since there were no lines yet that far out. No phones, of course. You had to drive five miles to find one. And mostly outdoor plumbing, except for the Mr. and Mrs.

You kind of took it for granted that you'd use outhouses if you went into the country on vacation. Hell, a lot of people in Chicago were still using them in the twenties and thirties and even during the War.

I tell the kids—never can call them the grandkids because I'd mix them up with my own younger ones—about the outdoor privies and they think I'm being gross. Indoor plumbing, they seem to think, has been with us since we left the Garden of Eden.

Anyway, Daniel—that's the boy about my age, you understand—and I became pretty good friends, even if he was a Republican. Probably because we were both a little wild. Nothing much by today's standards. Roadhouse booze when we were in our middle teens before FDR did in Mr. Hoover's noble experiment of prohibition. That kind of thing.

Want another sip of Jameson's? 'Course not you, you're driving. I forgot.

He was a hell of a fine fellow, Daniel Enright. Light as a snowflake, mind you. Always had everything. Always expected everything. Tall, good-looking, charming—women adored him. Wavy blond hair, aquamarine eyes that almost hypnotized you every time you looked at him. He would have been a more successful politician than his father. There was talk of the Senate. First Catholic from Illinois. We haven't elected one yet, you know. Talk about prejudice.

He was the life of every party up there in those days. The whole summer was a party. I still smell and taste those steak barbecues, pine aroma in the woods at night, the fresh Wisconsin mustard on the hot dogs, cheese right out of the dairy. It never seemed to rain and the water was always warm and the moon was always full. Nostalgia, I suppose. Kate, your mother, said that the fun I had with Daniel in Eagle River was the reason I bought the house at Grand Beach as soon as I could after the War.

"And," she used to say, "you had the sense to know it would be even more fun if it were closer to Chicago than Eagle River."

And I'd say something about the same kind of sense I displayed when I married you.

He wasn't hungry, Daniel Enright. Didn't have to be. But then a lot of other folks who didn't have to be were hungry, if you know what I mean. I went off for a year in Europe, Austria mostly, up in Salzburg because I thought I was going to be a musician, if you can imagine that. But you've heard that story before, haven't you, Johnny? Helen? Right.

I watched Europe come apart. I went to Berlin after Hitler was elected. I saw what Roosevelt did to them when he sunk the London economic conference. Later he turned to free trade, and it looks like that damn movie actor has remembered one thing from his New Deal days anyway. But it was too late, the harm had been done. The Depression was even worse over there. In Germany it was pretty obvious that the Versailles peace treaty from 1919 and the Depression would give them an excuse for another war. So I came home, a pretty sober and thoughtful fellow.

I tried to explain it all to Daniel, but it was a waste of time. "The country needs a war to teach it a little discipline," he'd say with a big laugh, which you knew he only meant half of.

He didn't have much depth, like I say, but he was the most loyal friend you could ever ask for. When Vinney Nelligan's father went bottoms up in the Depression, Daniel found Vinney a job somewhere, lent him money, gave him a new start. I never could figure out what he saw in Vinney. All right, I suppose, but kind of dull. Nerd, the kids would say. Always has been, always will be. Can't help it, I guess. If there's one thing worse than a Republican, it's a Republican banker!

We all romanticize our youth, you know the great days when we were growing up. Can't say I've noticed you growing up, Johnny, but that's beside the point, isn't it?

I'm not insulting him, Helen. It's a compliment and he knows it.

As I was saying, it does seem to me that we had more fun then than kids do today. Walking along the shore of the lake when the sun was coming up, feeling the sand or the grass beneath your feet, hiking along the old narrow-gauge–lumber-railroad right-of-way, swimming out to the raft and sitting on it all day, hugging a girl in the moonlight on the edge of the woods. Somehow seemed simpler then. Probably wasn't. Most likely we were just as confused as kids are today.

Anyhow, the Great Depression wasn't bad for everyone. It wasn't too bad for most of us who flocked up to the Enrights' summer camp in those days. And if you were like Daniel and could ignore the rest of the world, it was a great time. Nothing to worry about, like the bomb or inflation or terrorists or that sort of thing.

For a lot of people it was hell. And I knew that and wanted to do something about it. That may have been why we kind of drifted apart after I came home.

And then there was Vi. I told you I'd get around to her eventually. Thing is, you have to understand the times and the Enrights to figure her out. Doubt that you can even then, poor woman, God be good to her.

If He possibly can? Helen, I'm surprised at you.

Well, okay, I was thinking the same thing. You don't want to shock the priest, do you?

She was hungry, you see. Like your mother. Like me, but a lot more so. Only it was a pretty limited kind of hunger—money and property, especially property. She was short and kind of cute, you know. No, not at all like her granddaughter, who is short and pretty if not beautiful. Reminds me of that lovely little Italian kid in the movies. What's her name? Yes, Mia Sara. Bet she's got a last name they don't tell us. My Sara. Why should anyone be ashamed of an Italian name?

The grandmother was nowhere near that class. You kinda had to wonder why Daniel, who had the pick of them, would fall for her. He regretted it later on, of course, but that's the way of things, isn't it?

She was a sort of servant too. Her father was out of work, she didn't go to college. The family was in Old Dan's ward, so on impulse—he was as impulsive as Daniel but not nearly so lightweight—Dan hires her for the summer.

Daniel falls for her. His family were good sports about it. They even seemed to like her. Thought she'd settle their son down. And she was from a Republican family in the Thirty-seventh Ward. Even Republicans were loyal to their own. In those days, I mean.

It was the year I met your mother. She wasn't staying with the Enrights, but at another "camp," not that walls or long walks in the dead of night stopped her for a minute. So the four of us became a team.

We had a great time that summer of 1935, even if I was the only Democrat and they were convinced that FDR would be swept out by a landslide the next year. I showed them. 'Course, by then your mother had discovered poverty and become a Communist. Only up to the Hitler-Stalin pact, three years. Tell the truth, I think the party was glad when she walked out. Never took to discipline.

There wasn't a wild thing that you could do in northern Wisconsin that summer that we didn't do. Your mother in the lead, naturally. Excuse me for misting up; I always do when I remember that year. There have been better times since then, but nothing ever quite so much fun.

Vi was a tagalong. Interested only in estimating the

value of houses and land and how much property would be worth in two years. And what she'd buy if she had the money. There are Irish women like that, you know. Women of property, they call them in the old country; addicted to buying and selling. And always turn a profit. The poor man of the house fades away to nothing, he gets so worn out from moving every time she sells the place out from under him.

Your cousin, Catherine Curran, is like that a little bit. Lucky she has her art. 'Course, she doesn't move her family around either. But she always makes a bit of extra on her deals.

Well, poor Daniel thinks it's hilarious, a big joke. Someone who talks about property on a date. Great joke, huh? He finds out too late that it's not a joke.

I pass the bar and hang up my shingle. And he doesn't pass, laughs it off, goes to work for the Chicago Sanitary District and takes flying lessons while I'm hanging out with the Naval Reserve down at the armory because I'm convinced there's going to be a war.

And we never go back to Eagle River together because we're both married when the next summer rolls around. They close the place during the War, and she sells it after the War, probably because she hates the memory of being the kid who had to work in the kitchen before she left on a date.

It wasn't easy for her, I don't suppose.

Maybe he wouldn't have married her if your mother and I hadn't married that winter. He might have been the kind of man, extrovert on the outside, who panics when he thinks he's being left behind in the marriage game. I never could figure that out. Maybe I was too certain that he'd get over her. Which he did eventually. When it was too late.

So Daniel and I drifted apart. Nothing explicit, you understand. The way lots of friends do when they grow up and discover they have nothing much in common except good times when they were young.

Well, pretty soon, as you know, there's Mary Kate and Eileen and Nancy and Packy. You come later.

Only things are not progressing so smoothly over at the

Enright house—it wasn't Harrington Enright then, believe you me. And the middle name of all the kids, even poor dippy Rita, wasn't added till after Daniel was dead.

Old Dan, you see, was a bit of a nut.

I mean, we thought he was a character, always doing outlandish things, like appearing at a party in red flannel underwear and a cook's hat.

He was probably a bit of a psychotic too, as your sister Mary Kate would say, but not so nutty that he belonged in an institution.

What he did was announce on their wedding day that he'd written his will so that if they produced a son, they'd receive half of his fortune. And if they produced a daughter too, they'd get the other half. No son, nothing. A son and no daughter, half. Son and daughter, everything. What they fail to earn with their kids goes to the church.

Daniel is old Dan's only son, you remember.

Crazy, but not illegal.

Nothing wrong with that the way the Irish were reproducing in those days, so long as they had a little bit of money. Only the young Enrights don't reproduce.

Then bing, bing, bing, in forty, forty-one, and forty-two, they turn out the three boys, first two of them locked into the priesthood from the moment the doctor announces their sex.

Vi was not backward about necking and petting, but she was always pious.

Then Rita came along in forty-four, about the same time as you. There's always been a bit of a cloud around that birth. Something not quite right. It was during the War, most of us were away. Vi had already locked herself up in the apartment at the Edgewater Beach—she's got her hands on the old man's money now. And then there was Rita. Poor pretty little drip. No doubt about her father; she's the spitting image of Daniel, without any of his laughter and enthusiasm, but with his aquamarine eyes. The fun turns up again in the granddaughter. Seen it happen that way lots of times.

She had to have been conceived just before he left for England.

So now they're entitled to all the inheritance when Old Dan dies. Not a hell of a lot, mind you, because the old man lived high off the hog. Enough to begin building her real estate empire. She bought everything she could get her hands on out beyond the suburbs even before he came home.

You see, she already controls all the money and is investing it in Old Dan's name. With Vinney Nelligan helping her. Investing it in real estate. Property, do you understand?

How does she get the money? She has the poor old guy declared legally incompetent, which he probably was by 1944, brushes away his wife, and takes control of the family money. I'm sure she and Vinney bribed half the judges on the Superior Court, as we called it then, even though it wasn't very superior. Like I say, a lot of us were away and things happened that no one noticed.

Daniel seems to have signed a document agreeing to it just before he left with a platoon of rangers for a pre–D-Day diversionary landing in Brittany. Probably figured he'd never come back and wants to make sure he's taken care of his three sons.

In a way he never did come back. He had a bad bout with pneumonia in Northern Ireland before the invasion and was wounded twice after that. So when he finally came home, he looked like the shadow of the kid I'd played softball with up in Eagle River. Same old smile, but nothing behind it. No more talk of running for the Senate. Or anything else.

He was a very wealthy man by 1946, but it never meant much to him. Hung around the Chicago Athletic Club, kept an office in the Loop and a separate apartment from her in the Edgewater Beach. Maybe he never forgave himself for what they did to his parents. They were both dead, you see, before he came back in forty-six. So maybe that's why he was such a wreck. Died in 1953. Cancer, they said. And I wouldn't doubt it.

She didn't visit him in the hospital and, I guess, spent as little time at his bedside when he came home to die as she possibly could. That Irish nurse woman, Mary Feehan— married the fireman later—took care of him at the end.

I always felt that he died of a broken heart too. Not that she destroyed any deep love he had for her. What she did was destroy his love of life.

I visited him the week before he died. I'll say one thing for that Feehan woman, I think her name was O'Brien then, she took good care of him.

"Didn't we have fun in the old days, Ned?" he asked me. "You and Kate and me?"

Great fun, I tell him. Of course, a few years later, right after Kennedy was nominated, your mother is dead too, which is neither here nor there for this story, God be good to her. Which if She's not, She'll hear about it!

So that's a very prejudiced version, Johnny, of the life and times of Violet Enright Harrington. God be good to her too.

I suppose God will ask her for an explanation of why she destroyed a whole family that had befriended her.

And she'll give the same answer she always gave for every shady deal she ever pulled.

She did it for her kiddies.

BLACKIE RYAN'S STORY

6

"No arraignment today, then." I sipped the apple cinnamon tea, which is a moderately acceptable substitute for the real thing if you are prepared to concede the wisdom of a substitute, which I am not. "Isn't that interesting?"

"There seem to be a number of reasons for this caution, despite the fact that all the other members of the Harrington Enright family eagerly reported the young woman's violent threats against her grandmother on both Saturday and Sunday"—Mike Casey the Cop blew gently on the surface of his own teacup—"not the least of which is that my sometime colleagues in the department and their allies at the State's Attorney's office do not wish to repeat the mistakes of yesterday, especially since they must face the wrath of your good friend, that inestimable young hellion, Patty Slattery."

"Indeed." I sighed enigmatically.

It was the Monday afternoon of Violet Enright's wake. Mike and I were sitting in the spacious, sunlit room, which smelled of oil crayons, at the back of his wife's art gallery, where Mike does his painting. We were sparring for information. Mike's friends in the department—he had been acting superintendent before he retired—were confused by the Harrington Enright case and were looking for hints. I was looking for facts. We would, of course, exchange information. Cautiously, as befits two Chicago micks.

"Gorgeous redhead hellion." Annie placed four chocolate chip cookies next to my cup, compensation for the herbal tea.

Annie is herself a gorgeous woman in her middle fifties—slim, gray blond, lithe and well curved, in jeans and a Monet water lily T-shirt. Mike—tall, lean, silver hair, in a double-breasted Italian suit with light stripes to emphasize its elegance—looks like an Irish Basil Rathbone playing Sherlock Holmes.

Mike the Cop endeavored to sigh as loudly as I do. "There is also the matter of the fingerprints on the gun."

"Only Fionna's prints?"

"Indeed." Mike's shrewd blue eyes narrowed.

We were seated in leather chairs next to Mike's latest painting, a row of post–Chicago Fire houses glowing in the sunrise like an outpost of fairyland—Belden Street, I was willing to bet.

Annie removed my glasses and, with tiny spray container and tissue, devoted herself to cleaning them, a pious work to which a number of attractive women are dedicated, on the premise—utterly accurate—that I am incapable of doing it myself.

"Since the gun was, according to the testimony of both Ms. Downs and Luisa the maid, the property of Mrs. Harrington Enright, it is odd that there are no other fingerprints on it." I did my best to convey the impression of confused innocence, an effort utterly wasted on Mike the Cop. "It might have been cleaned, wiped free of prints, and remained untouched till Ms. Downs picked it up and shot her grandmother. But since Mrs. Harrington Enright seems to have carried it in her vast purse at all times, that does not seem likely."

"So my sometime colleagues argue." Mike nodded his assent.

Annie replaced my glasses and kissed my forehead. "There, Father Blackie, you'll be able to enjoy the blue sky for another week. I'll leave you two men to your games. Unlike you, I have to work for a living."

She flounced out of the room. Mike's eyes followed her

posterior with the hungry concentration of a bird dog looking for quail, or of a recent husband who can hardly believe
that such a paragon is actually his wife.

"There is also the matter of the lie detector test that Ms.
Slattery is demanding." Reluctantly he forced his attention
to return from the living to the dead. "The State's Attorney is
aware that it's not admissible in court. Nonetheless, he
would certainly take it into account in determining whether
to oppose bail."

"Obviously."

Mike is my cousin, his mother was my father's sister. We
call him Mike Casey the Cop so as to distinguish him, it is
often presumed by those not in the clan, from another Mike
Casey we know.

But we don't know another Mike Casey.

He rearranged his notes on the clear plastic coffee table
that Annie had pushed between us for our tea and my cookies. "There is finally the matter of the paraffin test."

"Which proves or purports to prove that Fionna Downs
had not recently fired a weapon."

"Someone told you?" Mike carefully put his notes down
again, so as not to appear too surprised. "I received the call
from my sometime colleagues just before you walked in the
door."

"No one told me." I was sure I was smiling beatifically.
"And there were also no carbon remnants on the hands of the
deceased?"

"No. . . . The test is not absolutely conclusive, as you
know, but still . . ."

"It gives your sometime colleagues pause?"

"Decidedly. But don't you see, Blackie, what that might
mean?"

"That there was someone else in the salon of the *Violetta*
yesterday at four o'clock and that someone else fired the
weapon, wiped his/her prints off it, threw it on the bed, and
then escaped from the room and subsequently the ship without being seen by Ms. Downs, Luisa Without-a-Surname, my
good sister, a devout and virtuous woman if there ever was

one, her equally good spouse, and perhaps half a thousand people in Monroe Street harbor?"

"Precisely."

We both greeted that possibility with reverent silence. I refilled Mike's cup and my own from the Irish Belleek teapot Annie had left on the table. Mind you, apple cinnamon tea is not totally unacceptable.

"It's impossible." Mike folded his arms across his chest as if to protect himself from demons. "Joe Murphy searched the cabin. . . ."

"A diligent and responsible man . . ."

"The police later searched the boat and found no one. Moreover, the only access across a half mile of water was the *Violetta*'s launch, which the police had impounded."

"And after all the TV attention, if a Sunday sailor had seen any other craft approach or leave the *Violetta*, they would certainly have informed the CPD by now."

"They've had a lot of calls. Surprising how many Sunday sailors were watching the *Violetta*. None of them saw anything that makes any difference."

"Uhm . . ." I replaced my cup on the table, spilling only a little tea and that nowhere near Mike's notes. "Perhaps a swimmer . . ."

"The windows and the panels of the salon were locked from the inside. They're too high above the water"—he passed me a remarkably detailed set of drawings of the *Violetta*—"to be closed from the water. Or even to be reached by a rather short young woman like Fionna Downs."

"Indeed."

"Don't ask me about a submarine." He shook his head in discouragement. "One of my most sane sometime colleagues seriously asked me that question only forty minutes ago."

"You are, after all, the author of the classic text *Principles of Detection*, in which you exclude the possibility of an authentic locked-room crime. I can't recall you discussing the possibility of the use of submarines in such cases."

He laughed, not altogether cheerfully. Mike the Cop, now a successful painter, would always be Mike the Cop. The department's problems would always be his problems. Not that his wife or his pastor would want him any different.

"Think about it, Blackie. A prominent and wealthy woman is murdered in her private yacht on a Sunday afternoon in high August, the yacht being in full view of hundreds of other craft in and around Monroe Street harbor, motorists on Lake Shore Drive, and apartment and condo dwellers all along the Chicago skyline. Either her niece, who had the motive and the opportunity, killed her—and now some of the evidence suggests that she did not—or she was murdered by person or persons unknown who boarded and departed the yacht without being seen and who escaped, seconds after the murder, from a locked room without being noticed by responsible and observant witnesses."

"Hardly Chesterton's mailman on a Sunday afternoon."

Mike the Cop ignored my reference to the classic Father Brown story. "And it is practically certain that only Luisa Flores, Fionna Downs, and Mrs. Harrington Enright were on the boat at four o'clock yesterday afternoon."

"The worthy, ah, Carlos and Tomas have yet to be found?"

"Ms. Flores tells my colleagues that they are very bad *hombres*, they carry switchblades, and she did not know them before she became Mrs. Harrington Enright's maid. While my aforementioned colleagues—Hispanic themselves, by the way—are disinclined to believe anything an undocumented says, they think that these statements are probably true."

"And Ms. Flores has been handed over to the tender mercies of the INS?"

The teapot was unaccountably empty and my four chocolate chip cookies were gone. A leprechaun or perhaps, in this ecumenical age, a golem must have eaten at least two of them. I stared around the room seeking traces of this naughty spirit.

"She has been incarcerated in a convent, protective custody. She is afraid to run away from the nuns. My Hispanic-American colleagues are not disposed to do the INS any favors."

"Their reward," I said with a sigh, "as one of my Polish classmates used to put it, will come great in heaven."

Annie reappeared, bringing with her a delicate trace of Givenchy. "More chocolate chips, Father Blackie? More tea?"

We accepted both dutifully, and I did not ask why the cookies were allotted to me in rations of four.

"Distracting, aren't they?" Mike grinned happily as she flounced out again.

"Cookies?" I replied with my most wide-eyed innocence.

"Bastard," he replied with little respect for my clerical cloth. Perhaps I should have worn the collar! "How would you like to try to work all day with a woman like that swishing in and out periodically to minister to your every want."

"Islamic paradise, save for the woman's ego strength. Now as to the matter at hand . . ."

He strove to concentrate. "Consider the agenda for these yachting parties of Mrs. Harrington Enright—somehow Ms. does not seem correct for her. On Saturday afternoon she was ferried from her apartment at the Edgewater Beach to Montrose harbor. She boarded the boat with her daughter, Ms. Rita Downs, her granddaughter, Ms. Fionna Downs, a maid, and her two male servants. Caterers delivered a sumptuous cold supper and a large supply of various alcoholic beverages and departed. A captain arrived to pilot the boat. Then the other members of her family appeared—"

"Two couples"—I ticked them off on my fingers—"the D. and E. Harrington Enrights, and two unattached folk, the mysterious Mary O'Brien Feehan and my distinguished brother in the Lord, titular bishop of some forgotten spot now under the Aegean Sea, Bishop H. Harrington Enright."

"Nothing so mysterious about Mary Feehan. She's a nurse, the wife of a retired battalion chief in the CFD with several children living in various voting districts of Cook County."

"And she commutes back and forth from County Galway?"

"Mayo."

"God help us!" I added piously, as one always must when that most impoverished of Irish counties is mentioned. "But fortunate, isn't she, to be able to afford such a life-style on a battalion chief's retirement pension? The unions and the late mayor's generosity did well by you public servants, didn't they?"

"Not that well." Mike made a note. "I'll check. Mike Feehan was reputed to be an honest fireman, easier in their form of public service than in mine."

"Indeed."

"Then, finally, borne by his Mercedes 600 SL, Vincent C. Nelligan appears from Lake Forest."

"With his adored grandson?"

"When everyone is on board, they proceed from Montrose to Burnham harbor under the light of the August moon, eating the supper and drinking the assorted forms of booze." Mike continued to peer suspiciously at his notes. "Since Mrs. Harrington Enright was not an easy person to endure in the cramped quarters of the *Violetta*, most of the party would drink heavily so as to kill the pain of listening to her various obsessions. Mrs. Harrington Enright herself was a very heavy drinker."

"Indeed."

"Then they anchored off Monroe Street, the two servants put the captain ashore since he would not be required till the following afternoon, and they all retired."

"Where?" I leaned over the charts on Annie's coffee table.

"There are five cabins—staterooms if you wish—on the lower deck of the *Violetta*, in addition to the owner's specially designed two-deck salon in the stern. The bow cabin, the second most luxurious, was assigned to—"

"The good Bishop because of his dignity as a successor to the Apostles."

"Sometimes, Blackie, I think there are two different churches."

"Many. Of which his and mine are at the opposite ends

of the continuum. I distract you with my own obsessions. Pray, continue."

"On the port side with adjoining bath are the rooms that the two married couples occupied, Dr. and Mrs. D. Harrington Enright aft—"

"The nonmedical doctor or, as my niece the good Caitlin puts it of my Ph.D., the doctor kind that doesn't help people."

"And Dr. and Mrs. E. Harrington Enright forward. On the starboard side—I had to look these terms up to get them right—in the aft cabin Rita Downs shares the room with her daughter, and in the forward cabin Mary Feehan sleeps alone, Chief Feehan remaining in County Mayo this trip."

"I see. How fortunate. For him, I mean. And what of the worthy banker?"

"Normally no one is dispensed from the joys of the yachting party overnight. However, since Mrs. Feehan is an extra guest and since it would not be proper for her and Vinney Nelligan to occupy the same cabin, he is permitted to return to his invalid wife in Lake Forest. He returns the next morning early with his grandson Rick, whom he worships and to whom he can deny nothing. He too disapproves strongly of the liaison between Rick and Fionna, but nonetheless he brings the young man along on Sunday morning, despite Violet's warning the night before that he is not welcome. She ignores the young man, who retaliates by engaging, according to Luisa Flores, in a passionate exchange of affection with Fionna Downs in the galley, an exchange which is not pushed to completion because, young people of principle, they are not living together or even sleeping together."

"Virtue runs in strange cycles."

"If I were young and in love with that young woman, I would have a hard time keeping my hands off her."

"A problem that afflicts only the young."

Mike blushed and smiled contentedly. "No, *Monsignor*, not only the young. But they with less concern about the consequences."

"Such concerns among the young might signal the end of the species, but to continue the discussion . . . No, wait—what, if any, is Mr. Nelligan's military history?"

"Rick?"

"No, his grandfather. My Old Fella left that out in his story telling last night."

Mike shuffled through his stack of papers. "A year in the Canal Zone as an M.P. at the end of the War. Was drafted in forty-three when they were taking anyone that could walk. His job was cushy. Probably required a lot of clout to get it. My information is that he wasn't very eager to go. But lots of people weren't."

"In more recent times they would have been admired by many. . . ." I had no idea why I asked the question. I merely wanted to fill in the blank. "There is a connecting bathroom—the nautical term is head, by the way—between the two cabins set aside for the unattended women?"

None of the Ryans, as you may have noticed, can resist scoring points.

"Yes. Right here."

"And, of course, the Bishop must perform his natural functions in secure privacy up here."

"Precisely."

"And there are two doors to the main salon?"

"One on the lower deck, which is always locked to protect Mrs. Harrington Enright's privacy. And the other on the upper deck, the one through which Fionna Enright entered—to discover her grandmother's body, as she claims—to be followed almost instantly by Luisa Flores and a minute or two later by Doctor Joseph Murphy."

"A living saint if there ever was one, with all which he has to put up." I felt it appropriate to repeat the Ryan family respect for my trim, white-bearded brother-in-law.

("If my daddy were Jewish," Caitlin had informed us when she was an early teen, "he would be like a rabbi or maybe a prophet.")

"So the folks say . . . there are two keys, one securely in Mrs. Harrington Enright's commodious shoulder bag—"

"Next to the Beretta?"

"Perhaps. It's a big bag. And the other in the possession of her maid, Luisa Flores. The keys are made from a special stock, so neither Luisa nor the two bad *hombres* can have copies made."

"Indeed." I disposed of the last of my second ration of cookies. The golem—I was convinced that it was a Jewish spirit—had taken his two again.

I felt quite certain that I understood the locked-room trick. Indeed, I had understood it last night, hence my phone call from my sibling's house. If my analysis were correct, I also knew the identity of the killer, at least in all probability. Motives were another matter. As was proof—I was not an employee of either the Chicago Police Department or the State's Attorney of the County of Cook. So long as the innocent were not prosecuted and my sister's reputation not injured, it was not up to me to see that the guilty were captured.

Priests are not cops. Or disciplinarians. Or judges. Much harm has been done to the church and to the Christian people by our attempts to play any and all of these roles.

It would not do to have people think that their friendly, nearsighted, ineffectual parish priest is considering the criminal propensities of everyone to whom he gives the Eucharist or greets in the back of the parish church after Mass is concluded.

Go in peace—unless you are threatening others. I leave you to heaven and the State's Attorney.

"The *Violetta* has been searched for secret passages and the like?"

"Certainly."

"And this rather large bathroom carved out of the salon does not lead into the cabin occupied by Rita and Fionna Downs."

"No. And there are no sliding panels in the back of the closets. . . ."

"I see. So. What is the agenda for Sunday morning?"

"Champagne brunch, would you believe? Another orgy

of food and drink. Mrs. Harrington Enright holding sway from beneath a deck umbrella, rather like a mixture of Cleopatra and Catherine the Great. Swimming is frowned upon because Mrs. Harrington Enright believes the lake has been polluted by the coho salmon that the State of Michigan has introduced into the lake...."

"Polluted by the coho?" I spilled more tea. Mrs. Harrington Enright was a true loony. "And she buys bottled water to protect herself and her own from the ravages of fluoridation."

"How did you know that?" Mike demanded with some show of impatience.

"It figures. Nonetheless, the good Fionna did swim."

"She is a strong swimmer and possesses, as we all have been told, a strong will. I suspect she wanted to demonstrate her skills, as well as her charms in a wet bikini, to her young man."

"Grandmother was outraged by this display."

"Livid."

"And, of course, she disapproves of bikinis."

"Absolutely. Modern immorality."

"They appear in Roman and Greek frescoes, but that is not to the point, is it? So the good Fionna comes out of the lake, perhaps engages in more affection with her young man, dresses in jeans and a blouse, and like the others, is conveyed to the dock at Monroe Street harbor by the launch driven by Carlos or Tomas?"

"They ride back in cabs to Montrose harbor to pick up their own cars. Mrs. Harrington Enright took to her bed early in the afternoon, perhaps because too much of the drink had been taken and perhaps to show her displeasure with her stubborn grandchild."

"More and more do I like this Fionna Downs."

"She's a knockout and reputedly tough as hell."

"Yet she became hysterical when she finds the body? And surely she could not have deceived the inestimable Doctors Murphy?"

"You find your grandmother in bed with a hole in her head, it makes you hysterical."

"Indeed." I glanced through Mike's stack of notes. They were remarkably legible with my newly cleaned lenses. "Ah, these are the times of departure for the various members of the family. My, your colleagues in blue have been diligent."

"They try. . . . Each guest paid respects to Mrs. Harrington Enright as they left, leaving the door open for the one who came next. The leavetaking, by custom, is at half-hour intervals because Carlos and Tomas in the launch require that much time to bring visitors to the dock and return. The boat is able to carry three passengers but not four. All the visitors report that Mrs. Harrington Enright was uncommunicative but certainly alive. Well, not every guest said good-bye. Young Rick Nelligan was distinctly *persona non grata*, so his father expressed his regrets."

"The Nelligans left at two-thirty I note. And My Lord Henry, bishop of whatever submerged *in partibus infidelium*, withdrew before noon to return to the cathedral rectory, wherein he dwells in peace and amity with his fellow priests."

"Does he?"

"We never see him. He eats in his room."

"Did he return to the rectory as he said?"

I blinked my protest. "Of course I checked that with the young persons who guard the door of the rectory on Wabash Avenue. Juniors in Mundelein Cathedral High, best porteresses in the species. You may depend on it, My Lord Harry returned as he said."

"That lets him out then."

"Alas"—I sighed against the illogic that governs the world as opposed to the neat logic which reigns in mystery novels—"that does not follow. You know what a maze our place is. It would be simplicity itself to steal quietly along a corridor, slip unseen down the back stairs, open the door which leads to the cathedral sacristy, and exit through the cathedral onto State Street or out a side door and through the passageway to Chicago Avenue."

"You've questioned your staff?" He leaned back in his leather chair, his mind perhaps on something else. Annie? The painting? Both?

Very likely.

The painting, I had noted, was a major work. I don't know how one introduces universality into a row of houses on Belden, but he had done it.

"If I referred to them as 'my staff' they would very likely revolt. Nor do I dare wander about hinting at plots on the part of a guest who is already unwelcome. My colleagues are very uneasy about the possibility of our baroque dwelling being blown up by various characters in the shadow world who have a grudge against My Lord Harry."

"He's into them that bad?" Mike screwed up his face, hardly able to believe that bishops could be the object of hit contracts.

"It is said that no less a person than Licio Gelli himself—the master of the Propaganda Due and the impresario behind the Vatican Bank mess and, if you are to believe David Yallup, the man who ordered the murder of John Paul I—has put a price on Bishop H. Harrington Enright's handsome head."

"But your, uh, *pares*—as in *primus inter pares*—would have told you this morning if they noticed him sneaking out yesterday afternoon?"

Mike went to the seminary for a couple of years and is proud of his recollection of Latin, of which he knows more than most priests under forty. *O Tempora! O Mores!* you should excuse the expression.

"You bet your life. There has been no such report. From which it follows not that he did not leave but that he was not seen leaving."

"It'll be hard for the CPD to be suspicious about a bishop. I'll suggest they talk to Interpol about him."

I returned to the chart. "Dan and Lena left at three-thirty in company of Señorita Flores. Why was it necessary for her to go ashore and thus be available for Fionna Downs's return trip?"

"Tomas and Carlos were to purchase a bottle of J&B and tomorrow's *Tribune* and pick up the captain. She was to buy a bottle of Advil for Mrs. Harrington Enright's headache. She took a cab over to the Hilton and made the purchase."

"I won't even ask if you checked that story."

Mike nodded. "A pretty young woman in a uniform that makes her look like a commodore in the Bolivian Navy is easy to remember. And there was only one bottle of pain-killer on the boat."

"Her compadres came back with the captain, saw the commotion around *Violetta*, dumped the captain, and va-moosed?"

"In an Enright Ford for which we are still searching."

"So . . ." I continued to peer at Mike's neat chart. "The Edward Harrington Enrights took their leave at three and the Mss. Downs and Feehan departed at two o'clock—all re-porting that Mrs. Harrington Enright was alive if not partic-ularly well?"

"Rita Downs went home and straight to bed with a split-ting headache—confirmation of her return from the door-man at their building. Mary Feehan and Fionna Downs stopped for a milk shake in the café in the Fine Arts Building. No one remembers them, but no one there remembers any-one ever."

"A milk shake after all that food?"

"What can I tell you? Then Mary Feehan, who is staying at the Harrington Enright apartment this trip, takes a cab back to the apartment—arrival confirmed by the doorman—and Fionna Downs walks back to Monroe Street and prevails upon Luisa to ferry her out to the yacht."

Mike paused, expecting comment and perhaps illumina-tion from me.

Why, I wondered, was the nurse who took care of Daniel Enright in his final days such a close friend of his wife?

"Where she arrives about four o'clock to deliver, if we are to believe her hysterical story, a message to her grand-mother, to wit: 'You're no real grandmother.' What could that have meant and what relationship, if any, might it have to the crime?"

"I have no idea. Do you, Blackie?" He considered me with his shrewd, penetrating silver-blue eyes.

"None at all." An answer which was totally honest. The

main outlines of what had happened were clear enough. But there were several peculiar strands that baffled me and which I did not like.

"What else do you want to know?" Mike reordered his notes and put them into a transparent folder.

If he gave them to me, it would be a sign that his some-time colleagues wanted me to poke around. They would say something like "Hey, Mike, this one is off the wall. Why don't you see what that weird little priest of yours can do with it. Give him all we got."

Given the way cops talk, they probably would have said "fucking wall" and used that obscene but hardly sinful participle at least once more in the sentence. Possibly before "weird."

"Father of the fine-spirited Fionna? Bill Downs? That is his name, isn't it?"

"Professor William I. Downs, econometrics, UCLA." He opened his transparent folder. "Faculty dinner party in Manhattan Beach. He flew in this morning for the funeral."

"In that field he should find the object of his daughter's love appealing. They can talk to each other in calculus. Or Fortran."

"There is a report. . . ." Mike shrugged, meaning that it was not strictly a report from the investigation. Possibly something that his wife had heard around town earlier in the day. "That he wants to reclaim Rita. He has not remarried. There's been a divorce and an ecclesiastical annulment, but apparently he still loves her."

"That's interesting." What might there be in such an overwhelmed middle-aged woman still to love? A tiny spark perhaps of what had flared in her daughter? One more inexplicable strand.

"Most of the money goes to Fionna, of course. From a girl with nothing but what her grandmother chose to give her, she becomes one of the wealthiest women in America."

"That *is* interesting." I sat up straight. "This was not known?"

"Oh, yes indeed it was known. It was not liked, but it was

known. Mrs. Harrington Enright kept changing her will as the patterns of antagonism in her family ebbed and flowed, but she was very explicit about its arrangements each time she made a change. There are trust funds of various odd shapes and sizes for everyone. None of the family will ever need to worry about money again. But Fionna receives the lion's—or should I say the lioness's?—share. Mrs. Harrington Enright believed that she was the one most like her."

"Which may very well be true. Any information that she threatened changes in the will because of Fionna's infatuation, as Mrs. Harrington Enright must have seen it, with young Richard Nelligan?"

"Very explicit threats, made on the deck in the presence of everyone just before she descended to her stateroom for the last time."

I pondered that bit of information. If the police and the prosecutors were reluctant to push ahead with an indictment when they possessed that testimony, they must be very uncertain indeed. "I presume," I said to Mike, "that she had often made such threats?"

He nodded. "Not quite so angry as this time. Or so it is said."

"And La Belle Fionna's response?"

"Said she didn't want the money, never wanted it, and would give it all away if she received it."

"Fearsome." I sighed. It would play well in court, however. At minimum it might be argued that anyone who said that about tens of millions, perhaps hundreds of millions, was suffering from diminished responsibility. "Do any of the beneficiaries need money?"

"Rita Downs lived with her mother, as did Fionna. Apparently she did nothing at all except sit on some charitable and artistic boards—you know the kind, the sort of lean and intense women who meet for lunch at the Arts Club once every couple of weeks, passionately committed to the pursuit of good works."

"Tell me about it. The others?"

"Lena and Dan"—Mike crossed his legs and folded his

arms again—"live above their faculty salaries, but not by a hell of a lot. He wants to launch a highbrow literary magazine—*Chicago Writers*, it is called. Prospecti for it are floating around town. He has some Illinois Arts Council seed money. He'd be the editor, of course, and one of the writers. It's a way to get your essays and poetry and stories published."

"But hardly grounds for murder."

Mike picked up an oil crayon and examined his painting. He dabbed a small black line. It transformed the picture.

Genius.

Fucking genius, his sometime fellow cops would say.

And the best I can do is write books about William James. Oh well, God is good.

"Who knows why people commit murder?" he asked glumly. "But under ordinary circumstances, no. Still Dan Enright does fancy himself a very distinguished writer, even if the New York publishing companies won't give him a second glance. Ed Enright has much better motives."

"Ah?" My interest picked up. He had dared to assail the reputation of one of my siblings in public. Bad guys deserve to finish last.

"He makes a nice living as a surgeon and has an allowance from Mrs. Harrington Enright to boot. But he thinks he's a financial wizard too. Some M.D.'s, as you know, assume that because they're good in their own field they're good in every other field too."

"Some clerics think that. Even some cops . . ."

Mike grinned. "Touché, but with Ed it's an obsession. He has to fight lawyers and traders and everyone else on the streets of Chicago."

"Traders?"

Only a slightly less dangerous occupation than gambling with the Outfit in Vegas.

"He's currently taken a very heavy long position in dollars. There are margin calls. Instead of taking his loss and getting out, he's hanging on. And everyone in America but him knows that since Jim Baker moved over to Treasury from the White House, the strategy has been to cut the value of the dollar."

"He can be wiped out?"

"Sunk. Permanently. His mother's death saves him. For the moment. He'll probably blow the legacy too, eventually."

Those whom the gods would destroy, they first make mad. Or attract to the commodity markets.

Often the same thing.

The strands were even more complicated than I had thought. Yet the picture was clear, was it not? Could not the police be expected in time to cast aside the trees of the massive data they had assembled and see the obvious forest?

"You want to take this stuff with you?" Mike stood up; we both knew that we had covered all the bases.

"Thanks but no thanks. I have a good memory."

Good enough so that if I raced back to my room at the rectory and wrote quickly, I could get most of the high points down on paper. If I took Mike's notes and charts, I would be committing myself to the Chicago Police Department. He knew as well as I did that it wasn't time for that yet.

I don't like to make notes of my own. Bad enough that a priest pokes around, without him writing down the results of his poking for all to see.

Besides, did Father Brown take notes?

Annie Reilly hugged me and gave me a bag of chocolate chip cookies.

"Don't eat them till you get home. You don't want people to say that the rector of the cathedral is an absentminded little priest who wanders down the Magnificent Mile gobbling chocolate chip cookies, do you?"

"Thoughtful," I said, clutching the cookies. "Not absentminded."

They both laughed. I left them, arms around each other, walked down Oak Street, turned the corner, and in a few minutes found myself on the Oak Street Beach instead of approaching the cathedral.

Wrong turn.

Ignoring Annie's warning, I started in on the cookies. My *pares*, I argued, would take them from me if there were any left when I arrived at the rectory.

Sophistry.

Having married her childhood sweetheart in the late middle years of life, Anne O'Brien Reilly Casey had decided to enjoy him as often as she could. She was also faced with the necessity of managing an art gallery. So she combined the two needs by ensconcing Mike the Cop in the back room of her gallery. Thus the poor man found himself being seduced all day every day.

Which may be what God had in mind when He foresaw that the species would eventually reach a stage where life expectancy was prolonged decades after the end of fertility.

How clever of Her.

Not that Lady Wisdom required my praise of Her wisdom.

Was this sort of environment interfering with his painting? If it's true that, as some of my sibling's fellow Freudians believe, creativity requires frustration, then trying to paint with Annie around all day must surely impede his work.

On the other hand, Doctor James (William) would have argued that great art often is created in a burst of joy and contentment.

In re Mike Casey the Cop: game, set, and match to Dr. James.

As usual.

The cookies finished, I turned down Wabash. The case of the murder of Violet Harrington Enright could safely be left for the present to the Chicago Police Department. They didn't need my wisdom. And they probably wouldn't appreciate what it meant if I told it to them.

All would work out in due course.

I could not have been more wrong.

However, looking back on the case, I cannot fault myself—as I had in the case of Lisa Malone—for gross and inculpable stupidity.

I knew how the locked-room puzzle worked. I knew who

set it up. Or so I thought. I was unclear about the motives. There were obscure strands that I did not understand, but they seemed to be irrelevant to the murder, however puzzling they otherwise might be.

More time would be required before I could possibly understand the full horror and the full confusion of the Harrington Enright story.

More time and more deaths.

■

FIRST INTERMEZZO

Mary Kate

7

She was too preoccupied to be driving home from Little Company on 95th Street on a hot summer afternoon. Always lectured the kids about paying attention at the wheel of a car and wasn't paying attention herself.

She just barely missed running a red at 95th and Western, a risk like jumping off a high-speed train. Or walking the rim of the parapet on the observation deck of the Sears Tower.

Fionna had passed the lie detector test with flying colors, God bless her. She still had been arraigned and charged with murder, but Patty Slattery demanded and got a low bail. The Assistant State's Attorney had not argued very strongly against releasing Fionna. Nor did there seem to be any great rush to obtain a grand jury indictment. According to the Punk, the cops and the prosecutors knew they had a case which, while strong in some ways, could be torn apart by a smart young defense attorney like Patty.

So Fionna was home with her mother—and her father, who had appeared out of the west and was staying at the Enright apartment.

Should she go to the funeral? Fionna had asked on the telephone. "I mean with all my uncle said on TV the other night?"

"Do you want to?"

"Yes, Doctor. I hated her but I loved her too. And I did NOT kill her."

"If you want to go to the Mass, then go. Ignore your uncle. And ignore the TV people. You have a right to be there and they don't."

"Are you really suing him?"

"My father is. He's a lawyer."

"Good! What he said was totally gross!"

Totally gross. How like her own children. Just out of college, a year younger than Caitlin. And she has to put up with all this horse manure.

A more personal question was whether she and Joe should go to the wake at Carroll's, the funeral home without which you were never really dead in the cathedral parish. Even though the Harrington Enrights lived in St. Ita's, it would be unthinkable for the Bishop to say the funeral Mass anywhere else but the cathedral. Mary Kate's deepest Irish instincts said you always go to wakes. On the other hand, given the nature of the charges and countercharges about her professional behavior in treating Fionna, it would probably be in good taste to stay away.

Occasionally, she told herself, I do opt for good taste.

A horn honked behind her. All right, idiot, so the light has turned green. You probably need to see a shrink.

She glanced at the car next to her. Not the one which had honked.

A black Ford.

Funny. No, it couldn't be them.

The two dark-skinned men in the Ford looked like Carlos and Tomas, the two pilots of Vi Enright's launch.

8

"May I have a word with you, Monsignor?" Bishop Henry Harrington Enright stood at the door of my study, dressed in Roman collar, pectoral cross, episcopal ring (not just a gold band but a jewel), and underneath his clerical vest, a white shirt (surely tailor-made) that displayed French cuffs and cuff links with a papal crest. A touch of purple marked the junction of white collar and black vest. Impeccably groomed, impeccably dressed and pressed, a gray tinge at the edge of his impeccably razor-cut thick black hair, Harry Enright was a handsome bishop right out of the twenties, a mannequin in the window of a "church goods" store, an ad for a clerical clothier in a magazine for priests, a travel agency's promotion for a "pilgrimage to Lourdes, Rome, and the Holy Land."

"Sure, Harry, come on in. Would you care for a wee drop of the crayture?"

"No, thank you, Monsignor. . . ." His patronizing voice was rich baritone, like those which one heard on fine-arts FM stations. "Well, perhaps some of your fabled Jameson."

Even more fabled was my Bushmill's Black, but he hadn't heard that fable.

And wouldn't get any if he did.

My Christian name is John. No one calls me that save for an occasional radical nun. The Old Fella calls me Johnny. My Lord Cronin calls me Blackwood most of the time. My siblings call me Punk normally. So do my many nieces and nephews, as in "Uncle Punk." Helen's kids—my half siblings—and most of the rest of the world call me by my proper name: Blackie. Sometimes as in "Father Blackie," or if they wished to be disrespectful, "Monsignor Blackie." My *pares*, to use Mike the Cop's term, sometimes—when they're giving me orders—call me "Boss."

No one—I repeat, *no one*—calls me "Monsignor."

Not twice anyway.

I motioned Harry to a chair, removed the stacks of papers about William James which made it impossible for him to sit on it, poured him a modest ration of John Jameson's, and sat back to listen.

"I want to thank you and your staff for all the courtesies during this tragic interlude."

M.K. was right: he did talk like he was translating for the Pope.

I assayed a response in the same language even though I am innocent of even a single virus of *Romanita*.

"It's been our privilege to serve your family in whatever way we can to alleviate your great pain at this time."

Not bad, huh?

He crossed his legs, carefully arranging the knife-sharp crease on his trousers, and relaxed a tad. Probably thought he was back with his own kind of people.

"It would appear that I must ask you a favor." He hesitated, a delicate pause so that I might express with equal delicacy my surprise, dismay, disapproval, understanding, or whatever other reaction I had prepared beforehand.

"His Eminence spoke to me about a small problem. . . ."

Better and better, Blackie Ryan.

He waved his fingers, like indeed he was a member of the Curia. Of course, he had been just that and technically still was.

Then the clean, sharp lines of his face seemed to dissolve and his hard brown eyes to melt. "It's the matter of the, ah, revolver with which my mother was killed."

"An automatic, wasn't it?"

I warned you about my genetic tendency to correct minor mistakes.

"Yes, certainly. An, ah, nine-millimeter Beretta automatic."

"M-38, short?" I said nothing about James Bond.

"I believe so."

"With a silencer, I am told."

Why do you need a silencer to protect yourself? You don't, not unless someone is trying to set you up.

"Yes, I could never understand the reason for it. Nonetheless, certain men associated with the Vatican gendarmes insisted that I must be armed. I failed to see what difference that would make. The others—"

"Clavi, Sidona?" The names of those who already had been eliminated by orders of the invisible but deadly Licio Gelli. "John Paul I?"

"I don't think the last."

"Nor do I. But we can't be sure."

"No, we can't." He tasted his Jameson's and seemed surprised that it was, after all, better than Campari and soda. "Can we? I sometimes think I would have been much better off if I had remained a curate in Chicago. But Mother had such high hopes, you know. Poor woman."

"God be good to her." I did not, however, make the sign of the cross.

I almost did, to tell the truth.

"Mother very properly demanded that I not carry it in this country. She hired those two dreadful Hispanic persons to protect me. She took the gun and the silencer. I had no idea she was carrying it herself."

If, as I suspected, Carlos and Tomas were recruits from the cocaine world, they would be better qualified than most security types to deal with the professional killers of the shadow world. But they were probably lightweights up against real heavies. Licio Gelli used only the best hit men available on the planet. He made the Chicago Outfit look timid.

"They cut him loose," Sean Cronin had moaned before the funeral Mass earlier in the day. "Can you imagine that, Blackwood? They cut the poor bastard loose. Gave him a gun and a silencer and sent him home. Stay alive if you can. And the gun is probably a setup anyway. He was too dumb to throw it over the side of a Tiber bridge before he left Rome."

His graying blond hair was in wild disarray, his hooded Celtic warrior's eyes shining wildly, his handsome haggard face alight with fury or battle lust or who knows what other demonic emotion.

My Lord Cronin carries his crozier like a pike.

"The gendarmes leave something to be desired," I admitted. "They're not as competent, I am told, as the Swiss Guard."

"The Swiss Guard, Blackwood, are Swiss."

"So I am told."

"The son of a bitch calls the Pope 'the Vicar of Christ' every time he talks about him. Can you imagine that, Blackwood?" My Lord Cronin pulled his clerical collar off and tossed it on the floor next to my easy chair, which, out of perversity, he always occupies when he comes to my room.

"And you told him that if the title implies an identification of the Pope with the Lord Jesus, it follows that the Lord Jesus sired children during the Borgia papacy, committed many other errors and mistakes down through history, and on some occasions may even have been gay? You also told him that for the first twelve hundred years of the papacy the title 'Vicar of Peter' was deemed more appropriate and that you think it is to be preferred because it stresses the human frailty of the church and its leadership?"

"Of course I told him that. It's true, isn't it? You gave the lines to me."

"Once or twice in error," I modified his description of me ever so slightly, "long, long ago, but never in doubt."

"Precisely. It had no effect. He didn't hear me. He's the kind of guy who thirty years ago, after a life of dedicated ministry, would make a pilgrimage to Rome, which his parishioners had funded as a silver anniversary present, and then come home to tell them in all sincerity that his general audience with the Vicar of Christ—along with thirty thousand other shouting pilgrims, mind you—was the most moving experience of his life."

"Indeed."

"Except, Blackwood, it is 1985."

"So I am told."

"They say to me, he's washed up over here. One or two small errors in judgment, you know, nothing serious, but it was not well done. No *bella figura*. What they mean is that he trusted his bosses a little too much. Something went wrong over which he had no control, maybe because one of the bosses was on the take, and so they feed him to the lions."

"Deplorable. But an ancient Roman custom."

"A pagan custom." He threw his long legs over the side of my chair, treatment for which it is not designed. "But then those guys have never been Christianized, have they? Don't misunderstand me, Blackwood." We moved into the second phase of My Lord Cronin's blowing off steam, a phase in which his rationality and balance are permitted to express their perspective. "It's not quite the time of the Borgias. And the Vatican is not shot through with corruption. The problems are mostly at the middle and the lower level and don't affect all but a tiny minority. But damn it"— exit rationality and balance—"how can you pretend it doesn't exist when there's half a dozen best-sellers in English, to say nothing of other European languages, revealing in rich and persuasive detail the involvement of some curial types in the shadow world: with Mafia hit men, Turkish drug dealers, Bulgarian double agents, international arms merchants, terrorists of various ilks and colors, bent Italian Masonic lodges with cardinals as members, CIA, KGB, MI-6, the Mossad, and hell only knows how many other crazies with guns."

"Shocking." As My Lord Cronin knows very well, I haven't been shocked since I was nine years old.

"Not well-organized conspiracies within conspiracies presided over by a single evil genius, as your friend Malachi Martin would have us believe, but a loose and fluid world of shifting alliances among lunatics, a world which makes Ludlum and le Carré seem like religious-education teachers."

"Fascinating. And the inestimable Malachi is no friend of mine."

A comment, delivered in the name of accuracy, which

was not likely to slow down My Lord Cronin for a second. Not when he's wound up.

"So they send this naive punk from the Gold Coast into that world, allegedly with money for Solidarity in Poland—hell, I don't know anything about that—and something goes wrong. He follows orders too literally; he doesn't understand a wink of an eye or a pregnant silence. So he ends up allegedly on someone's hit list. Without telling me any of this, they say, 'Seano, me boy, will you take him off our hands? After all, he's from your city. He's washed up—and honest, he's not a spy, nor is he supposed to replace you.' One look at the poor bastard tells me that he knows he's finished. So I say, 'What the hell, I'll take him, so long as he stays out of my hair.' I find out that there's a contract out on him only after he shows up here in my home."

"My home. Yours is up on North State."

"Too many ghosts." He waved a deranged hand in the direction of the old mansion at 1555 North State.

"But surely they exaggerate." I leaned back comfortably on the couch to which I had been banished, prepared for my own lecture. "We do know that the elusive Signor Gelli moves with ruthless speed. If he were of a mind to—I believe the term currently in use is—*put down* Bishop Harry, he would have already done so with ruthless cunning. The story might be designed to keep the good Bishop silent and frightened. Moreover, this clumsy business with the gun and silencer, does it not sound like a primitive charade to sustain his fear? Is it not arguable that his late mother acted prudently in removing the gun from his possession?"

"Maybe." He seemed impressed by this line of reasoning. "And maybe not. The point is that it was supremely imprudent of her to leave the gun lying around. She was killed with it."

"It would appear so."

"Killed with a gun that might be traced by Interpol to the Vatican and to Harry Harrington Enright."

"If they gave him a weapon that they had registered. Would they do that?"

"They might, Blackwood. Either out of stupidity or cunning or both. Are the Chicago cops checking with Interpol?"

"I believe that they are."

It was, I thought, entirely inappropriate to note that they were doing so as a result of a remark I made to Mike the Cop.

"Did he kill her, Blackie?"

"It is possible, but I doubt it. What motive?"

"Money to pay them off."

"She didn't leave him that kind of money. Besides I'm not sure you pay those folks off."

"Did they kill her, as a warning or perhaps as a punishment?"

I paused. Carlos and Tomas? Maybe even Luisa?

"Candidly, I'm not sure. It's not very probable."

"All of this shadow world in the Vatican is recent, you see." His legs came off the arm of my chair and back on to the floor as he moved into the final phase of his lecture. "You had minor corruption all along, like in every bureaucracy, and some kinky stuff, like in all Mediterranean-culture bureaucracy; but it only got bad after the War when they began to get a little money again for the first time since the Piedmontese finally took over Rome in 1870. And it only got really bad under Paul VI, who was too innocent to grasp what was happening. My Polish friend is afraid to touch it because he thinks the church is already facing too many other enemies and attacks. Polish siege mentality. I tell him he's got to clean it out, and he just rolls his frosty blue eyes at me."

"Which means?"

"How the hell do I know? Am I Polish?"

"I don't believe so."

"What will happen if the five o'clock news should learn that a murder has been committed with a gun—minus silencer—issued by the Vatican to one of my auxiliary bishops?"

The five o'clock news is My Lord's *bête noire*. This does not mean dislike for Mr. Jacobson or Ms. Esposito or any of the other anchorpersons, but a more generalized resentment at being constrained to preside over an archdiocese in which general understanding of what is happening on the Bark of Peter is shaped by thirty-second news clips.

"I am a patient man, Blackwood." As he spoke this patent falsehood, the Cardinal swung his tall frame out of my short-person chair. "Do I not tolerate activists and passivists, right and left, Opus Dei and Call to Action, radicals and conservatives, feminists and chauvinists, women who want to be ordained and women who don't want to be ordained, ERA protesters and Right to Life protesters, Liberationists and Catholics United for the Faith, and virtually every other form of trouble in the contemporary church?"

"Indisputably."

"What don't I tolerate?"

"Ghosts," I repeated his pet aversion, "especially on the five o'clock news."

"I now add another category to the list—auxiliary bishops who are either murderers or murderees. Is that plain?"

"Reasonably so."

"Then"—wild Irish grin "see to it, Blackwood!"

He swept out of the room.

Indeed.

So like it or not, I was on the case.

Did I like it?

On the whole I liked it much less than other messes that the Lord Cardinal had dumped into my lap.

He poked his head back into my room. "Another locked-room puzzle, like that one up at Long Beach?"

"Now that you mention it . . ."

"Enjoy yourself."

But I had already solved the puzzle.

Or so I thought.

There was nothing in my subsequent conversation with My Lord Harry to contribute to my enjoyment.

"Did your mother have reason to think her life was in jeopardy?" I asked cautiously.

"Not that I know of." He rested his chin on his index

fingers, the picture of a prince of the church being coopera-
tive. "She was a strong woman, as you know, and had many
enemies. But I never heard her express fear for her own wel-
fare."

"I see. And the dispute on the boat last Sunday?"

"You're from a strong family too, Monsignor." He
smiled disarmingly. "You are aware of the ambivalences
that slip into such relationships?"

"Tell me about it."

"I beg pardon?" He seemed baffled.

"Yes, I am well aware of such problems."

"I see. . . ." He still couldn't solve the puzzle of my odd
choice of words. "Then, you can understand it when I say
that my mother and my niece were women formed from the
same mold. They loved each other and they hated each
other. I'm sure that the love was stronger than the hate."

Cool, huh? No endorsement of Fionna, but no condem-
nation either. They must make you practice that sort of
statement in Rome the way they make college basketball
players practice free throws.

"I'm happy to hear that."

"Then you will be able to, ah, assist in the solution of
this mystery? My family has agreed to cooperate in every
way possible. Quite coincidentally, I might remark that my
brother Ed has agreed to, ah, withdraw his unfortunate remarks of last Sunday night. He was under great strain."

"I am happy to hear that too."

He damn well better withdraw them.

"We all hope that you will be able to put this dreadful
matter to rest."

The way you just put Mama to rest.

"I'll certainly endeavor to do so. One question, Harry, if
you don't mind. Was there any question in your mind of your
mother making payments to your enemies?"

"Of course not." He dismissed the question with an angry frown and a brusque wave of his carefully manicured
hand. Then his face fell apart again. "I'm afraid that we

don't have the kind of money they would want if that were the issue."

"I see. Might your mother have, on her own initiative and perhaps against your advice, entered into negotiations with these enemies of yours?"

He fell apart: his shoulders slumped, his head curved downward, his crossed legs separated, his reply came in a voice choked with pain. "I don't know, Monsignor. I advised her not to involve herself. She rarely took our advice or even listened to us. She was quite skillful in working with local politicians and, ah, businessmen. I could not persuade her that these people are . . . different. If she did approach them, I fear she would have been out of her depth."

"I see."

"I would hate to think . . ." He pulled himself together. "But that is not very likely, is it, Monsignor?"

"Possible, Harry, but not likely."

He stood up, rather shakily.

"My family and I will greatly appreciate your assistance. Whatever you are able to do will help us enormously."

He offered me a firm and confident hand. I took it. I somehow had the feeling he wanted me to kiss his ring.

No way.

I felt sorry for the poor bastard when he had left. His remark that he would have been better off in a Chicago parish than in the Curia was surely accurate. It was probably too late for him now. He would never have either the red hat or the Chicago parish.

He had also displayed more sensitivity than I had expected when he attributed his decision to go the route of Vatican politics to his mother.

She had forced him into the priesthood, then ruined it for him. Might he know that, in almost so many words?

It was possible, if beneath the smooth veneer there was not a completely hollow man.

Could you murder a woman who had ruined your life? Why not?

Especially if the Vatican had given you a 9mm M-38, short, automatic pistol.

■

SECOND INTERMEZZO

Dan Enright

■───────────────────────────■

9

"We shouldn't talk to that little priest." Lena drew heavily on her cigarette. "He's part of the establishment. We can't trust him."

His wife, Dan Enright reflected expansively, was blessed with a wonderful freedom in her hatreds. So long as there was a simple target for her rage, she needed no more elaborate templates to guide her through life.

"He's not important." Dan sipped his Danish beer slowly. "A minor ecclesiastical bureaucrat who has earned himself a reputation as a detective. I think we ought to invite him to one of our cocktail parties. Our friends would agree with me that he is an excellent example of how fact imitates fiction. Savor, if you will, Lena my dear, that innocent little shanty-Irish priest in the same room with Saul and Studs and Mike and the gang."

Her haggard face lit up in a brilliant smile. Those who did not know the smile could not appreciate how beautiful his wife was.

"They'd kill him."

"So discreetly he would not even know it. A mere twist of the wrist and the razor does its job."

Her smile broadened into a happy laugh. It was good to

see her laugh again. The events of Sunday afternoon had been a strain on Lena. She was not equipped constitutionally for either violence or conspiracy, whatever her ideological convictions might be.

"But he might stumble on the truth about your mother. . . ."

"No fear of that." He emptied the beer bottle and considered the possibility of asking Lena to bring him another one from the fridge. "As I've explained to you, we have nothing to worry about as long as we keep our stories clear and consistent."

"You're not sorry that she's dead." Lena lighted another cigarette and ground out the butt of the one she had finished. Her ideologies did not extend to opposition to nicotine.

"I am"—he paused, seeking for the precise word to express complex thoughts, as any good writer must—"frankly ambivalent. Obviously we benefit from her demise. Obviously she made our life difficult for us. Yet one must respect her for the authenticity of her posture toward life and the integrity of her value system, admittedly different from ours. Moreover, one must admit that love for the mother, however misguided it may be, is absorbed quite early by the human organism—"

"Bullshit." Lena jumped up and ran to the window. "You're talking like there's a TV camera in the room."

Dan laughed easily. "Not at all, my dear. Or rather"—he relished a new idea—"we must realize that all of life is merely a series of thirty-second TV clips. Is that not the case?"

"That priest is coming down the street. He's missed our building, the little dummy. No, he's turning back. He looks lost."

"John B. Ryan always looks like he's lost, my dear . . . and try while he's here to give some appearance of mourning."

"Why should I?" She whirled away from the window. "You're not mourning, are you?"

"Yes, my dear." He felt that he was speaking a deep truth that he himself had hardly recognized before. "In a very real sense I am."

10

"Actually, John, the old girl was a unique Chicago type." Dan Enright waved his crystal beer mug, shaking off some of the suds but not freeing that which clung to the edges of his mouth, perhaps the largest mouth—literally as well as metaphorically—that I had ever seen. "Only in this city do such combinations of virtue and vice survive. Her passing represents the end of an era."

I could see another Illinois Humanities Council paper in the works. For Dan Enright eras were always ending and beginning.

He waved his beer mug, propelling more suds onto the already multiply stained carpet. "Only in Chicago could a woman say to her son, 'You're not going to be a goddamn priest, you're going to be a goddamn Jesuit and a goddamn good one.' You know, John, she was right. I became a Jesuit and a good one till it was time for a mid-life career change. She was not only a Chicago landmark, she was a Chicago symbol. Chicago is a great powerful crude city, hog butcher of the world, and she was a great powerful crude woman. The last of her kind."

"Three thirty-three Wacker, the Art Institute, the Chicago Symphony," I sighed.

"That's right, John." He heard my words, but missed my meaning. "The goddamn hog butcher of the world. It's the end of an era."

I repressed a powerful urge to label his comments, in Mary Kate's favorite denunciatory phrase—horse manure. Carl Sandburg's line long ago had become a cliché and for the last quarter century an inaccurate cliché. The hogs were butchered elsewhere. But Dan Enright's outpourings sounded insightful because they flowed as smoothly as chocolate syrup and as confidently as though he were Lionel Trilling lecturing a class at Columbia. Among the self-professed "literati" with whom he associated, he had become an "important Chicago writer," which meant that one was expected to listen to his pompous horse manure as if it were unassailable wisdom.

"Actually, she was as much part of the Chicago that will soon be forgotten, and tragically forgotten"—he raised a magisterial finger—"as Roman Puchinski, 'Pops' Panzcko, George Halas, and Franklin McMahon. Nelson Algren said it to me on his deathbed, John: The great characters are being replaced by yuppie Personalities and bureaucracy-created Celebrities."

Dan Enright looked like a somewhat younger and greatly overweight Bob Hope—snapping brown eyes, big, swaying jaw. Though the air conditioner was humming in his North Wells apartment—unnecessarily since the temperature was not above eighty on that August afternoon—he was dressed in red and white striped golf shorts, perhaps two sizes too small, and a gray T-shirt, also too small, which announced in purple letters "Old Town is the Most!" His belly hung precariously over the unbelted waistband of his shorts and his feet were stuffed into leather sandals.

His toenails needed clipping.

"You left out Everett McKinley Dirksen and Dick Daley."

"As I was telling Studs the other night at Riccardo's—Terkel, you know—New York or L.A. could never produce a Violet Harrington Enright, John," he ranted on, like Bob Hope in his pauses too, as if waiting for laughter and applause. "They're too much part of the post-1980 world. Actually you have to come to Chicago with its raw, uncouth power, its untamed hatreds and loves, its thick dirt and rank smell, to find the last great symbols of the world that used to be." He drained his beer glass.

What was the difference between the pre-1980 world and the post-1980 world? I didn't ask for fear he would tell me. The Enright condo, in a skyscraper in the 1600 block on Wells, overlooking Lincoln Park with the lake a flat blue mirror in the distance, had its own thick dirt and rank smell.

Lena and Dan Enright lived like two undergraduates, in the midst of unwashed dishes, flashily modern Scandinavian furniture marked with cigarette burns and uncountable glass and bottle stains, stacks of unopened copies of the *New York Times* and *The Reader*, and a huge stereo system whose unplugged cord hinted that it hadn't functioned for months. A badly tuned portable—the kind teens bring to a beach—played WFTM classical music, absolutely required twenty-four hours a day if you are part of the Chicago literati.

The carpet, which before it had been scarred beyond recognition might have been beige, was littered with cigarette ashes, scraps of paper, and unopened envelopes. The ottoman, on which Dan rested his running shoes, was split with a tear from top to bottom, and had spilled some of its stuffing on the floor. The "rank smell" was, as best I could decipher it, a blend of burned vegetables, unwashed sheets, and thousands of cigarettes, whose butts filled every available container in the front room of the condo.

Lena stared at me hatefully from the pillow on which she sat in the middle of the floor, legs crossed under her, a cigarette in one hand and a gin and tonic in the other. She added to the undergraduate atmosphere with her cut-off jeans and T-shirt (matching Dan's), both of which ill became her round and dumpy little body.

She was wearing three or four rings, two bracelets, and a double string of pearls—a walking insurance casualty.

Neither of them had undergone the rigors of the shower or the bath recently.

A former priest and a spinster professor trying to persuade the world that they were young and important and "with it," they succeeded only in updating the stereotype of shanty Irish.

"I was telling Bill Kurtiss, from Channel Two, you know, when he called to express his sympathy, that the pain of our loss is mitigated somewhat by the assurance that her death was a loss to the whole city, the end of an era."

He opened a second beer, kept in reserve on top of a mammoth *Webster's Unabridged*, and with a vast dramatic gesture emptied it into his crystal mug.

"A star has fallen in Israel," I murmured.

"What do you mean by that?" Lena exploded in anger. "What's that supposed to mean? She wasn't Jewish."

"Only that a great woman has died."

As my nieces and nephews would put it, Lena was not too swift. Her posture toward reality, therefore, was to attack it with intermittent outbursts of rage. If you cannot impress people with your intelligence, then you intimidate them with your anger.

"This tragedy," Dan continued sententiously, "has been harder on Lena than on me. I knew Mother all my life, of course. So I have better perspective. I'm able to articulate my grief with history, if that doesn't offend your clerical sensibilities, John."

"I'm not really very sensible."

For a moment I feared that Lena was about to demand what I meant by that remark.

"The point of these reflections, as I'm sure a man of your intelligence and cosmopolitan experience comprehends immediately, is that I am enormously indebted to Mother for all that she passed on to me, especially her sense of the raw, primal greatness of this city and its people. Crude, undeniably, as she was crude, undeniably. Embarrassing on occasion, quite wrong on other occasions, but nonetheless treasured and loved for all the struggle—the blood, sweat, and tears—that she summarized."

"His mother and the city," Lena cautioned me with a savage frown.

"Father"—he smiled tolerantly—"understands, dear."

Until ten years before—and long after the Vatican Council traumas in the Catholic church—Dan Enright had been as much a model Jesuit as Harry Enright had been a model ecclesiastical diplomat. With superb training at Berkeley and later at Oxford and a published article or two on nineteenth-century American novelists, he was a smooth, refined, literate clerical scholar and occasional retreat master for Catholic women's groups—exactly what his mother had designed him to be. Now, as Sean Cronin had remarked to me before I set out on this first interview, he had become a Chicago Catholic Sammy Glick. He had abandoned the pursuit of a reputation as a careful scholar for the quest of celebrity stardom. He cultivated the columnists and the commentators, the reviewers and the critics, the pols and the literary editors. By the sheer agony and energy of his self-promotion and name-dropping he had become a "Chicago writer," a label which the real Chicago writers desperately avoided because it was jealously protected by those who were not read anywhere else.

He had put on a mirror image of the mask his mother created for him. So she was responsible, with reverse spin, for Dan as much as she was for Harry.

"I'm impressed, Doctor Enright, by the fact that, unlike so many others of her generation and background and piety, she seemed to have accepted quite gracefully your mid-life career change."

Lady Wisdom, pardon the euphemism.

Lena, however, was not about to pardon it. "What the hell do you mean by that?" She lurched forward like a linebacker about to blitz, a short, white Otis Wilson.

A spasm of displeasure moved slowly across Dan Enright's face. "Father is only remarking that Mother continued to support me in my new role the way she did in the old one.... Actually, John, that she was able to do it so gracefully is in part because she was so fond of Lena. I think we have to remember about the Great Characters, of which she was certifiably the last, that for all their limitations of time and space and for all the restrictions their own life histories placed on their perceptibilities, they were often much more flexible than their college-educated children and grandchildren. There was a raw, primal pragmatism in their personalities, a good thick, heavy willingness to adjust and compromise, to accept the future because it was here, a strong dose of—what should I say, animal shrewdness which freed them from ideological constraints. All her life Mother disliked the blacks, as she called them even when it was a term of disrespect, long before it became expected and even required terminology." He gulped a big swallow of beer. "Yet when my friend Harold—he's been in this apartment many times—was nominated, Mom promptly poured money into his campaign. He was black, but he was also a Democrat and that was what counted."

"I thought your family was Republican."

"Nationally perhaps, but not locally."

The important fact about Harold was not that he was black or a Democrat but that he was going to win. Don't make no waves, don't back no losers.

"So she supported you in your new vocation as a writer?"

"Absolutely," he belched as though he were trying out for Falstaff. "I'm sure you agree, John, that in this time of transition, in this post-1975 Catholic church, the forms and the styles of the past must be viewed with the same sympathetic nostalgia that we feel for the peasant cottages of mid-nineteenth-century Ireland. Sean represents the last of the ecclesiastical leaders in the Mundelein style. What we see next will be very different."

"Sean? You mean John Paul II?" Lena exploded again. "That chauvinist bastard!"

"Sean Cronin," I said with a sigh, "Cardinal priest of the Church of St. Agnes Outside the Walls and, by the grace of God and the tolerant inattention of the Apostolic See, Archbishop of Chicago."

"Precisely!" Dan threw up his hands as though his brilliantly reasoned argument had won me over to his point of view.

I wondered if George William Mundelein raided his cathedral rector's liquor cabinet on the grounds that "Blackwood, you're richer than I am!"

A patent falsehood, incidentally, one of the many myths that My Lord Cardinal wove around his cathedral rector.

"And of course she was supporting your interesting concept for a new magazine?"

He looked at me cautiously. "She made some small initial investments, of course. It would have been improper and unwise for her to give anything more than that."

"Why?" I asked, trying to sound innocent.

"Neither Lena nor I wanted people to say that my mother had given me this magazine as a toy to play with." He put his beer mug on the *Unabridged* next to the two empty cans. "Once it became profitable—and there's no question that Chicago is able to support a magazine in which writers who deserve to be published are finally in fact published—it would have been entirely proper for Mother to put more money into it to improve layout, distribution, promotion, national advertising so that it might become more important and even more profitable. She understood this and so did I."

Horse manure.

"She valued her dollars," Lena snarled.

"Don't we all, dear," Dan belched again, "don't we all?"

Did either Harry or Dan Enright feel anything beneath their carefully cultivated veneers? Were they hollow men, all self-conscious style and no substance? Was there any grief lurking behind the masks they presented to the world? Could they answer those questions themselves?

And how did an essentially hollow man like Dan work up the courage to kick off the traces, seduce Lena, and reverse his mask?

Give the old lady credit—she stuck with him. Must have been furious at him for not seeking her permission. Must have felt betrayed. Must have thought that he was a damn fool. But he was still *her* damn fool, so she stuck by him.

Just like she had contributed heavily to Harold Washington's campaign when a lot of others had sat it out or even voted for Bernie Epton—which she could have done in good conscience since her roots, despite Dan's rewriting of history, were Republican.

Conscience was not the issue. Winning was. I'm sure she called him a nigger. But when he was elected with the aid of her money he became *her* nigger. So a woman who had begun life with corrupt Republican money, filtered out of the sanitary district sludge pumps, ended it by contributing money to a Reform (sic) Democrat.

And from her viewpoint, with perfect, indeed exquisite consistency.

"Who killed her?"

Dan seemed surprised, as if he did not expect me to ask such a question. Had I not come on a social rather than a professional visit?

"What do you mean by *that* question?" Lena leaped to her feet and glared at me furiously.

"Relax, dear," Dan barked. "We all know that Father is thought by many to be Chicago's Father Brown and that Harry has asked him to play that role for us. For which we are grateful." He smiled at me and recaptured his beer mug. "Well, I should have thought it obvious, John; my niece is the murderer. Or rather the killer. Poor girl, she had yet to learn that you never argue with Mother. You present her with an accomplished fact. Become pregnant by   what's his name?"

He snapped his fingers impatiently at his wife.

"Rick," Lena growled and reluctantly resumed her Buddhist posture on the floor.

"That's right. Become pregnant by Rick Nelligan and confront Mother, or Grandmother, if you will, with that phenomenon. She would have acquiesced. Noisily perhaps, but that was her privilege. Indeed, she would have made a hundred-and-eighty-degree turn and poured money into his career."

Was this strategy autobiographical? Had Lena been pregnant and perhaps lost the baby? Or had they faked it? Or had they merely gone through a marriage ceremony? I would have to check.

"Indeed."

"Who else could it have been?" He finished the beer and folded his hands across his untidy belly. "I'm surprised that she hasn't been indicted yet. Presumably there'll be a plea bargain on a manslaughter charge, don't you think? A year or two in prison?"

That would suit you fine, wouldn't it? Wipe the crime out of the papers as quickly as possible.

"That would be the usual prospect. I'm sure there's no question of seeking the electric chair."

"I should hope not!" He frowned ponderously. "I don't see how it is possible to have any ill will against the poor child. Her father was not a stable individual, you know. I picture Mother's death as accidental, more than anything else."

"No more a murder than as though she had fallen down the steps of the companionway?"

"As if," he corrected me.

Okay, I do it too, but with leprechaunish wit, not with supercilious pomposity. And never for secondary but approved constructions.

"As if," I agreed.

"That's a very good image."

"She was drunk enough to have done just that," Lena snarled. "She really tied one on last Sunday. Plastered out of her mind."

"Wasted," I whispered.

"Mother was not a heavy drinker, John"—he smiled ingratiatingly—"not by Irish standards. Normally she settled for one or two, three at the most, cocktails at the end of a hard day's work. And she worked up to the end, as you know. Occasionally, and always on appropriate occasions like her annual August yacht party, she would dedicate herself to vodka with the consuming passion that marked everything she did. But, don't you see, this is in line with my model of her as the last of the Great Chicago Characters. Who else but a unique and special person would keep a ninety-five-foot motor yacht—fifty years old and worth almost a million dollars—in perfect condition merely for the purposes of an occasional high-quality beer bash? Doesn't that show a flair, a style, a *joie de vivre* that you would never find in our college-educated *nouveau riche*?"

We were back to the Humanities Council paper, complete with a phony French accent.

"And the uniforms," I sighed.

"Like Nixon's presidential guard, were they not?" he demanded exultantly.

"She was alive then when you visited her stateroom to say good-bye to her?"

"Alive and well and feisty as hell. I resolved after we left that I would have a friendly word with Fionna the next day—not with Rita, since that would be a waste of time—about modifying her strategies. Alas, by then, as you know, John, it was too late."

"Indeed."

"I can't say that we had any premonition as we left, did we, Lena dear? I fully expected to see her at dinner at her apartment the following Saturday—our usual custom, as you know. The conflicts of the day would be forgotten. Mother was very good at writing off foolish quarrels. The era that she represented was an era of the Great Pragmatists— Roosevelt, Kennedy, Harry Truman, none of them were ideologues."

"Dick Daley," I said again, and was again ignored. Lena had not confirmed the absence of premonitions.

"So it really is a great tragedy, a series of unfortunate misunderstandings culminating in a senseless death for which no one is really to blame. Life is a great mystery, isn't it, John?"

"St. Paul would agree," I said with inexcusable smugness. "And the door was locked when you left?"

"Locked-room puzzle, eh?" He winked. "Those things don't happen in real life. Any more than my episcopal brother's shadow world exists outside of trash fiction."

"Indeed."

"Come now, John, you're a man of the world. You don't really believe in legends about *Propaganda Due*, and Licio Gelli, do you? Why do we need to assume such monsters when the explanation for Mother's death can be found in the sexual hungers of an inexperienced young woman?"

P-2 was the corrupt Masonic lodge to which many Cardinals and Italian financiers belonged.

"Both could be true." I permitted my eyes to blink faster than their normal rate.

"The Masonic-lodge conspiracy theory helps my poor

brother to ease his personal defeat at falling out of favor in Rome. Actually he probably offended a gay Cardinal over there and surely will fall into favor again, won't he?"

"Perhaps."

He swept both hands away from his body in a dramatic, politician's gesture: Richard Nixon dissociating movement from content. "Does not Licio Gelli play for men like my brother and Malachi Martin the same role that the devil played in the medieval church? Does he not account for the accidents and mischances that no one else is available to blame? Is it not better to see the enemy as a bad person rather than bad luck? Given sufficient time, do not all human activities end badly?"

The statement, as true today as when Gustave Weigel made it a quarter century ago, was not pertinent to the death of his mother, even if a lot of luck—bad or good, depending on your point of view—was involved in the locked-room puzzle. Dan Enright was deeply concerned that the investigation of his mother's death might continue. He had inundated me with words, partly because it was in his nature to inundate everyone with words and partly to turn me away from the subject.

I'm sure he thought he had succeeded.

Both Dan and Harry were essentially trivial people, men without depth and without character. They were concerned about the manipulation of their images. They lacked an overriding hunger to do well that which they did best. Their ambitions were stylistic rather than substantial. Both had at first been effective image manipulators in their currently chosen worlds, successfully imposing their chosen image on the pertinent audience. But Harry had failed, perhaps because finally, even in the corridors of the Curia Romana, a little *substantia* is required to go along with the *stylus*. And surely Dan would fail, even by the standards of the self-professed "Chicago writers," for the same reason.

Neither of them were capable of understanding substance. So had their mother made them.

Did either have the ruthless nerve and/or the passion that my theory postulated for the killer?

It did not seem likely. Yet if I was right about the two shots and the two guns . . .

My visit to the D. Harrington Enrights had been a matter of routine. I had confirmed the report that he was, not to put too fine an edge on things, a loudmouthed slob, a phony who wasn't even smart enough to know that he was a phony.

He was also a grand deceiver, which was not a surprise either. He had probably deceived his mother at the time of his marriage, though I couldn't be sure about the method; he had tried to deceive me about his mother's support for his magazine. I remembered items in Chicago columns at the time his book of essays had been published which reported that the book would be on the *New York Times* best-seller list the following week.

But the book did not appear on the list. Could it be that Dan had planted the story, hoping that the item in the press would be father of the fact?

A touch of the psychopath?

Doubtless. The kind of man who might be cheerfully about the death of his mother, from which he would certainly profit?

Why not?

I didn't believe a word he said.

So he thought he had succeeded in throwing me off the track, and he actually—to use his favorite word—made me more suspicious than I had been before.

Try to mess with Blackie Ryan, will you?

He continued to babble—either a Humanities Council paper or an editorial for *Chicago Writer*. How could a mere quarterly provide him enough room for all his insights?

I confess that I may have dozed off, despite the fact I had declined his offer of a beer. I am likely to do that any hour of the day, no matter what I have or have not eaten or drunk. It made no difference to Dan Enright whether I was asleep or awake.

"Actually part of our problem is that those who write for the popular media and the trash racks in the pharmacies and supermarkets are innocent not only of literary sensitivity, John, but of history. They cannot see persons like Mother against the full, rich tapestry of their historical epoch and as part of the passing parade of life. Hence they write an obituary that treats her as a curiosity rather than a landmark, a simple woman who made a lot of money instead of a symbol of an era whose passing is rather more lamentable than not. Don't you agree?"

Absolutely.

I had several more interviews to accomplish before the day was over. Nonetheless, I desired with a great thirst a sip of smooth and mellow Jameson's Twelve Year Special Reserve (now, as you doubtless understand, more than twenty years old) to cleanse the taste of the Dan Enright apartment out of my mouth and perhaps to protect me from any infectious diseases that might be lurking there.

The sip, perhaps even a wee jar as the saying goes, would have to wait till later. But it was nonetheless imperative that I get out of that nuthouse as quickly as my legs would carry me.

I offered my sympathy again, bid them a polite farewell, and fled for my life.

Only in the pure air of a thirteen-mile-an-hour northeast wind off the lake did I breathe easily again. As a substitute for the postponed wee jar, I bought a large Lindt dark chocolate bar and disposed of it handily. Chocolate, especially dark chocolate, provides energy. Right? It looked like I was going to need a lot of energy to cope with the Harrington Enrights. Even to stay awake.

I placed a call from an outdoor booth, one which had lost its phone books but still, miraculously, functioned.

"Cronin."

"Ryan."

"Blackwood, you scare the hell out of me."

"A wise reaction. I was correct then?"

"My certain friend in a certain position in a certain building in a small city-state somewhere in Eurasia informs me that indeed Vincent Nelligan was in the aforementioned city-state at the end of July before the city closes down and goes on vacation. He did indeed make certain substantial payments to certain people who act as links and conduits to certain other people, some of them very shadowy and very heavy. There were hints of *very* substantial payments if certain yet more heavy and more shadowy personages were available for conversation and for the reception of *extremely* substantial payments. Nothing came of these hints."

"Indeed. I must go back to work now."

"The real question is how you knew."

"Genius," I replied, and hung up.

Vinney Nelligan had gone to Rome with money from Violet to pay off Licio Gelli. And had been rejected, probably because he had made the pitch with *bruta figura*. Had he given all the money back to Violet?

An interesting question.

In my concern to escape from Dan and Lena I had hardly noticed the two dark-skinned gentlemen in black jackets who were waiting outside the 1610 North Wells apartment building when I left.

11

"Why did you not avail yourself of Luisa's generous offer to dispose of your grandmother?"

The young woman, officially charged with her grandmother's murder but not yet indicted by a grand jury for the crime, studied my face carefully. Was I a good leprechaun or a bad leprechaun? She decided that I was a good leprechaun and smiled. "Maybe I should call Patty Slattery before I answer that question."

"I will seek permission from My Lord Cronin to perform the rite of exorcism over that hellion."

We laughed together. One more attractive young woman had decided that Father Blackie was "cute."

It can get to be a cross. Especially when the young woman is also "cute" and you are supposed to suspect her of murder. Especially when "Rosalita" is turned off immediately after you knock on her door.

But the odds against the coincidence that would have made her the murderer were absurdly high.

She returned to her shrewd appraisal of my countenance. "Doesn't that prove that I didn't kill Grandmother? Why should I do it when Luisa was prepared to have it done for me?"

It was dark outside her window. Perhaps the stars were looking down, but on Sheridan Road, you don't see the stars, only lights in apartment windows. The steady hum of traffic six floors down provided the background music, substituted, I suspected, for the rock and roll she had turned off out of deference to my clerical status.

I strolled over to her stack of cassette tapes—the Who, the Police, the Psychedelic Furs, the Boss (of course, but in his early manifestations), Guard Twelve and the Harbor Masters. I put the last-named tape into the deck and punched the appropriate buttons.

Both the names and the skills came from listening to and watching the behavior of my nieces and nephews, especially Nicole Curran, who had become even as a preteen an expert on all things rock and roll.

"Perhaps you were afraid that Luisa and her friends might blackmail you."

"Would I, having committed one murder, hesitate to commit others if their demands became unreasonable?"

"You are sure you're not going to law school?"

Another joint laugh.

"I think I might change my mind. Patty is such a wonderful human being as well as a fine lawyer. I'd love to be like her."

That was as good a summary as any of Fionna Violet Downs—one moment she was a poised woman of the world, ready to defend herself smoothly and persuasively in court;

the next moment she was a kid, heroine-worshiping an older woman (and not that much older). Too young to face murder charges and the responsibilities of an enormous fortune, too old to rush to her room and drown out her anxieties in rock and roll music.

She was arrestingly pretty, in the strict sense of the adverb: it was impossible to take your eyes away from her face. Like the visage of my sister Mary Kate, Fionna's expression was never at rest. Mirth, anxiety, resolve, sympathy, affection raced back and forth, chasing one another like a pack of puppies turned loose in a backyard. She enchanted you not so much with her blue eyes, pert nose, even white teeth, challenging lips, and pointed chin—though they constituted a pleasing enough blend—but with the wondrous movements in which these features engaged as they strove to keep up with the ebb and flow of her emotions.

Similarly her youthful and undeniably nubile body exercised its charm not by the neat flow of its lines or the pertness of her breasts, but by the vitality of its movement as if she were a trained dancer or mime. The energies that propelled Fionna Downs, most of them sexual, were balanced in precarious harmony. Disturb the balance and she might tear herself apart.

As you watched her bounce back into the parlor with a glass of "really yummy chocolate soda," you wanted to pray that she would be protected from such self-destruction.

Her black hair was cut short, her pale white skin touched with a minute amount of makeup, her perfume barely noticeable, her light gray summer dress only hinting at a trim and subtle figure. Fionna Downs was a tasteful, intelligent, vivacious young woman poised confidently on a diving board above the pool of life.

The question was whether she knew how to dive.

A killer?

Hardly.

A fabulously wealthy young woman?

Of course not. Rather a niece's weekend houseguest at Grand Beach or a nephew's new date for a summer dance.

"I was horrified at Luisa's suggestion," she frowned. "I do so worry about her. She's an intelligent girl, but she must learn that our customs are different here. Not better maybe, and possibly not worse. But different."

"You were lamenting your conflicts with your late grandmother and admitted that sometimes you felt like killing her?"

"But I didn't mean it literally, Father Blackie. Honestly I didn't. You know, how you go about a friend at whom you're mad, I could kill her, but it's . . . hyperbole?"

"Rhetorical exaggeration." The child, like her age peers, used the verb *to go* as a substitute for the archaic *to say*. (This sometimes creates linguistic problems, as in such constructions as "So I go let's go and he goes I don't wanna go till I find the men's room because I have to go." Dig?) But she also knew what hyperbole meant. Well, there's some things Leland Stanford Junior Memorial University can teach you and some things it cannot.

"Fersure." She smiled, complacent that she'd used the ten-dollar word accurately.

"Fersure" means merely "for sure." It can be roughly translated as "that's right." A synonym, though rarely used in the presence of clergy, is "no shit."

"I guess in Luisa's world they don't use hyperbole." She paused to make sure she had pronounced the word correctly. "Anyway, she goes, 'Oh, señorita, you should not do that. Tell me that you want her killed and I will have Carlos and Tomas kill her. They are very bad *hombres.*'" Her mimic's face became as Hispanic in its movements as Luisa's. "'They will not charge much if I ask them to do it for you.' Well, Father Blackie, it totally zonked me out, and I go, 'LUISA, don't talk that way. I wasn't serious.' And she goes, 'I would do anything for you, señorita, because you have been so kind to me.' And I go, 'Well, promise me that you won't say anything like that again. People may live that way in Sonora but not in Illinois.'"

The late Violet Harrington Enright had appropriated for her family an entire wing of the sixth floor in the Edgewater

Beach Apartments, a pink and white art deco relic of the roaring twenties. It was once a companion to the Edgewater Beach Hotel. In front of the hotel stretched the famous Beach Walk, a classy nightclub to which to take your date, until progress in the form of a northward extension of Lake Shore Drive to Hollywood Avenue wiped it out in 1959. The hotel itself survived into the late sixties, when it succumbed to the need to build more profitable condominium apartments on the lakefront. In my admittedly romantic memory of it, the Edgewater Beach was the sort of place where you might encounter Al Capone or Greta Garbo or George Halas or any one of a number of faintly crooked appellate court judges or high-priced call girls.

Any or all of whom might have walked over from the apartments—where in fact Martin Kennelly, Richard Daley's predecessor as mayor, had lived. (The Old Fella once said of him. "He was so honest that he couldn't imagine how easy it was for the boys to steal from him; you don't have to be on the take to be a good mayor, but you have to be able to imagine what it is like to be on the take.")

Vi Enright poured large sums into Kennelly's first two campaigns. When she judged that he was going to lose to Daley, she jumped ship without losing a step. Don't back no losers.

The apartments, pink and beige and off-white and faintly Floridian and so ancient as to require window air conditioners, manage to convey to the visitor the impression that, while they are still utterly plush and respectable, they have seen if not better, at least more colorful days.

The late Mrs. Harrington Enright's personal apartment occupied most of the lakefront side of her wing. Her daughter, Rita Downs, lived in a sitting room and bedroom at the north end of the lakefront side. Across the corridor were five smaller apartments in which guests, clients, hangers-on, and family members dwelled. Fionna's apartment, across the hall from her mother, looked out on Sheridan Road and the city to the west. ("Mom wanted me to live in her rooms so I could see the lake, because she didn't appreciate it anymore.

Poor Mom. I told her that was silly. I'd rather look at the city instead of the creepy old lake.")

Her quarters looked like a tastefully expensive thirties hotel suite, doubtless furnished by an interior decorator hired by her grandmother. Save for a stack of rock records and a tennis racket, there was little to hint at Fionna's personality. Would that change now that she owned it all?

"Were you at all tempted to consider seriously Ms. Flores's well-intentioned offer?"

"Do you think"—the puppies paused in dead seriousness—"that I killed Grandmother, Father Blackie?"

"I think it most unlikely."

She nodded, and the puppies began to frolic again. "I was scared more than anything else. I realized how angry I was at Grandmother to make Luisa think I wanted Grandmother dead. My shrink"—sunny face—"says that it's all right to acknowledge such feelings, especially if you know you're not going to act on them."

No mention that the shrink was my sister. Maybe she didn't know. Unlikely. She was too smart not to be informed on the connection.

"My task, Fionna, is to try to understand the world of the Enright family so that no one else will die. I don't want to send anyone to prison or punish anyone."

"How did you know about me and Luisa?" She tilted her jaw in my direction, a very tough young woman if you had to fight her. "The police never asked about that."

"Because Doctor Joseph Murphy didn't tell them what Luisa shouted when you came out of your grandmother's cabin."

She nodded. "They'd really love that. I told Patty about it, just in case poor Luisa panics."

"You're a very clever young woman, Fionna."

She waved aside my compliment. "Not so clever that I didn't freak out when I saw the gun, and pick it up even though I knew it was crazy. Real moron. . . ."

"Like you were in a dream?"

"Now how did you know THAT?"

"I know a little about compulsions."

"We're a crazy bunch, Father Blackie." She opened another can of Diet Fudge Soda and poured it on the ice cubes in my glass. "Last year at Stanford it finally dawned on me how different we are from everyone else I know. I mean, other kids have nutty grandmothers, but not like Grandmother. I got scared. So I made up my mind I would find a shrink as soon as I came home."

"You met Richard Nelligan at Stanford?"

"Uh-huh. Isn't he the cutest boy? I fell in love with him right away, even if his grandfather is such a geek, poor man. He was a junior when I was a freshman, and he stayed at Stanford for his M.B.A. It took me two years to make him notice me. Then he fell as hard as I did. Last year was terrible with him in Chicago and me out there."

"His family does not live in Chicago?"

"No way. They live in central California someplace, would you believe? I think all the children wanted to get as far away as they could from Mr. Nelligan. They didn't even want Rick to come to Chicago to work. And his father and mother didn't like me because of Grandmother." She grinned like a conspiratorial elf. "Until they met me. I won them over real good. Rick was supposed to work in New York on the Comex." A triumphant smirk. "But somehow he decided that the Chicago Board of Trade was more interesting. AND"—she beamed—"he gets along fine with his grandfather and grandmother. He feels sorry for them because they're so old and so lonely. He really is the sweetest, kindest boy." A lingering expression of infinite sadness. "Sometimes I think that he's too good for me. . . . BUT"—joy returns—"he doesn't think so. Why should I argue? Right?"

"Why, indeed?"

"He didn't have to live up there with them, did he? I mean, wasn't that the most totally generous thing? He could have been a yuppie and had a real good time in bars on Halsted. Instead he takes care of them."

"How could your grandmother object to him? His prospects are excellent. His family has known your family for generations. He is, I gather, a presentable, respectful young man. I should have thought she would be delighted."

"Tell me about it!" Fionna sighed, and tugged at the hem of her skirt—a movement, I am told, still taught in Catholic high schools for women even in this our time. "You could never predict Grandmother, Father Blackie. I don't see how she can stand Aunt Min or Aunt Lena, but she liked them. She liked Daddy at first too, I guess. She's always feuding and making up with people. Was, I mean." She discovered a tissue on the desk next to her chair and dabbed at her eyes. "I do miss her, Father Blackie. She was a terrible old woman sometimes. And she tried to ruin my life. But I still loved her."

I waited patiently for the tears to run their course. I did not doubt that Fionna had loved her grandmother. Maybe the only one in the family that really mourned her. And the one that profited the most from her death.

"Anyway—" She folded the tissue neatly and rested it on the arm of the chair, certain that it would be needed again. "I didn't tell her about Rick till he moved to Chicago last year. She was furious at me. Wouldn't talk to me for weeks. I thought she'd change her mind as she usually did, so I didn't make a big thing about it. Then we wanted to get engaged in June so we could be married after Christmas. We're not sleeping together, Father, or anything like that." Shy blush. "But we really love each other and we really want to make love, so we have to get married soon, don't we?"

There is still innocence left in the world. But what a strange place to find it.

"Indeed."

"WELL. Grandmother totally freaked out. And I stood up to her. She only respected you when you fought back. Mom's trouble is that she doesn't fight back. But this time fighting back didn't do any good. So I compromised a little and said, 'All right, September for an engagement but the wedding is still after Christmas.' And that made her even more angry. She tried to make them fire Rick. Took some of her money out of the company. They wouldn't give in. She said she would take it all out. They asked Rick to resign for the good of the firm. They knew him really well." She turned bitter. "He was about to quit until I go, 'No way.' She goes that no firm in Chicago would hire him unless I postponed the wedding for five years. FIVE years, would you believe it?"

"I still don't understand why. What did she have against him?"

"She wouldn't tell me."

"Nothing?"

"Not a word, Father Blackie. Nothing. Rick goes, 'Even my grandfather doesn't know what's wrong with her.'"

"You were supposed to give up the man you love merely because she said you should, without any explanation?"

"That's right." She reached for her tissue. "It was terrible. She always said I was the only one of the children and grandchildren who was like her. I hope I never do that to my children or grandchildren. Do you think I will?"

"I think you will at least give them reasons for your stubborn stands."

She wondered whether to laugh or cry. So she laughed. "Fersure! Really!"

"What other plans did you have for the year?"

"Well . . ." Her eyes danced with excitement—a Virginia reel, not a fox trot. "I want to be a writer. I mean a real writer that real people read, not a pretend writer like Uncle Dan. I got straight A's in my creative writing courses. I . . ." She blushed. "I was going to get a job at Marshall Field's, so I could meet people, you know, and then write at night."

"No graduate school?"

"My teacher goes, 'If you want to write, Fionna, write. If you want to teach, go to graduate school.'"

"What happens now, Fionna?"

Her jaw tilted again, this time toward the world. "If he still wants me with all this terrible money, I'm going to marry him the week after Christmas, probably in your church, Father Blackie."

"Does your mother approve?"

She nodded vigorously. "She totally likes him. . . . Oh, 'scuse me, I'll get more Canfields. I'm so glad I finally found someone else who likes it. Rick thinks it's gross . . . plastic chocolate." She bounced off to the kitchen and bounced back with a six-pack of the marvelous liquid, a supply of which I resolved to lay in at once. "EVERYone likes him, Father. Except poor Grandmother."

She poured another can into my glass and reached for her tissue.

"And Daddy adores him. He says that Rick is totally brilliant and a nice boy besides and that we ought to get married as soon as we can."

"I see."

"Daddy is sweet too, Father. I wish he and Mom . . ."

She paused.

"Yes?"

"Grandmother drove him away. Mom should have gone with him."

"I see. And now? . . ."

"He still loves her. He wants her to come back to California with him."

Someone else who would benefit greatly from the death of Grandmother.

"Do you want her to do that?"

"Oh yes!" She clapped her hands. "I think it would be totally WONDERFUL! Mama's really neat. I like her a lot, even if sometimes she's so creepy that she really freaks me out."

"Will she return to your father?"

"I don't know," she said, with a weary shake of her head. "Mom can never make up her mind about anything. She's totally smart and reads everything, but she has like no confidence in herself or her own judgments, you know? She'll change her mind back and forth a hundred times and then decide not to decide. Which is what she did when Dad went to UCLA. I go, 'If you don't decide, you really decide,' and she goes, 'I don't know what to do so I can't make up my mind until I do know what to do' and I go, 'Then you'll never do anything.' Right, Father Blackie?"

"He who hesitates is lost."

"Right . . . know what?"

"No, what?"

Giggle. "I think they're sleeping together. Mom and Dad, I mean. Since he came back for the funeral. Isn't that too neat? And they're divorced and annulled and everything! Is that a sin?"

"God is probably laughing just like you are. She has a great sense of humor."

"Right. Anyway, they like totally can't keep their hands off one another. I think it's really neat."

"They've been divorced for . . . ?"

"Eight years, ever since I graduated from St. Ita's and Daddy got the job offer from UCLA. Grandmother forbade him to take it."

"I see."

"And she forbade Mom to go with him. I was so angry at them both. But they didn't pay any attention to me then."

Devouring mother indeed.

And a man and woman in the middle years of life who were still in love with each other, enough in love to jump into a bed of fornication (technical) as soon as the devouring mother was dead, after all the conflicts of separation and divorce.

"Daddy says that if you want to talk to him, even though he's not really part of the family anymore, he'll be glad to see you after you're finished talking to me."

"I should very much like to meet him."

Fersure.

"No problem." She refilled my fudge-soda glass.

"What was your grandmother like, Fionna?"

"Really like?"

"Yes."

"She was a terrible old woman." Fionna made a wry face, dissatisfied both with her grandmother and with herself for speaking the truth about the old woman. "She was an alcoholic; she interfered in everyone's life; she had no moral principles, even if she went to Mass every morning; she

made my daddy go away; she ruined Mom's life; she terror-
ized all of us with temper tantrums like a little baby. But I
still, like, loved her, you know, Father Blackie. Does that
sound weird?"

"Totally, but love is weird, Fionna. Why did you love
her?"

"I don't know exactly. She gave me everything I wanted
and a lot of things I didn't want. Would you believe a
Mercedes convertible? Ugh! Yucky! . . . She was lonely and
sad and needed someone to love her. And she loved me; I
mean, it was a crazy love and possessive, but not all the
time. And it was those times when it wasn't possessive that I
had to love her back. I knew I was hurting her because of
Rick, and I didn't want to do that, but it wasn't my fault or
his, you know? And I wasn't going to give him up. . . ."

Her voice trailed off in uncertainty. Grandmother
Enright should have been content with such simple youthful
devotion.

"Did she say he had bad blood?"

Fionna's eyes popped open. "How did you know THAT,
Father Blackie? I mean, do you read minds?"

Before I could say that I didn't but that I did know how
elderly Irish women thought, she rushed on.

"There's nothing wrong with his blood. He doesn't have
any diseases or anything. It's good old American type-A
blood. What did she mean bad blood?"

"What we'd mean by bad genes."

"There's nothing wrong with Rick's genes." Fionna still
did not understand, but she was working on it. "He's
nearsighted—and I'm going to make him wear contacts so I
don't have to gaze into his soft brown eyes through a window
pane—but . . ." She snickered complacently at the thought of
staring into her lover's eyes.

"She probably didn't really like his grandfather."

"So that's it!" Fionna's finger touched her lip thoughtfully, as if she were trying to remember details to fit into the
new picture. "Of course! They were business partners and
they talked on the phone every day and they made a lot of

money together, but I always thought that she couldn't stand him. But she never said that, and we all had to treat him respectfully. And it never occurred to me that she hated Rick because she hated Mr. Nelligan. Ugh." She shivered. "How terrible."

"She hated most people, I think, Fionna."

"She HAD to, Father Blackie, to protect herself."

"And someone she hated killed her. Who? I wonder."

"I wish I could figure it out. Then I wouldn't have to worry about going to jail and being raped, and maybe I'd stop dreaming about her at night. And maybe she'd be free to go to heaven. Will she go to heaven, Father? Will God forgive her for all the terrible things she did?"

"Have you forgiven her?"

"Of COURSE!"

"And you think you're better than God?"

"All RIGHT!" She smiled happily. "God or the Blessed Mother or someone will get Grandmother into heaven."

A position about forgiveness that no one ought to challenge and still claim to be a follower of Jesus.

"I know the police have asked you this time after time—and Pretty Patricia, as one of her old swains calls her even now—but . . ."

"WELL." She straightened up like a sixth grader asked to perform a familiar recitation for Mother Superior—in the good old days when we had such beings. "Luisa opened the door and ran away because the fighting made her cry—she really is a dear, poor girl—and I walked into the salon and started in at the top of the steps. I go, 'Grandmother, you're no real grandmother and I'm like totally . . .' and then I hear the gun. At first I don't know what to think about it and then I look down and I see it on the floor and notice that Grandmother is lying like kind of funny. And I smell that terrible odor, as if someone has lighted a hundred wooden matches. So I run down the stairs and see the hole in her head and then freak out completely and act like some teenage moron or something."

"No one in the room?"

"Honest, Father Blackie, I didn't look. I saw the gun and

Grandmother lying funny and then the hole in her head. Like I told Patty, there could have been the whole Stanford football team in the bathroom and I wouldn't have noticed. The next thing I know, Doctor Murphy is holding me in her arms and I'm wailing like a baby."

"Do you have any idea how close the gun was when it was fired?"

"I thought it was right next to me."

"Which side?"

She hesitated. And then moved her left hand in the direction of Sheridan Road—"Like over there, by the window."

That figured.

"But I didn't see anyone."

"Or hear the gun when it was thrown to the floor?"

Another long pause.

"No, Father Blackie. But it's thick carpet."

"Indeed. The windows to the stateroom were closed?"

"I think so. The smell was terrible . . . but, Father Blackie . . . I've been thinking. . . ."

"Ah?"

"WELL." Her eyes ignited like fireworks on the Fourth. "Do you think . . . I mean the boat was close to Meigs Field, right?"

"Right."

"Couldn't someone jump out the window and swim over to the island and get on an airplane and fly away? I mean, suppose he had scuba stuff and stayed underwater. And don't say, like Patty, that I've seen too many James Bond movies."

And the Pope is Irish, I thought.

"Anything might have happened, Fionna. But who would have closed the windows?"

"I know, but there had to be someone else in the room, didn't there? I mean, if I didn't kill her—and you said that you don't think I did, and I know I didn't—then how . . . ?"

She bowed her head discouraged.

"I don't want to go to jail. I know what happens to

young girls in jail, especially girls like me. I wouldn't be any good for Rick. . . ."

"No way we're going to let you go to jail."

She nodded, dubiously. "I hope not. Patty says they have six months to indict me."

"I wouldn't worry about that."

As it turned out, there was something much more serious about which Fionna Violet Downs might well have worried.

■

THIRD INTERMEZZO

Richard

■—————————————————■

12

Rick Nelligan listened to the babble at the other end of the telephone line with a tolerant and loving smile. Fee's problem was that she thought symbolically rather than discursively.

"You're sure he's on our side? I don't care whether he's neat and cute and likes fudge soda. He's dangerously intelligent, priest or not, and—"

He was silenced by another fierce defense of Father Blackie. There was nothing wrong with symbolic thought. Quite the contrary. The best programmers were men who thought in symbols, and so too the most brilliant of theoretical physicists. Fee was not quite in either class. But Rick knew that she was more intelligent than—and anything but —the scatterbrain that he had once written off.

She did, on occasion, he had to admit, *sound* like a scatterbrain.

He assured her that he loved her, exchanged kissing sounds over the phone, and with his head thick with possible scenarios for which he ought to prepare contingency responses, walked back to his grandfather's study.

"How does this death affect you?" he asked, sitting in a dimly lighted corner of the grim old room.

Vincent Nelligan moved a bayonet on his thick mahogany desk, a relic of his army days during the War. "I've been independent of her financially, Richard, for many years. Many, many years."

"But how does it affect you personally?" Rick leaned forward trying to read the eyes behind the thick glasses. "You've known her for most of your life."

Rick was well aware that, despite his abilities and training in economics, he was a sentimentalist, a passionate sentimentalist. He knew it because Fee had told him so and she was rarely wrong. He knew it because of her evidence: "Like, Rick, I MEAN, is there anyone you don't like? Is there anyone whose story doesn't interest you?"

"At my age, Richard"—he smiled that faint, frosty smile that always meant that his grandson amused him—"you assume that people you've known all your life will die. Most of them have already died. Another death is no more surprising or dismaying than the dawn of another day."

"But"—Rick was also a romantic—"you knew her as a girl Fee's age. Surely you must feel some irony at the changes which made her the person we saw on the boat the other night."

Grandfather's dry lips moved slightly, as if he wanted to say something but had thought better of it. Finally he murmured, "She was never like your frivolous little friend, Richard. I don't think she changed much at all. In any event, I shall, I trust, soon be joining her in that final sleep that wipes out all our dreams and all our nightmares."

"Are you worried about the questions the police are asking? And Father Ryan?"

"Ned Ryan is a very dangerous man, very dangerous. He

purports to believe that the world should be constrained to follow his principles. Not that those principles kept his wife alive. His son, I feel, is a fool."

"The police?" Rick was very worried about the police, very worried indeed.

"I think the death of Vi Harrington will continue to be an unsolved mystery." His sigh sounded like a rasping file. "As will her life, for that matter."

"You don't care who killed her?"

"What does it matter? She's equally dead either way, isn't she?"

13

I considered Daniel Enright, Major, Army of the United States, his beret set at a rakish angle, his Ike jacket perfectly fitted, his battle ribbons neatly arrayed, his lips parted in a devil-may-care smile, his brown eyes twinkling cheerfully.

"Something missing, isn't there?" Bill Downs asked. "I put in nine months in 'Nam, right after Fionna was born. Mostly tending a computer in the basement of a concrete building in Saigon. I met some of those fellows, green berets by our time, in the drinking spots around town. There was something missing in them too. But I don't think it was quite the same thing."

"Indeed."

Bill Downs, a man who wanted back the wife he had lost eight years before. Badly enough to kill for her?

I would have to find that out.

There *was* something wrong about the painting. And maybe about the man in the painting. It was a good portrait. The artist had caught the recklessness, the vulnerability, the wit, but also the sadness.

"I wonder if he wanted to come home alive." Bill Downs gestured with his martini glass. "I gather from Rita that he lost his political ambition over there, but that must have been something she heard about him. She was born when he was overseas."

A broken heart, the Old Fella had said in an uncharacteristic romantic phrase.

"A man with a broken heart?"

Bill Downs glanced at me curiously. "Maybe. I had been thinking that he was a man without character. Not that my performance with this family would lead anyone to think I had character. But 'broken heart' might do it better. The fun gone out of life?"

"And not enough hunger to put it back."

"Maybe."

Bill Downs and I were standing in the mammoth parlor of the Violet Harrington Enright suite, examining the "official" portrait of Major Enright, commissioned by his wife after the Second World War. You could not help but feel that Daniel Enright thought the painting and life itself were both a laugh, a melancholy laugh.

"Let's go into the big room," Bill Downs had suggested, after his giggling daughter had introduced us. "Either way, the old girl won't mind."

Fionna had inherited her energy legitimately enough. Professor Downs was a short, stocky man with receding brown hair, bright blue eyes, a square, open face, and enough enthusiasm and wit to keep a class of five hundred freshmen awake the first day of the second semester. He might have been a union organizer of thirty years ago, or a precinct captain about to be promoted to ward committeeman, or a successful automobile salesman (new, not used, cars). Or a pastor in a suburban parish, universally loved by his people and viewed with great suspicion by the Chancery because they knew but could not prove that he broke almost all the rules in the service of his people.

Bill Downs you could not help but like. And you could not help wondering what he was doing in the Enright clan—

even if, as he put it with a wink, he was "civilly and ecclesiastically separated from it."

"Not from the wee lass."

He rolled his eyes admiringly. "What a pistol she is! Young Master Nelligan has found himself a handful." He flopped on an enormous beige couch. "Sure you don't want a drink, Father? This is my single martini, permitted three days a week, not counting Saturday, but every day during periods of official mourning."

"Reasonable rules. You do not seem prostrated by grief."

"The old girl was a ball-breaker, Father. I don't like to see anyone die"—he shrugged his shoulders and lifted his drink, perhaps in farewell to the dead—"but the world is undeniably a better place without her. Incidentally, I've looked forward to meeting you since I read your book. I checked with a colleague in our philosophy department when Fionna said you were coming over. He tells me that you're the outstanding man in the younger generation of William James scholars."

I had been convinced for some time that no one outside of the family, including the reviewers, had read *Criteria of Truth in William James: An Irishman's Best Guess*—a book for which you need not search, by the way, on the *New York Times* best-seller lists.

"An easy enough task when you exhaust the population."

One disarms Blackie Ryan by reading his book. Very clever. And very virtuous!

"You know that James was at Stanford during the San Francisco Earthquake?"

"Examining Starbuck's collection of stories about religious experiences."

"And promptly boarded the train to ride into town—when most folks were trying to escape."

"What's an empiricist to do?"

Mrs. Harrington Enright's "living room" could have been a suite at an antique show. It was the sort of place that you could not assemble by yourself after years of careful collecting—too perfect in its harmony to be the result of anything else but orders to an antique dealer and interior decorator to build a perfect Queen Anne parlor and hang the cost.

Outside, Lake Michigan, in one of its more reflective moods, basked quietly under the orange globe of the harvest moon, unperturbed for this night at any rate by the relentless traffic on Lake Shore Drive.

"Like I said, the old girl was a ball-crusher, Father. Hated men, despised them. For our weakness, I suppose. She was furious at me for getting Rita pregnant, but she turned on her charm and lured me into the family. We even lived here while I was teaching at Chicago Circle. It was great—no rent, when you're an assistant professor. She began to take Rita back while I was in 'Nam, but even when I came home, I still thought I was welcome. Then it became evident that I mattered only because I had been necessary to produce the wee lass. The fly knew the spider had him trapped almost too late. I would have been emasculated just like those three hormoneless sons of hers. I lucked out, or God saved me, or something, with that offer from UCLA. I was sure Rita would come with me."

"And she did not?"

"The old girl won, as she always did. I think she might have even beat Fionna down. Maybe not. That kid is one tough customer, hell of a lot tougher than her old man."

"Indeed." Like most of us academics and quasi academics, clerics and quasi clerics, Bill Downs liked to talk and to listen to himself talking. I let him talk.

"Chicago is home. Garfield Boulevard. Visitation parish. Worst kind of South Side Irish. I didn't want to leave. But they offered me a distinguished chair, research funds, the works. If I turned it down, no one else in the country would offer me anything like that ever again, because the word would go out that I couldn't be moved. I had to take it."

"Surely."

"Vi saw her chance to go for the jugular. She was the kind of hunter who could wait patiently for years till the prey gave her an opening. I told Rita my good news about the phone call from UCLA, and she turned pale. 'I can't leave Mother when she's in ill health!' That was the beginning of the end."

"Mrs. Harrington Enright was sick at that time?"

"She was *always* sick! That was part of the game. I told Rita that, and she became even more angry at me. What the hell, you marry an academic, you know you may have to move. I'd told her that often, though in the middle seventies the old marketplace was drying up and I thought I'd be riding those creaky elevators over at Circle for the rest of my life."

"You were ready to give up your wife for your career?"

"Hell no." He looked at his empty martini glass as though he too suspected elves or golems or other creatures had sipped half of it. "If I'd known it would end that way, I would have told them to forget it after the first phone call. I loved her. I still love her, damnit. I should have forgotten about her, but Rita is not the kind of woman you can forget."

"I see."

I did not see at all. The diffident woman in the dowdy black suit I had noted at a distance during the funeral Mass did not seem the sort who could create such sustained emotion in any man.

"I bumble through life, Father, making big and simple assumptions about how others will behave. I was being offered one of the best business-school jobs in the country, a distinguished chair that would mark me as one of the top men in my kind of statistical analysis. I was so happy that I took for granted everyone else would be happy too. It just didn't seem possible that my wife would not rejoice the way I did."

"A statistical improbability."

"Yeah, but in the real world, it's zero-sum. She doesn't come with you, she comes with you. I went out there for the recruiting ritual, knocked them dead, came home, told the family the good news—Fionna at least was happy for me—and hardly noticed the gleam of triumph in Vi's cold little blue eyes. When they made the offer, I accepted by return mail. I was sure Rita would come with me, even up to the last minute the following summer when I got on the plane to fly out there to stay. Even then I thought that in a week or two, she and Fionna would join me. Certainly before school started. They never came."

"Because of Mrs. Harrington Enright's ill health?"

"That's what she said. To be fair, she never told me that she would come eventually, when her mother felt better. She knew pretty well that any attempt to move would cause a return of ill health. The old girl had a heart attack when Fionna decided to go to Stanford. She didn't want the child anywhere near me. No one could explain to her that Palo Alto is hundreds of miles from L.A."

"Fionna was not dissuaded?"

"It was a near thing, but I laid down the law. Unlike her mother, Fionna responded."

"Yet you still love her?"

"You bet, Father." He slouched lower in the couch. "She loves me too. I suppose that little imp has told you we're in the same bedroom these nights? She doesn't miss a thing."

"Indeed."

"One look at each other and all the old chemistry went into action. Like the first night we saw each other at the Hyde Park party her mother didn't know she was going to." He grinned mischievously. "Interesting theological question, Father: given our ecclesiastical annulment, are we committing fornication?"

"An even more interesting question, though not theological, is why she sought an annulment. Was there a question of another marriage?"

"Rita will never marry again. She doesn't have the stamina to be caught between her mother and her husband for a second time. I guess Vi wanted the annulment to make everything final."

"But now that her mother is dead . . ."

"Is she really dead, Father?" He looked up at me quizzically. "I'm not sure she will ever be dead as far as Rita is concerned."

"Indeed."

"I used to think that when Vi died, Rita would hop on the first plane. I consoled myself that way for the first four years. Then I told myself that the old girl was too mean to die. The last year or two I began to face the truth: I'd lost Rita for good. Dead or alive, she'd never let Rita go."

His workman's face was sullen, angry for a moment. Then he dismissed his failure with a laugh. "Maybe I'm wrong. If I could once get her out in L.A., I'd have her again for the rest of my life. Rita can't make decisions. At the final moment she can't board the plane. She's basically a passive person, vulnerable, frightened, kind, you know the sort. But if somehow she decided to join me now, she'd never leave me again."

"I see. And your predictions?"

He held out his hand and moved it up and down, a gambler's gesture at estimating odds. "Two to one against."

"Not too bad."

"Not too good."

"Better than the last time."

"I miscalculated them the last time too." He smiled wanly. "Of course, this time there is Fionna, who is like totally convinced that Rita and I should try again. She'll push and I'll pull and we'll both hope that passion is stronger than fear of the dead."

"Her mother's death gives you another opportunity, one you've been waiting for, possibly the last one."

"I know." He picked up his glass and sipped at the melted ice cubes. "But I was at a party in Beverly Hills—the one out there. So I couldn't be the solution to your locked room, could I?"

"Not unless you acted through an agent."

Locked room—everyone these days knows mystery genres. And thinks they're a modern Sherlock Holmes.

Or, if you're Sean Cronin, a tall Blackie Ryan.

He laughed, not altogether pleasantly. "Kill her mother to get my wife back. Not a bad thought and not one I didn't have, but only—you should excuse the expression—academically.

The two of us almost went crazy at Fionna's graduation. We pretended to be cold and distant, and both of us wanted desperately to find a bed somewhere into which we could fall. We didn't then, but at O'Hare on Monday, we collapsed into each other's arms like a pair of horny teenagers. She came to my room that night, but if she had waited another quarter hour, I would have gone to her room."

"If we are to believe the folklore, a very traditional Irish way of responding to death."

"I sometimes think—a little more seriously than I thought about killing the old girl—that I ought to kidnap Rita. The way they did in the old days. Male chauvinist fantasy." He laughed mirthlessly again.

"But not altogether unpleasant?"

"Hardly." His eyes drifted far away and then returned abruptly. "Don't worry, Father, I won't do it. Everything up to it, but I'll stop short of physical force."

"Just short of it, I trust."

He looked surprised and then grinned, a true South Side Irish barbarian, Ph.D. or not. "Just short."

We both were alone with our thoughts.

"The bitch not only took away my wife, she took away my manhood. That was the kind of woman she was. She would beat you and then humiliate you. I was offered a damn good position at Northwestern last year. More money, less work, almost no work, which, as you know, is what we academics want most in the world. If I'd come back, Rita would have moved in with me almost immediately. I was sure of it. But I was afraid of another fight with Vi, and another loss. Fear was stronger than passion then, Father."

"The kind of woman she was." I sighed.

"The kind of woman she was. The kind, as you're certainly thinking, a clever man might plot to kill from two thousand miles away."

"The thought had occurred to me," I admitted, with yet another sigh.

"Be my guest, Father. If you can find a solution that points at me and make it stick, go ahead and do it."

"In lieu of an immediate response to that interesting challenge, whom would you suggest I seek as the most likely suspect?"

"Vinney Nelligan," he said promptly. "That son of a bitch is capable of anything. Nail him"—he jabbed a stubby finger at me—"and I'll vote for you for Pope."

"Why Mr. Nelligan?"

"No reason, more than anyone else." He lifted his hands and then let them fall helplessly. "Except that I hate the pious fraud so much. Your classic dirty old man. I don't like the way he looks at Fionna and Rita, but maybe I'm imagining it because I despise him. He has less motive than the others. He doesn't need the money, God knows, but he's the kind that loves to be kinky not because it's in his interest to be kinky but because it's in his nature to be kinky."

A sentiment not unlike the one expressed by the Old Fella.

"How would you think he did it?"

"The locked-room bit?" Bill Downs shifted in the couch, trying unsuccessfully to sit up straight. "Maybe with the help of those Mexicans or Colombians or whatever the papers say the police are seeking."

"They could have been in your employ?"

"Make it stick, Father." He chuckled. "I can't believe that congruence, usefulness, and ... what's the other Jamesian criterion?"

"Luminosity."

"Right ... I can't believe that they point at me."

Another silence, both with our own thoughts again. Mine uncertain and obscure, his surely about the charms of his sometime wife.

"Does it sound sick, Father? I mean the thing between Rita and me?"

"Its proper name is fidelity."

"Really?" He did sit up straight this time. "I would have called it obsession."

"The line is thin."

"I guess. . . . I told her the first time the other night that I was going to take her back to California with me."

"And she said?"

"Nothing, which is what she usually says. Her mother is scarcely in the grave, but what did the fella say?"

"Let the dead bury their dead?"

"Yeah."

It might not, in the last analysis, be Rita Downs's decision. Bill would have to make up his mind whether his hunger was strong enough to insist implacably. How much of his masculinity can a man throw into the balance in such a contest?

The wild card in this game of bluff and counterbluff, as he well knew, was the ineffable Fionna, possibly as tough a good angel as her grandmother was a bad angel.

"I want her back, Father. I won't say that I'll stop at nothing. But I'll do almost anything to get her back."

Good hunting.

For both father and daughter the death of Violet Harrington Enright had opened the curtain on a stage on which the drama of their lives might notably change.

And perhaps a new curtain also had risen for the wife and mother, the mysteriously compelling Rita.

Whom I would have to get to know better.

14

EQUAL JUSTICE UNDER THE LAW?
(An excerpt from Farley Strangler's column)

I don't understand what it's like to be rich. I grew up in a working-class neighborhood. I live in a working-class suburb. I drink in a working-class bar. I've never had enough money to know that I can pay next year's bills.

I don't mind not being rich. Life would be a lot easier if we had a cook to make our meals and a maid to serve them.

As it is, I have to sweat over the barbecue grill on Sunday afternoon. But that's all right. I can sleep peacefully Sunday night and live with myself on Monday morning. I don't have to worry about whether I'm enjoying the good life because other people are not enjoying life at all, that my comfort is purchased by other people's sweat, that my ease is paid for by their suffering.

And the nice thing about not being rich is you know you have to keep the laws. I don't dare run a red light, because if the cops stop me, they'll put a punch in my license, and two more of those and they'll take the license away from me. It's good to know that you're bound by the laws. The nuns in grammar school—when they weren't hammering independence out of our characters and thought out of our heads—said that the fear of the Lord was only the beginning of wisdom. But fear is still a pretty good beginning

I hope I keep the laws for better reasons than fear. But back me into a corner with temptation to take one more drink before I drive home and fear of a DWI charge is useful motivation to force me to turn away from the drink.

If you're rich, you can do anything you want, because the law doesn't apply to you the same way. You can walk the streets of Chicago, unindicted and free on a low bail, even if they find you in your grandmother's bedroom—on her ninety-five-foot yacht, no less—with a gun in your hand and a hole in her head.

If I were rich, maybe one of my children or grandchildren could get mad at me and put a hole in my head without any fear that they are going to be kept in jail or indicted for murder.

They're saying over at the State's Attorney's office that they have lie detector tests and paraffin tests which make them hesitate about going up to a grand jury.

Lie detector tests are not admissible in court. Paraffin tests or not, Fionna Downs's fingerprints—and hers alone—are on the gun. Maybe twelve good citizens of the County of Cook should be given a chance to decide whether she's guilty or innocent.

But I'm not rich, so maybe I don't understand these things.

■

FOURTH INTERMEZZO

Mary Kate

15

Mary Kate was worried about Fionna. Farley Strangler's column in the early edition of the morning's paper had been mean-spirited and nasty, like everything Strangler wrote. "He's got one column," someone had said: "It's about himself and he writes it over and over with different targets to blame for his troubles."

This time the target already had more than enough guilts about being rich to last her a lifetime. Now that Strangler had found her a good target for envy, the other media vultures would close in.

Mary Kate turned off 95th Street and onto Longwood Drive. A car turned behind, following much too closely. What was the matter with the idiot?

Nine-thirty was too late to be coming home from Little Company. Unlike more orthodox analysts, she had continued to maintain a hospital practice, arguing that analytic techniques and methods were sometimes appropriate for hospital contexts. Perhaps her case load was too heavy. Maybe she ought to cut back and spend more time at home with Joe.

There'd been a call on her answering service from Fionna canceling their appointment this afternoon. Was the young woman backing off from treatment? She shouldn't quit yet: there was a lot of work left to be done to free her essentially sound and healthy personality from some of the constraints under which it labored.

It was remarkable that the poor kid had survived at all.

The car was still right behind her. Bastard!

She was also worried about her own professional responsibility for the death of Vi Enright. The Punk insisted that Fionna had not killed her grandmother, and Punk was almost always right. Ed Enright had apologized, rather ungraciously, for his outburst the day of his mother's death. There had been no indictment yet, but the Strangler column might be the first step in a media blitz to demand that the case be brought to a grand jury.

So for the moment Mary Kate must contend only with the judge in her head—a hanging judge, as Joe had often said.

Speaking of Joe, she hoped he was home already, preparing to wrap his strong arms around her.

That was his job, wasn't it? She laughed contentedly to herself.

Except the poor dear man has lots of worries on his mind these days. And he won't talk about them.

The car behind her was now riding her bumper.

Furious at his stupidity, Mary Kate jammed her brake pedal down. The car behind her skidded to a stop, bumper touching her bumper. Then she hit the gas pedal, and, like crazy Biddy, peeled away.

She didn't look back as she swept into the driveway of the house. Joe pulled up right behind her. Home from work at the same instant, God bless him.

She bounded out of the car and embraced him passionately, a sure cure for uncertainty and fear.

"Anyone else home?" he asked, when she finally freed his lips.

"No."

"Will we make it to the bedroom this time?"

"Who cares?"

As they walked into the house, arm in arm, she glanced back down the drive. The dark car had disappeared.

16

"Dan Enright was killed last night," Mike Casey's voice, as somber as Gabriel's will be when he announces the day of judgment, burst into my vague, disturbing dreams. "And his wife. Throats slashed with knives."

"That wasn't supposed to happen," I replied, struggling for consciousness. "It doesn't fit."

"I know it doesn't." Mike's voice sounded hollow. "The police have put guards on the rest of the family."

"Where did it happen?"

"On Wells Street in front of their apartment, early this morning. They were coming home from a meeting of Chicago writers. A couple of kids saw two men leap from a car, run up to Dan and Lena, swing their arms, and then flee. The kids called the police and an ambulance. Both of them bled to death before help arrived."

"Is it foolish to ask who the killers were?"

"Knives rather than twenty-five-caliber bullets. Looks like the m.o. of cocaine professionals."

"Carlos and Tomas?"

"Could be. When was the last time we caught a professional hit man?"

"I presume the media are going wild."

"The pressure to indict Fionna will be pretty strong."

"She is being blamed?"

"She's the only one they have."

It was not a good day in the cathedral rectory. My Lord Cronin received a call from the Pro-Nuncio, a creepy character whom he despised, informing him that the Holy See was concerned about the deaths in Bishop Enright's family. With characteristic tact, he responded with the suggestion that the Holy See might want to send a contingent of the Swiss Guard to protect the Archbishop of Chicago from assassins who might confuse him with Bishop Enright, and slammed the phone down.

"Did you see those poor slobs last night?" he demanded of me.

"And two gentlemen in black jackets loitering outside their building."

"They tell you anything?" He paced up and down restlessly, a caged Irish wolfhound.

"Nothing important."

"They didn't kill the old woman?"

"I don't think so. Now at any rate."

"Are the killings linked?"

"I believe the police are taking the stand that they have no evidence linking them. Money was taken from the most recent victims, indicating that it might have been a mugging. The various media seem to dissent."

"The kid?" He jabbed a finger at me.

"Might she have hired the slashers? I think not; some of the media mavens, most notably the wondrous Farley Strangler, think otherwise."

"I don't like it, Blackwood, not at all. I want it solved. See to it."

"Naturally."

I turned on the TV.

Followed in and out by phalanxes of camera persons and reporters, a pale and tense Fionna was interviewed, at her attorney's insistence, by the police at 11th and State. She had no comment for the cameras.

"There is no evidence linking my client to these most recent deaths," red-haired Patty Anne—as I properly call the young hellion, much to her dismay—snapped at the reporters. "Please leave her alone."

Patty Anne would have used much stronger language off camera, but such a modest plea was calculated to win sympathy for her client.

My Lord Harry, walking and talking like a zombie, came to my room to seek permission for another funeral at the cathedral.

"I believe they lived technically in Immaculate Conception parish"—he smiled automatically, the curialist discussing the infinitely flexible law—"although they attended church at St. Michael's, the German parish, you know. The Cardinal has given permission. . . ."

"Of course I have no objection. I'm sorry, Harry."

"Thank you, Monsignor. I am very grateful. I don't suppose you have any, ah, clues."

"None, I'm afraid."

"It . . ." He hesitated, his face lined with shock if not grief. "It makes no sense at all. Why them and not me?"

"You think your former associates are involved?"

"Who else? The method is theirs. I fear that they may kill all my family first and then me." He sagged against the doorjamb of my suite. "They are capable of that, you know, Monsignor."

"There are police guards."

"My, ah, associates are not inhibited by police guards. Remember Clavi, Sidona? One was under guard, the other in prison. And perhaps John Paul I in the Vatican itself. If they want to kill you, they will do so."

"Indeed."

"One more point. You are aware perhaps that my brother and Lena were not canonically married. I managed to obtain a dispensation for him from his priestly vows, but he refused to avail himself of the opportunity to enter a valid marriage. If I myself were making the decision, I would be concerned about the possibility of grave scandal to the faithful. Cardinal Cronin does not seem anxious about the matter, but if you think it a subject for solicitude, I would quite understand. . . ."

"The faithful, Harry, have not been scandalized since 1968, the birth control encyclical, you may remember."

When he left my room, I phoned Mike Casey. "Bishop Enright is convinced that some of his former associates— read the P-Two lodge—are killing his family one by one as preparation for killing him."

"In Chicago?"

"They have a reputation for killing anywhere they want."

"The Outfit does not like anyone poaching on their territory." He laughed. "Besides, the boys are all good Catholics. Would they put down a bishop?"

"There was the matter a number of years ago of a provincial of a certain Italy-based religious order who was strangled by person or persons unknown."

"A provincial is not a bishop. I'll suggest to my former colleagues that they make some inquiries. If there is an outside firm at work, our friends on the West Side will be able to tell us."

The term *our friends* or *your friends* (or, when Jane Byrne was mayor, *her friends*) accompanied by a nod in the general direction of Halstead and the Congress Expressway—as we Democrats persist in referring to the Eisenhower Expressway—means, of course, the Boys, the Mob, the Outfit, the Syndicate (but never the Mafia or the Cosa Nostra, media names not favored in Chicago).

Next I placed a call to Rome, to a certain journalist I know in a comfortable old apartment on the Piazza Collegio Romano, a man who knows more about what is happening in the Curia than does the Pope himself.

As usual, there was much frantic and confused shouting before the Italian operators were able to complete the call.

"The Gelli crowd is capable of it," my friend said in his light Wexford brogue. "They're capable of anything."

"Do they really have a contract out on Harry Enright?"

"I shouldn't have thought so. He's a pretty small fish, hardly worth worrying about. They're strange men. Sometimes they go after small fish to teach other small fish a lesson. Or they might do it just for practice. But on the whole I think not. Harry Enright is more an embarrassment than a threat."

"Could you check around and see if there are any reasons to think that they might have changed their minds since his mother sent a delegate to deal with them?"

"Did she really do that?" He seemed tolerantly amused. "What happened?"

"She's dead."

"Oh my."

I told him the story.

"They might indeed attempt to eliminate a whole family. It would fit their sense of the family-structured nature of the world. Yet they are under considerable pressure from even more powerful forces now. The shadow world does not like publicity, as you know. I should have thought that if they wanted to dispose of Bishop Enright, they would have done so promptly and without fanfare. Still, you can't tell about those men."

I was not reassured.

I replaced the phone and, my hand still on it, attempted mentally to review the bidding.

Fionna Downs, she of the Harbor Masters and Diet Fudge Soda, was still the prime suspect of the officers-at-arms. She had made threats; she was in the cabin when the shot was fired; she had rushed out of the cabin, gun in hand.

I did not, for a number of obvious reasons, think that she was guilty. That meant a locked-room—or a locked-cabin, if you will—crime. I thought I knew how the locked-cabin affair had been managed, or rather how it had happened.

I reconsidered my solution. It was hard to shake its main supports.

I also had thought I knew, in all probability, who the criminal was. But the events of the previous night cast doubt on that suspicion, to put the matter mildly. The locked-cabin event now pointed in the direction of a number of people, quite possibly a complicated conspiracy of various actors, all with motivations—but not sufficient, or so it seemed to me, to account for two crimes.

My confidence of the previous day that I knew all (which

had diminished notably before the day had ended) now evaporated. I was as much at a loss as Chicago's Finest.

Then one of my junior colleagues, a fierce-looking young man with a thick black beard and handlebar mustache, appeared at my doorway.

"I thought I'd better turn this in, Boss." He laid on my desk a pistol, which, from the safe distance at which I regarded it, looked very much like a 9mm Beretta M-38 automatic.

Not that I had ever touched such a weapon.

"That is a real gun?" I pointed at it with, I confess, a certain amount of fear.

"Not at all." My bearded associate grinned. "It's a perfect replica. You can find them in mail order catalogues these days. Uzis, Walthers, all of them."

"How reassuring. And this was used for the teen club play?" I picked it up gingerly. It was light and fit snugly into my hand. Blackie Ryan as gunman? IRA underground? CIA agent? Modern Fenimore Cooper character?

Most improbable.

"I thought that with the cops hanging around everywhere, this ought to be in your possession."

"So that I might be arrested for carrying a firearm without a permit?"

"It's not a firearm and you don't need a permit and it's parish property."

"Indeed." I placed the weapon with some caution in the center drawer of my desk—the saucy medieval Madonna on my wall did not approve of it at all. "I assume that we have no parish switchblades or razors?"

"Maybe next year's play."

"A delightful prospect to contemplate."

I said the noon Mass, preached on confidence in God's love, consumed a modest midday repast of corned beef sandwiches, dill pickles, and chocolate chip ice cream with chocolate sauce, and departed in my trusty Chevy Nova for the convent in South Shore where Luisa Flores was in "protective custody." A wild thunderstorm, autumn's warning that it would soon be upon us, was racing across the city and whipping up the lake. Perfect weather for a day of murder.

Luisa was in tears when she joined me in the parlor of the convent, an old-style convent parlor with paintings of Leo XIII and Benedict XV on the wall, where they had doubtless been placed by the pastor who built the place three-quarters of a century ago.

The black patrol officer—Clarissa Day—who sat at the end of the corridor, chair comfortably tilted against the wall, reading a "Spenser" mystery, had told me before the nuns fetched Luisa that (a) there had been no trouble; (b) Luisa was a little doll; (c) she—Patrol Officer Day—had gone to the school next door; and (d) "Hawk is cool."

I think that in most circumstances I would rather have Mike Casey at my side, but I would not mind Hawk in reserve.

No way.

As I might have anticipated, one of the elderly nuns brought cookies and lemonade.

The nuns were very nice to Luisa, but the police had come today and asked terrible questions. She knew nothing about the murders last night. Carlos and Tomas were not friends of hers. She had not met them before La Señora hired them. They were not from her village, not even from her state, Sonora, but from Guadalajara (that spoken in a tone of voice which indicated that their origins should explain everything).

They were bad *hombres*. They threatened her with their knives. They felt her body. Only the Señorita saved her from being raped.

The Señorita was a saint. Luisa loved her. She treated her like a sister.

Would she kill the Señora for the Señorita?

"No, Padre, killing is a sin."

Uh-huh.

So is lying, but let it go.

So I asked her about her home and family.

They lived in Sonora, fifty kilometers south of the border. Her brothers had worked on the farms in Arizona. Because she was smart and quick and knew a little English, they took her with them. She became a maid for some rich gringos in Tucson and ran away when the gringo man tried to do things with her. A friend said there were jobs in Chicago. Another friend in Chicago took her to La Señora. Life was very good, working for her, even if she was a bit *loca*. Never in all her life had Luisa lived so comfortably. She sent most of her money home to her family because they were poor. Would the Padre please tell the police not to turn her over to the *Inmigración* when they were finished with her. She would like to go to school, learn to speak English properly, perhaps own her own restaurant and serve Sonoran food. It is so much better, Padre, than the Tex/Mex—an epithet from the way she spoke it—food they cook in Chicago restaurants.

She did not remember the names of her friends.

She was very old, Padre. Sixteen. Almost.

Because she looked so much like the tragic young woman in the film *El Norte*, Luisa won my sympathy, not that I believed much of what she told me.

The coyotes, the smugglers who exploit the undocumented workers, call them *pollos*—chickens—because they are frightened, defenseless people, easily used by everyone, smugglers, employers, the Mexican government, the American government. Our young people demonstrate, appropriately enough, against racial oppression in South Africa, but ignore our nation's treatment of the *pollos*, an exploitation and an oppression that comes dangerously close to genocide. And Father Hesburgh, that great Catholic folk hero, presides over a presidential commission that tells Americans what they want to hear—that the *pollos* are a threat and laws can keep them out. The commission does not tell Americans what they ought to hear—that as long as you have a labor supply on one side and a labor demand on the other side of a long border, you will have immigration, even if you shoot the immigrants you catch; that the *pollos* are an asset to the

American economy and not a liability; and that our nation is shamelessly using and exploiting them.

Just as the late Mrs. Harrington Enright had exploited Luisa.

At the cathedral we are not part of the sanctuary movement. Break the law? And get publicity for breaking the law? Don't be ridiculous!

We merely protect people as best we can from the gestapo tactics of the INS. Quite effectively, I might add.

The point is that I was disposed to be sympathetic to my little brown-skinned friend, even if she was lying.

How else can a *polla* protect herself?

Who killed the Señora?

Wide innocent eyes. She did not know. Maybe the ghost of her husband, the handsome young señor in the painting? At first, Padre, she thought it was the Señorita. But the Señorita said that she had not done it, and the Señorita would not lie. She, Luisa, might lie sometimes—shy smile—but not the Señorita. No way, Padre.

What had happened that afternoon?

She told me the story I already knew. When had she last seen the Señora alive? After Señor Nelligan left. She asked her to go ashore with the last of her guests and buy a bottle of "Adveel" for her headache. She was angry and very drunk, Padre, *loca* really. Totally *loca*, but she was alive.

She had seen the body of La Señora from the top of the companionway. There was a tiny mark on her head. But Luisa was very much afraid of the dead, so she did not go near the body. Besides there must have been a ghost, must there not? Who else could have killed La Señora?

Luisa was doubtless a trial to Mike Casey's former colleagues. She was vague on names and places and took refuge, as a *polla* must, in poor comprehension of English when they challenged her with tough questions. They might threaten her with the INS if she did not tell the truth, but there were others she feared even more than *Imigración*.

If there was nothing else to do with her, they might well deliver her up to the INS when they were finished with her.

But Fionna Downs would have enough clout to hire her as a maid and find her a green card. Luisa would become the young matriarch's first child and be treated with generous affection. She also would be constrained to do what she was supposed to do: master English, perhaps go to school, and to tell the truth most of the time.

Become a good American, in other words, and perhaps a neurotic in the process.

Better than being returned to Sonora and thus constrained to trust herself again to the coyotes for another attempt at crossing the border. And another and another.

On the way back to the cathedral and chaos, I turned off Lake Shore Drive to Northly Island, site of the 1933 fair and now of Meigs Field and the Adler Planetarium. Having cleansed the city of pollution, the thunderstorm had departed to the eastern horizon. The skyline glowed, spanking clean, like a postcard picture or a film clip from *My Bodyguard*, red and white and black and bronze and gold.

But I gave it little heed as I sat near the planetarium, in contemplation of Monroe Street harbor.

Lake Michigan was, I reflected, one of Lady Wisdom's playful tricks. Twenty-five thousand years ago, the Michigan Basin had been a vast area of wooded lowlands, drained by a complex river system. Then the Wisconsin glaciation had pushed its way south with massive glaciers, including one ten thousand feet high that for some ten thousand years occupied the space where Northly Island and everything else in the area now lay. Then the glaciers melted, forming first Lake Chicago and then, some twelve thousand years ago, Lake Michigan, 923 feet deep, 579 of those feet above sea level.

It made for cooling lake breezes in the summertime.

None of these reflections helped me to understand the problem of who was attacking the Harrington Enright family.

I considered the possibility of making an assault on the dessert table at the Chicago Yacht Club, but abandoned the scheme—reluctantly, to tell the truth—because of the late hour and my other responsibilities.

Not that the cathedral does not run even more smoothly in my absence, when I am engaged in my efforts to make the Cardinal's life less troublesome than it already is.

Fionna Downs's scenario was childish, but that did not mean it was wrong. Truth is not only often stranger than fiction, it is often stranger even than a James Bond film.

Let us examine it, I thought, as a model. First we presume that a Bond-like character sneaks on the boat, perhaps the night before in darkness, and hides himself, perhaps in the engine room or some other such obscure place. Then, perhaps, when the late Mrs. Harrington Enright was holding court on the bow under a deck umbrella that matched her caftan, he could slip through the open door and into her stateroom. He hides there, in a closet perhaps. I checked the police department's excellent diagram of the yacht; yes, the closets were big enough to hide in.

He waits till the last of the guests have left. There is no one, he thinks, on the yacht. He has heard Mrs. Harrington Enright tell Luisa to purchase a bottle of "Adveel." He tiptoes out of his hiding place and, perhaps with a touch of inspiration, kills his victim with her own gun, which he has seen in her purse. Just as he raises the automatic to fire, he sees, or perhaps only hears, Fionna. It is too late now to hesitate.

Here the scenario breaks down. Why not kill Fionna in case she has seen him?

Perhaps because she flees in hysteria too quickly. Perhaps he knows that she will alarm the whole of Monroe Street harbor. He knows he must bid his farewell to the *Violetta* quickly. He pulls on his scuba suit, yanks himself up the wall of the stateroom, and slips back into the water, before the sainted Joseph Murphy, M.D., appears in the room and the whole of Monroe harbor converges on the *Violetta*.

How does he close the window?

Perhaps there is someone on the boat to close it for him. But who?

Fionna? She has already hastened from the room and will not return.

Luisa? She will not reenter the room because she is afraid of the dead. She lies about that? Perhaps, but when does she have the opportunity to reenter?

Joe Murphy?

And the Pope is a Mormon.

Until we find how the window was closed, Fionna's scenario, or variants thereof, will not fly.

Perhaps this Bondish hypothetical character has a confederate on the yacht. Fine, that simplifies his concealment, but it doesn't answer the window question.

The windows slide back and forth. According to my notes, they are moved either by hand, if the mover is a tall person, or by a window pole if one is a short person—like Mrs. Harrington Enright, Luisa, and Fionna. They lock themselves when they are fully closed and hence cannot be opened from the outside. But could they be closed from the outside?

Not, if the police diagram is to be believed, by someone in the water.

By someone clinging magically, and perhaps invisibly, to the side of the boat?

Probably not. Surely the police must have considered that possibility.

After the funeral, I must explore the *Violetta*, impounded now at the wharf at the Chicago Yacht Club. Not that there is any reason to think that I'll find what the police have missed. My abilities at the Father Brown game, such as these may be, consist in insight and not Sherlockian observation.

Still, it wouldn't hurt.

And in the process I could raid the dessert table.

There was still the matter of the second gun.

Might that be harmonized with this scenario?

Perhaps, but only if the scuba person was brilliantly ingenious and immensely resourceful.

And more perceptive than anyone else in Monroe Street harbor that Sunday afternoon.

Although there was no one but Lady Wisdom to hear me, I sighed noisily.

Even if the Fionna scenario could be sustained—doubtless considered with more sophistication, if less enthusiasm, by the citizens-at-arms—there was still the matter of the second gunshot.

I pondered that. Surely two guns. And two gunshots, one heard—patently—and the other? Perhaps not heard because of the silencer. Or perhaps, for reasons that had seemed obvious to me all along, heard but not noticed.

My explanation of the locked-room puzzle, you see, had been battered by the terrible murder of the Dan Enrights. Nothing computed anymore.

I might be matching wits with a madman.

17

"There's something strange happening," my Roman friend whispered, as if the agents of the Inquisition were listening outside his door. "They are very upset with your friend Harry Enright."

"*They?*"

"The people that matter. They do not know why he sent that old man to offer money. Very much the *bruta figura*"—the Italian antonym for *bella figura* spoken with a thicker Irish brogue than usual—"if you take my meaning."

"Indeed." "The people that matter" were not high-level curial bureaucrats but the parasitic hangers-on from the shadow world who were exploiting the inefficiency of the Curia and the venality of some of its members. The kind of people who had cleaned up on the Vatican Bank scandal and were waiting, carrionlike, for more bones to pick.

"Harry's superiors thought Harry understood that he was to accept his disgrace and go home quietly. They thought they had made it clear that they would not protect him from the Others, but that he need not worry too much so long as he remained silent. Now this old man appears and it looks very bad. Moreover, the Others are upset too."

The "Others" were "the people who mattered"—sleek, brilliantly tailored characters out of Fellini movies who hung around the golf clubs with expensive watches on their wrists and dazzling women on their arms. Shadow world.

"I see. Can it be communicated to them that Harry did not know that his mother would attempt this intervention?"

"They would ask whether the woman could not be controlled. What sort of family is it in which the woman can't be controlled."

"Irish."

"You know that and, glory be to God, I know it, but they would not understand."

"Ah. But the woman is dead."

"That worries them all the more. They do not understand how Harry permitted that to happen."

Sweethearts, real sweethearts, these Masonic Cardinals.

"Perhaps the Others did it."

"They do not rule out the possibility. The Others were very upset, if you take my meaning."

"Oh, I take it all right."

"It is believed in very high places here that the Others have taken steps to clarify the situation."

"Sent someone over here?"

"Yes, but for purposes which are not yet clear. That's about all I know at the present. I don't think my friends know much else, but they're scared. For their own asses."

"As well they might be. Tell me, what was Harry's offense, other than *bruta figura*?"

"It would seem"—my friend paused, evaluating his information—"that he was assigned to deliver a certain sum of money to a certain recipient. He delivered the money in full."

"When part of it was supposed to be skimmed off and consigned to others, as a service charge perhaps?"

"You understand these people very well, my friend."

"Tell me about it."

On the television, Studs was bemoaning the senseless slaying of a great Chicago writer. A police spokesperson informed the world that the switchblades used by the alleged perpetrators had been found near the bodies without fingerprints. The knives, of Colombian make, were of the sort used by criminals engaged in traffic in illegal drugs.

I turned the set off.

It was, for some reason, impossible to think. Too many loose ends, too many possibilities.

Who might have hired my fantastical scuba diver?

The police department continued to insist that they had no evidence linking the murder of Dr. and Mrs. Dan Harrington Enright and the murder of Mrs. Violet Harrington Enright. And indeed they did not. But the media were calling for an end of the "blood bath." Farley Strangler was beside himself with rage, wondering whether all writers, including himself, were fair game for hit men hired by pubescent female killers. Farley's single narcissistic column admitted of infinite varieties of hatred and paranoia.

My Lord Cardinal would be upset. Thus it would be wise to avoid him.

By going to the wake.

I had a hunch that, while Carroll's had been packed at Violet's wake, it would be quite empty tonight. A simple parish priest would be welcome.

And would have an opportunity to study all the mourners.

If there were any mourners.

So I ate a wholesome supper, followed by one large dish of chocolate ice cream to compensate for my failure to arrive at the pastry table of the CYC in time, and drifted over to Carroll's.

The big old Victorian-home-turned-funeral-parlor was virtually deserted, save for a number of young men and women, soberly attired and of somber demeanor, who were scattered about the premises.

Some of our more presentable and intelligent citizens-at-arms.

You mourned a Great Chicago Writer on TV and in the press, but you didn't show up at his wake to offer sympathy to his family.

Perhaps because you knew that they were not suffering all that much.

Only Rita Downs, wearing the same dowdy black suit and sitting quietly in a remote corner of the room, into which the smell of mums had been impregnated decades ago, was weeping, quietly and steadily, as her sometime husband (once and future husband if he had his way) watched her with silent protectiveness, ready to fend off anyone who would violate the privacy of her grief.

Why did the family, I wondered, act as if Rita hardly existed? Was she that much of a cipher? A harmless and useless part of the scenery? A piece of furniture? A bush or a tree in the backyard that no one ever noticed?

Perversely, perhaps, I offered my sympathy to her first. Her protective Lancelot winked at me.

"Thank you, Father," she said through her tears "He was the only one of them that was ever nice to me. Till he married that woman. She seduced him and pretended to be pregnant. He never wanted to leave the priesthood."

"Easy." Bill Downs's right hand touched her shoulder.

"I'll be happy to talk with you after the funeral, Father." Her tears seemed to increase as she touched Bill's hand with tentative gratitude. "I'm not quite up to it now."

"Of course." I continued to wonder what her appeal was to Downs. She was not unattractive, surely; impressively well preserved and, like her daughter, with natural and durable finespun Irish-linen attractiveness. But about as sexually exciting, it seemed, as a mannequin in the Bonwit Teller display window.

On the other hand, what did I know about such matters?

"I'll be staying indefinitely, Father Ryan." Downs's square jaw was determined, a rock not to be moved. "Until this mess is cleared up."

"A very wise decision," I agreed in my most bland voice.

"I do not intend to permit my wife's throat to be cut."

I was in no position to deny the danger.

"In Father's eyes," she sniffled, "I'm not your wife."

"Matrimonial court judges," I said with a sigh, "are a necessary evil, but God is not a matrimonial judge, and neither am I."

For some reason they both thought that was funny.

She was somewhat more attractive when she laughed, but still not a woman you might wait for through seven long years in hopes that her matriarchal mother might die.

Differences of opinion, I supposed, are what make for horse races, beauty contests, and marriages.

"It was *so* good of you to come, Monsignor."

I turned around and found my pudgy right hand firmly grasped by Bishop H. Harrington Enright.

"I'm afraid," he went on unctuously, "that his Jesuit colleagues must have decided that it was not appropriate for them to appear. I am grateful that my mother is not here to see this empty room. As you know, Monsignor, she was a very devout woman; she went to Mass and Communion every day, rain or shine. Of course, she supported Dan's decision to leave the priesthood. If it was what he thought was best, then she thought it was best too. But it hurt her terribly. I'm sure you understand."

"Indeed."

Harry Enright's handsome face was drawn, as if he had been fasting for a month, and tight—a death mask.

"Lena's family disowned her." He grimaced. "They would not come to the wake or funeral from Oregon. Her sister told me that as far as they were concerned she had died the day she married Dan."

"Deplorable."

Which indeed it was. At least Vi stuck by her own.

"I spoke with some of my colleagues in Rome, former colleagues, you understand."

"Ah."   .

"They were not helpful."

"Did you expect them to be?"

A spasm of pain leaped across the death mask. "I suppose not. I wonder who will be the next victim. Rita? Poor Ed? The girl?"

"The Chicago police are watching them closely, I understand."

"Every police force in the world—and, Monsignor, I mean in the world—can be corrupted by these men."

Poor Harry.

I eased away and found Fionna, in a severe but flattering black jersey suit, at the closed caskets, in charge of the wake. Her own Lancelot was stalwart at her side, a tall, point-guard type in a double-breasted dark suit and thick glasses. His dense, neatly trimmed brown hair hinted at firmly restrained curl and his big hands, big enough I think to palm a basketball, suggested gentle strength. A nerd, but without the plastic protective liner for his multicolored pens.

"Father Ryan, this is my fiancé, Richard Nelligan, Rick, this is Father Blackie Ryan."

"Doing his best"—there was a saving glint of mischief in the young man's eyes—"to look like an American Father Brown, though perhaps even more bumbling and incompetent."

"My nieces and nephews have betrayed me." I took his massive hand, which was firm but not overpowering.

"I'll gladly match wits with you after the funeral Mass at your convenience." The mischief remained. The young would-be hero was looking forward to it.

"On-line? In Pascal?"

"Actually I tend to think in Basic."

"Cut it out, you two," Fionna demanded. "This is a wake. You're supposed to be serious."

"Not," I argued, "if you're Irish."

What had the fair Fionna meant when she said Vi was not a "real" grandmother? I had not asked her because I was sure I'd be given the same answer the police were given—she was just terribly angry at Grandmother. And I didn't believe it.

"Still, this is terrible, Father Blackie. Poor Uncle Dan was a flake, but he was not a bad man. He deserved to live out his years. When will it stop? Who's next?"

Understandably the Enrights were worried about serial killing.

"Do you mind advice about your future"—I changed the subject because I didn't know the answer to her question—"from a weird old priest?"

"From a cute little priest," she corrected me promptly.

The next step would be the tissue and the glasses, and I wasn't ready for that from someone who was technically still a suspect.

"I would turn your inheritance over to this young robber baron and take that job at Marshall Field's—or whatever other job that might facilitate your career as a writer."

"See?" Rick permitted himself a small smile.

"That's what the young baron here thinks too," she said, nodding at her intended.

"With a board of three trustees to moderate me," he added, his face turning crimson. "I'm marrying her for her money, of course, but we should keep up appearances."

"I don't want the money to ruin him"—her lips narrowed in a stubborn line—"the way it ruined us."

"The point is, darling, it won't ruin me." He extended his arm around her briefly. "It's not an end, only a means."

"Like Monopoly™ money. Or Eurodollars, which, as I understand them, come to the same thing. Or options or futures on a stock market index."

"But you do agree?" Rick asked anxiously, suspecting but not knowing for sure that I had trumped his Father Brown comment.

"Most certainly. The fair Fionna should be a lady bountiful, not a woman of property."

We were prevented from pursuing this point by the appearance of Mary O'Brien Feehan, the mystery woman of the Enright family, the nurse turned family friend, and a family friend whose elegant reserve was distinctly out of place in this contentious, new-rich American Irish clan.

Fionna introduced us and, her hero in tow, walked to the far end of the room to greet a new batch of mourners—when there were so few, each one was precious.

"A terrible thing, Father," Ms. Feehan said with a sigh that, unlike mine, was authentic West of Ireland. "A terrible thing."

She pronounced "thing" as "ting," the way all good Celts must, since their language lacked the letter *thorn*, from the Greek *theta* which provides us with our "th" sound.

"Indeed."

She was a tall, handsome woman of about sixty, with the professional self-confidence and restraint of the first-rate nurse. There was no nonsense about her neatly combed gray hair, tied in a severe bun, but also no absence of kindness in her light blue eyes. Her long thin face suggested dignity and something more than intelligence—wisdom.

Mary Feehan was the reassuring presence you wanted to see in the hospital room when you woke up from your anesthetic, or in the recovery ward when you came down from surgery.

Or perhaps next to you in bed when you were in your sixties and still craved reassurance and affection and competent love.

"As though there were some terrible family curse."

"My God has no part of such things."

"I suppose." She smiled, not altogether convinced, but too respectful of the clergy to disagree.

"You're from Mayo." I omitted the prescribed "God help us," lest it give offense.

"Born and raised there and living there half the year with my husband. But I'm an American citizen and my five children are Yanks, Chicagoans. Saint Thomas More."

So much a Chicagoan that she defined herself by the parish in which she had lived.

"Did your hospital training in the U.K.?"

"Oh, no," she said lightly, "nothing so grand as all that. St. Mary's in Castlebar."

"A town called Castlebar." I hummed a bit from the song—badly, as I do all things requiring physical skills. "Norman name, of course."

"Of course."

"Fine psychiatric unit there."

"And wouldn't we be after needing it in the West of Ireland?"

We sighed in unison.

"You were Mr. Enright's nurse in his last days, as I understand."

"Major Enright," she corrected me. "Right after I immigrated and before I met Chief Feehan, my husband."

"A man with a grand reputation in the department."

"And deserved it is too, isn't it?"

Another matriarch. Surrounded by them.

"Of course. So you knew them all as children."

"Every one of them. . . . I'll be glad to talk to you, Father, once this terrible ordeal is over. But I don't know how much I can add."

Everyone wanted to talk to me. Please protect us from the killers on the loose, Father Ryan.

Better that you pray to Lady Wisdom, who must be upset with me because she's permitted me to be befuddled, even though I smell a lot of things I don't like.

Totally befuddled. Really.

The Bishop asked me to say some prayers. Combining the new with the old, I recited the Twenty-second (ecumenically the Twenty-third) Psalm with them antiphonally and led them in a decade of the rosary.

Then I exercised the pastor's right to preach, even if he intends to preach more to himself than to anyone else.

"There are no good ways to die. Some are worse than others. Dan and Lena left us in one of the more ugly ways. There is nothing in our faith that enables us to pretty over either the tragedy or the senselessness of their death. We think of them as children filled with bright dreams, as a young man and a young woman of talent and promise, as dedicated servants of the church, as contestants for new ways of serving God and their fellow humans, and we ask why they were not given more time.

"To that question I propose no answer other than to say that it must be tabled till that day we are able to demand an account from God of how he has arranged our lives and our deaths. His answer will doubtless be like that of any lover backed into a corner—he loves us and he will take care of us and wipe away all the tears and make us happy again and forever. It is a promise that we believe even now through the dark glass of faith. We cling to this dark glass and assert that tomorrow will be different, no matter how bad today is. Even when today is the last day of our life.

"Life and death are inseparable on earth, as the poet says, for they are twain, yet one. And death is birth."

Harry Harrington stared at me oddly when I was finished. I actually believed that stuff, he was thinking. Not that he didn't believe it. But his years in the bureaucracy of the church had moved such pieties not only to the back burner but out of the kitchen.

I prepared to take my leave, having been hugged by the fair Fionna, burdened with even more uncertainty than when I came. I had answered no questions and had indeed uncovered several new ones.

On my way to the door of the funeral home, I was intercepted by Dr. Edward Harrington Enright, his Rock Hudson face lined by pain, his leonine head bowed, his small body bent with fatigue, his soulful brown eyes haunted by anxiety.

"Please, Father Ryan. May I have a few words with you before my wife joins us—she's driving in from Elmhurst and I walked over from the hospital. I don't want to alarm her unduly. You see, I have a confession to make."

18

"I was stealing from my mother." Ed Enright spoke in small choked gasps, part sob, part anxious wheeze. "Large sums, I fear. We have serious financial needs in our family,

and I happened to have made an extremely fortunate investment. But there have been some temporary setbacks. You
know how these things happen, I'm sure, Father. . . ." He
was racing through his little speech as if he wanted to finish
it before he was felled by a fatal heart attack. "If one takes a
firm, long-run position in certain financial transactions, one
must accept the necessity of meeting certain interim obliga-
tions."

"Margin calls?"

We were sitting in the ornate Victorian office of the funeral parlor, also permanently steeped in the smell of mums
and lighted by lamps whose shades cast a rose glow throughout the room. Ed was behind the desk—isn't that where doctors always sit?—and I on a couch at the other side of the
room, as though he were the priest and I the troubled
counselee.

"Er, yes, something of that sort. Temporary problems,
you understand. Well." He breathed deeply as if to steady his
nerves. "I asked mother for money. She told me I was a fool,
a riverboat gambler, that I deserved to lose all my money
and that she wouldn't give me a penny. She believed in punishing us severely when we erred. I assume you know what
she did to Rita. There was no changing her mind. She would
continue the usual allowance, but I would have to find a way
out of my investment problems myself."

"I see." This quivering, quaking man made me sick to
my stomach. The smell of the mums didn't help. Nor the rose
light. "I assume that if your investments were successful,
you would no longer have been financially dependent on
her."

"I will be a wealthy man." He preened himself, a vest-
pocket peacock puffing his chest. "I will never have to do another operation for the rest of my life. I am a good surgeon,
Father. I'm sure you will find that out if you inquire among
my colleagues. But, frankly, I no longer find medicine of
compelling interest. I would have much preferred . . . But
that is not the point at the present."

He had not wanted to be a doctor, any more than Dan

wanted to be a priest or Harry wanted to be a Vatican diplomat.

And what had she done to punish Rita? Ruin her marriage or something else? And arguably worse?

"So you took money from her?"

"On a temporary basis, you understand. Mother gives us—well, gave us—a check every month, a not insubstantial amount. I merely increased the amount with some erasures. Vincent Nelligan noticed the change—Mother never pays any attention to canceled checks—and called it to her attention. He is such an upright and honorable man that nothing can shake him from the path of what he thinks is his duty. I begged him not to tell her, but it made no difference. 'I have to do what I have to do,' he said."

"Your mother was displeased, I assume?"

"She was irrational when she was told. I feared that she might stop her allowance to us, that she might even turn me over to the police. She did neither of these things, but what she demanded as a price was even worse: she insisted that I terminate my investments completely, not only this excellent opportunity but all future opportunities. She wanted . . ." He sniffed, and shook his quivering head in disbelief. "She wanted me to agree that she be appointed conservator of all my money and property. Just as she had been conservator of my poor grandfather. The humiliation . . ."

Vi was right about her youngest son. He was a compulsive riverboat gambler. Gaylord Ravenal in Elmhurst. When the problem is gambling addiction, the CBOT is no different from the late and lamented Arlington Park Race Track.

Or Las Vegas.

A place where you can prove you're a man and at the same time punish yourself for rebelling against the parent figure.

"She threatened this during the yachting party?"

He nodded miserably. "The first night, in the presence of my wife. I was beside myself with shame and grief. I . . . I made threats. Only Min and I know of them. Still, the police are no doubt aware of my problem with the checks. I am expecting to be arrested for the murder of my mother momentarily. I need help, Father," he begged. "I'm innocent, you see. I could not have killed her."

"You benefit greatly from her death, however, do you not?"

"Probate will require months. I still will not be able to meet my margin calls. Not without selling my house, my cars, my wife's furs . . ."

"She can't prosecute you for check kiting now. And you will receive your inheritance."

"But already the police think I'm a killer. That's much worse than—"

"Forgery?"

"I suppose that's the right name." He buried his face in his hands. "Only a few more days, another week at the most, and it will all turn around."

"You fought with your mother on this subject the day of her death, as well as the day before?"

"What?" He looked up from his protective hands, an unfortunate sniveling wretch. "Oh, yes. The last day. I'm afraid she was too inebriated and too angry at Fionna to devote much time to me and my problems . . . but my contention, Father, is that I do not stand to gain by her death. The allowance will stop; the money she has left us is not adequate to my responsibilities; I have children to educate; there will be marriages to pay for, certain debts to pay. Her death solves neither my short-run nor my long-run problems. Could you not point this out to the police? And there is certainly no reason I would want to kill Dan. His death does not increase my inheritance."

His head returned to his hands.

"Was it not possible to obtain a loan against your prospects? I mean a loan to meet your margin calls?"

"Hmmm? A loan?" He was distracted, completely absorbed by his fear of the police. "I'm afraid, Father Ryan, that my credit is not very good with the banks. And Vincent would discourage reputable bankers from advancing me more money. I lack the courage to seek money from organized crime."

"A wise decision," I murmured.

No matter how despicable the man and how disgusting his anxiety, his argument was not unpersuasive. His mother's death did not help him out of his financial crisis.

On the contrary, her death guaranteed that the crisis would be permanent. On the other hand, he was a successful surgeon, which meant that he had a source of steady and considerable income. Almost certainly Fionna would bail him out of trouble in the years to come, more readily perhaps than his mother would. And she would not insist on becoming conservator of all his money, humiliating him before his wife and friends. On balance, Ed Enright was better off with his mother dead.

Moreover, as far as I knew, the police were not closing in on him. They knew he had a strong motive for killing his mother and that he was the last one to see her alive. Yet they had made no arrests. It was, in fact, most unlikely that they knew about his check kiting and her threat to reduce him to the same state of servitude that she had imposed on his grandfather. Stern ethics or not, Vincent Nelligan apparently had not seen fit to tell them these components of the story.

"She was a hard woman, Father." He strove to pull himself together. "She had no respect for any of us as men. Rita didn't matter obviously. She punished us according to her own standards, which were often harsh. Yet I grieve for her passing." He choked again. "I loved her. In her own ways, frequently misguided but always well intentioned, she was generous and loving. I . . . I feel like a huge door has slammed shut in my life and can never be opened again. I regret with all my soul that the last days were marred by her regrettable misunderstanding of the opportunities in this investment I have made. Until the, ah, reversal recently, I had made a very considerable sum of money."

Paper profits, already eaten up.

"You hoped that she would be proud of this accomplishment?"

"Nothing I could do," he groaned, "would ever impress

her. I was always the feckless child, the baby who never grew up."

Grounds enough for murder, it seemed to me.

"If you can explain these matters to the police . . ." he pleaded, his voice appropriate for a man on his knees begging, let us say, Genghis Khan, for his life. "They seem so insensitive to the nuances of family emotion. They seem to believe that my grief is not sincere."

"Who do you think killed your mother?" I asked cautiously, trying to change his focus from himself to others.

"Oh." He dismissed *that* question as unimportant and unwelcome. "I would have thought that was obvious. That wretched girl, of course. I don't see why the police are dubious. Was she not apprehended with the gun in her hand? Does she not benefit the most from Mother's death? She is much like Rita, worthless in every way. Hardly worth noticing. In one respect, however, she is different from her mother. She is capable of brief outbursts of destructive rage."

"Indeed."

Everyone in the family seemed to want to point a finger at Fionna. Did they think that a jury verdict or a plea bargain would cost her the family fortune? Or did they hope they could break the will?

"But you will intercede for me with the police?"

If the police knew what I knew now, they might well arrest him on the spot. He had ample reason to want his mother to die. But his motives for killing his brother and sister-in-law were less obvious. While he could be pictured shooting his mother in a moment of deep despair, it was hard to imagine this quivering little man giving a cold-blooded order to two slashers to slit the throats of the man and woman in the closed caskets outside the office in which we were sitting.

"I will certainly keep in mind your reasoning," I said tentatively, "which in its broad outline does not seem unpersuasive."

It was a weak promise, but one which reduced him to

tearful gratitude. I was afraid he would attempt to kiss my hand, so I rose and made a hasty retreat from the office. He trailed along after me like a lapdog afraid to be abandoned by his owner.

In the lobby of the funeral parlor we encountered Vincent Nelligan and Minnie Enright. Ed introduced me to his wife and his nemesis.

Unlike Rita Downs, Min Enright presented no great mysteries as to the nature of her eroticism. Boyish figure, thin face, artificially blond hair, black silk dress with a deeply plunging neckline, heavy makeup, false eyelashes— the components of her appeal were much less impressive than their total: an invitation and a promise. The former was blatant, the latter suggested rich rewards for those who accepted the former.

"Vamp" would have been the word in the past. More clinical obscene descriptions would be used in our day. "Trouble" would have been appropriate at any time, especially trouble for middle-aged men who were seeking a change of pace from a faithful but unchallenging wife.

The victim falling into her spider web would know that he was destined to be seduced, played with, captured, and then cruelly dismissed as no longer interesting. Even that prospect, however, added to her allure.

She barely acknowledged my existence. I was no longer a "cute little priest" but an uninteresting fly on the wall. Her green eyes flashed hatred and contempt for her husband. He had, I suspected, been warned *not* to talk to me. He had broken the rules and would receive a fierce tongue-lashing as soon as they were alone.

The lapdog became a hangdog.

Poor man had traded one dominating woman for another. More reason for murder.

"Good evening, Father," she said with notable lack of enthusiasm. "Nice of you to come."

I mumbled something Brownishly—ineffectual and obscure. She was unimpressed.

"I've been wanting to meet you for some time, Father."

Vincent Nelligan's voice was rich and powerful, the sound of a wide river plunging confidently over a waterfall. Not Niagara, but possibly Iguaçu. A voice which implied the forward plunge of the economy—and your part in it, if you deposited your money in his bank.

It was the only vestige of youth and vigor left in the desiccated old man. His skin was brown and parched like the pages of an old book, his eyes a faded blue, his hair white and transparent, his back, once firm and upright, curved sharply forward—an exclamation point turned into a question mark—his hand as dry as a desert under the summer sun.

One felt the urge to suggest that the corpse return to the coffin for the rest of his wake.

He was dressed like a corpse too, black three-piece suit, white shirt, careful tie, handkerchief in his jacket pocket, a solid, old-fashioned banker about to be laid to rest.

Vinney Nelligan, perhaps a year or two older than the Old Fella, looked twenty years older, a man on whom the chill hand of death was already resting. Only his voice suggested that he was still fighting whatever sickness it was that had wasted him.

"I am delighted," he continued, his eyes shifting nervously from the guilty and embarrassed Ed Enright to me, "that Harry has persuaded you to take an interest in this most unfortunate matter. Perhaps I might have a word with you before the funeral Mass in the morning?"

On the edge of death he might be, but still no fool. The splendid Minerva had found me no threat; Vincent Nelligan knew better.

"Of course. Nine o'clock?"

"That would be perfect." He removed an expensive leather-bound notebook and made a minute note in it. I would have wagered that the handwriting was fine and graceful, but now unsteady. "I shall be looking forward to it." He paused, not for lack of words but to impress the rest of us. "I find it unfortunate that Violet should have passed on at a time when there was so much trouble in the family. Perhaps I may be able to disentangle the various threads for you."

"I would welcome that."

His bleached blue eyes flashed for a fraction of a second; briefly he was a shrewd businessman gauging an adversary. And not underestimating him either. Ned Ryan's son, for all his harmless appearance. And Ned could be poison when he was angry. Pure poison.

"Tomorrow morning then, Father?"

"Indeed."

"I'll be looking forward to it."

We are two sensible businessmen, you in God's business and I in Mammon's. We'll sit down for a few casual moments' conversation and settle this unfortunate affair, won't we?

I wondered what had happened to the money that was not used to bribe that group in the shadow world whom my Irish friend in Rome called "the Others."

That would be a good question with which to begin the next morning.

Outside the funeral parlor I met Annie and Mike Casey, the former gorgeous, the latter grim.

"See you in the rectory afterward, Blackie?"

"Only if you bring your lovely date."

Neither of them laughed. A bad sign.

19

"There's a hit man in town," Mike said, frowning at me over his Waterford goblet (Powerscourt pattern) of Jameson's. "From Europe. Very heavy. He is either a Franciscan priest—Padre Adolpho—or is disguised as one. Our friends on the West Side are impressed but unhappy. Otherwise"—his lips moved into a thin mirthless smile—"my sometime colleagues would not have learned about him."

"I think it's terrible," Annie protested. "A priest being a hit man. It must be a disguise."

It is perhaps revelatory of my psychosexual condition that I was baffled by the apparent sensual appeal of Rita Downs, affronted by Min Enright's blatant eroticism, barely moved by Fionna's nubile enthusiasm for "cute little priests," and overwhelmed by Annie Reilly's mature charms. I was breathless because of her presence in my rooms, and could not concentrate on her husband's face because my errant eyes insisted on straying to her. From her carefully shaped hair to her elegant shoes, she demanded constant attention.

And knew it. And reveled in it.

Priests must not be hit persons, she might say to me, but they can fantasize about me to their heart's content. Unfortunately for you, Father Ryan, you're going to have to wait till heaven to see me with my clothes off.

To which I thought, in imaginary reply, that such a splendor alone would be enough to attract one to the heavenly city.

Mike Casey was—I told myself for perhaps the millionth time—a lucky man.

"Some houses of the Sicilian Franciscans have been allies of the Mafia since the War. According to the history of the matter, they combined forces to fight the Nazis and continued the joint venture afterward for purposes of mutual benefit. I assume that the Poverello of Assisi would hardly approve. In the late fifties, the police arrested most of the friars in a couple of monasteries and charged them with virtually every crime that it was possible to commit—not excluding murder and rape. Pope Pius XII, profoundly shocked, denounced them in no uncertain terms and demanded prosecution. Then, presumably using the old argument about the 'good of the church,' he reversed himself privately and pressured the government to drop the cases. Under Pope John, at least some of them were convicted. Visitors from Rome have repeatedly tried to effect reforms, apparently with some success. But one hears that the last traces of the Mafia interlude have yet to be eliminated."

"But why, Father Ryan"—she smoothed out her black skirt, appropriate for a wake and for many other events too, no doubt—"would priests become thieves and rapists and murderers?"

"For the same reason that other men do—power, money, pleasure. We are not immune to desires for such things, Annie."

"I know that." She blushed, thinking of her own unhappy experiences with priests. "But they gave their lives to God."

"It is not a gift that cannot be withdrawn when age and discouragement intervene to blight the dreams of youth. The man we prayed for tonight is evidence of that."

"He was a flake who thought he was an important writer." She sipped a tiny drop of the half shot of Jameson's her husband had poured for her. "Padre Adolpho is a killer."

"I admit the difference in the outcome, not in the cause: weariness in the pursuit of the work of a very unpredictable Lover."

"We are not sure that he's come to put down anyone or even that he's a priest," Mike interrupted our theological discussion. "It would seem that he's here to evaluate and make some decisions."

"Indeed."

"He has told these friends of ours, whom he treats as if they are unlettered bumpkins, that his friends are very embarrassed by the publicity the Enright family is receiving."

"Do they think he might be responsible for causing the publicity?"

"It's not always clear"—Mike was watching his wife too—"even on the West Side what their words mean. In the other parts of that world, they become yet more obscure. I'll say one thing: our friends don't like it."

"It may be possible to take certain steps with regard to that part of the problem. My concern is still with the narrow issue of who is killing off the Enrights. Candidly, I thought I had an explanation, now I'm as much befuddled as your sometime colleagues in the CPD."

"The walls of the rectory will collapse." Annie giggled into her drink. "And on all this mess."

"Drink your whiskey, woman," I responded. "I didn't say *permanently* befuddled."

"They're looking for the two slashers, of course." Mike was unconscionably amused at the exchange between me and his wife. "When was the last time we found professional hit men?"

"And the fabled Fionna?"

"They may have to hand down an indictment if only to shut up the media. But no one thinks they could get a conviction. That wild Slattery woman is threatening suits for malicious prosecution which she might just win."

"Beautiful child—Patty Anne, I mean," his wife mused. "I hear that she has agreed to model for one of Cathy Curran's nudes."

"That will fill the gallery if we exhibit it."

"I *had* thought of such an outcome," Annie admitted.

"If Fionna is not the murderer," I asked, noting that once again the golem had been at work on my drink and Mike's, "who then did kill Violet Harrington Enright?"

"They've gone over every inch of the yacht. It's at the Coast Guard station now, by the way, if you still want to poke around it. Yes, thanks, another couple of drops. My wife will lead me home."

"Not for me, Father." She put her tastefully jeweled hand over her glass. "My husband says I get giggly. I think he means more giggly."

"What about Ed Enright?" I asked lightly. "His financial problems, I am told, are acute."

"They could bring him in, book him, charge him, and even indict him. A smart lawyer could probably get the case thrown out by the trial judge. Still it might distract the Farley Strangler types from Fionna, who is even less probable."

In twenty-four hours the pressure on the police and the State's Attorney to indict *la belle* Fionna would be much less.

No one, however, would be any closer to a solution of the murders.

Without interrupting our conversation, Annie removed my glasses and performed her usual cleaning operation. She had brought tissue and cleansing liquid in her purse.

See, I might tell the Pope, women are not all that bad after all, are they? They have some uses besides childbearing, do they not?

"Stonewall?" I sighed in the direction of her husband.

"With the threat of more violence in the wind coming over the wall."

An accurate prediction.

We finished our drinks, I walked down to the Wabash Avenue door of the rectory, Annie hugged me appropriately, and the Reillys departed.

I went to the Cardinal's room instead of my own. He was reading the Bible. My Lord Cronin is about ninety-five percent agnostic and five percent mystic, an appropriate blend for a bishop these days.

No one, however, would ever persuade him to be silent in the presence of evil in the name of the "good of the church."

"I have two small favors to request?"

"Huh? Oh, Blackwood. I was trying to figure out St. Luke."

"Interesting Greek." I spoke from my past as a classics instructor in the seminary. "Not a literary great, but a supple command of the koine, the common language of the day all around the Mediterranean. Now as to my favors . . ."

"*Two* did you say?" He closed the Bible, his finger at the page of St. Luke he had been reading. "That's a lot for one day."

"The first is perhaps the more difficult. As soon as you arise in the morning, call your friends in the Vatican, the higher the better, including possibly your Polish friend with the frosty eyes. There is a very heavy hit man in town, alleging to be a Franciscan from Sicily named Padre Adolpho. He is messing in the Enright affair. The Chicago police know about him. If there is another crime—and only a fool would exclude that possibility now, since the murder of Dan and Lena Enright seems gratuitous—Adolpho may well be arrested. That opens the possibility of a media scandal about Harry Enright and his former superiors in Rome."

"Wonderful." The Cardinal put aside his Bible. "Damn fools!"

"Decidedly. You should make it clear to the relevant parties that Padre Adolpho should be withdrawn *permanently* on the first Alitalia flight out of O'Hare and that the games with Harry Enright should stop or you won't be responsible for what the American media may make of the whole matter. You should convey the impression, not inaccurate, by the way, that you are sitting on a crate of high explosives that would destroy the Peter's Pence collection next year. Possible?"

"They won't like it one bit"—the Cardinal's brown eyes escaped from their hoods, glowing with battle light—"but they'll buy it eventually. They have no choice. And"—he shook his head—"they'll lament that the present condition of the church, under attack by so many enemies all around the world, precludes a permanent solution to the whole problem."

"We will at least push it out of our city."

"That we will do. Is your second favor that simple?"

"A phone call to your colleague the Bishop of Down and Conor, the esteemed Ed Dailey, should do it."

I told him what I wanted.

And, his being a Cardinal, why I wanted it.

"Do you think that a likely solution?"

"As to whether it's a solution to the whole puzzle, I am not sure. As to whether it's likely, all I can say is that the numbers fit."

"You are definitely scary, Blackwood. I'm glad I'm on your side." He smiled up at me. "At least I think I am."

"For the present." I sighed loudly.

The answers to those questions might help to find the key to the puzzle.

They would not, however, prevent the next bizarre bloodletting.

■

FIFTH INTERMEZZO

Bill Downs

■————————————————————■

20

Rita's eyes were red with tears—mourning after all. Bill Downs touched the back of her neck, gently, reassuringly. Her back stiffened in immediate response and his own body tensed in quickly awakened need.

Would they never have enough of one another?

Well, so what if they didn't?

"You have to mourn, Rit; unless you permit yourself to do that, you will never be able to start the next phase of your life."

She had been sitting at her vanity table, in black bra and slip, garments of both mourning and seduction, death and life, staring vacantly at her own reflection. They maintained the fiction of separate bedrooms but were more intimate now than they had ever been when they were married—a relaxed intimacy in which all the old conflicts had been settled by unspoken assumptions.

Love on the night of a wake? An old Irish custom, was it not? Fuck you, Death!

"You know me better than I know myself. I don't know why I feel sad. No, that's not true. Of course I do. She ruined my life and our marriage and almost ruined Fee's life too. I'm crying for us and not for her."

"Your life is not ruined." He sat down next to her. "And you are weeping for her. Grief can't be sorted out that neatly, Rit. You're glad you're free of her, but sorry that she's gone and sorry that there was not more love between you."

"Typical of you"—she leaned against his arm—"to feel sorry for a woman who took your wife away from you."

He drew her closer. "I like my new mistress much better than my old wife."

Bill Downs was not exaggerating. His ardor for Rita had never cooled completely. But now it was a firestorm. If this mix of pleasure and love could be sustained, with the normal ups and downs, then the years of separation would have been a small price to pay.

During the many fantasies in which he had imagined Vi Enright's death, he had consoled himself with the daydream of renewed love. Now the daydream was coming true.

"That's sweet, Bill, but it's not the way the world is."

He felt that he was close—oh, so close—to conquering this woman completely. If he was careful in his approach to her now, she would be his, without any doubt or question, for the rest of their lives. Wife or mistress did not matter. He wanted her.

"Do you think if we had not been apart for so long, we'd feel this way now?" He began to nuzzle her shoulders and arms.

"Crooked lines of God?" She sighed deeply.

His fingers moved to the hook between her breasts. Yes indeed, he would cheerfully kill to reclaim this woman. And Blackie Ryan knew that and somehow understood it. She is mine and I must have her back. Now and forever.

"Let the dead bury the dead." The words exploded from his mouth—hunger, rage, and love rushing together like three streams merging into a mighty river.

"Love me, Bill." She drew his lips to her bare breast. "Love me!"

This time she would be his and no one would take her away.

Vi had won the battle. He was about to win the war.

■

SIXTH INTERMEZZO
Min Enright

■————————————————————————————■

21

Min Enright poured herself a stiff shot of gin, walked on bare feet into the kitchen, added ice to the drink, pushed open the screen door, and entered the enclosed patio in their backyard. The grass under her feet, the light breeze stirring her thin nightgown, the tart taste of her drink—slowly combined to still her nerves. She sank into one of the garden chairs, too shaken to sleep, too drained to weep.

She and Edward had fought again, an almost nightly occurrence now. He was furious at her for behaving like a "cheap tart" at the wake, and she at him for breaking down and spilling his problems to that silly little priest.

How, she wondered, shivering, could a man who was a brilliant surgeon and often a breathtaking lover fall apart so completely?

Her husband's decline had been slow at first—he found excuses not to attend professional meetings, then excuses to decline patients, and finally excuses not to make love. She had been faithful to him until then, not even thinking of infidelity.

When he had challenged her last year, she had fired back at him, "You brought sex into my life, and now I can't do without it. It's your fault, not mine."

He had moved out of their bedroom then, nominally because she was a cheap tart, actually because his impotency was habitual.

It was all the mother, of course. She had broken him

down slowly with her persistent attacks on his manhood:
"Be a man for a change, Edward, will you?"

It was a strategy well calculated to erode Ed's precarious confidence in himself. And, Min knew, she had cooperated unintentionally. The end of their intimacy confirmed Vi Enright's diagnosis. Poor Ed's crazy speculations on the Board of Trade were designed to impress her as well as his mother.

She sipped at her drink, cautiously, carefully. There was no point in becoming an alcoholic.

This murder could be the last straw for Ed. He had cracked up completely on the boat, blaming that Murphy woman on television for Vi's death—as though he did not know what had really happened. But when the subject was his mother, poor Ed never behaved rationally.

"You actually believed that when you were shouting at the TV cameras, didn't you?" she had demanded when they were driving home late that night.

"She was responsible," Ed began. "If she hadn't taken that little bitch as a patient . . ."

"Come on, Ed, you know better than that."

"It's my mother that's dead." He had begun to weep. "You don't care, but I do. I never had a chance to win her respect."

So she had argued about his professional accomplishments, about the respect of his colleagues, about his national reputation.

"None of that means anything," he sobbed. "Mom's dead."

Irrational, but still pathetically real for her husband. They all wanted to please the old woman—Ed by earning money, the Bishop by achieving power, Dan by winning fame. None of them would ever have done it, no matter how rich or powerful or famous they had become.

And now it was too late.

Poor Rita didn't want anything. She had given up early, which was probably the better way out.

"All right," Min had replied. "She's dead and I'm sorry

for you. But you have to keep your head these next few days. The police will release that girl and start looking for someone else. Another blowup from you and they'll think you're the most likely someone."

So he had screwed up his nerve and kept his mouth shut. Until tonight.

"If I were that snoopy priest," she had barked at him, "I'd suspect that you knew the whole story."

"Don't I?"

"Not everything."

"Maybe I do know everything."

"Then go to the police and tell them. Get it over with. Put me and the kids through a trial. Spend the rest of your life in prison. Maybe you'll get to like being buggered."

And more recriminations followed, each of them bitterly blaming the other.

There was only one person to blame, and she was dead, much good it would do Ed or Min now.

Good riddance to her. And damn her to hell too.

Min rose from the lawn chair and walked back to the house for another drink. As she went into the kitchen, she saw in the western sky a brief flash of lightning.

Heat lightning, her mother would have said when they were young.

Whatever happened—she wondered as she filled her glass again—to my youth? It had vanished before I even knew it was there.

22

"I regret to have to say it, Father." Vincent Nelligan's cough was dry too, the penalty of a long life of heavy smoking. "She was both a remarkable and a terrible woman. I've known her since she was a child in her First Communion dress. While I cannot say I introduced her to her husband, I was certainly present when he was attracted by her beauty and her intelligence. They were well matched. He possessed the charm, she the business sense. If it had not been for the destruction of his body by the War . . . well, that was a given, I suppose."

He paused to hack again. I hoped it wasn't catching.

We were in one of the first-floor offices of the rectory, looking out on the wind- and rain-swept surfaces of Wabash Avenue. I was not quite sure I wanted any of the members of the Enright family or their intimate friends in my suite, not since it still smelled faintly of Annie Reilly Casey's scent from the previous night, an aroma I did not want contaminated.

Ah, as the Irish would say, the woman is a "divil."

An angel to be exact, but that was not the point just now.

"It was a love match, then?"

"Absolutely, Father, love at first sight for both parties. And, as I say, a good match it would have been if poor Daniel had come home from the War with some of his vitality. But he was a broken man. I'm surprised he lasted eight more years. . . . In any case, Vi had to be mother and father to the children and, of course, financial administrator as well. She was, as I hope you understand, always that. If I may say so, I never knew anyone, man or woman, who had more powerful insights into the intricate and complex world of real estate investment. I confess that as an individual and then as the president of my own bank, I rode to success and wealth on her shoulders. I was not an adviser, Father—" Another dry rasp. "Pardon, rain in the early morning has this effect on me. . . . I was an agent, and a very profitable role that was."

Although Vinney Nelligan was not part of the elite downtown banking world—First Chicago, Continental, Harris—he was known and appreciated in that world. His own West Side neighborhood bank (now relocated in Oak Brook; secure, as he would see it, from the threat of racial integration) had been successful, often when the downtown institutions required government help to keep their doors open. Nonetheless, his seriousness of manner and dress—stopping just short of caricature—seemed more appropriate for the board room of the First Chicago than for a bank whose origins had been at Madison and Crawford, next to the Marboro Theater of happy memory.

"Less successful in family life, I would gather?"

He shook his head sadly. "When the subject was her children, rather than her investments, her shrewdness deserted her. And that ... I hesitate to use the word lest it sound pejorative ... ruthlessness, utterly appropriate in the world of investment, seemed to increase and become inappropriate when she was dealing with her children. Oddly—I might even say, paradoxically"—he played nervously with the large ruby ring on his right hand—"all the financial efforts were directed at assuring the comfort and happiness of her children."

"Indeed. No love of the game for its own sake?"

His dry, pale lips moved in what might be taken for a smile. "There is that for all of us, and it is harmless until it runs out of control. Then, as in the example of poor Edward, it becomes an addiction. All the more dangerous in his case, because he lacks the skills and the talent for the game."

"Indeed."

"Every mistake that one can make in the rearing of children, she made, Father." He shook his head sadly. "And then compounded the mistake by vigorously and sometimes even cruelly punishing them for being nothing more than what she had made them."

"She would not let them go?" I ventured. "Like many parents, she wanted to keep them dependent on her for all her life?"

"I'm afraid," he said, removing a handkerchief from his pocket and coughing into it, "that you have summarized the situation perfectly. None of them, Father, is an adult. The poor Bishop did not, in the final analysis, have the strength of character to be an effective Vatican diplomat; Dan, Lord have mercy on him, has always been a shallow poseur, and Ed ... well, I'm sure you saw what Ed was last night."

"Yet they all had talent, did they not?" I rearranged a stack of baptismal books piled up on the office desk, because this seemed to be an appropriately pastoral thing to do while I was waiting for him to get to the point.

"Oh yes, but the talents they have are not the ones their mother wanted, you see. My wife and I have five children, Father, three sons and two daughters, all of whom are a source of pride and joy to us. We made mistakes, like all parents do, but each of them is an adult able to fend for himself or herself—and indeed, far away from us. We were prepared to let them go. As a result, I am blessed"—he smiled happily and twenty years vanished from his ancient face—"with a wonderful grandson to stand by me in my old age. Violet did not let her children go. And as a result, she was killed by an ungrateful granddaughter."

"You assume that Fionna is the criminal?"

Yes, they all wanted it to be her. Did Vinney Nelligan fear that Fionna would take her money, once it became hers, out of her husband's grandfather's bank?

Perhaps she would if she found irregularities. And Rick would support her decision. There was no doubt as to whom that point guard owed his loyalty, God bless him.

"Certainly," he replied promptly. "She is as tough-minded as Violet was at that age. Because of her mother's influence, I presume, she lacks the instinctive shrewdness that prevented Violet from going too far. The child saw Violet as an obstacle to what she thought would be her happiness. She removed that obstacle. There might have been other less violent ways of achieving her goal." He shrugged his thin old shoulders. "I'm sure the child never thought of them."

"Did you share Mrs. Harrington Enright's opposition to the match between grandchildren?"

He shrugged again and hacked into his handkerchief. "Excuse me, Father, this humid weather is hard on an old man's weak lungs. . . . It is part of the fate of the species that the young must marry and reproduce. Rarely, if ever, do their romantic dreams survive the traumas of the first year of intimacy. I would have preferred that Richard had found a young woman who was better matched to his intelligence and goodness, but rarely are marriages in this modern world based on the appropriateness of the matches. I presume that he will find other relationships that are satisfying in ways that marriage to Rita Downs's daughter cannot be. To answer your question, I had no strong objections and no great expectations either."

"But you were angry that she endeavored to have your grandson dismissed from his job?"

"Furious. As furious as I had been at her during the more than six decades we have known one another. My grandson was in a position, and may still be in a position, where he would be forced to leave Chicago to exercise his great skills as an investor." He beamed happily at the thought of his adored grandson. "I do not pretend to understand these modern computer methods, but there is no doubt that he is brilliant in their use. He can sit there at his terminal in the attic room of our house and deal with the exchange in Singapore in the middle of the night, making a profit while most other traders are asleep. Even that pitiable weakling William Downs tells me that Richard's technical skills are awesome."

"Totally awesome."

"Pardon?"

"Adolescent slang. . . . And her objection to Richard was a reflection on your family too, was it not?"

"I presume so." His fingers twitched nervously. "She would not specify the reasons for her objections to him. Rather she said, as she always did, that she need not give any reason for not liking a proposed spouse. I feel that she would have been opposed to anyone whom Fionna had chosen. She did not want to lose her."

"Ah?"

"I felt—and in truth, I told Richard—that there was a simple way out. Dan, Edward, and Rita had all taken it. If the woman became pregnant, then Violet would change her position and insist on marriage. All he need do was to impregnate his little piece of fluff and the problem would be solved."

"You used those words?"

"Obviously not." His lean nose continued to point toward the ceiling. "Words to that effect which Richard would find more palatable. He was quite upset with me, closer to anger than his sweet disposition normally permits. He would not, he told me, engage in sexual congress with her until they were married. I do not know what is happening with young people these days, Father, when they permit such absurd idealism to interfere with the realities of life."

I will demand many points from Lady Wisdom in the final accounting for letting that one pass.

And I was willing to wager that Rick, as befits the idealists of his generation, used one of the available Anglo-Saxon one-syllable words instead of "sexual congress."

So all I said was, "Lena, God be good to her, was pregnant at the time of her marriage to Dan?"

"It was alleged that she was and that she subsequently suffered a miscarriage. One is permitted to have one's doubts."

"Henry wanted, I think, merely to be a parish priest. Ed, it would seem, wanted to be a businessman. What did Dan want to be?"

"A high school teacher. He was never happier than when he was teaching at St. Ignatius before his ordination. All of them are empty men, lacking the courage to be anything other than what their mother wanted them to be."

"Not hungry?"

"Not in the least. Of course, she did not permit them to be hungry." He folded his handkerchief neatly and put it back into his pants pocket. Then he consulted his watch. A few more seconds closer to his own date with the cemetery. "I pleaded with her to give them some elbowroom. I don't believe she even heard my words. Yet"—he looked at the watch again—"I must insist, Father, that however crude her methods and inappropriate her goals, she nonetheless acted out of the most powerful of loves."

"I understand." Lady Wisdom protect me from such love. "Do you think the conflict about Richard would have ended your friendship with Mrs. Harrington Enright?"

"I told her solemnly that our relationship would be terminated if she drove Richard out of Chicago." He sighed. "I fear the years had dimmed her intelligence, Father. She did not find that outcome at all objectionable."

"So you had good reason to want her dead?"

His tired old eyes widened in surprise. "I? Oh my, Father, you can't believe that at my age someone would engage in a foolish crime of passion, can you?" His laugh turned into another hack. "I would miss Richard if he had to leave Chicago. However, I have suffered other disappointments and survived. Moreover, I suspect that he would have found some other position in the general business area in which her influence was not so great. No, I did not kill her. That is absurd."

"Indeed."

"My purpose in this visit is to speak about poor Eddie. I assume that he told you his sad tale last night?"

"He seemed quite distraught."

"He made a very bad investment, Father. The best thing he could do is to take his losses like a man and abandon his position. However, as much as he might have made an excellent investor if his mother had permitted him to pursue such a career, he is now quite incompetent. He ought rather to continue as a surgeon, build up his capital again, husband the money which he will receive from his legacy, and entrust his investments to someone who is not compelled to go for the long shot at every opportunity."

"He apparently believes that the dollar will rally."

He smiled thinly. "Not when our friend in Washington, a man whose political views are somewhat too liberal for Edward, insists that the dollar is too high."

Never fight the Great Communicator. Ask Tip O'Neill.

"You do not then see his plight as desperate as he sees it?"

"Fortunately for Edward, his wife is a strong and vigorous woman, much stronger than he deserved." He smiled briefly, amused and pleased at the image of Minnie in his head. "Normally she keeps him under careful restraint. She was in Paris when he made this most recent plunge into the commodities market."

"One hears it said that she is not completely faithful to him."

"How can a strong person"—he lifted a dried-up hand in weak protest against injustice—"be expected to be faithful to a weak one? Min fulfills her wifely and motherly duties better than most women of her generation. What she might do in the time that is left over is hardly anyone's affair but hers. Especially," he added with a sickly leer, "when her husband's compulsive interest in interns—male interns, I hasten to add—is no secret. Those with powerful sexual needs must find outlets for them. So long as they act with taste and discretion, I cannot see any sound reasons for objection."

Had he slept with Min earlier in his life?

If she was as omnivorous as I thought she was, he certainly had.

"A remarkable woman," I said tentatively. Well suited to play Dracula's twin sister, I did not add.

"Indeed she is." His complacent smile was appropriate for a dirty old man.

"You have not said much about Rita. It is almost as though she does not matter in the family, save as Fionna's mother."

"Rita is worthless."

"Fluff?"

"Not even much use as that. She could not hold on to her husband. She does not count."

"Indeed."

"The purpose of this visit"—he glanced at his watch again—"is to explain that I did not feel it necessary to inform the police about Edward's forgery of checks from his mother. I assume he told you that last night, in quivering panic?"

"He seemed quite worried about the police."

"I'm sure he is. After all, he was the last person to see his mother alive, although it is impossible to picture him as a killer, is it not, Father?"

"An unlikely image, I would admit."

"Exactly. The police already know about his unfortunate position in dollars. If they knew about the forgery, they would certainly arrest him. He would experience a nervous collapse, inundate the police station with his tears, destroy himself and what little reputation he has left, and all to no avail. The police would not be able to connect him in any certain way with the crime, and he would never be able to act as a surgeon again. I saw no reason to submit him to such a fate."

"Indeed."

We both rose. A dirty old man and a clever old man. Kinky, as the Old Fella had said.

Very kinky indeed. He had come to protect Edward, or so he said. But had he in fact intended to dig Edward's grave for him?

Vincent Nelligan had been convoluted for so many years that he probably did not know anymore whether he was coming or going. And frequently met himself on the way.

He was not to be trusted or believed. He had certain very special tastes in women, it would seem; all other women were worthless, save as the bearers of children and the objects of routine lust.

A dirty, kinky old man, by his own admission more or less.

But why kill anyone at the very end of his own life? Especially when, as he himself had said, there were other ways to arrange matters?

What was his relationship with Violet Harrington Enright? Merely business? Surely she represented the kind of woman that he did not dismiss as fluff. But was she the kind that aroused perverse desire in him?

Probably not, but it would be worth exploring.

"Why did Dan and Lena have to die?" I asked him at the door of the office.

"Gratuitous, was it not, Father? I cannot comprehend . . ." His voice trailed off, then picked up again. "It makes no sense at all. He may have been a useless poseur, but he harmed no one."

"Do you think Fionna is behind this crime too?"

"I cannot imagine why." He reached again for his handkerchief. "Her crime was one of impulse, passion. She lacks self-control, but she is not a monster surely. This crime speaks of deliberate depravity. It is possible that some of her associates feared exposure. . . ."

He looked at his watch once again, clinging to every second, and then walked cautiously down the still slippery sidewalk and turned west on Superior to enter the cathedral for Mass.

The pieces of the puzzle were not fitting together. Indeed, there were no more pieces.

My Lord Cronin, however, added yet another heap of puzzle pieces in the sacristy as we were preparing for the Mass of Resurrection (as we now, with dazzling hope skirting close to presumption, call the funeral Mass).

"The first assignment, Your Riverence," he spoke with the Irish brogue he assays when he feels impish, "progresses. I have them worried. As to the second—" He winked. "If you take my meaning, your friend in Down and Conor called back within a half hour. Incredible efficiency, especially in Ireland."

"The influence of the occupying power, perhaps."

"As you doubtless know already, he confirmed your suspicion in every detail. An old nun, I take it, remembered everything."

The plot thickened.

■

SEVENTH INTERMEZZO

Mary Kate

■───────────────────────────■

23

Mary Kate glanced over the list of the patient population in the psych unit. Not even Labor Day and already crowded. What would it be like the second week in September, the real, if not the symbolic, beginning of a new year as vacations ended and the kids went back to school? It was the time of new beginnings which made people review their pasts and turn neurotic with guilt over wasted opportunities, real or imagined.

Just like a silver wedding.

Two orderlies entered the elevator with a gantry cart. Collecting someone for surgery, no doubt. She glanced at her watch. A little late for surgery.

Back to the list. Definitely she ought to withdraw from hospital practice. Cut back on her case load. You could only help other people when you were sound of mind and body yourself. When her training analyst came back from his August vacation and forced her to face decisions about her life and marriage, she would make that decision anyhow. Why not be mature, impress the old dear, and make it before you see him?

He would, of course, want to know why you had made the decision so soon.

The two orderlies had passed the floor for the surgical cases. What was the matter with them?

She felt better about Fionna. Despite Farley Strangler

and his friends, there was no way Fionna could have been responsible for the death of her uncle and aunt. She felt no rage against them.

And she had called Mary Kate finally. "I was afraid to talk to you, Doctor Murphy. There's something I have to tell you, and I had to think it out first. It's why I was so mad at poor Grandma that Sunday. But I didn't kill her."

She would keep her first appointment next week.

The door of the elevator opened. One of the orderlies jammed the cart between the doors so they could not close.

What the hell?

She dropped her clipboard with the patient list. As she stooped to pick it up, she saw the two switchblades and the two orgasmic grins. She raised her left arm to ward off a descending blade and felt it slice into her arm and the hot flow of blood.

She knew with absolute certainty what would happen next.

24

"She was not a bad woman, Father Ryan. Truly she wasn't. She was hard to get close to, you know, and even harder to like. God knows"—she laughed lightly—"she might have benefited from ten years or so of psychotherapy. But she might not have been able to tie her shoes by then. She was tied together by only a few tight links. Cut one of them and she would have fallen apart."

Mary Feehan and I were walking through the graves of the older plots of Mount Carmel Cemetery, now long since filled. She was leaving from the burial for O'Hare and the flight home to Chief Feehan in their home on Lough Corrib. I asked if we might talk for a few minutes before she left. She agreed, if I would accompany her to the grave of Major Daniel Enright.

And near that grave I would drop my bomb.

"God knows the poor man stopped needing my prayers long ago—he was a gallant man to the end, Father—but I still need to pray for him."

"You were a friend to her?" I asked, struggling to keep up with the woman's long military strides.

"Not to say friend, exactly. More of a confidante. I never pushed my opinion on her, which is probably why she felt free to ask me an occasional question, don't you know?"

"Everyone was pushing opinions on her?"

"Wasn't everyone? Her children, that wee gombeen man Vinney Nelligan, the clergy who followed her around like flies follow a dog in the summer, the people she gave money to?"

"She gave money away?"

"Didn't she give millions, Father, and all of it anonymously? Will you be finding any hospital pavilions named after her or the Major? But aren't there enough that might be."

"Yet she was harsh on her children."

"Didn't she destroy them? All but Rita, who has managed to survive, somehow or the other. Poor thing. Maybe she'll be all right now."

"You believe that she will rejoin her husband?"

"She'd be a damn fool if she didn't, wouldn't she now?"

"That's an arguable position."

"Were you after telling himself and he telling the wee one and she telling me that their sleeping with one another since he came home from the funeral was not fornication, but fidelity?"

"Ah no." I found myself slipping into the mimic's imitation of her soft brogue. "Didn't I say God would consider it fidelity? I made no commitments in the name of the church."

We both laughed.

"There's the grave." She gestured. "Would you lead us in a decade of the rosary, Father?"

So on a sunny, cool, late-August day, we knelt under an

immense oak tree on a carefully trimmed hill, with the hum of the Congress (Eisenhower) Expressway in the distance, and prayed for the repose of the soul of Major Daniel T. Enright, Army of the United States, born August 1, 1915, died December 14, 1953.

"A good man, Father." I helped her to stand up. "Too good for this world."

"Ill treated by your friend Violet."

"Weren't there two sides of it, Father? Two sides? Neither one of them knew how to draw the line on the other, if you take my meaning."

"An essential requirement in a marriage," I agreed as we walked down the shady hill.

"Is it ever?" She laughed. "And among us Irish easy enough usually for the woman and hard enough usually for the man."

"Indeed."

"Ah," she sighed contentedly, "wasn't I after being the lucky one with Tom, my wonderful fire chief?"

"I'm sure you were. . . . Did not Daniel, however, have reason to be upset about the way his parents were treated?"

"Two sides to that too, an't'ather," she said, using the Gaelic for *Father*. "Daniel should have faced the problem before he left. Didn't a lot of their friends, not just that gombeen man from the bank, tell me that the father was round the bend altogether by 1940?"

"So I have heard."

"Daniel was too light-hearted, Violet was too serious," she summed it up, "and they both deteriorated. By the time I came along it was too late altogether. He was glad to die and she was glad to be rid of him. 'Twas a terrible pity, now wasn't it?"

"It was indeed."

We sighed in unison.

"Nonetheless"—I sighed again, a distinctive sigh of my own—"it was, I think, very wise of you to tell Fionna that you were her grandmother. Whatever promises you might have made certainly did not hold under such circumstances.

It eliminated all possible motivation for her to kill her putative grandmother, didn't it?"

She stared straight ahead, face expressionless, head unbowed. We continued to walk down the road toward the cemetery office.

"You're daft, Father," she said finally.

"Come now, Mrs. Feehan, surely you can do better than that. You did not train at St. Mary's in Castlebar as you told me at the wake. Rather you trained at the Royal Victoria in Belfast. You left there shortly before graduation because you were pregnant. Later you returned and finished your work. Then, perhaps, you went to Castlebar. When he knew he was dying, Daniel Enright pleaded that, as the only real love of his life, you come to America to take care of him. Violet, party to the old arrangement by which your daughter became her daughter, accepted this new arrangement, perhaps willingly, because then she did not have to care for her dying husband in his last painful agonies. You were nicely rewarded in his will for your love and care. You remained in America to marry—happily, I take it—and raise your own family. Yet your first love for Daniel has not been eroded by time and never will be."

"She told you?" Her voice was as steady and hard as her face.

"Fionna? You underestimate your granddaughter. If she has not been given permission to tell practically perfect Rick, she has not done so. You may depend on that."

"Then how do you know?"

"Insight."

"Of what sort?"

"You were eighteen in 1944 when Daniel Enright was stricken with pneumonia in Northern Ireland. Then you appear eight years later to take care of him in his death agony. You have a very special relationship with his family which even the hardened Violet is either unwilling or unable to end. Both Rita and Fionna like you, which means that you have been kind to them, as well you might. You tell me you trained in Castlebar when I ask you if your nursing school was in the U.K.—which includes the six counties, as you well know. You engage in a tête-à-tête with the fair Fionna immediately before she tries to tell Mrs. Harrington Enright that she is not her real grandmother. Doubtless you had revealed the secret so Fionna might counter the threat against Richard with a threat of her own, a threat which would call into question half of the Enright inheritance. To check my suspicions I needed only determine whether a Mary O'Brien from County Mayo was in training at the Royal Victoria in Belfast in 1944 and if perchance she had to drop out of school for a time. Sickness in the family was the given explanation. Being a Protestant hospital, the Royal Victoria keeps excellent records."

"You're going to tell the whole world?"

"I'm not going to tell anyone unless I need to so that no one else will be killed. Fionna knows, the Cardinal knows, I know."

"And Richard. You can't expect a woman to keep a secret like that from her man." She laughed lightly. "I had to tell her, Father. I was sure that Daniel wouldn't mind. I'll never forgive myself for not telling poor Rita. But I feared what it would have done to her."

"And Fionna?"

"She was delighted." The woman flushed and smiled, her humor and her common sense returning. "More that I was her grandmother than that Violet wasn't. Whatever doubts she had about resisting her were swept away. That was, of course, my intention. I hardly thought that she would return to the boat immediately and attempt to have it out with Violet."

"Not quite aware of how much of you there was in her?"

"Perhaps," she said ruefully. "Wasn't she after telling me later that she would have added, if the gun were not fired, 'But I love you anyway.' Isn't poor Fionna the sort of young woman who must do all things that are virtuous at once?"

"Fersure."

We were approaching the cemetery office. She glanced

at her watch and turned off down a side road back into the cemetery.

"I don't see how it can be related to the killings, do you, Father? Especially if, as I am, you are certain that Fionna is innocent."

"My exact words—"

"—were that it was most unlikely."

"The child has a photographic memory."

"Almost."

"Can you tell me about Daniel?"

"Of course, now that you know the heart of the story, why not the rest? His unit had been trained in the Mojave Desert for six months, on combat rations that included no fruits or vegetables. The men who planned the training had not the most elementary notion of the nutritional needs of the human body. If you send someone with an enormous vitamin-C deficiency into a climate like Northern Ireland's and house them in an old castle without central heating, you are inviting pneumonia. I found him in a library."

"In a library?"

She laughed, a happy eighteen-year-old again. "In a library, not that Daniel was ever much of a reader. Or that I am, for that matter, our Rita makes up for both of us. . . . Funny, Father, that's the first time I have called her our Rita."

"She is an interesting woman."

"The only one of the family who still has a chance. Anyway, Daniel went to the library to stay warm, and I went to find a book I needed for class. I found him lying asleep in the stacks with a high fever—a hundred and four when we finally got him into the hospital. He'd been there for two days, too weak to walk or even call for help. I summoned an ambulance and took him to the hospital. One of his friends stole some penicillin from the American hospital and we saved his life. Just barely."

I listened. There was nothing to say.

"You can imagine what happened after that. He was a delightful, generous American, and I was an innocent, lovestruck virgin from a poor farm in Mayo. He expected to die in the landings. I thought I had saved him from one death to deliver him over to another. I knew there was a wife somewhere whom he did not love, but that he did not love her was not the point. I loved him with every ounce of my underweight body. That was all that mattered. I suppose we were sinning, though some priests your age now talk about compassion, which God knows we needed."

"God is not a moral theologian, for which we all may be grateful."

"Daniel went off to war. I didn't tell him I was pregnant. He was wounded in the first landing and somehow managed to find me in Dublin just before our little girl was born. I told him I would have to put her in an orphanage—we didn't have many adoptions in Ireland in those days, people were too poor. He wanted to take her home with him. He explained about the inheritance and that his wife had had a miscarriage and a hysterectomy. I remember his exact words: 'She won't care where the little girl came from or that I'm her father. So long as we can pretend that she's the mother, it'll be all right. It's the money that counts in her life.' "

"Did you come to believe later that he was judging her too harshly?"

"Yes, I did. She was ready to raise the child and forgive him. She wanted the money, that's the kind of woman she was. But she loved the little girl as much as her own children."

"An often misguided love."

"But never ungenerous."

We paused at the end of the road.

"I loved him, Father. I still do, as much as when I was a silly, green teenager. Not the same kind of love I feel for my husband, not a better love, not a poorer love. Just love. But I never had to hate her. I still don't."

Again I said nothing.

"I don't know how Rita was flown back to America or how it was made to seem that she was Vi's child. Later on, when I asked him, he said that many people were away in the War and that it was easy to do things that you couldn't do a few years later. He asked that I never tell Rita, or anyone who might tell her, the truth about her origins. He didn't make me promise—Daniel was not that kind of man. He asked me and I agreed. He was worried that it might hurt her if she knew. Now I'm not sure."

It was none of my business, but I was sure that if Daniel Enright knew what would happen in the years after he died, he would have made her promise just the opposite.

"She loves you as a good friend?"

"I tried as best I could to persuade her to follow poor Bill to California. She couldn't do it. I was afraid that she would be destroyed altogether if I told her the truth."

"And now?"

"Would I be knowing the answer to that? What do you think?"

"More to the point, what does the fair Fionna think?"

She smiled happily. "If you have to ask that, you either don't know our Fionna or you're really not the legendary Blackie Ryan."

"Who killed Vi?"

"The Hispanics?"

"Why?"

"She was about to turn them over to Immigration?"

A simple, rational explanation from a simple, rational woman.

And a loyal and incredibly brave woman who seemed to be free of both hatred and regrets.

Would she have killed her rival—for that was surely what Vi was—to protect her daughter and her granddaughter?

Backed into a corner, sure, especially if she saw it as some form of self-defense. But why wait for so many years?

"Were you resentful that you could never marry him?"

"Resentful?" We began to walk back to the cemetery office. There was a cab waiting for her. "What good would that have done? I wished I could have married him, but that was not possible. And didn't he die too soon? Didn't God want him? Neither of us could have him."

"That's very reasonable, Mrs. Feehan."

Too reasonable for my suspicious mind.

"I'm not a reasonable person, Father Ryan. Not in the least. I'm at least as passionate—and I can say it now—as my daughter and my granddaughter. What you hear is a rationalization I have developed and lived with for more than thirty years. Daniel made me promise to marry just before he died. He looked up at me with those wonderful blue eyes and said, 'Mary, I won't take no for an answer. Find yourself a good man to love. Don't mourn me for more than six months.' "

"You agreed?"

"Without my heart being in the promise. He was right, as usual. I fell in love with Tom the first time I laid eyes on him. I never would have given him a second look if Daniel had not made me promise to look for a good man."

"Any regrets?"

"Our Rita—I like the words, Father—is not a happy woman. But I don't think she would be any happier if she grew up in an Irish orphanage. Do you, Father? And she still has a chance. God always gives us second chances, doesn't He? As long as we live."

Undeniable theology.

And a moving story. What did it contribute to a solution to the mystery?

Who would want to kill Vi Enright because of the secret of Rita's origins? Rita? But she apparently did not know the truth. Fionna? But by definition she was innocent, unless an astonishing coincidence had taken place. This handsome, poised woman? Maybe, but again, why wait so long?

More puzzles. No answers.

"You'll look after Fionna?" she asked as we shook hands at the cab.

"She can look after herself and she has Remarkable Rick."

"She needs a priest. I needed one and could never find the right one."

"I'll be around," I promised.

I watched the cab pull out on Manheim Road. In a few hours she would be back in County Mayo. If necessary, she could be extradited.

I drove back to the cathedral, bemused and confused by the complexity of humankind. What could one make of the love between Mary O'Brien and Daniel Enright?

Sinful according to the old textbooks. A maturational experience according to some of the new psychological ethicians. Or perhaps another case of Lady Wisdom up to her favorite trick of drawing straight with crooked lines.

On the crowded expressway I prepared a mental list of the possible suspects:

Fionna Downs? Statistically improbable, but with the motive now of rage over a life of deception.

Rita Downs? Also with a very powerful revenge motive. If she knew about it. Moreover, her presumed mother had destroyed her marriage, a passionate love match.

Harry Enright? In a fit of outrage about his mother's intervention in his career problems.

Dan Enright? For money to start a magazine? But why would he then be killed?

Ed Enright? Best motive and best opportunity. But hard to see as a killer.

Min Enright? Nothing on her except that she was kinky and ruthless.

Vincent Nelligan? To protect his admired grandson. To settle scores from the past. But the grandson could be salvaged less drastically—and why wait till you are on the edge of your own grave?

Richard Nelligan? To protect Fionna and his own career. Possibly. Love can drive one to violent action in the defense of the beloved.

Bill Downs? To reclaim the wife he still passionately loved. Why not? Except that he was at a dinner party in Beverly Hills, California. Through agents, the Hispanic servants, who might also be the hit men who had killed Dan and Lena? But why wait till now?

Mary O'Brien Feehan? An excellent reason to seek revenge. And the kind of person who would wait patiently and for a long time to destroy a rival, if she was of a mind to want revenge.

Fionna's scuba diver, on his own or in cooperation with the family, or as an agent for the shadow world, or in some mixture of the three? But then what of the problems of the windows? And the second gun?

That problem applied to all the previous scenarios.

And why kill Dan and Lena Enright?

Perhaps their deaths were totally unrelated. Another accident. Two guns. Two murders. One story of real and unreal grandmothers.

None of it made any sense.

I walked into the rectory, still confused and bemused.

"Judge Kane on the phone, Blackie." One of my associates shoved a portable phone into my hand. "She's been trying to find you all afternoon."

"Punk? Eileen. You'd better come right out to the Murphys'. The slashers attacked Mary Kate."

25

It was not like an Irish wake. The assembly of the Ryan/ Murphy clans in the Murphy house was too quiet for an Irish wake. We micks, the great Gaels of Ireland, the men whom God made mad, laugh at death—and make love in the fields outside a wake in defiance of death.

But a brush with death reduces us to silence. The nearness of death frightens us. Its presence makes us laugh. Don't ask me for an explanation.

The whole solemn high assembly, then, was silent. Except for the principal character, who was talking the proverbial blue streak. She was flanked by Eileen and Caitlin, the

former sibling rival and senior confidante, the latter pregnant elder daughter and junior confidante—the typical triune appearance of Irish matriarchal deities celebrated in the
New Grange circular symbols.

"I knew exactly what I had to do." Her eyes were
glowing brightly—morphine and exultation. "It was just like
the lesson the revered master taught us about resisting two
attackers in an elevator . . . the revered master, Red, is my
karate teacher, not my husband."

Red Kane, the famous columnist, an Irish Royko it is
said, was taking notes.

Mary Kathleen Ryan Murphy object to her story being
spread all over the papers?

And the Pope is Hindu!

"Actually," she continued, "it was easier than the exercise because the elevators at Little Company are bigger than
the box at karate class and those two geeks were not ready
for me. No way."

"Did you shout 'Ughhhhh' like they do in the karate
films?"

"Enter the Punk"—she beamed at me—"with the
insightful question as always. Of course I did. Well, I simply
hit the first geek in the throat with clipboard and kicked the
second one in the jaw. Then I stomped on their balls and
broke the wrists of their knife hands with the clipboard. That
pretty much took the fight out of them. So I shoved the cart
out the door and rode them down to Emergency."

"I should think so."

"Beat the shit out of them, Johnny." The Old Fella
beamed. "The absolute and total shit."

"Indeed."

Cathy Curran slipped a very small glass into my hand. It
was not Jameson's but the most special of celebratory
liquids—Bushmill's Black Label.

"When the elevator opened in Emergency"—Joe Murphy's eyes were moist—"they saw these two gentlemen on
the floor, screaming with pain and covered with blood, and
my good wife, controlling the bleeding in her left arm with

her right hand, still kicking her assailants. I don't think LCM will ever quite recover."

"Come over here and kiss me, Punk," my eldest sibling demanded. "And be careful of my left arm. I think I was driven to clobber those geeks by the image in the back of my head of you saying my funeral Mass."

It is reported that my eyes were moist too.

"Carlos and Tomas?"

"The same," she agreed. "I recognized them from the boat."

"Very dangerous *hombres*," Mike Casey spoke up. "Drug milieu. Same kind of knives that killed the Dan Enrights. And the police found part of a fingerprint on Lena's purse which they didn't announce to the world. It appears to match Carlos's. So they're saying the mysteries are solved."

"I think I had better watch my step from now on," Joe Murphy, who had been observing his wife for signs of shock, said easily, "especially around surgical carts."

Then the party began, and the glow in Mary Kate's eyes began to fade. Nine stitches, they said. The wound would hurt like hell for a few days. And there'd be some bad dreams.

And triumphant ones.

The glow faded out of her eyes. They began to glaze. But it would be a long time before Joe or anyone else could persuade her to go to bed.

It was patently not the case that the mysteries were solved. The heat was off the cops. Nothing more. The source of the problems was still at large. And now it would be a battle to the bitter end.

The killer had gone after one of my family. That was totally unacceptable.

All I had to do was to figure out who the killer was.

Before another and perhaps more successful attempt to kill.

26

Padre Adolpho looked like a malign Friar Tuck. He was a big man, six three or four, close to three hundred pounds, with thick ham hands, a bald head, and tiny dangerous eyes that stared out unblinkingly at the world through massive folds of flesh. Unlike American Franciscans whose uniform has become the 85-percent Dacron, white sport shirt hanging over the belt, he wore the traditional garb—brown habit and sandals. His robe had not been blemished by washing; the stains of many meals decorated it with more color than the uniform of a Russian general.

Mike the Cop and I watched him add more splotches to his garment as he consumed an immense plate of pasta—his eyes on not the food but the doorway.

It was said, according to my Irish friends in Rome, that he killed by strangling his victims. I didn't doubt it.

My Lord Cronin's contacts in Rome were moving slowly. Padre Adolpho was not a dangerous man, he was told. Bishop Enright was in no danger. There would be no scandal.

They were stonewalling for reasons of their own. Or perhaps for no reason at all, but because it was in their nature to stonewall.

Meanwhile, Mike learned that there had been a contact between Padre Adolpho and the two hit men who were recovering under guard in County Hospital from their ill-advised assault on my fearsome sibling, more recently turned Chicago folk heroine. He seemed to have made an offer to spring them from the jail, an offer which the citizens and officers-at-arms found very interesting.

"Get him the hell out of town," My Lord Cronin demanded, perhaps not altogether unreasonably. "I warned them there would be a scandal. They said there wouldn't be. So prove them wrong. See to it, Blackwood."

Naturally. What else?

It turned out that it would be relatively easy. From the point of view of the INS, Adolpho was that highly desirable person, the illegal alien. The police had learned from their "friends on the West Side" that the fat friar had slipped across the border from Canada. So Immigration would arrest him, TV cameras would be waiting for him after the arrest, and the media would describe him as a "priest–hit man," the ultimate in hyphenated clergy, and tell the tale of the long history of clerical involvement in Sicily with the Mafia.

They would even report the story of Pius XII's regrettable reversal on the prosecution of the criminal clerics before his death and John XXIII's reversal of that reversal.

One scandal whipped up and served to order.

Who fed the background to the media?

What else are gray eminences for?

So Mike the Cop and I were sitting at the back of a dark, homey Tailor Street restaurant that smelled of freshly made sausage, salami, and red peppers, not too far from the campus of the University of Illinois at Chicago—waiting for it to "go down," as they say in that part of the world. The floor and the tables were bare of covering, but the plates were piled high with some of the best Southern Italian food to be purchased west of the Hudson River.

Mike was too nervous to eat. I, on the other hand, was raised to think it was a sin to waste food. So I was dispatching my pasta and his and sipping on the contents of the bottle of Chianti that apparently came with the table— *classico speciale riservato*, which, of course, in the Italian way of things means an ordinary inexpensive table wine.

Adolpho, according to our "friends," or perhaps more appropriately "friends of friends," ate lunch and dinner at this restaurant every day, without going through the formalities of asking for a table or a check.

On the West Side not even Big Tuna himself got away without asking for a check.

INS wanted to pick him up in the evening after his incredibly large dinner. Mike's friends on the CPD insisted that the alleged perpetrator be apprehended—their words—at noon, for the obvious reason that the apprehension would then make both the five o'clock and the ten o'clock news.

MAFIA PRIEST ARRESTED! the *Sun Times* would announce. Not especially good for the church, but not as bad as establishing the precedent that denizens of the cages in the Vatican basements—I speak figuratively—were to be permitted to wander the streets of Chicago.

In point of fact, those streets were not especially safe even in the absence of Franciscan hit men.

"Where the hell are they?" my cousin demanded impatiently.

We were at the very back of the restaurant, wearing hats of course, *de rigueur*. I had traded in my clerical shirt for a polka-dot sport shirt, which I felt appropriate for the occasion and the environment. I saw no reason to forsake my Chicago Bears windbreaker, especially since I accepted the Old Fella's diagnosis that Jim McMahon was "hungry." Indeed, I pointed out to my worthy parent that if McMahon had not been injured at the time of the 'Niner game the previous year, we would have made Superbowl XIX.

I looked at my watch. "Don't worry, Mike," I mumbled through my mouthful of pasta-coated meat, "it will go down on time."

"Go down?" he exploded. "Blackie, you fit into this environment too well. You scare me."

"Alas, not nearly as much as my sister the now legendary Mary Kathleen scares half the city."

The windows of the restaurant, which as far as one could tell was nameless, had not been washed since before the Great Depression. Nonetheless, I observed a van pull up outside. Channel 9. All present and accounted for.

Adolpho was working his way with commendable system through a second plate of pasta. Outside there was a brief flicker of sapphire light. Chicago's Finest.

Was Adolpho involved in the Enright killings? Or was he merely trying to become involved? I inclined to the latter explanation. And I was reassured by his clumsiness. Even in the shadow world, bureaucracies were incompetent. And quite possibly irrelevant too.

The pressure on the police and the State's Attorney had declined since my sibling's memorable battle with the forces of evil. They had an indictment in the Dan and Lena killings as well as an "assault with deadly weapon" in the attack on Mary Kate.

"Assault *on* a deadly weapon," her virtuous and long-suffering husband had observed ruefully.

The media seemed satisfied with the conclusion that the unfortunate Carlos and Tomas had also killed Mrs. Violet Harrington Enright, a theory with several holes in it through which one could fly a 747. The State's Attorney knew this too, because despite Patty Anne Slattery's fierce admonitions about suits for malicious prosecution, charges against Fair Fionna had yet to be dropped.

A killer still lurked. I still did not know that person's name. Maybe Father Adolpho did.

The most curious event since the Amazon Queen of Longwood Drive had trashed her two would-be assailants (a phrase of the same solemnity as "alleged perpetrators") was a conversation in my study with Harry Enright.

He had appeared at my door, clad as usual in full clerical garb with ring and pectoral cross. I suspected that he wore them in bed at night. With purple pajamas.

"If you will permit me, Monsignor, I should like to comment again on your remarks at the wake of my brother and his wife. They were quite remarkable, you know."

"Standard Catholic teaching," I murmured, uneasy as I always am with unalloyed compliments.

"They were stark, almost harsh words. They did not hide the evil or the tragedy of death, as many funeral sermons, ah, homilies, do."

"We work for the crucified Jesus, not for Pollyanna."

"Yet your few comments, even the touch of wit about demanding an explanation from God—"

"No joke. She had better have some good ones."

"—ignited Christian hope in all of us. I am most appreciative. Fionna, with her photographic memory, has quoted you verbatim a number of times. It was most moving."

"The child could be dangerous."

"In addition to expressing our collective gratitude for your remarks and my own personal gratitude as well, I wondered if I might ask you a question. . . . No, no, there is no need for me to sit down. I will not consume any more than a few moments of your precious time. I have a rather simple question."

"Indeed."

"Do you think His Eminence would view with approval a request of mine to be named pastor of a parish in the black community? I fear," he smiled deprecatingly, "I would need a competent curate—I mean *associate* of course—to teach me the ways of such a parish, but if His Eminence did not object."

Brigid, Patrick, and Columkille!

Was the saucy medieval Madonna grinning behind me, her "I told you so" grin?

Is the Pope Bishop of Rome?

"I'm sure His Eminence would be most pleased with such a request. If you wish, I might have a quiet word with him."

"That would be very kind. I'd be most grateful."

The nice aspect of it all, don't you see, is that blacks with their admirable love of costume and ceremony (from which we micks, too much influenced by the somber Anglo-Saxon occupying power, ought to learn) would be ecstatic over Harry's formality and solemn robes.

My Lord Cronin would about die!

I would pass on the request to him at the same time I reported the success of our carefully staged scandal.

Right on schedule, three normal-sized men from the INS walked in, looking very official and very bureaucratic. They were asking for trouble. I would have appeared with half the border patrol, dressed like the red-neck sheriffs in the movies and talking pure red-neck like the curvaceous Cindasoo.

Adolpho was on his feet before they reached his table, ready and eager for a fight.

The leader of the Immigrations produced a card and began to read rights, something that has never bothered that organization much.

The big friar swept plates, glasses, and silverware from his table with a single mighty swing of his left hand, picked up the table with his right, and used it as a battering ram to brush aside the protectors of our nation's borders.

Three citizens-at-arms appeared at the door. "Halt, police!" they shouted.

In vain. Bellowing like an outraged cow elephant whose offspring were in danger, the Franciscan smashed a plate-glass window with an almost casual swipe of his battering ram—a thick wooden table in hands such as his can be a very deadly weapon—and plunged through the temporary exit he had created. Outside, a dozen or so sapphire lights began to whirl.

Mike Casey the Cop and I raced to the smashed window and arrived just in time to see Padre Adolpho demolish the Channel 2 minicam with a quick back-and-forth swing of his table. Then he turned on Channel 5.

Ah, it would look wonderful on the five o'clock news. Some of the best supper-table violence since the Vietnam war—a big, ugly priest in a medieval robe hurling a table at you through your TV screen. (While perhaps your cute blond daughter announced, "He's here.")

The stalwart citizens-at-arms regrouped and counterattacked. In the absence of Richard Dent and Dan Hampton and William "The Refrigerator" Perry, it required ten of them to bear Adolpho to the sidewalk. There was nervous cheering from the TV crews as the handcuffs were fixed to his thick wrists.

I would not have been surprised if, as in the Hercules films, he had not simply ripped the cuffs apart and attacked the citizens-at-arms again.

In this case, however, fact did not imitate fiction. The good Franciscan was dragged to a paddy wagon—an ethnic slur, I might add—and carried off to a cell in the nearest police station, a strongly locked cell, I devoutly hoped.

The clips would run at least three minutes that evening, delightful entertainment. They would end with a statement from a Chancery Office spokesperson that Cardinal Cronin deplored the presence of such men in the United States and was pleased that he would shortly be deported. Stronger remarks about Vatican corruption would be eliminated by the Cardinal's humble and self-effacing *éminence gris*.

Naturally.

"Well," Mike Casey whispered, "you wanted a scandal, you got one."

"Solemn high and in full color with four-track Dolby sound," I replied modestly. "That should dispose of the Vatican connection in the Enright case."

"Do you think there was ever such a connection?"

"Who knows?"

The killer, the real killer, was still at large. Did Adolpho know who he was? If he did, he was most unlikely to admit it before he was crammed into an Alitalia DC-10 and shipped back to where he belonged.

The killer had developed a taste for violence and death. He would strike again.

27

"I can hardly wait to get Fee into bed with me, Father Blackie," Rick Nelligan confessed as I brought him a second helping of Bavarian chocolate cake. "It's all I can do now not to tear her clothes off every time I see her. I dream at night of all the wonderfully obscene things I can do to her . . . I should say with her, shouldn't I? . . . when we are married. I hope that's not wrong?"

A candid young man, deeply in love. Ready to kill for that love?

"It seems to be the way Lady Wisdom has designed the species." I sighed in protest (totally false, in fact, because I think the whole process quite clever of Lady Wisdom).

We were eating lunch in the dining room of the Chicago Yacht Club, perhaps the most lovely place in all of the city to eat lunch, the skyline lurking proudly behind you, the lake with its picture-postcard toy boats pinned on the blue waters in front of you.

And the best pastry cook in Chicago—or so it seemed to my prejudiced tastes.

"I think I will always feel that way about her," he continued fervently, obviously finding the fair Fionna more attractive than the cake, understandably enough. "I know," he blushed, "that most swains are obsessed by their brides-to-be. But Fionna is different. She is smart and generous and talented."

"Indeed. Moreover, there is evidence that her mother is still extremely attractive to her father."

"Understandably." He cut a small piece of cake with his fork. "I suppose it's because I'm just sort of generally horny, but Rita drives me out of my mind too. I can imagine what it must be like for poor Bill."

Another vote for the eroticism, as yet invisible to me, of Rita Enright Downs.

"That relationship is on its way to renewed legitimacy?"

"Fee says"—he smiled amiably—"you called it fidelity, not fornication."

"Fionna has a dangerous memory."

"I'm not sure what will happen. Mrs. Downs is a very unhappy woman with extremely low self-esteem."

A future mother-in-law has low self-esteem: thus do our young people talk these days. Not necessarily inaccurately.

The charges against Fionna were still pending, but the papers and TV commentators had forgotten about them. Padre Adolpho had been transported, with considerable difficulty, back to Leonardo da Vinci airport at Fiumicino, where, perhaps regrettably, he had not been gunned down by Islamic terrorists desirous of a head start on the houri supply in paradise.

A vigorous debate raged in the press between Catholics as to whether it was anti-Catholic to accuse a priest of having Mafia connections. The history of the corruption of some Franciscan houses in Sicily, a documented fact, was simply denied by the Catholic right.

The dollar continued to fall and margin calls against Ed Enright grew more insistent. His house, already groaning under a double mortgage, was on the market. His Mercedes had already been sold.

A *very* highly placed Vatican official went so far as to admit to My Lord Cronin that he had been correct in predicting a scandal. He was congratulated on having responded to the unfortunate matter very well. A *bella figura* award for Sean Cronin. Rare enough. I'm sure he accepted it churlishly. He was also *given* to understand that there would be no more problems in the matter of Harry Enright.

Bill Downs was packing to return to UCLA after Labor Day. His wife's return with him was problematic. I suspected that there was some additional and secret reason for self-contempt that had prevented her from accompanying him before and still influenced her.

A reason that would justify murder?

I was saving the enigmatic Rita till the end of my list of suspects.

Luisa was still at the convent, assiduously studying English and learning to read and write that totally irrational language properly.

The stitches were out of Mary Kate's arm—the thin scar pronounced by all female relatives of whatever generation to be "distinguished."

Oh, I picked it up at Heidelberg dueling with Colombian drug hit men.

The killer was still at large.

And next weekend the Tri State Regatta would race from Chicago to St. Joseph to Michigan City and back to Chicago.

Rick Nelligan was crewing on one of the smaller boats.

"We did not have enough money for sailing when I was growing up," he said, with no trace of self-pity. "I bought a twelve-foot plastic boat when I was at Stanford and sailed in the bay on weekends. I'm looking forward to racing on Lake Michigan for the rest of my life. Maybe next year or the year after I can join the Mackinaw race."

"The fabled Fionna inherits the power craft too, does she not?"

He nodded gravely; everything about Rick Nelligan was grave, even his statement of desire for his beloved. "I don't think she wants to keep it. It's an old boat and the upkeep is enormous. On the other hand, because it's now something of a classic, its value appreciates every year." He smiled and some of the gravity disappeared. "Even with the costs of maintenance the boat is a reasonably good investment, not as much as a killing in gold futures, but better than S and L rates."

The *Violetta* had been transferred from the Monroe Street dock to the old Coast Guard station at the entrance to Chicago harbor at the mouth of the river. I would have to go out there this afternoon to perform my inspection ritual. Without magnifying glass, mind you.

"She will never lack wise financial counsel."

"I'm marrying her for her money." He laughed and the rest of his gravity was destroyed. "You know she thinks people will really believe that? How can anyone look at Fee and imagine that money would be in a man's mind? I had no idea when I first saw her at a party in Palo Alto that she had any money at all. She dressed as if she were the daughter of a poor dirt farmer. We fought all night over James Joyce, and I made up my mind I wanted her forever. It took me two years to work up enough nerve to tell her that. Anyway"—he shrugged his broad shoulders—"I wouldn't have needed the money. If I stayed at O'Rourke, I could have bought my own boat in a couple of years. Not as big as the *Violetta*, maybe, but all I'd ever need."

It would surely be said, despite her attractiveness and

energy and intelligence, that Fionna's principal charm for her husband was money. It did not, one must admit, make her any less attractive. Both young people would have to live with that charge. At least Rick was not so senseless as to refuse to touch any of her wealth. Quite the contrary, his plan to administrate it instead of earning his own wealth dialoguing via computer with Singapore late at night showed commendable wisdom.

"You did not know of the Enrights?"

"Sure, but my parents stayed away from Chicago. Grandpa Nelligan was not the world's most sympathetic father. So I had never met any of them. And the name Downs didn't mean a thing to me. She knew who I was, once she learned my last name, but that was at the end of the argument and after the kissing—and by then it didn't matter."

So much for the wisdom of Lady Wisdom's arrangements of human reproduction.

"Under the circumstances, is it not unusual that you should elect to live with your grandfather and indeed to take care of him?"

"My father wasn't very happy about it." He was now progressing nicely through the Bavarian chocolate cake. If chocolate cake, even from the best pastry cook in town, is no substitute for sex, still it must be candidly admitted that sex—either real or in the case of Rick Nelligan, fantastical—is no substitute for Bavarian chocolate cake.

"Your parents and your grandfather are estranged?"

"To put it mildly. Dad's in construction contracting, an up-and-down business the last ten years. He's never received a penny from Grandpa and wouldn't take it if it were offered. None of my aunts and uncles speak to him. At least they were able to get away from him, which is more than Mrs. Enright's children could do."

The young man was speaking frankly. Or appearing to speak frankly. He was bright and in love and hence likely to obscure any truth that might remotely threaten the fantastic Fionna.

"How would you evaluate your grandfather's relationship with Mrs. Enright?"

"Oh, they loved one another." He waved his fork. "Wasn't that obvious? Not the way Fionna and I love one another, not even the way I hope we will love each other fifty years from now, but they still loved each other."

"Romantically?"

"You're the one, Father Blackie"—he jabbed his finger at me—"who talks about the way Lady Wisdom arranges to keep the species going."

"*Touché.*" I conceded. "When they were young, there almost had to be a certain sensual, not to say erotic, element in their relationship. It does not follow that they were in love."

"You'd believe that it did if you could see the way the poor old fellow is moping around the house these days. Grandma isn't much help to him, never was, poor lady. He's lost a woman he loved and with whom he was once in love. It shows."

"You think they were lovers?"

He paused for a moment. "I doubt it, Father. Not in those times, the way they were raised. I'm sure they thought about it. However, money, not pleasure, held them together."

"Sounds a bit kinky."

"As kinky as a corkscrew. I didn't say it was an ordinary love affair. There was something a little perverse about both of them. But mildly twisted love is still love, isn't it?"

Strange philosophical talk from a specialist in computer science. Doubtless the vocabulary and perhaps the ideas themselves had been furnished by Fionna—at no extra charge.

"Lady Wisdom," I agreed, "is by definition a pluralist."

He nursed the last pieces of the chocolate cake and continued to quote trippingly on the tongue, the conclusions he had reached, probably in long and delightful discussion with his young woman. "I don't think that their love was necessarily good for them. They probably would have been happier and better human beings if they never met one another. But maybe there were times when they helped one another in positive ways. Anyway, he loved her, no question about that."

"Ambivalently?"

"Aren't all loves ambivalent?"

Fionna's philosophy, absorbed and made his own by her young man, smelled of inexperience and book reading, but it was not necessarily wrong.

"Even yours for the frothy Fionna?"

"I wondered what the next *f* word would be . . . flaky, fabulous, fantastic, frothy . . . I like that." He polished off the last bite of the cake. "Sometimes . . . well, not really, but I think I'd like to break the little bitch's neck. She is terribly bossy, Father. I guess it comes with being an Irish woman."

"Tell me about it."

"But I hold my own!"

"A man of remarkable fortitude."

He would have to be.

"You can't figure out me and my grandfather, can you, Father Blackie?"

"I'm supposed to ask the questions." I sighed, graciously admitting defeat. Fionna was, after all, well-matched with her match.

"The thing is—and yes, I will have another slice of cake—I like the poor old guy. He's at that age in life when most of the passion and all of the desire have gone out of life. He hungers only for someone to be nice to him, to listen to his stories, to assure him that he didn't live in vain. I enjoy the stories, even learn something about human nature from them, maybe only negatively, and it doesn't cost me anything to be pleasant to him. Anything wrong with that?"

"Nothing, except that others will find your good example offensive."

"I hope my children will visit me—us, I should say— when I'm about ready to die. But if things go wrong and they don't, then maybe your friend Lady Wisdom will send a grandson or a granddaughter to smile at me and cheer me up."

"Your father and mother think . . . ?"

"That he's a monster."

"And you respond . . . ?"

"That he was once, but now he's only a tired old man getting ready to die. He did a lot of bad things that a banker wouldn't dare try today, Father. But there are a lot of respectable, church-going bankers today, and not only in Florida—thanks for the cake—who launder drug money, blood-soaked drug money at that. And when the government finally blows the whistle on insider trading in leveraged buyouts and mergers, a lot of upstanding citizens might find themselves in jail. Grandpa was no worse than them."

"Not necessarily better."

"I won't do those things, Father." He laid down his fork. "I don't believe in them. If I ever did, Fee would leave me."

"You merely argue for sympathy and kindness toward an old man with many regrets. . . . Do you think he killed Mrs. Enright?"

"Impossible." Rick picked up the fork again. "I told you that he loved her and is dragging around the house mourning for her. Besides, why kill her?"

"She was threatening your future?"

"He wouldn't kill for such an unimportant reason, Father." The possibility was so unlikely to Rick Nelligan that he dug into the second helping of cake with gusto. If Fionna were to be loved with comparable enjoyment and determination, she would be a very fortunate young woman. And very busy.

"Why unimportant?"

"Mrs. Enright was overreacting, as I told Fee almost every day when she cried about it. She could have had me fired at O'Rourke and maybe a few other Chicago-based firms, but the nationals? Citicorp? Merrill, Lynch? Paine Webber? Everyone associated with her seems to have an exaggerated notion of her power, probably because she did too."

"So you would not have had to leave Chicago."

"I would *not* leave. Someone has to help Grandpa to die and Fee to live. This is my city now, Father, and a wonderful, beautiful city—look at the lake and the skyline and the Buckingham Fountain over there! I will not be driven out of it. *Ever.*"

"Did your grandfather and the frenzied Fionna believe you?"

"Sometimes. They were afraid of Mrs. Enright's ruthlessness. She was that kind of woman."

"But you liked her too?"

He stirred uneasily. "Not as much as Grandfather, but she was going to die soon too, Father. And she had a lot of regrets too. And"—he brightened a bit—"she sure was interesting."

"Who killed her?"

"Not Fionna. You yourself said that it was most unlikely, though I don't understand why."

"I'll explain someday perhaps. But if not the fine-spun Fionna, then who?"

"Dan to get the money for his magazine and then he was killed by the Colombians because he wouldn't pay them off?"

A bold theory and with some plausibility to it.

"Fionna's mother to avenge her ruined life."

"Of course not," he snapped, a little too quickly.

"But you wonder, because she is a complex and perhaps deeply angry woman?"

His jaw set grimly, like he was about to shoot a game-tying free throw. "If she killed Violet, it was justified killing, not murder."

"Indeed. Your grandfather was sympathetic to your suit of his friend's granddaughter?"

"He didn't seem to care much one way or another. . . ." Rick hesitated, reluctant to say anything unpleasant about his grandfather. "He has kind of odd notions about marriage and women. I try to explain to him that all marriages don't end badly; certainly my parents' marriage seems to become better every year, and he tells me I'm a romantic. He thought it was all right to marry Fee so I could have a family and slake some of my youthful passion, his exact words, but he predicted that I would find her rather unsatisfactory. Can you imagine Fee ever being unsatisfactory, Father Blackie?"

"Often unbearable, but never unsatisfactory."

We both laughed at that truism.

"And your parents, I take it that they were initially opposed to any relationship that might bring you back under the sway of your grandfather and Mrs. Harrington Enright?"

"Violently opposed, till they met Fee. She won them over, the little imp, in her first half hour in our house. You should see her in the kitchen."

"An ice-box stuffer? The bottom one-tenth of a potato salad container, a single dill pickle in a gallon bottle?"

"You know the kind, Father. Mom's the same way."

"Irish."

All in all, a charming lunch.

The most important conclusion of which was that this admirable and intelligent young man feared that his future mother-in-law might be the murderer of her own mother. Putative mother.

Her reasons for killing Mrs. Harrington Enright need not be related to the truth about her origins, a point to keep in mind. Mary Feehan's story, however true it certainly was, might be an unintentional red herring in the mystery of Violet Enright's death.

And what sort of woman was this middle-aged matron who was sexually appealing even to a young man whose bloodstream was drenched with hormones incited by her daughter?

To most of those involved, Rita Enright was the dullest person in the family. Worth nothing, according to Vinney Enright.

The more I heard about her, however, the more interesting this daughter of Daniel Enright and Mary O'Brien seemed to be.

She would remain at the bottom of my list, but not at all because she was the least likely suspect.

If she had killed, she killed with good reason, her prospective son-in-law had argued.

What reason? A lie about her birth? A destroyed marriage?

Or something even more terrible?

■

EIGHTH INTERMEZZO

Fionna Downs

■————————————————————————■

28

Fionna was unaware of the whitecaps on the lake or the wind blowing through her hair as she drove up Lake Shore Drive in her Mercedes convertible.

It had not been an easy session with Doctor Murphy. Fionna was burdened with guilts. Doctor Murphy was not ready to provide absolution for any of them.

"So you feel responsible for your grandmother's death even though you did not personally kill her?

"And you feel responsible for the attack on me?

"And you also feel responsible for your mother's refusal to accompany your father back to Los Angeles?

"Why do you feel responsible?

"What are the reasons for your sense of guilt?

"Is your guilt realistic, Fionna?"

Realistic, SHIT!

"Why does it hurt so much to grow up, Doctor Murphy? When you're older does it still hurt?"

"You mean REAL old?"

"Not REAL old, just older."

"It always hurts."

Then she told her about her real grandmother.

"How do you feel about that, Fionna?"

Doctor Murphy didn't seem even a little bit shocked.

"Freaked out!"

"Why?"

Always why, why, why!

"Do you want a therapist, Fionna, or a mother?"

Really!

She was so busy being angry at Dr. Murphy that she hardly noticed the black car until it pulled even with her and began to nudge her toward the concrete median divider.

Geek!

She slowed down to fall behind him. He slowed down and nudged her again.

Was it a yucky boy trying to be fresh?

She glanced at him as he nudged her a third time. He was wearing a ski mask.

Fionna slammed the accelerator to the floor. Her obedient convertible leaped forward. She swerved in front of her tormentor, crossed to the next lane, and roared toward the Diversey Avenue exit.

The big black car—for Fionna, cars were coded "Mercedes" and "all other"—slipped into the exit lane, now far behind her. At the last minute, she turned back to the left and accelerated out of the exit lane. The other car was hemmed in and forced to leave the Drive.

Geek!

29

"Does it have a resident ghost, Sergeant?" I asked the young black officer-at-arms.

"The boat or the station, Father?" he asked with a polite grin.

Both the Sergeant and I knew that the abandoned Coast Guard station at the breakwater entrance to Chicago harbor *had* to have a ghost.

"Either."

"I wouldn't want to go on that boat after dark," the Sergeant said, laughing easily. "But no one has heard anything."

"Indeed."

The three-story, clapboard Victorian station, with a lighthouse cupola, also abandoned, looked like a setting for a thirties Coast Guard movie, set in the Florida keys, in which the commander and the lieutenant commander were in love with the same woman (maybe the widow of the former commander, who died in the last hurricane). Pressed against the hazy blue late-afternoon sky and the whitecaps pounding against the breakwater, it belonged in San Juan not in Chicago.

And it had not been painted in years. The USCG covered downtown Chicago now with a helicopter from Glenview, such are the advantages of technology and the disadvantages of presidential budget trimming. The red-striped cutters were gone, to be replaced by the blue and white cop boats.

For which someone had to pay.

It seemed much more useful to reflect on politics and the plot for my thirties film—smugglers or drug runners could be the bad guys—than to board the *Violetta* and search for ghosts and/or clues.

I protested with a sigh. The officer-at-arms replied antiphonally, and I walked down the dock to the gangplank of the *Violetta*. The Sergeant preceded me across the plank and extended his hand to help me board the *Violetta*.

Can't have a funny little priest fall into Lake Michigan, can you?

He removed the Chicago Police Department seal and waved his hand in the general direction of the stern. "It's all yours, Father."

"Thank you, no."

"Sinful to own a boat like this?" He paused on the gangplank.

"Only to own it and not use it."

Violetta was an old boat, solidly made of the best oak, but still—I suspected as I began, somewhat aimlessly, to prowl its decks—subject to dry rot and requiring constant maintenance. Did Mrs. Harrington Enright keep it as a status symbol or because she loved boats? Or perhaps because her late husband had enjoyed it during his last years?

Who was this woman? I asked myself as I turned the key in the door leading to her stateroom.

The devout Catholic laywoman of her son Harry? A generous but irrationally repressive grandmother whom Fionna both loved and hated? The dangerous Señora whom Luisa feared even more dead than alive? The improbable friend of her rival Mary Feehan? The Old Fella's gauche girl who talked about property on dates? The ruthless operator who seized money from her husband's family while he was away at war? Vinney Nelligan's shrewd business partner who made tragic mistakes with her children? Dan Enright's "last of the Great Chicago Characters"? Ed Enright's castrating mother? Rick Nelligan's woman whom his grandfather certainly loved?

All of the above? And more?

Which of us fits into the single definitions of our friends and enemies? Or into the sum of them?

But which, more to the point, was the woman who was murdered? Was she the victim of an old feud or a contemporary conflict?

Or both?

I thought I knew the answer to the locked-room puzzle. That answer must point at the killer, but I didn't see the direction of the pointer yet, especially since Dan's death.

And the killer was quite capable of striking again.

I stumbled down the stairs to the floor of her stateroom. The bed was made but a coat of dust was already forming on the flat surfaces. Not a very tasteful room, as the saintly Joe Murphy had reported. Money given to an interior decorator who knew the client's inclinations and didn't see any difference between a bedroom on a boat and in a lakefront apartment.

I consulted Mike Casey's notes, on which I had made some observations of my own in handwriting that I could hardly read.

The poor future generation of priests who would have to struggle through my baptismal book entries.

My brother in the Lord, Harry Harrington Enright, soon to be a pastor on the South Side, had left early. Around noon it was said. Fionna, Rita, and Mary—three generations, another triune goddess—had departed at two. Violet was certainly alive at that time. Vinney saw her at two-thirty. As he was leaving she asked Luisa to purchase "Adveel." Dan and Lena took their leave at three. Both swore she was alive then.

At three-thirty Ed and Min said good-bye, he still pleading for help and mercy. She was still alive and unyielding at that time.

At four, Fionna, flushed with the news which had "freaked me out," appeared to shout that Violet was not her real grandmother; a gun was fired; a hole appeared in Mrs. Harrington Enright's head; Fionna—caught up in a compulsive dream or so she felt—ran screaming from the cabin with the murder weapon in her hand, and the admirable Joe Murphy boarded the boat, followed by Chicago's version of Grace O'Malley the pirate queen.

A wayward scruple tickled the farthest corner of my brain. There was something wrong with that summary. The killer had missed a trick, an important trick.

But, try as I might, I could not quite locate the trick, like hunting for a name from the past that one has forgotten.

It would come. Hopefully in time. But it could not be forced.

I tried the door of the salon that opened from the bedroom deck, as locked as it was when Joe Murphy tried it a week before. Could someone have taken the key that was later found in Mrs. Harrington Enright's purse, opened the door after Joe tried to get in from the outside, rushed back to the purse to deposit the key, and then snuck out into the gangway while Joe, redirected by Luisa, came back to the main deck and entered the salon from there?

Theoretically it was possible. I opened the door with the key the Sergeant had given me and peered down the dark gangway. There was no natural lighting in the passage. Was there a light switch? I fumbled on the wall and found one, then flicked the switch, illuminating a cramped, narrow corridor, barely room for one person. Naval architects knew how to conserve space. If the lights were out, someone could have hidden in the corridor or, even more likely, in one of the staterooms. I peered down the corridor: married couples on the left, single persons on the right, bishop in the bow. The killer could have hidden in any cabin or in the cabin he or she had occupied the night before. In the darkness here in the bowels of the ship, you could hide a long time.

Then slip out before the police began their systematic search two hours later.

Over the side of the boat and into the blue waters of Lake Michigan.

With most of Monroe Street harbor watching.

And how had the killer come on board, unless s/he was my Roger Moore/Sean Connery in a scuba suit?

Fionna and Mary Feehan were in the Fine Arts Building café, unrecognized, be it noted, by the staff. My Lord Harry was back in the cathedral. Dan and Lena had returned to their apartment in Old Town. Ed and Min were on the expressway riding to Elmhurst. Vincent and Rick were just arriving home in Lake Forest.

Uncertain alibis because the other person might readily lie to protect a loved one, but alibis that would be hard to shake nonetheless.

Only Rita, the inexplicably appealing Rita, more of a mystery woman even than Mary Feehan, did not have an alibi. I had placed her at the end of my list of interviews, just before her brother Doctor Edward. Ed had managed to violate the order and symmetry of my list, like the others eager to be done with the weird little priest. Rita seemed to be in no rush. It would be a most interesting interview.

There was, I felt certain, more to her divorce from the

faithful Bill Downs than I had been told. To some she was "nothing," to others "worthless," to Bill and Rick an irresistibly sensual woman, and to Fionna a mother whom you liked and admired, even if you lost patience with her.

Did she know, had she known all along, who her mother, her "real" mother, was?

Or had she learned the truth, not from Fionna after the death of her presumed mother, but from someone else before the death of Mrs. Harrington Enright?

Motive for murder? Not by itself, unless there was a touch of madness in Rita Downs. But combined with the wreckage of a passionate marriage?

Possibly?

And why did not Fionna have siblings?

A delicate question, the answer to which might be totally unimportant.

I poked along the gangway, opening the doors to the staterooms, dark because drapes had been drawn at the portholes. They were tiny rooms, the size of a Pullman compartment from days of yore. A husband and wife who were in conflict with one another might be tempted to murder in such cramped quarters. Each other, not their hostess.

Each room was decorated in a different vulgar color—turquoise, lime, crimson, pink, purple.

Ugh.

I continued to poke but found nothing. There was no reason to think I might discover what the police had missed.

I went back to the salon, sat on the edge of the bed, and reviewed the Sunday afternoon again. Still nothing.

Except the one glitch. And that would probably fit into place only after I found the key to the puzzle.

I had the key: the locked-room solution. It obviously pointed to one person with excellent motivation. Perhaps the obvious was still true. Even if it seemed very unlikely that my principal suspect from the very beginning was not the sort of person who would order, for totally inexplicable reasons, the killing of Dan and Lena and the attempted killing of the Last Great Pirate Queen of the Western World.

I stuffed the notes in my Chicago Bulls windbreaker pocket and struggled up the companionway to the deck, locked the appropriate doors, replaced the police seal, and tottered across the gangplank—without, you will note, the help of the officer-at-arms.

He ruined it all by yelling "Careful there, Father! We don't want a sure-enough monsignor falling into the lake!"

Indeed.

I drove back to the cathedral in the rose and gold light of a Chicago sunset, still confused and bemused. The puzzle was essentially solved, but not the murder. Too many clues, too many motives, too many suspects with dubious alibis. Too many secrets.

So I should go to Mike Casey, explain the puzzle of the locked room, and my solution to it.

And then the officers-at-arms would arrest my suspect and the State's Attorney would drop the charges against Fantastic Fionna.

Not a chance.

My Lord Cronin was waiting in my study, a tumbler of my Jameson's on his knee.

"More trouble, Blackwood. Harry rushed out to Elmhurst Community Hospital an hour ago. His brother Ed tried to force the hand of the Almighty with an OD of Valium. He said you might want to drive out there too. His sister-in-law, Mickey, wants to talk to you."

"Wrong mouse. Minnie."

"A woman with a name like that"—he toasted me with my own liquor—"has to be the criminal. See to it, Blackwood."

30

"He's not a bad man, Father," Min Enright insisted. "He's a good surgeon and a good husband and father. He'd even have been a smart investor if she'd left him alone. He knew he should get out of dollars weeks ago. He was afraid she'd call him a coward. He had to stick it out to please her."

"Indeed."

Minerva Enright was not on my list to be interviewed. Just as her husband had intruded and destroyed the logic of the list, so she had intruded and destroyed its purity.

Dr. James (William, that is) would have been disappointed at my efforts to reduce his "blooming, buzzing pluralism" to order and purity.

Especially since Minerva Enright, a woman transformed in the antiseptic pink of the hospital's "family lounge," was proving an excellent witness, answering my questions before I asked them. She was defending her husband, but without any illusions about him or herself.

I struggled to adjust to the change in her. The vamp of the wake had disappeared completely. She had been replaced by an anxious, rather plain suburban housewife, in Notre Dame sweat shirt, white jeans, and running shoes, who had been suddenly summoned from her home to the hospital emergency room. When I entered the waiting room and peered around looking for her, a tall boy in his late teens hovered protectively near.

"It's all right, Johnny. Dad's out of danger. You drive home and calm down the little kids. I'll talk to Father Ryan for a few minutes."

The lad, shaken and troubled, but still his mother's good right arm, kissed her forehead, nodded politely to me, and departed.

The Bishop had returned to the cathedral when he learned that his brother was out of danger.

I did not doubt, as we discussed her unconscious husband, that the persona of the night before was real. Min Enright could play the sexual-tiger role expertly. But the middle-aged matron, without makeup or pretense, was a more basic role.

"He wanted help, of course." Her hazel eyes were direct, her voice casual and professional. "I'm a nurse, Father. That's how I met Ed. I worked in a psychiatric unit for several years. I gave it up because Ed doesn't believe in psychiatry. Poor goof, what he really means is that he's afraid of it. Like a lot of suicide attempts we used to get in the unit, he pushed his luck. He told me on the phone he was in a motel. He didn't say which one. Another half hour and it would have been too late."

"No suicide note?"

"Of course not. He didn't expect to die, didn't want to die, but almost died anyway, poor bastard. I suppose you've heard the stories about homosexual relationships?" She inspected my face carefully.

I admitted that I had.

"All of us are a mix of sexualities, Father. I'm sure you don't need to be told that. The bisexual component is a little stronger in Ed. When he feels good about himself, it's no problem. When she emasculated him—and she did it as often as she could—then he lost interest in me. Not surprising, is it?"

"No."

"I haven't been perfect either." She lifted her shoulders wearily. "The things she did to him infuriated me and I kicked over the traces—until I figured out that that was what the old bitch wanted. I loved him. I still love him. He loves me. I won't give him up. I'm glad she's dead."

She reached in the purse she must have thrown over her shoulder as she rushed out of the house and found a pack of tissues.

"But Ed didn't kill her. Neither did I. We can survive without the money. He's a damn fine doctor. I wanted to go back to nursing anyway, now that the kids are older. I just hope we can keep this out of the papers. Thank God he did it out here and not in Chicago. Publicity would kill his career. We've already had too much of it. That idiocy on TV about malpractice insurance was her idea. 'Why don't you fight them, Ed darling, if they're so bad. Aren't you man enough to take on the lawyers?' "

"Constant attacks on his manhood?"

"I can't remember a time when we were with her that she didn't go after him. The Bishop was always treated with respect, maybe a question or two about when he was going to replace Cronin." Min smiled wryly. "Fat chance of that now. Then she'd go after Dan about why his book hadn't made the best-seller lists yet and Rita about whether she was dating anyone. They'd all wince but never fight back. Well, Rita wouldn't wince. She's just a dull lump anyway. I don't think she heard the old bitch half the time."

"Ah."

"Then it was Ed's turn. He'd be sweating, literally sweating like he was being given the third degree by the police. She'd go right for his testicles. And he'd sit there and take it, tears in his eyes, fists clenched, and never fight back. She'd chew him up and spit him out. God, did she have a feast with this investment of his in dollars. She knew he'd be afraid to abandon his position if she beat him over the head with her club: 'Don't have the manhood to stick it out, eh, Edward? Just like your father, no guts.' Otherwise he would have taken his losses a couple of weeks ago and still made a lot of money."

"She wanted him to lose his money?"

"She wanted him to have to crawl to her for every cent. She was a shrewd old whore, ready to grab at the slightest opportunity. When Ed went long in dollars, she saw her chance to finish him off. Finally he had a choice of jail or turning everything over to her, as his poor grandfather did. You could see those terrible blue eyes of hers burning with pleasure."

"Why?" I asked, admiring the woman's cool self-control and wondering whether I was not witnessing a superb dramatic performance.

One thing was no longer in doubt: she loved her husband.

"She'd say to make a man out of him. Or to protect him from himself because he'd never be a man. She wanted to keep all her children under her thumb. Ed's the only one who had a spark of resistance, and she was about to destroy that too."

"So."

"And punish him too," she rushed on. "She was big on punishment, Father."

"For what was he being punished?"

"For seducing me, what else? And the joke is that I seduced him, poor man. I was pretty good at it. He was a frightened virgin. It was easy and even kind of fun." She dabbed at her eyes. "I wanted him, you see, Father. I still want him. He's improved a lot. He's a good lover now, when she leaves him alone. Not spectacular, but all I want."

"And Mrs. Harrington Enright was still punishing him after all these years?"

"Isn't it strange that all three of her children were involved in premarital pregnancies, even if Lena's was a fake? It was the only way they could marry, and at the same time it guaranteed them a life of punishment. She really messed them up, Father. And that little brat Fionna is certainly having it on with her dumb boyfriend. Lucky little bitch won't be punished for the rest of her life either."

"Indeed."

"She killed Vi. Obviously. And it looks like she might get away with it too."

"You're certain of that?"

"Who else could have done it? She had the gun in her hand, didn't she? She gets most of the money, doesn't she? And poor Ed ODs on Valium because he's afraid that he's about to be arrested." She paused and looked at me cautiously. "He's not going to be arrested, is he, Father?"

"Not that I know. . . . Tell me, did your mother-in-law renew her threats when you last saw her that Sunday afternoon on the yacht?"

"She was mostly angry at the brat. I give the kid credit for one thing: she's the only member of the family who fought back. In spades. Maybe we should have killed her long ago. We didn't, but I'm not sure that we shouldn't have. I don't think it would be a sin."

"Oh?"

"Legitimate self-defense. At least that's what I think." She laughed bitterly. "I wouldn't even confess it. Anyway, someone else beat us to it. I don't mind the brat getting away with it, so long as my Ed doesn't have to take the blame."

"But she did make threats that afternoon?"

"She told him she wanted the papers assenting to her becoming his conservator signed by the end of the week or she'd call in the FBI. That would mean she'd have *all* his money, Father, even what he received for his surgery. She could dictate how he spent his money on me, the kids, the house, vacations, everything. He would have to ask for her permission to pay college tuition, to buy me a new coat, to breathe."

"You advised your husband to resist?"

"To call her bluff? She wasn't bluffing, Father. She would have sent him to jail if she had to." Min's grim face twitched with venomous hatred. "She was really mean."

"I'm sure he could have plea-bargained out of a jail sentence."

"And have his reputation as a doctor destroyed? The only choice was to sign the damn papers and hope she died soon."

"You are certainly being candid, Mrs. Enright," I said softly.

"What else can I do?" She held out her empty hands. "There's no point in hiding our motives."

"Was Vincent Nelligan involved in this matter?"

"Nelligan?" She frowned. "He's an odd duck, Father. Reported the forged checks to Vi and then urged her not to take legal action against Ed. He tried to talk her out of the conservatorship idea. I don't think he would have changed her mind. He never did before. He would usually defend the children and try to persuade her to leave us alone. Never got to first base with her."

"Is he a hypocrite?"

"Hard to say." Her eyes flickered. "I think he has some principles, narrow ones. You don't kite checks, for example. But he wouldn't hesitate to rob you blind on a kinky deal if he could."

" 'Kinky' is a word I hear often about him."

"You'd have to be a little odd to work with Violet all these years."

"You think they were lovers?"

"Are you kidding? The two of them? That's what my kids would call gross."

She seemed genuinely appalled by the thought.

"I suppose."

"Besides . . ." She hesitated. "The rumor I hear is that he's into light S and M stuff. Not chains or whips, but spanking and bondage, humiliation sort of thing."

I must have gulped.

She laughed. "Don't be shocked, Father. Hookers will do anything for a score. And some women actually enjoy it, so long as it doesn't get out of hand. No one has ever said it gets out of hand with Vinney."

The mystery became more sordid. But the sordid was not necessarily relevant.

Was she, I wondered, speaking from personal experience? A furious and hateful woman seeking revenge?

"Do you think he might be the killer?"

She frowned thoughtfully. "Why? What would be in it for him? He didn't inherit any money. I don't think the brat and the jerk she's fucking will keep Vinney on retainer. Vi and Vinney were probably not finished making money. Why kill the goose that laid the golden egg?"

"A valid point."

"Besides, how could he have done it? An old man climbing out the window of the yacht and swimming across Monroe Street harbor? You can't be serious, Father."

"Perhaps not."

A plump, cheerful young nurse interrupted us. "Mrs. Enright, your husband is regaining consciousness now."

"This is going to be important," she said firmly, rising from her chair with dedicated determination. "Thanks for listening, Father. Wish me luck. Pray for me. Whatever."

"All of the above."

It had been a spirited defense of her husband. She knew that the police, still not satisfied that the knife wielders had acted on their own initiative, would find Ed Enright's attempted suicide incriminating.

So hunt up Blackie Ryan, bumbling American Father Brown, and co-opt him with more candor than he would expect.

Her love for her pitiable husband was, however, not an act. There was a lot of love in this mystery, much of it convoluted or unattractive or mysterious or unusual. Daniel and Mary. Violet and Vincent. Lena and Dan. Ed and Min. Perhaps Vinney and Min. Violet for her children. Fionna for her putative grandmother. Rick for his grandfather. Mary for her daughter and her granddaughter. Bill and Rita for each other. Mary for Violet.

The straightforward, hormone-induced, reproductively oriented passion between Rick and Fionna seemed delightfully innocent by comparison.

One wonders occasionally if Lady Wisdom has erred in persuading us that love is a human emotion that is a valid metaphor, even a sacrament, for Her attitude toward us. It is a messy, violent, difficult, erratic, unpredictable, frequently convoluted passion toward unity.

Can that be God?

If Lady Wisdom says so, then it must be true.

Min's defense of Vincent Nelligan was low-key and effective. Why indeed should he kill the goose who laid the golden egg? But was she also defending a part-time lover? Minerva Enright was a suburban housewife who loved her husband

and would do almost anything to help and protect him. She had been the spine in his back, what little there was, throughout the marriage.

But she would not be the only suburban matron who, loving her husband, also found an occasional bout of "light S and M", entertaining and diverting as a recreational experience. One which, like murder with good cause, you really didn't have to confess.

What business was it of the church if once in a while you permitted a man who was not your husband to tie you up and spank you? You were still a good wife and mother, weren't you?

And maybe you were even purchasing freedom for your husband.

However, Vinney Nelligan's alleged propensity for kinky sex, of which I had heard from no one else, seemed to have no relationship to the murder of Mrs. Harrington Enright.

Unless, long ago, he had done the same things to her. Might she—like, by hypothesis, her daughter-in-law—have found such occasional amusements diverting?

But so what?

She might want to kill him for revenge, though why wait so long?

But why would such past interludes give him reason to kill her?

I must now face the responsibility of my last interview, with the mysterious and potentially difficult Rita Downs, a suspect who, I thought, might have the strongest reasons for wanting her presumed mother dead. And if the reactions of some men to her were any indication, she might well be possessed by the slumbering passions and submerged intelligence that would make three murders and an attempt at a fourth possible and attractive.

And safe.

31

"I had the best reason of all to kill her, Father Blackie." Rita Enright Downs, a sleek, sinuous feline, rose from the chaise lounge on which she had been reclining, walked to the compact glass and chrome liquor cabinet by the window, and prepared for herself a second vodka martini, with rather more Martini than your typical Irish female alcoholic would normally use.

"I hated her more than the others. I had better reason for revenge. I thought of it often. If I do say so"—she brought me a second container of Canfield's Diet Fudge Soda—"I could probably have figured out a way to do it that would fool even you."

"I don't doubt it."

"My Fionna"—she said the name with a complacent and proud smile—"says you enjoy this terrible plastic chocolate stuff."

She refilled my glass.

"Like totally."

She laughed, returned leisurely to her chaise, and arranged herself elegantly on it. "You approve of my Fionna?"

"Like totally."

"So do I. She's the one part of my life of which I am quite proud. . . . Don't worry, Father Blackie—may I call you that? Fionna said it was the proper title. . . . I'm not a drunk. Two of these—and this is my second—put me to sleep. I am"—her tone turned bitter—"not even a successful alcoholic."

In the privacy of her chrome and glass and leather suite, there was no longer any doubt about the fact of Rita's eroticism or the nature of it. She could hide it with effort on public occasions. In private this woman, just my own age, had the same effect on me as the lovely Annie Casey.

Not at all blatant, her intense sensual appeal was as obvious as sunrise. When she opened the door, in scuffed loafers, designer jeans, a big white shirt hanging over the jeans, a trace of makeup on her lips and at her eyes, and a very faint perfume, you did not notice any special attractiveness. Then you looked at her oval, timeless face with its wide eyes and clear complexion and you thought you had a metaphor for her. The face should be surrounded by a wimple and a veil, preferably the brown veil of a contemplative Carmelite. The touch of pain that seemed to lurk in her eyes and in her sad smile suggested a life of penance and suffering and all-night prayer: Sister Mary Rita of the Infant Jesus, O.C.D.

Only when she had poured your fudge soda, picked up her first martini, and disposed herself modestly on the chaise did her full impact hit you. Just as from funeral home to hospital Min Enright had been transformed from vamp to housewife/nurse, so from funeral home to apartment overlooking the gray lake had Rita Downs been transformed from a drab and lackluster middle-aged woman, whom you might hardly notice, to a dazzling vision whose sensuality permeates her environment the way the aroma of fresh bread fills a room.

Her appeal was not in the least perverse. Rather it arose from straightforward and intense womanliness. Passive and perhaps even lazy she might be, a woman who would give and not take, but you knew that when she gave herself in response to someone who was taking her, she would give all that she had and was, body and soul. Rita would hold back nothing from a man to whom she belonged. Her passion would not be inhibited by modesty or fear or shame or restraint. She would be an abandoned lover because she would know of no other way to love, a wanton lover because that was the only way to love, a demanding lover because her passivity would be a devastating challenge.

In every cell of her body she was a tank of flammable and explosive sexual energy waiting for a spark to ignite her. The right spark.

The wrong spark would have no effect at all.

Fionna's womanly appeal was energetic, vital, animated. Her mother, perhaps a little taller, was blessed with the same compact, well-engineered female body: trim legs, slim hips, flat belly, narrow waist, small and exquisite breasts (all preserved probably with very little effort). But her appeal was the opposite of her daughter's; her eroticism was submissive, patient, unresisting, engulfing.

The County Mayo genes had produced two quite remarkable women. No, counting the grandmother, three quite remarkable women.

No wonder Rick Nelligan could not keep his eyes off Rita. And Bill Downs his hands off her.

Blackie Ryan was bowled over, you say?

Oh yes indeed. He realized, funny little priest, that he was in the presence of one of the most remarkable women he had ever met.

Was she aware of her impact on me?

Almost certainly. She could not have lived four decades without knowing that she had a powerful effect on men.

Did she orchestrate that impact?

I doubt that she was capable of it.

Did she understand the nature of her appeal?

Most improbably. It was simply a given in her life, which was part of the appeal: the very unselfconsciousness of her eroticism heightened its effectiveness.

Even women on a jury would sympathize with her.

"You seem to have a good relationship with your daughter."

"With Fee?" She leaned back comfortably on her chaise. "More like a big sister. And she's the big sister. Orders, suggestions, commands, hints, furious denunciations . . . One of the benefits of Violet was that all of Fionna's rebelling was against her. The worst she aimed in my direction was contempt." She grimaced. "Well-deserved contempt, I might add."

"You approve of her marriage?"

"To Rick?" She grinned. "I told her that I saw him first

and that made her very angry—for five seconds. Then I was embraced and proclaimed a wonderful mother. A label to which I am not entitled. I'm hardly a mother at all."

"And her career plans?"

"I read a lot, as you can tell, Father Blackie"—she gestured at the stacks of books and magazines around her: mysteries, SF, Westerns, romances, best-sellers, college press novels, literary reviews—"without much taste or discrimination, I'm afraid. I know good writers. I knew that my poor brother couldn't write worth a damn despite all his posing. And I know that my Fionna"—she beamed—"is very good and, if she works at it, maybe great. I'm prejudiced about her, but I don't let that interfere with my taste."

"I'm sure not. You were close to Dan?"

"He was the only one who didn't treat me like a freak. He and Mary Feehan, but she isn't around all the time. Dan meant well. He escaped Mother by pretending to be a poseur. He pretended so well that he became one."

She sipped her martini, very slowly, perhaps so as not to fall asleep.

"And you think you could design a murder that even the legendary Blackie Ryan could not solve?"

"Design, yes." She smiled at me, a very winning smile. "Not execute. I live in a world of fantasy, of daydreams and Spanish castles, Father Blackie. In the real world I'd fail as a killer like I have failed at everything else." She considered her drink meditatively. "A man came out of the dream world once—Irish, not Spanish—and claimed me. I lost him like I've lost everything else in my life."

"Except Fionna."

"Except Fionna," she agreed sadly. "Give me time and I'll lose her too."

"Why would you have killed your mother?"

"Why? When I was bringing Fionna into the world, she bribed the doctor to cut my tubes. She told me years later. It was a punishment for my premarital pleasures. She thought it was very amusing. Bill loved children. He wanted more Fionnas; so did I. I didn't tell him because I was afraid he would be angry at me. I decided not to go to California with him so that he could find a woman who would give him more children. He didn't want me badly enough to make me come with him."

The whole story was told in quick, sharp narrative.

"And he didn't choose to exercise his opportunity?"

She shifted uneasily on her chaise. "I can't understand that."

"Can't you?"

"Other women are good lays too. I worked at it when we were first married. I guess I must have been pretty good. But not that good. Then when he left, I drew a line through that part of my life. Whenever he's around, it all comes back."

"Your decision then was wrong?"

"Was it?" She swirled her martini. "I don't know that. He wants me but not enough. He could still find another woman who would give him children."

"You told him the truth now."

"Yes."

"And?"

"Are you investigating a murder, Father Blackie, or trying to help a badly confused woman?"

You take a deep breath, drop back, and punt.

"Both, unless they become inconsistent. And maybe even then."

She studied me intently. I was emerging as not only a cute little priest but a nice little priest. And I was beginning to react to her the way I do to Annie Casey. I insisted to myself that no way was she to be permitted to do the glasses-cleansing routine.

Enough is enough already.

Unless she positively insisted.

"And he was very angry at me." She averted her eyes. "For thinking that it would make any difference to him and for not finding a doctor who might do some repair work and for insisting that it was too late now for the repairs."

"I see."

"Do you, Father? You think my self-hatred and self-contempt is pathological. I think it's realistic."

"My judgment is not pertinent."

"I know," she snapped. "Bill's judgment is what matters. But I do not want to be a wife who sleeps late, buys clothes, exercises enough to stay in condition, and lounges around a California pool all day reading books and fantasizing about the wonderful things her husband will do to her when he comes home from his university."

"I should think that paragraph raises doubts as to whether Fionna is the only one in the family with literary talent."

"I must have read it someplace." She colored at my compliment. "I want to have something to give to a man."

"Most men would be more than content with the woman you have described, especially if she could afford to pay for her own clothes."

"Playmate?"

"A myth that is inaccurate mostly because of its incompleteness."

"I wanted to be an actress." She finished her martini. "Can you imagine that, Father? An actress? Maybe I'm an actress now, at this very moment. Maybe I have concocted a splendid performance to persuade you that my acedia—good word, isn't it, Father?—is so great I could never murder my mother. I don't suppose that idea has even occurred to you?"

"You do me an injustice."

I never had the chance to use that line before.

She struggled out of her lounge and stood up, one hand on her hip, the other holding her martini glass, her splendidly crafted breasts pushing against the fabric of her shirt.

"And your conclusion?" she demanded.

"I'm reserving judgment."

"You *are* a funny little priest." She walked uncertainly back to the bar. "Third drink. I'll fall asleep on my chaise. All your fault, Father Blackie."

Fortunately she did not forget my fudge soda.

"So?"

"So I'll never go to California with him." Her lips became a thin, harsh line. "Never." She paused thoughtfully. "Not unless he wants me enough to make me come. And he doesn't. No, never."

"In the words of Harry S . . ."

"Never say never because never is a hell of a long time." She giggled, the vodka now having its effect. Apparently.

I had to push the conversation if I were to obtain the necessary answers.

"Maybe I will join him eventually. But I'll have to make up my own mind. And I've never made up my mind to anything in all my life except to go to bed with him the first time. And," she sniggered, "every time he's wanted since then."

"So your never is negotiable?"

"Depends on how much I've had to drink." She smiled peacefully as she gulped a major portion of her martini. "The hangover is on your soul, Father Blackie Ryan. Anyway it's probably up to that little bitch I brought into the world. My ex-husband doesn't believe in kidnapping women. His liberal principles. She's quite capable of drugging me and dragging me off to California. . . . Drugging and Dragging, Father Blackie, alliteration . . ."

"You would not, however, object to your husband kidnapping you?"

"Off the record? Promise? Scout's honor? I think I'd love it, like a romance novel, or medieval fantasy. He'll never do it, the creep. And I suppose"—heavy sigh—"it would not be a good way to resume a relationship, would it?"

She was not as drunk as she wanted me to think she was. Vodka works fast, but not that fast.

"Who killed your mother?"

"I don't know and I don't care. Fionna didn't do it. I didn't do it, though I almost wish I did. Other than that, it's up to the police and priest-detectives to figure it out."

"Someone in the family?"

She closed her eyes, as if she was about to fall asleep. "Maybe. She hated us all. Does that surprise you?" She was mumbling incoherently, not a bad actress at all. "She hated us because we were younger than she was and would outlive her. She was terribly afraid of death. So she wanted to kill us, spiritually anyway, before she died. All that crap . . . sorry, Father . . . all that nonsense about misguided love was shit—"

"Ms. Downs," I barked at her. "Most of your third drink was water. I suspect that the first drink, which you were consuming when I arrived, was entirely water. You are not drunk, you are not anywhere near drunk. Don't try to play the fool with me, even though you are both an attractive and persuasive fool, quite possibly because you've had practice acting like one all your life."

"You goddamn bastard!" She opened up her eyes, sat up straight, and glared at me in cold fury. "How dare you say those things about me?"

Even more dazzling when enraged.

"Because they're true. Now answer my questions or I'll tell Fionna on you."

Her reaction was, blessedly, laughter.

"You are a terrible priest, Father Blackie, just terrible. I want to get rid of you because your questions hurt. I almost fooled you too, didn't I?"

"No."

"But I can play a pretty good drunk?"

"Excellent."

"And you're right about the damn fool."

"No, I'm not. Now tell me about the last time you saw your mother."

"Yes, Father." She turned crimson. "I'm sorry for trying to fake you out—Fee's English, not mine—and for using such terrible language to a priest."

That merited more quite sober laughter. I had already become a wonderful little priest. In a moment she would begin to flirt, very mildly, with me.

"Your last minutes with your mother?"

"Last Sunday, about two o'clock, wasn't it? She was drunk. Mary and Fionna and I paid our respects. Luisa was there too, terribly worried about La Señora, poor little frightened child. Fionna was in one of her stubborn moods. Wouldn't say a word. Rick will have his hands full when she's in that mood. I never hated my mother more. I almost told her that. Now I'm glad I didn't. Mary soft-talked her in that smooth Irish brogue. Told Luisa to get Mother some Advil for her headache. We left. I had my own headache, so I came straight back here and went to bed. Dreamed of Bill, naturally. I woke up for the five o'clock news and saw the pictures of our boat in the harbor. No one in the family thought it worth the effort to call me. I was never so happy in my life. The evil old woman was dead."

"Indeed."

She was leaning forward eagerly, her eyes were shining brightly. "The first thing I thought of was Bill. What kind of a woman is it that can't reclaim her husband until her mother is dead? How could any man want that kind of love?"

"Presumably he can speak for himself?"

"Can and has," she sniffed, "and does, *ad nauseam*. I don't really mean that. Would it have been a sin if I killed her, Father Blackie?"

"You had reason to be angry, not to murder."

She considered that for a couple of seconds and then changed the subject.

"Any more questions?"

"Your mother's relationship to Vincent Nelligan?"

"Partners in evil. And rivals. They both would steal each other blind if they could."

"Lovers?"

"Not in any meaning that word may have to me."

"Did Vinney . . ."

"Hit on me?" She grinned crookedly. "Monthly at least. I was married to a man who knew all my quirks, not that there are many. So I brushed Vinney off politely. When I wasn't married anymore, I thought he was a dirty old man and told him so. I also told him what I'd do to him if he made the smallest pass at Fionna."

"Your brother the Bishop?"

"Harry? Poor geek. He thinks I'm a notorious sinner, that's the word, isn't it? Because I didn't have any more children, he thought I was doing birth control. I've never had the heart to tell him the awful truth about his sainted mother."

"Dan?"

"Harmless flake. Couldn't hurt a fly."

"Ed?"

"Min's a bitch, but she stands by him, which is more than I might do. Doesn't have the balls for murder."

"Mary?"

"Mary who? Feehan? She's a sweet pious lady, whom I dearly love. But she doesn't have any passion, Father. I bet she conceived those five kids without a single orgasm."

"Who's the most likely suspect in your judgment?"

"I told you that in the beginning: I am. If the police knew what she did to me, they'd arrest me on the spot."

There was no further reason to bask in the charms of Rita Downs. Pleasantly exhausted, I took my leave after a cordial handshake.

"I may just call you someday, Father Blackie Ryan, for some quick spiritual advice."

"In anticipation of such a call, I'll determine the location of the nearest United Airlines ticket counter."

We both laughed. She with her fears and her hopes. I with my prayers.

If the police knew both of her secrets, the first about her birth and the second about why she had produced no more Fionnas, they would certainly think seriously about arresting her.

She was surely the only one of all the suspects who seemed to have the motives and the intelligence and the toughness of spirit to kill Violet Harrington Enright.

And no jury in the world would convict her.

Not of that murder. But the others?

■

NINTH INTERMEZZO
Fionna Downs

■────────────────────────────■

32

Fionna was driving very carefully through Lincoln Park on the hottest day of the summer. The park, like North Avenue Beach and the zoo, was wall to wall people, grandmothers to babies, searching for shade under the leafy trees or strolling down its walks and across its lawns.

Like in that great flick *My Bodyguard*.

She and Patty and Luisa had taken Clarissa Day to lunch at the Belmont Plaza. Fionna had one glass of Cabernet Sauvignon, the most she would permit herself when she was driving, even if she now was legal. She didn't want some geeky cop stopping her and making her try to walk a straight line. Fionna had a hard time doing *that* even when she didn't have one drink.

Rick didn't drink at all, which was a good idea. He would not tell her to give up booze or ask her either, but she would do it anyway. Grandma, poor woman, was disgusting when she was wasted, and Mom drank too much even if she wasn't a drunk.

Thinking about Rick was a very bad mistake when you were driving. She tried to concentrate even harder on the street. There were so many kids running back and forth.

Although the charges against her had not yet been dropped, Patty was convinced there was nothing to worry about. Now the problem was keeping Luisa in America. She had ensconced the girl in a room in their apartments as a maid, but she had made up her mind that when Mom and Dad were together again, they would have to adopt Luisa, providing Fionna with an instant little sister.

It would be hard for Luisa to give up Mexican ways and become American. She'd lose some important things. But she couldn't go back, not now. And she would be able to help her family.

And help us too, Fionna told her uncertain conscience resolutely.

The lunch was for Clarissa because she had been so kind to Luisa when she had been locked up in that nice convent.

Suddenly the black car was in front of them, roaring down the wrong side of the street.

Fionna swerved to avoid it, but the big car clipped the little Mercedes and whirled it around so it was facing the opposite direction.

People were screaming all around her. Children running. The other women in the car shouting. Clarissa struggling for her service revolver.

The black car drove off the street, turned on the grass, and hurtled back toward them.

Fionna deliberately spun in the opposite direction, jumped the curb, raced across the grass, dodged around crowds of children, and flew through space right into the Lincoln Park Lagoon.

The force of their landing knocked her out momentarily, but the slap of the water against her face revived her. Instinctively, she pressed her seat belt buckle and struggled to the surface. She saw Patty's carrot top and her strong arms clutching a terrified Luisa.

Where was Patrol Officer Day?

Fionna kicked off her Reeboks and her skirt and dove back to the car. In the murky muddy waters of the lagoon, she had a hard time finding it. Then she saw an inert form in the back seat, reached for the seat belt holding the young woman in the car, lost her breath, and struggled back to the surface.

There were sirens and shouts and screams. No time to

wait. This is my last chance. Deep breath. Please, God, help me.

She dove again, found the car after a desperate search in the muck, and caught her foot on the steering wheel. Lungs aching, her chest in a vice, she fought free, tore at the seat belt around the young black woman, and with every bit of strength she still possessed, dragged her back to the surface.

Clarissa was choking and vomiting, but still alive.

How do I get her out of here now?

There were hands to help.

Thank you, God. I owe you one.

Fionna looked around. The Reeboks were lost, but she had to find her skirt.

It was expensive.

33

Fionna Downs made the instant transition from crime suspect to folk heroine with effortless grace. She replaced the Last Great Pirate Queen of the Western World without so much as batting one of her (natural) eyelashes. On television, her mother and father beaming proudly behind her, she told the story of the black car in standard English in which the verb *to go* was replaced by its archaic form *to say.*

The only slip into TE (teen English) was the comment, "Totally no way were they going to kill Patrol Officer Day."

The driver of the black Thunderbird, the "alleged perpetrator," had been apprehended "fleeing the scene" after his car had plunged into the lagoon. He was refusing to explain his behavior to police investigators.

Third-rate hit man.

Patrol Officer Day and Patricia Anne Slattery had been treated at Swedish Covenant Hospital and released.

No one in Chicago was betting that charges pending against Fionna Downs would survive another sunset.

And a crazy killer was at large.

Might the dazzling Rita Downs have ordered an assault on her Fionna?

And the Pope was Amish.

Which didn't help me to prevent the killer from having another shot at her.

Holmes had the cocaine bottle. I have my cassette tape deck. It plays twin two-hour tapes and then plays them again and yet again for five repeats, twenty-four hours of uninterrupted background music, mostly Mozart. My colleagues make fun of me—the Boss uses Mozart for background. What, I demand, if I switched to Gustave Mahler?

We'd quit, they reply. Or fire you.

What can I tell you?

I turned the tape deck on, poured myself a large, frosty glass of lime Perrier water, and reclined on my favorite chair. Across the room the Johns of my adolescence watched me—Kennedy, XXIII, Unitas. The saucy medieval Madonna, who is alleged to look like my mother, with her saucy child, who doesn't look like me at all, also watched me. They all seemed to regard me with disapproval.

As well they might.

On the opposite wall hung Catherine Curran's recent painting, *Cuz*, which purported to be me in a Cubs windbreaker and Coast Guard cap (provided for the occasion by Cindasoo) on a stormy day at Grand Beach. If you can't make him handsome, make him colorful, heroically colorful.

It won her some kind of prize last year, a phenomenon that baffles me. Perhaps they thought it was an on-site painting of a sawed-off St. Brendan of Clonfert sailing home from Barbados.

I felt neither heroic nor colorful, nor very much like the steely-eyed cleric in Cathy's painting.

The Madonna did not seem pleased with me. At all. At all. Well she might not be. I had not been praying nearly enough. So you think you can do it all yourself, huh, Blackie Ryan?

No, ma'am.

I found a rosary in my pocket, untangled it from a crumpled five-dollar bill, hooked the separated links together, and said a decade of the beads. The Madonna looked less unhappy.

I was as confused as I ever had been in my life. Unlike most mysteries, where you start out with a puzzle and find eventually a solution, I had started out with what I took to be the solution to a puzzle and found another puzzle.

There were at least three puzzles in the case, all of them imposed by forces outside the motives and the intents of the persons involved:

1. The initial locked-room puzzle itself. I knew the answer to that from the first night, immediately after the crime. Had the answer confused or blinded me? Perhaps. On the other hand, the police did not know the solution and they had done no better than I. The indictment of Fionna Downs had been postponed. I had my primary suspect, and the rationale for this explanation was as strong as ever, but that particular person seemed an unlikely killer and an even more unlikely force behind the murder of Dan and Lena and the attacks on Mary Kate and Fionna.

2. The Vatican connection. I had been preoccupied by the impact of Vinney Nelligan's trip to the Vatican on subsequent events. I still was not convinced that Harry Enright was in real danger because of the simple fact that he yet lived. The forces of the shadow world, however, had their own logic, timing, and methods. Surely a twisted locked-room story, a puzzle within a puzzle, would be typical of the convoluted machinations of P-Two lodge. If they were playing in this game, we would no more find a definite solution than we did to the death of John Paul I.

3. The discovery by Fionna of her "real" grandmother. If Rita Downs had been told the truth about her own background, she might have yet another good reason to murder

her mother. As best as I could determine, neither Mary Feehan nor Fionna, the only two people in the world besides me (and I presumed the Doctors Murphy) who knew this story, had not and would not tell her. Rita might still seek revenge for the children of which she had been deprived in an act of horrific cruelty. But why wait for so many years?

Would Mary Feehan finally seek revenge? Why bother to kill an old woman after all these years of acceptance of the inevitable? And for Fionna wasn't the truth about her origins not bad but good, liberation from the shackles of her ambivalence? It was no longer necessary to kill the bad grandmother because she wasn't the real grandmother.

Right?

I reached for a pen and a piece of paper, found the latter, and was forced out of my chair to hunt for the former. On the way back I collected Mike Casey's stack of notes. I returned to the comforts of my chair, discovered that my Perrier glass was empty, and with a sigh of protest to Lady Wisdom rose again, proceeded to the fridge, obtained a six-pack of the bubbling liquid, and went back permanently to the chair.

Why did I want the pen and paper?

Yet another puzzle.

Oh yes.

I wrote the names of the three puzzles on the note sheet: "locked room, Vatican, real grandmother."

I added three names—"Mary Kate, Dan, Fionna."

Someone wanted them dead. Those murders and attempted murders also seemed to be red herrings to the solution of the original crime. Surely my primary suspect would not want to . . .

Well, maybe, that person or the person from whom that person was taking orders, would want to dispose of the three of them, each for a slightly different reason. But then what about the Vatican and Mary Feehan?

Completely irrelevant.

Maybe.

After all, perhaps the most simple answer is also the best.

Right?

Except that I never liked this particular simple answer because it seemed so instinctively wrong. As probable as it was and as deeply motivated as the person might be, it somehow didn't fit. Even if the person was pushed by the one who might have pushed.

Of course . . . that person might have been pushed to a lesser crime. Would this suspect, then, possess guilty knowledge? Why would the suspect continue in silence? For a number of reasons. . . .

The suspect would know that the original suspicions that had occurred were certainly false. And hence the killer most likely was . . .

For a moment I saw a picture in which it all made sense—the kind of sense which shapes the actions of a dangerous lunatic perhaps, but still sense.

I lost the picture and then tried to force it back into my conscious mind. It had disappeared.

There were two guns involved, of course. As Doctor James would have predicted, the witnesses were deceived by their perceptions about that. Two guns . . . and two shots, the second one heard. The first one maybe silenced or maybe heard and not noticed. Either way it would work. Two guns, two shots.

And one secret.

Or possibly two secrets? About which the participants were also confused. What were the two secrets? I knew one. What might be the other?

I saw the picture again. It faded and then—of its own, so to speak—it reappeared.

As I have described the experience before, the elevator door opened and the solution came out, fully grown like Venus from the sea (to use an utterly inappropriate metaphor).

Lunacy, absolute lunacy!

But it fit. The puzzle of the second gun and the puzzle of the second secret!

Then I tried to analyze the component parts rationally. If I turned everything upside down from the way I had looked at it before—I turned my notes symbolically upside down—then *all* the data fit.

Upside down and inside out.

But that meant . . .

Yes, of course it did.

I worked through the story line again.

And felt sick. Dear God, what an ugly, terrible story. Evil multiplied, reinforced, and come home again.

I could never prove it.

Not so fast.

You can prove it to yourself first. A couple of ways. Moreover, you can prove it to the cops and the State's Attorney if not a trial jury.

Why do that?

Because other lives are in danger, that's why, dummy.

And I might be able to get a confession. A bit dangerous?

Not really. Not if it were done properly.

And others were still in danger.

I must make some phone calls.

First the Old Fella.

He confirmed my recollection.

Then to M.K.

She answered my question.

Then to my primary suspect's agent. There was no time to waste, so I laid it out bluntly—what had happened and how the suspect and the agent had responded.

The agent, relieved to spill it all, admitted that I was correct. I made another charge.

That was admitted to—with a desperate plea to which I gave some reassurance.

Then to a sad victim. Tell me the truth, I demanded, or you will regret it forever.

Please.

No pleases. Tell me.

I was told. I gave some more reassurance.

Then to Mike Casey.

He agreed with my plan.

Then the killer.

Tomorrow morning at ten o'clock? Certainly.
Pleasant dreams.

34

"Nice of you to come." Seated behind my desk, I waved
my visitor toward the chair nearest my bedroom door.

"I'm happy to do whatever I can to be of assistance."

I had slept the sleep of the just and was eager for action.
I might as well throw the fastest pitch first. Or to change the
image to the old submarine movies, fire the first torpedo.

"Do you have any regrets because you ordered the murder of your son?"

"I beg your pardon?"

"Dan Harrington Enright was your son, wasn't he? They
all were. Don't bother denying it. We can prove it. I suppose
you were the one that arranged for the eyes in that portrait
to be repainted. Vi was not well educated enough to know
that two blue-eyed parents cannot produce brown-eyed sons.
But you knew it—and feared the boys might wonder about
the problem in years to come. So you had the eyes changed,
probably when Daniel was dying in the other apartment,
right down the hall."

"You're out of your mind." Vincent Nelligan's face had
turned from chalk to dirty gray. "This is outrageous."

He was impeccably dressed as always, dark suit with a
very light hint of stripe, vest, white shirt, dark tie. The
clothes you'd see in a coffin.

And the face to match.

How would we know when he was dead?

"Is it even more outrageous," I demanded, "to tell you
that Fionna's secret is about not her uncles' parentage, but
about her mother's? Rita Downs is the daughter of Mary

O'Brien Feehan, the only true child of Daniel Enright. The others are not only adulterous bastards, they are fake sons."

Fire two.

Rita was an adulterous bastard too, as far as that goes, but she nonetheless was the only child of the seed of Daniel Enright.

"That is absolute nonsense." He rose unsteadily from the chair. "I will listen to no more of it."

Fire three!

"You had Dan and Lena killed by the two Colombian knife men you hired out of the drug world to provide protection Violet demanded for Harry. Your son and his wife found their mother dead in her bed with a bullet through her head. So they knew you did it. He talked a lot, endlessly. Maybe, poor fool, he hinted to you that in return for money for his magazine, he'd continue to say that she was alive when he and Lena saw her. I understand also why you wanted Fionna dead. You mistakenly thought her secret was about you instead of Mary O'Brien Feehan. But why my sister?"

He staggered back into the chair. Third direct hit.

"You're mad."

"No, I'm not mad, but you are—or so your lawyers will contend when they move for a ruling that you are not fit to stand trial."

"I am *perfectly* sane," he croaked at me as his face melted from frozen crags to dissolving snowbanks.

Fire four!

"Presumably you thought Dr. Murphy knew your secret too, having learned it from Fionna. But neither she nor Fionna knew it at all. Fionna knew a secret, but she knew a different secret. Your big mistake, Vinney, was to attack my sister. We Ryans have a thing about family loyalty. If you had left her alone, you might have been able to get away with this lunacy."

"I had nothing to do with any of this!" he gasped for breath, his heart literally no longer in the fight.

The lives of others were still in danger, so I fired five!

"Your motives for killing Vi were mixed. She was trying

to destroy the promising career of your beloved grandson, the only accomplishment of your life in which you could take pride in your final days. She had found out"—wild stab in the dark—"that you had kept the money she gave you to buy off Harry's enemies and was furious with you. Perhaps she threatened some kind of public scandal. She certainly knew where all your skeletons were buried. So you killed her— something you'd been wanting to do for a long time any- way."

"*No*, it was not that way at all!"

"Did you threaten to tell the secret yourself, to scare her away from Rick? And was she dumb enough to believe you meant it? Is that why she pulled the gun on you in her drunken stupor?"

"She was never really intelligent where her children were involved." His whole body was shaking, his voice a whisper. "Especially when she was drunk. I acted in self- defense. She was going to kill me. I had no choice. I never had a choice."

I felt, all of a sudden, very tired. It was all over now. I had beat up on a weak old man.

Weak but dangerous. I eased open the middle drawer of my desk.

"A drunken woman who had never fired a gun in her life, a woman from whose hand you easily wrested the weapon because, as you noticed, the safety was on? You were in the military police, weren't you? And you knew about guns?"

"She said that she would have her security guards—the Colombians I had hired to protect her—cut my throat and throw my body in the lake."

The man was dying before my eyes. Had I any right to press ahead?

The lives of others were in danger until we had a clear confession.

"The threat of a drunken and angry woman?"

"She was going mad, crazy in her old age, absolutely in- sane on the subject of that worthless piece of fluff. I didn't care what Rick did. A man can always have fluff. I did not want his career ruined. Or his life ended. She was crazy enough to kill us both."

"So you killed her?"

"I had no choice." Miraculously rejuvenated, he regained his composure, an urbane, self-possessed retired banker. About to go 'round the bend completely. "I never had a choice."

"Blame it all on the woman? Especially when she is dead?"

I slipped the contents of my drawer onto my lap. My Madonna looked very uneasy.

"It was her idea. . . . I mean about the . . . the children. She was convinced that Daniel was sterile. . . ." He sniggered wildly. "I guess she was wrong, after all. How angry she must have been if what you tell me about the other woman is true. I always thought that Rita was mine like the others."

"So she forced you to make love to her?"

"It wasn't love. There was no pleasure in it for me. Only humiliation. She reveled in that. And in tormenting my wife with her vulgar hints. I never thought of them as my sons. I was ashamed of them. She destroyed my marriage, my family, my life. A totally evil woman. I should have killed her long ago." He began to laugh. "But I finally did, didn't I? I've had my revenge at last."

"How did she force you?"

"I had made a small mistake"—he snapped his fingers, a trivial, unimportant matter—"at the bank. I might have gone to jail for a couple of years. She found out about it and threatened to go to the examiners. She gave me a choice— her bed or prison." He smiled suavely. "You know, I should have chosen prison." He laughed and crossed his legs, a man recounting a story in the lounge of the Chicago Club. "She corrupted me. I couldn't quit after that. She owned me body and soul and she knew it. She made me a rich and powerful man." He laughed merrily. "She also corrupted me and ruined my life . . . and ruined my life."

His hand strayed toward his coat, as I had expected it would.

"I have another scenario, Vinney. The 'little matter' was taking money from Daniel's account for her. You proposed a solution to her fertility problem because you saw it giving you a grip on the family money, though you had no idea that the money would ever be as much as it became. She was corruptible and probably would have been corrupted anyway, but you were the one who corrupted her. You enjoyed taking your benefactor's wife away from him. You enjoyed cheating on your own wife. You enjoyed debasing Vi. Just as you debased your son Edward's wife and wanted to debase Rita, even though you thought she was your daughter. There was always something a little perverse and perverted about you, Vinney. You loved every minute of it. Did you tie Violet up the first time? Did she enjoy that? Probably she did. Now in your old age you wanted to leave something clean behind you. So you killed her."

He relaxed a bit and leaned back in the chair. "Of course, I tied her up. Women are meant to be used that way." He smiled, a pleasant bit of nostalgia. "She was frightened—of God and her husband and of me of course. She needed to be punished and so I obliged her. It was pure ecstasy. I evened the score with that bastard Daniel Enright and debauched a woman who needed to be debauched. Each time was more pleasant than the previous one. I went off to war, leaving her sick and pregnant. I assumed that Rita was my child. When I came back, she refused me because her goal of a boy and a girl child had been achieved." He leered. "I think she missed it, however. She soon turned to drink. War hero or not, Daniel had no notion of how to deal with a woman such as his wife."

"You corrupted her, then?"

"She required corruption." His hand drifted toward his coat, the last kinky move. "But she had her revenge. I did not anticipate that she would be so perversely evil as to tell my wife. She ruined my happiness. I killed her because she deserved it, just like I'm going to kill—"

"Don't think about it, Vinney." I jumped up, whipped the Beretta into position with both my hands, and jammed it across my desk into his forehead. "Don't even think about it."

Mike Casey and the three cops in my bedroom had no trouble putting the cuffs on him and taking away his gun, a mirror image of mine.

Vincent C. Nelligan howled like a raving madman. Which he had become. Which perhaps he always was.

Deadly pale and angry at me, Mike waited till the cops had led the shrieking Vinney from the room.

"Do you have a permit for that thing, Blackie? You could hurt someone with it, most likely yourself."

"Oh, this." I tossed the nine-millimeter casually on my desk. "It's only a model. I figured it might give you an extra two or three seconds' leeway to get out of the bedroom, which was all I needed."

On the various walls of my room there were a lot of approving grins—John Kennedy, John XXIII, John Unitas, and of course *Cuz*. With his Coast Guard hat.

The Madonna seemed to be smiling again. The kid too.

So I winked at them.

Coda

Joe Murphy

On Monday, September 19, 1985, in the Hubert Humphrey Metrodome on national TV, Jim McMahon came off the bench in the second half. In the first eight plays he threw touchdown passes of seventy, twenty-five, and forty-three yards. Willy Gault caught six passes for two hundred and thirty-six yards.

Ned Ryan was right. The kid *was* hungry. We were on our way.

And Mary Kate and I were on our way to Ireland for a pre–silver jubilee honeymoon. Our respective case loads were screaming, but as she put it, "To hell with them."

We were also well on our way to discovering each other again. Or perhaps for the first time. It was, to both our surprises, a mostly delightful process. As she added, "To hell with death too."

Instead of her usual agonistic and adversarial style, and instead of insisting that I was a saint for putting up with her, she laughed affectionately as I told her about her wife/mother role in bringing nourishing sweetness to my life—much as she had laughed as she had undressed for me on our wedding night.

Why this utterly unanticipated response?

Perversity perhaps, like the five pounds she did not put on when the chart changes provided the occasion for my unspoken prophecy.

She would own me body and soul for the next quarter century.

We were leaving for Ireland on Wednesday, first class all the way this time. Tuesday we spent at Grand Beach. We board-sailed at Pine Lake, a new form of water madness into which I had been inveigled by my offspring and spouse. Afterward we shopped at Brennen's Book Shop for secondhand mysteries to read on the plane. That night, having talked the whole day about our life together, we treated ourselves to dinner at the Hunter, a marvelous Wiener Wald–type restaurant in Michiana, the next village over.

We persuaded my brother-in-law to join us. He filled in the lacunae of the Harrington Enright case.

"Which one corrupted the other, Punk?" My mate was polishing off a plate of Jaeger Schnitzel. "I bet it was Vinney. It's always the man."

Vinney was in a psychiatric institution where he would spend his few remaining days; there had been no need to reveal the story of his relationship with Vi Harrington Enright. The dead were left to bury their dead.

Prognosis: hopeless.

Bill Downs had returned to Beverly Hills without his former wife. Then the previous Tuesday, Fionna had returned home from her job at Marshall Field's to discover a note pinned to her pillow.

> *I'll call from California. Daddy doesn't know I'm coming. I love you, you wonderful little brat.*
> *P.S. Don't bother looking for your "Brazilian bikini." I stole it.*

One school of thought contended that Rita had engaged in a long telephone conversation with Monsignor John Blackwood Ryan, S.T.L., Ph.D., before departing for O'Hare.

Prognosis: guarded.

Mary Feehan went quietly back to County Mayo.

Bishop Harry Harrington Enright had asked for and received an assignment to a poor black parish.

Prognosis: hopeful.

Ed Harrington Enright abandoned his position in dollars and went into therapy at the insistence of his niece, who had paid his margin calls.

Prognosis: poor.

Luisa Flores was ensconced at the Enright apartment with the technical title of maid but was being tutored in high school courses so that she could eventually attend Mundelein College down the street.

Prognosis: excellent.

The engagement of Fionna Downs and Richard Nelligan had been announced. They would be married at Christmas.

Prognosis: guarded but excellent. (What more can you say about any marriage?)

Blackie sighed and wolfed down the last Yorkshire biscuit in the basket in front of me. "I don't think either of them could remember toward the end. They corrupted one another. Leave them to heaven, as Hamlet wisely suggested. The two of them were predators, both using the culpable innocence of Daniel Enright to seize what they wanted in life. They destroyed him, but not before he knew what it is like to be loved and to produce a child out of that love. The War shattered his health. His realization of what he had let them do to his father and mother finished him when he came home. I doubt that he knew the boys were not his sons. Maybe he did. Perhaps if he did, he didn't care. He loved little Rita and was certain as he died that there was an angel to look after her just as she looked after him up to the end.

"I disagree with your prognosis about Rita. I boost it to hopeful. She doesn't have to unlearn much. There's no law that says you can't grow up at forty-two. . . . Ah, Linzertorte please, Karel, and while you're at it, two of them."

"Perhaps she will. There must be something worth waiting for in her, or Bill Downs wouldn't have waited," my wife said, with a nod. "For me too, Karel. No, *two* of them for each of us."

Blackie's eyes followed the waiter carefully, waiting for the tortes. "I'm told that some epidemiologists say that it takes three generations for a family system to work through a problem—schizophrenia, alcoholism, the like. Perhaps Fionna and Richard represent a new beginning for both families.

"In any case, it's now clear what happened on that Sunday a month ago. The lifelong love/hate—I think it's fair to call it that—between Vi and Vinney finally became intolerable for both of them. She threatened to kill him. He took the gun and killed her, a mixture of passion and opportunism that demonstrated how ruthless he had been all his life. As I remarked previously, his spur-of-the-moment scheme should have worked well, either if one of his illegitimate sons had reported her death or if he had not. The return of our good Fionna was an utterly unanticipated intervention. Still, he might have carried the day if he had been content. But he had begun to enjoy killing. Dan and Lena had to go because they might talk, and well they might; but it was surely to Dan's interest to be quiet. Fionna had to go because she knew the secret, and you because she was presumed to have told you the secret. Only it was the wrong secret. He knew he could count on Minnie to keep the nervous Doctor Edward in line. My Lord Harry didn't figure in it at all, save that when Vi discovered, heaven knows how, that Vinney was keeping money that was supposed to pay off the shadow world, her anger reached critical mass."

"So it was the mistakes after Sunday," I said, "that did him in? Poor mad fool."

Blackie's eyes lighted at the arrival of the Linzertortes. "I don't think I would have ever thought that two sons could both walk out of their mother's death room without a word to anyone. They were hollow men—the way she made all three of them—but I wouldn't have thought that hollow."

"She suppressed Rita"—Mary Kate dug into her torte, keeping pace with her beloved Punk—"but she didn't hollow her out."

(I was eating chocolate mousse, but only one.)

"Initially I assumed, naturally enough, that since

Fionna patently did not kill her unreal grandmother, that Ed must have done so with Minnie's collaboration. He was the last one in the room before Fionna. He was almost broke and he needed money desperately to meet his margin calls. I didn't like that theory, however, especially because his outburst of anger—free-floating and omnidirectional—did not sound like that of a weak man turned murderer. Moreover, he was too weak a man to be capable of what seemed like a ruthless and cunning crime of opportunity.

"Nonetheless, I assumed that at the end of my poking around, I'd pass on my suspicions to Mike the Cop, and the police would arrest Dr. Edward Harrington Enright for the murder of his mother—making, I might remark, good sibling, his case against you moot. But before I had an opportunity to do that, all hell broke loose, quite literally as it turns out.

"The Dan Enrights were killed. Why would Ed do that? I could think of no reason. So I was in the unusual position of knowing how the locked-room affair worked but not knowing for whose advantage it worked. That night at your house I was supremely confident, perhaps obnoxiously so. The day after the killing of Dan and Lena I was as baffled as the Chicago police.

"Then you were attacked. Carlos and Tomas were put out of action. Vinney's trip to Rome was revealed. I learned the truth about Rita's mother and Fionna's grandmother and about Vi's obscene punishment of Rita. Fionna was attacked. How do these facts and events fit? Why would Edward want to kill Dan? He might be angry at you and Fionna, but what possible motive was there for killing his brother? And Rita certainly had no reason to attack her beloved daughter, even if now she knew the secret.

"In fact, the three male offspring of the Harrington Enrights all seemed much too hollow to kill anyone. And, while not hollow, Rita is too sad a sack to work up the energy for a crime against anyone except possibly her false mother. But she doesn't even know about the false mother.

"So perhaps the secret is irrelevant? But then why attack Fionna? Then it occurs to me that just as there were two gunshots, there might be two secrets."

"Two gunshots?" Mary Kate paused over her torte.

"Of course. But the point is, what if there were another secret about a real grandmother? Or what if someone thought Fionna was talking about another, totally different, parental secret? What if, in short, Daniel Enright was not the father of those reputed to be his sons? That seemed absurd at first inspection. Then I remembered that something seemed wrong about the painting of Daniel Enright in the family apartment. Could it have been the eyes? I asked. They were brown, like his sons'. But had not the Old Fella told me that Daniel's eyes were aquamarine?

"I called said Old Fella about that point and you, M.K., about the color of Vi's eyes, since it never had been my pleasure to look into them. It's a truism, of course, but nonetheless true that two people with blue eyes cannot produce brown-eyed children."

"So the money Vi and Daniel inherited was never rightfully theirs."

"Precisely. The church is not going to try to recover the money, of course. My Lord Cronin recognizes that the fabled Fionna is a good future in which to invest. Because I told him so.

"I didn't have too much proof yet, but I phoned Min Enright and forced her to admit that she and Ed had gone softly into the good night with his mother's dead body lying in her stateroom. He thought at first that Dan was the killer, and after Dan's death knew that it had to be Vinney. He was afraid to say anything because he was afraid that he and Min would go the way of Dan and Lena. Vinney, for his part, had one more weapon to keep Min in line as his virtual slave, a position that she despised but did not totally reject.

"It was then only necessary to confront Vinney. He has been going mad for some time now, but with the quiet dignity that behooves a banker, even a crooked banker. I merely had to force him to admit the truth. A confession that perhaps one part of him wanted to make. He did not appreciate the irony that he tried to kill over the wrong secret."

"And pulled your toy pistol on him?"

"A sensible precaution on my part." Blackie lifted his hand, like a little boy in a sixth-grade classroom. "It gave me a couple of extra seconds. If he had moved a millimeter closer to the gun he was in fact carrying, I would have bashed him, weak old man or not, on the skull."

"You're scary, Punk," Mary Kate whispered softly.

"A position on which you seem to agree, as in so many others, with my Lord Cronin. . . . Ah, Karel, could you perhaps wrap three or maybe four of these in a doggy bag for me to take along? Doctor Murphy will pay. Thank you very much."

The impressed Karel shook his head as he walked away from our table. "One last question. How did you know that Fionna was innocent?"

"My sister's diagnosis could not be wrong." He folded his hands piously.

"Yes, it could, Punk. I've made mistakes before."

"Unthinkable. But there was also—you should excuse me for sounding like a character from A. Conan Doyle—the curious matter of the second gunshot at four o'clock."

"There wasn't any second gunshot!" I insisted.

"That," the Punk said, beaming merrily, "was what was curious."

"I beg pardon." M.K. put down her coffee cup. "What was the second gunshot supposed to be?"

"The one which killed Violet Harrington Enright when you were passing her yacht."

"And the first one?" I demanded.

Blackie was smiling like the offspring of a leprechaun and a cherub. "Patently the first shot and indeed the only shot at that time was the starting gun for the four o'clock boat race. I called the yacht club from your house that night to make sure. There was indeed a four o'clock race. For juniors. By which I presume they mean teens. You were, by your own testimony, very close to the starting line. A shot rang out over the water, just as other shots had rung out earlier in the day. You would have taken no notice of it, just as you had ignored the other reports of the starter's pistol earlier in the day, if it were not followed almost instantly by the screams of two young women."

My wife's jaw and my own hung open, hers attractively.

"No shot on the boat?" we said in unison.

"Certainly not. Those who hang around yacht clubs on Sunday afternoons in summer become accustomed to starter's guns and do not react to them. Such explosions are analogous to Chesterton's mailman in the classic Father Brown story. If Fionna, almost at the same time as the shot, had not run out of the cabin screaming and clutching a gun in her hand, neither you nor the luscious Luisa would have noticed the shot at all.

"In the given circumstances, however, your brains interpreted the shot which you had heard as connected with the screams on the *Violetta* and the gun in Fionna's hand. As shortly did the brain of everyone else in the harbor because they had heard the screams and seen the unusual commotion aboard the *Violetta*. Explosive noises carry over the water on calm days with deceptive power. It is hard to locate the source of the explosion unless you know where to look. Your perceptions were accurate enough. Your interpretations were flawed by an illusion that linked the shot with the scream.

"Doctor James—William, that is—noted such phenomena long ago and discussed them at great length. Since I was not present in the harbor, I was more immune to the illusion. Hence I thought instantly of the starting gun. Perhaps my studies of the good Doctor James, uh, facilitated my immunity to the illusion. There was only one shot at four o'clock and Fionna didn't fire it. The paraffin test insisted on by the redoubtable Patty Slattery was certain to be negative."

"So, if there was no second shot at four, no murder shot that is, the real second shot must have been fired earlier."

"If Vinney was the probable killer, why did I think that Violet Harrington Enright was alive when he left her cabin?

"It was an assumption that had never been examined. Why did I assume it? Because Luisa, poor girl, had told everyone that she talked with La Señora when Señor Vincente was leaving. It was at that time she was instructed to buy Advil for La Señora. But Rita told me that she was present when that instruction was given. So either Luisa was lying or Rita. *Ex hypothese*, it was Luisa, who did not understand the purpose behind the lie. She told me that Señor Vincente threatened to have her breasts cut off and sent to her family in Mexico, and her drowned in the lake. A threat which he was quite capable of carrying out, I believe. If she had not added the extra touch about the 'Adveel,' I would not have suspected the lie. That touch, a desperate attempt at verisimilitude from a terrified child, was fatal to Vincent Nelligan.

"Under promise of my protection, she admitted that the last time she saw La Señora alive was when Señorita Feehona and Señoras Rita and Maria were in the room."

"What happens if Fionna finds out?"

"I'm sure Luisa has told her the truth now, with many tears. And has been promptly forgiven as all penitent children are promptly forgiven by good matriarchs."

"The curious matter of the shot that wasn't fired." I picked up my spoon, which somehow had fallen into the remains of my chocolate mousse.

"Indeed. The murder had patently taken place, it seemed to me, earlier. Unless there was a silencer available at four o'clock. But I was assured there was none to be found. The windows were too high for Fionna to open one and throw the silencer out. You and Luisa would have seen it if she had tried to dispose of it when she came out of the door of the stateroom. And why would such a temporarily disoriented young woman make such an effort? Especially since she would burn her hand on the hot silencer? She too thought she heard the gun in the stateroom."

"So the silencer was used earlier? Vincent waited till it was cool enough to remove or used a towel and tossed it out the window." I was filling in some of the blanks myself. "He was tall enough to close the window. And the closed windows, incidentally, kept the room hot, so when I touched the corpse, it was still warm."

I finished my tea and signaled for the check. Mary Kate would pay for the second week of the vacation and I for the first. Tonight was technically my treat. Would that all the problems we were sorting out were that simple.

"He did use the silencer, I suspect, but he did not need to, though it would have been asking too much to expect that he realized that fact. If a weapon was heard earlier on a Sunday afternoon in August and was unaccompanied by a scream, the boaters, in perfect support for Doctor James's theories in the matter, would have thought it the starting pistol."

Blackie folded his hands reverently over his "doggy bag."

"Really scary, Punk. Totally."

"A position"—he rolled his eyes complacently—"with which our friend the good Karel now seems to agree. On the other hand, five Linzertortes are not an illusion. Are they not, after all, hints, even sacraments, of the Sweetness ever ancient, ever new, for which we all hunger, not always in the wisest or the sanest fashion? And which, under Her appellation, Lady Wisdom seems to have given most of us a second chance in this bloody and sordid tale of love run amok."

"Sounds like a sermon, Punk."

"What else are priests for except to preach about the second-chance-bestowing goodness that lurks in the sun and the stars and the lake and the sky and the Hubert Humphrey Metrodome and in the body of the passionate lover."

"And in Linzertortes?" Mary Kate put her arm around me.

"Indeed." I chose Blackie's favorite word. "Even in Boston Celtic fans."

—Grand Beach
—Midsummer's night, 1986